HIS NEXT VICTIM

The Bloodsucker stood in the breezeway, beer in hand, and watched Ty walk Jillian down the sidewalk. He drew his tongue over the smooth, cool lip of the bottle, enjoying the pleasure of the moment—the taste of the beer, the feel of the cool breeze on the hot July night against the back of his neck, the sight of the lovely amnesia victim. . . .

The moment he saw her, he had known they were meant to be together. She was quiet, but kind. She had the personality of a person who had been through a war and survived. He could only imagine the strength that had to be running through Jillian Deere's blood. He let his eyes drift shut, almost intoxicated by the thought.

The Bloodsucker saw Jillian and Ty halt beside the motorcycle. They were talking too quietly for him to hear.

Suddenly, Jillian turned her head toward him, almost as if sensing he was there. He quickly lowered his head, reaching out to fondle the leaves of a potted plant on a stand beside him. The light was out on the breezeway, and a street lamp illluminated Ty and the bike and Jillian. The Bloodsucker knew she couldn't see him, but still . . .

Out of the corner of his eye he stole one more look at her lovely face and then headed back toward the party. . . .

Books by Hunter Morgan

THE OTHER TWIN

SHE'LL NEVER TELL

SHE'LL NEVER KNOW

Published by Kensington Publishing Corporation

SHE'LL NEVER KNOW

HUNTER MORGAN

ZEBRA BOOKS
KENSINGTON PUBLISHING CORP.
http://www.kensingtonbooks.com

ZEBRA BOOKS are published by

Kensington Publishing Corp.
850 Third Avenue
New York, NY 10022

All Kensington titles, imprints and distributed lines are available at special quantity discounts for bulk purchases for sales promotion, premiums, fund-raising, educational or institutional use.

Special book excerpts or customized printings can also be created to fit specific needs. For details, write or phone the office of the Kensington Special Sales Manager: Kensington Publishing Corp., 850 Third Avenue, New York, NY 10022. Attn. Special Sales Department. Phone: 1-800-221-2647.

First Printing: August 2004
10 9 8 7 6 5 4 3 2 1

Printed in the United States of America

Prologue

The Bloodsucker opened the refrigerator and the interior light spilled onto the tiled floor at his sneakers. Holding the door with one hand, he peered inside, pushing aside a can of soda, an apple with one bite taken out of it, and a half empty bottle of ketchup. Spotting the plastic container of yogurt he sought, he reached for it. As his pulled his hand out, he accidentally struck the two vials of blood. He could see what was about to happen, but he reacted a split second too late. He dropped the yogurt and caught one of the vials in midair, but the second hit the floor with a crack and a splinter of glass.

Suddenly, the Bloodsucker was trembling all over. He stared at the blood splattered on the floor. The thick, rich, red blood with its white and red cells, its life-sustaining plasma . . .

Slowly, feeling like a character in one of Hitchcock's old movies, the Bloodsucker eased his hand into the refrigerator and carefully set down the rescued vial. His yogurt and hunger forgotten, he eased the door shut, unable to tear his gaze from the puddle of blood at his feet.

He had to clean it up. He knew he couldn't leave it

there. But it was so lovely, so utterly perfect in its existence that he couldn't help but take this moment to admire it. That was what life was all about, wasn't it? Living in the beauty of the moment? He felt his chest tighten with joy. Tears sprang to his eyes.

He stooped over the blood that glistened with shards of glass. The puddle had taken on the shape of its own living cell . . . an amoeba or one of those very first single-cell organisms that the whole world, universe maybe, had been created from. To the Bloodsucker, it was alive . . . quivering, shimmering in the light that came from the fluorescent tubes overhead.

Knowing he mustn't touch the blood, but unable to resist its beauty, he ever so slowly lowered his hand, his finger extended. The cool wetness on his fingertip was so exquisite that he gasped with pleasure. His eyelids fluttered and he felt that tightness in his groin. "Oh," he breathed.

His finger still in the blood, he opened his eyes, trembling. Slowly he drew his finger across the tile to form a letter. P . . . Then another. H. It was as if his hand had taken on a life of its own. No . . . it was the blood . . . the power of the precious elixir.

O . . . E . . . B . . . E

He stared at the name written in the blood on the floor. *Phoebe.* He smiled. It was time to let bygones be bygones. Phoebe had not been exactly what he had wanted. He had been so sure of that when he had carried her from his car. When he had cut her. When he had watched the blood flow from her veins. But maybe she had been what he *needed.*

And now it was time to put Phoebe aside. To move on.

He took another shuddering breath.

It was time to clean up the blood. To begin anew.

He rose and turned away from the puddle of blood with purpose. He grabbed a handful of paper towels and went back to mop it up. It seemed like lot of blood on the floor, but really it wasn't. Four super-soaker paper towels and the blood was completely gone. At least no one else could see it. He tossed the paper towels in the trashcan, pulled the bag out, tied it, and left it near the door, then added a fresh bag to the can.

Last, he grabbed a bottle of cleaner from beneath the sink, took two more paper towels, and went back to the place where the blood had been. He squirted some cleaner. Lemon fresh. He wiped the tile, tossed the paper towels that showed no evidence of blood into the fresh trash bag, and returned the cleaner to its place, taking care to be sure the nozzle was off. A person could never be too careful with cleaning fluids.

At the sink, the Bloodsucker turned on the hot water and squirted some antibacterial soap on his hands. He washed them with the care of a surgeon, then rinsed in the hot water and grabbed another paper towel, using it to turn off the faucet. He started to dry off his hands but halted, staring at his finger. The finger that had touched the blood.

Again his breathing became shallow. He stared at the finger until he could see the blood. Smell it. Slowly he lifted the finger to his mouth and suckled it like a baby.

Chapter One

There were times when a woman realized she was at a defining moment in her life, and Jillian sensed that when she walked into the old-fashioned diner in Albany Beach, Delaware, that hot, July first afternoon. She didn't know a soul in the diner. Didn't know a soul in the town . . . or on the earth for that matter, except for the doctors and nurses who had treated her in the hospital in Portsmouth, Virginia, and Mrs. Angelina Jefferson of the Amnesia Society. Still, even being a stranger in an unfamiliar town, Jillian felt an overwhelming sense of exhilaration when she stepped through the door. Something was going to happen to her in this town, something wonderful. She could feel it in her bones.

As Jillian made her way to one of the stools at the lunch counter, she took in her surroundings. The diner was right out of the fifties, like a scene from Mayberry with its shiny chrome trim, Formica counters, and out-of-date Naugahyde-upholstered booths. Close to five in the afternoon, the place was busy with what looked to be tourists and locals alike. Among others, she spotted a woman in a beach cover-up sharing a milkshake with her daughter, a nice-looking blond man in his mid-thirties drinking a cup of coffee while he read the paper, and a scruffy young guy, mid-twenties, in sunglasses, eating scrambled eggs and bacon, who appeared to have a serious hangover.

No one seemed to give her any mind as she settled on the stool; it was almost as if she belonged there. As if she had been there before.

"'Lo there, little lady." A man in his mid-fifties, with thinning salt-and-pepper hair, leaned on the counter opposite Jillian. "What can I get you for?"

She hesitated, glancing at the large, poofy-haired waitress in a floral apron at the cash register, then back at the man in the dirty, wet, white apron. "I was wondering if I could get a soda?"

"You bet. See, I'm a jack-of-all-trades 'round here. Loretta"—he indicated the obese woman at the cash register laughing with a young, good-looking uniformed cop—"she owns this place, but she can't run it without me. Can you, Loretta?" he called to her.

Loretta flapped a pudgy hand, dismissing him without a glance, and went on ringing up the cop's bill.

"See, I can get your drink, bus your table when you're through, and then wash that glass, clean as a whistle." The jack-of-all trades, who looked more like a dishwasher to her, pursed his lips and gave a low whistle.

Jillian half smiled, forcing herself not to pull back from the stranger, who frightened her a little. She was still on shaky ground here. She felt uncomfortable everywhere, with everyone, but yesterday when Angelina Jefferson had come to the hotel to see Jillian off, she'd been straightforward with her advice. Angel, her advisor with the Amnesia Society who had turned out to be a true angel sent from heaven, said the only way for an amnesia victim to become a part of society again was to immerse herself in it. Jillian had to go to public places like restaurants and museums, and she had to talk to people in libraries, in line at the grocery store, even if she had to make herself do it. Angel said that some form of paranoia was common with most amnesia victims and that Jillian would just have to work through it. It was the only way to become a part of the world again, one of the living.

"I was hoping I could get that soda to go, if it's not too much trouble," Jillian said, making eye contact with the dishwasher.

"No problem, sweet thing. I got Styrofoam cups here with lids." He grinned as he picked one off the top of a stack. "What would you like old Ralph to get you?"

"Cola, high test," she answered, proud of herself for knowing the answer. Six weeks ago when she woke in the hospital, she couldn't have responded to his question. She hadn't known who she was or how she got there, much less what cold beverage she preferred. Now, at least, she knew a few things about herself. She knew she loved the color blue, and the Beatles, and despised diet soda. It was a little thing, but one more "baby step," as Angel called it.

"Coming right up." Ralph filled the cup with ice, leaned on the rear counter, and hit the button to dispense the soda. "Staying the week on vacation? Longer, maybe?"

"Actually, I don't know. I didn't have any specific plans," she said, trying to be vague without sounding like a fruitcake. "I have a few weeks off, and I'm just driving up the coast, stopping here and there." It was only a half lie. She *was* driving up the coast, stopping here and there. Only right now, she had the rest of her life off because she didn't know what job she was supposed to be returning to in what state.

"Albany Beach is a great little town." Ralph popped a plastic lid onto her cup and grabbed a straw from a box. "We still got a few vacancies, but you better grab one up quick, if you mean to stay. Fourth of July is a big holiday here. We have a parade with fire trucks, a band, the whole enchilada. And some say we got the best view of the Atlantic Ocean of anyone." He winked.

Jillian took the cup from Ralph's hand. When his

fingertips brushed her skin, she didn't recoil the way she had whenever someone touched her the first few days in the hospital after she woke from her surgery. Angel said it was normal for an amnesia victim to get spooked by human touch and that it would fade with time and regular contact with others. "Thanks for the soda." She slid off the bar stool.

"You bet." Ralph followed her to the cash register, where Loretta was just handing the cop his change.

"Have a good day, Patrolman McCormick." Loretta punched the drawer of the ancient cash register closed.

"You bet." The officer picked up his paper to-go bag and turned to Jillian. He nodded, acknowledging her, as he slid his wallet into the rear pocket of his pressed khaki uniform pants.

Jillian smiled and nodded shyly as she turned to the woman behind the cash register. "Just the drink."

"Large Coke," Ralph offered, looking over the proprietor's shoulder at the cash register.

"You've got a stack of dirty dishes calling your name, Ralph." Loretta hooked a thumb in the direction of the kitchen behind the lunch counter. "Hop to it."

Ralph looked to Jillian. "You have a fine day—sorry, I didn't catch your name."

Jillian hesitated, a little uncomfortable with giving the stranger her name. But then she thought, what the heck, it wasn't her real name. What did she care? She'd probably be gone by morning, anyway. "Jillian," she said. "Jillian Deere."

"Nice to meet you, Jillian Deere." Loretta handed her the change from her dollar bill and a big smile. "You come back and have breakfast with us, you get the chance. I make the best blueberry hotcakes on the East Coast. Ask anyone."

Jillian picked up her drink. "I just might do that. Thanks. Have a good day." On her way out, a blond man in his mid-thirties coming in the door held it open for her.

"Good afternoon," he said, smiling wider than she liked. He was wearing a navy blazer with a name tag with a realty company name on it. She only caught his first name. *Seth.* He didn't look like a Seth to her. He was a little too polished, his teeth a little too white.

She offered a quick, perfunctory smile, walking through the doorway onto the stair landing. She didn't make eye contact purposely. "Thanks."

He turned to watch her go the way she had observed that construction workers and highway employees often did when a pretty woman passed. "You bet."

He was still ogling her when she took a quick look over her shoulder halfway across the parking lot. Jillian picked up her pace, hurrying to her car. A loaner from the Amnesia Society. The private organization did what it could to help "unidentified" amnesia victims rebuild a normal life. They provided places to live, cash, even used Hondas with a hundred and twenty thousand miles on them. The only stipulation the organization had was that if recipients ever got back on their feet again, they were to make a donation to help others in the same predicament they had experienced. *If they ever got on their feet again.* Angel's ominous words still terrified Jillian.

In the car, she dropped her drink into the cup holder on the console, rolled down the window, and slipped the key in the ignition. The late model Honda's engine turned over and purred. She backed out of the parking space and pulled out of the parking lot. As she turned onto the street, she noticed the police officer from the diner sitting in his marked green and tan car, still in the parking lot. Again he nodded solemnly, but this time he flashed a cocky smile.

Jillian gripped the wheel and buzzed down the street. The cop was flirting with her. Sort of. And she didn't know how she felt about it. In the last few weeks, she'd run into men in the hospital, in stores, who flirted with her, but she still wasn't certain how to respond. She could look in the mirror and see that she was beautiful, by present standards, with her long blond hair, slightly up-turned nose, and bright blue eyes, but it really didn't mean anything to her. Right now, she'd have exchanged this face and her Coke for a few memories in a heartbeat. How could she flirt with a man not knowing who she was or who she had relationships with? What if she was married?

Of course she had entered the emergency room wearing no wedding ring, and as Angel had pointed out, she didn't even have an indentation from a wedding band on her left ring finger. Women who were recently divorced, or even robbed, had at least the imprint of a ring. Jillian had no proof she was married or had a significant other, just a weird feeling that there had been someone in her life. A man she loved.

That, of course, led to the next question. Where the hell was he? She signaled and turned off the main road onto a tree-lined street. She had no idea where she was going, only that she was getting closer to the ocean. She could smell it on the hot, humid, late afternoon breeze.

If Jillian had a husband, why hadn't he been looking for her? No one had called or come to the hospital in search of a blond, blue-eyed woman in her mid-thirties in the days after she turned up at the hospital. No one had contacted the Portsmouth police, or any police in the state, not even weeks later when she had recovered and had nowhere to go.

In the days following her mysterious arrival at the door of the Portsmouth ER, Jillian had talked with a psychiatrist, and several psychologists, and had even been hypnotized, but no one had been able to help her draw any conclusions. She didn't know who she was or where she had come from, and she didn't know who had shot her or why. She had continued to be listed as a Jane Doe until the hospital put her in contact with the Amnesia Society and Angel had come to her rescue. Literally.

And now, here she was, on her quest to find herself.

Angel had suggested taking a few days to drive around the area and see if anything looked familiar, or perhaps jolted her memory. She said that many amnesia victims who did not have a friend or relative identify them, often found their identity on their own just this way. Either they spotted a familiar house that turned out to be theirs, or they bumped into an old friend in a grocery store who asked them if they'd been on vacation. Angel said the world was full of surprises; it was just a matter of going out and looking for them.

Full of surprises? The elderly woman with her flamered hair and ever-present cigarette dangling from the corner of her lipsticked mouth had that one right. Jillian was surprised every day, nearly every hour, as she slowly uncovered aspects of the personality that was somehow locked inside her head.

Jillian spotted a small green street sign that read *Juniper*. She turned onto it without signaling, a sense of excitement coursing through her blood. There was something about the street name . . . or maybe the street. The way the maple trees hung over. Checking to be sure no one was behind her, she slowed down to less than twenty miles an hour, gazing from one side of the street to the other. She was obviously in an older section of town. The multi-story condos had given way to small, square, cedar-sided and whitewashed cottages. Some were freshly painted, while others were a little the worse for wear. On other streets, she had seen tourists walking with children in bathing suits in tow, carrying armfuls of chairs and wet beach towels. On this little side street, she spotted an elderly woman in her side yard taking down laundry from a clothesline. A middle-aged couple sat on a porch snapping fresh beans. They both waved as she drove by as if they had known her her whole life.

Jillian's heart skipped a beat. Did they? That was silly, of course, to think that in two days' time she could get in a car and drive home. But it was fun to fantasize about, if only for a moment.

Ahead, she spotted beach dunes covered in sea grass to prevent erosion and signs warning that cars would be towed for parking in unmarked spaces. It was a dead end. She pulled into the last parking spot on the end of the street, parallel to the sidewalk, just in front of an old restored motorcycle—vintage fifties. She got out of the car, leaving her purse and locking the door. Jillian had no idea where she was going or why. Her new sneakers seemed to have a life of their own.

Gazing up at the brilliant blue sky, she heard the crash of ocean waves and smelled the tangy salt air. The wind whipped at her hair as she stepped off the cement sidewalk onto a wooden one that led around the cottage directly ahead of her. She followed the creaky path around to the front of the house that faced the ocean. It was small, with a painted white front porch, flowerless window boxes, and pale green shutters that looked like they still worked. An orange *Vacancy* sign hung in the window, framed by pale yellow gingham curtains.

Jillian gazed up at the house, at the single small window on the second story that faced the ocean. She hesitated, glanced over her shoulder to see if anyone was watching her, and then mounted the steps to the porch. Obviously, no one was staying here if there was a vacancy sign in the window. What harm would it be to have a look?

The painted gray floorboards beneath her feet creaked and gave way slightly as she walked to the window, cupped her hands over her eyes and looked in. There was a bright, cheery kitchen with a round wooden table and dish cupboards with glass fronts. She crossed in front of the front door to look in the other window. It was a living room or maybe a parlor. Furniture was covered in pale sheets, but instead of seeming ghostly, the room beckoned her.

"Have I been here before?" she whispered, pressing her fingertips to the cool glass windowpane.

The house gave no reply.

After a moment, Jillian turned around and hooked her arm around one of the wooden posts that fortified the porch. A path led directly from the steps, through a break in sand dunes, onto the beach. It was a breath-taking sight, the mounds of fine white sand, the waving dune grass, the wide beach that fanned out in either direction as far as the eye could see, all leading directly to the Atlantic Ocean's edge.

She smiled and slid down to perch on the top step. The wind tangled her hair, but it was a hot, humid wind. On impulse, she slipped her feet out of her sneakers and peeled off her new white athletic socks. She wiggled her toes, enjoying the freedom. This was a nice place. Maybe a nice place to stay a few days? Ralph's description of the upcoming Independence Day parade sounded charming.

She thought of the vacancy sign in the window behind her and wondered how much the cottage would cost to rent for a few days, maybe a week. Probably too much. She had money, but her resources, for now, were dependent on Angel and the Amnesia Society. She didn't want anyone to think she was trying to take advantage of the generosity of her benefactors, staying in an ocean-front house when she could very well take a room a few streets back at a budget motel.

But there was something about this cottage. . . .

A long shadow fell over the sand in front of Jillian, and she glanced up to see a young man with sun-bleached blond hair, wraparound sunglasses, and a great tan walking over the crest of the dunes. He was shirtless, wearing fluorescent orange swim trunks and carrying a gym bag that had the Red Cross symbol on the side. A lifeguard.

She found it fascinating that she could recognize the symbol for the Red Cross, or a vintage motorcycle, but she couldn't remember her own name. Funny how the mind worked.

The lifeguard stepped onto the wooden walk that ran directly in front of the cottage. As he approached the house, he gave a nod and offered a lopsided, boyish grin. He had a nice smile that made her want to smile back.

"Hey," he greeted her.

She nodded.

He walked past the front steps, barefooted, swinging the bag. He looked like he was headed home. It had to be five-thirty by now. Quitting time?

She watched him pass, admiring his muscular, tanned shoulders. It was one of the interesting quirks she had learned quickly about herself. She obviously liked men. Found many sexually attractive. She couldn't remember having sex, yet she knew, innately, that she had enjoyed it a great deal.

The lifeguard got to the end in the walkway, about to disappear around the side of the house, when he turned around. "Can I help you with something?"

Before she could reply, he lifted a tanned shoulder in an easy-going half shrug. "You look kind of lost."

Jillian threw her head back and laughed, surprising not only the young man, but herself as well. He walked back toward her. He was still smiling, but obviously puzzled.

"I'm sorry," Jillian said, pressing her hand to her mouth, still chuckling. "I didn't mean to be rude. No, I'm fine. Thanks for asking."

But the lifeguard didn't go. He stood there, all six-foot-something of him, looking down on her sitting on the step, still smiling. "I gotta ask. What's so funny?"

She looked up, squinting in the bright sunlight, still amused. "What you said, it was just so . . . apropos." *Apropos?* What kind of person had she been that she used words like *apropos*?

"Why's that?" He slid the bag off his shoulder and parked one bare foot on the bottom step beside hers.

"I just—" She shook her head, burying her face in her hands for a minute. How pathetic was it for a woman her age to be spilling her guts to a kid who looked to be young enough to be her son?

"Got lost on I-95? Thought you were in Maine, and you wound up in little old Delaware?" he prodded teasingly.

She lifted her head. "Actually, even more bizarre than that." She hesitated, but there was something about the lifeguard's warm hazel eyes that just made her want to tell him her whole wretched story. "Before I go on with the crazy story, do you mind if I ask you a crazy question?"

"Shoot."

"Have you ever seen me before? I mean, I realize that obviously you don't know me, but I don't suppose, by any chance, you've seen me around town?" She sounded so pathetically hopeful.

He shook his head. "Nope. I'd remember your eyes if I had." He seemed to sense her disappointment. "But I only live here in the summer," he went on quickly. "I grew up here, but I've been gone a while. I just graduated from Penn State."

Jillian did the quick calculations in her head. That only made him twenty-two or twenty-three. He was young, all right . . . but not young enough to be her son.

"So tell me your crazy story," he said. "I'm dying to hear it now."

She took a deep breath. "Well, I am sort of lost because . . . because, I'm not exactly sure who I am." She said it without giving herself time to think, to get the words out of her mouth before she lost her nerve. She hadn't told many people about her predicament yet. So far, most people she encountered already knew.

"Interesting." He nodded his head, not sounding as if he quite believed her, but intrigued.

"Amnesia," she explained. She threw up her hands and let them fall to her pale, bare knees. "I know. Sounds like something out of a soap opera, but I was injured and left at a hospital without any identification on me. When I woke, I didn't know who I was. I still don't," she finished, thinking it sounded pretty far-fetched to her, too.

"Wow." He thrust out his hand. "I'm Ty."

She clasped his hand, warm and firm. He smelled faintly of coconut suntan lotion. "Jillian Deere."

He looked at her as if to say *Are you for real?* "As in Jane Doe?" he asked.

She laughed. "You know, you're the first person that's gotten it." She made a face. "I just couldn't see myself spending the rest of my life as *Jane Doe.* It would be like toting a red flag around that said, *I'm an idiot. I don't who I am or how I got here.*"

"Nah, I don't think anyone would say that. But I like it." He waggled the finger he pointed at her. "Pretty cool, actually." He dropped his bag in the sand and crossed his arms over his chest. "Out of curiosity, how did you find your way to Albany Beach, *Jillian Deere?*"

She liked the way he said her name. "I just got in the car and drove here. I've been in Virginia recuperating in a hospital; I was in a coma for a few days. Then I woke up with the amnesia. When I was released, some nice people helped me out. They loaned me a car and some money."

"Sounds pretty scary." He leaned on the porch rail, closer to her than he had been before. "I don't know if I would have had the guts to do it."

"It didn't seem like I had much of a choice."

"And no one came to the hospital looking for you? No one contacted the police or some missing persons bureau or anything?"

She shook her head. "The police said it could be that I was there in Portsmouth on vacation or business. But who knows? I just could have gotten off the interstate in the wrong place, or had a change in flight plans and wandered from a nearby airport into some kind of trouble. Someone could be looking for me, but in another part of the country. They say it happens."

"Wow, spooky," Ty said thoughtfully. He glanced at

her. "So you could, like, have a husband, kids, and not know it?"

"Well, the doctors say I've never given birth, so I suppose that's good." She lifted her left hand. "And no wedding ring, either." She stared at her finger. "Somehow that seems a little sad to me."

Jillian met his hazel-eyed gaze for a moment, then looked away, surprised by the emotion that stuck in her throat. Most of the time she could remain pretty removed from all this. Often it was as if it was happening to someone else. Like she was watching a movie.

"Well, I just got off work." Ty broke the silence. "Lifeguard. And I'm starved so I'm going to get something to eat." He paused, then pointed in the direction of the street. "You wanna come?"

"Oh, no, I couldn't." She raised her hand. "Thanks, but—"

"But what? You've got someone holding dinner for you? Got somewhere else better to go? Or are you just trying to get me the hell off your porch?"

She laughed. "Well, obviously it's not my porch."

He tilted his head in the direction of the street. "Then come have something to eat with me."

Jillian hesitated. What kind of thirty-something woman went to dinner with a twenty-two-year-old?

"Come on, it'll be fun," he dared her.

He was cute. And nice. And she didn't like eating alone; it reminded her of just how alone she was. "Okay." She hopped up, grabbing her sneakers, stuffed with her socks. "Sure. Why not? It's not like I have anywhere to be, is it?"

On the street, Ty walked up to the motorcycle she had parked in front of and strapped down his bag with a couple of bungee cords.

"So that's yours. I was admiring it earlier."

He rubbed something akin to rust on the gas tank with

the heel of his hand. "An old Chief made by the Indian Company."

"A 1958," she said. "The last year they really made them until the company was bought in '99.'"

"How'd you know that?" he asked, obviously surprised.

Not as surprised as she was. She stood there staring at the red and black painted motorcycle. "I have no idea," she murmured.

He studied her, blond brows furrowed as he slipped into a pair of ratty sneakers from his bag. "You recognize a bike from the fifties, know its obscure history, but you don't know your name?"

She opened her arms; his easy-going nature seemed to be contagious. "I told you it was a crazy story."

He laughed as he mounted the bike. "You just want to follow me?"

"Sure." Jillian jumped into the Honda and made a U-turn in the street. Ty pulled out, and she followed him back toward the center of town. They ended up in the parking lot of the diner she'd been at less than an hour ago.

"What's so funny?" Ty asked, waiting for her when she climbed out of the car. He'd pulled on a wrinkled Radio Head concert T-shirt.

"I was just here." She pointed at the silver building that looked as if it had been constructed from an old railway car, with an addition tacked to the back. "When I came into town, I stopped for a drink."

"Two-for-one burger night. Loretta makes a mean quarter pounder with cheddar cheese. None of that American crap."

They walked side by side across the gravel parking lot.

"Hey, Ty!" A blond woman about his age stuck her head out the window of a car in the parking lot.

Ty took a second look and broke into a smile. "Anne. I didn't know you were home." He hooked his thumb in

Jillian's direction. "This is Jillian. That's Anne." He pointed. "We went to high school together. She's at Virginia Tech now."

The blonde lifted her hand in greeting. "Nice to meet you." She started the engine of her car. "I have to run, Ty. Take-out for my mom and dad. But I'll catch up with you. You'll be home a while, right?"

" 'Till August tenth." He thrust his hands into his pockets, and he and Jillian headed across the parking lot for the diner.

"So what degree did you graduate with?" she asked.

"American literature." He glanced at her, a wicked grin. "I know. What the hell am I going to do with that? My dad says the same thing about twice a week."

"You know, I wasn't going to ask you that."

"What's that?"

"I wasn't going to ask you what the hell you were going to do with the degree."

He grinned. "I like you already, Jillian Deere."

She thought for a minute. "Although I guess that *should* be my response."

He lifted one shoulder in what she now recognized as one of his favorite gestures. "As much as I hate to admit it, I can see my dad's point. He paid sixty-some thou for four years of partying, and I'm now qualified to lifeguard on a beach—the same thing I've been doing since I was seventeen. My older sister is an engineer making bo-coo bucks in Texas for some oil rig company." They walked up the steps, and he held open the diner's door for her. "But I'm going back and getting a master's—I've been accepted into a program that will pick up most of the tab. I think I'd like to teach high school, but not in a regular high school. Maybe on an Indian reservation, or one of those schools for problem kids. You know, the kind where you make them climb mountains, live in the desert. I want to do something cool like that before I really have to become an adult."

She laughed.

"You know what I mean."

She nodded. "I don't know how I do, but I do."

Inside, they passed the cash register with Loretta at the helm and took a booth toward the rear. There was new assortment of customers from the ones she had seen before, but somehow they all seemed like friendly faces. In addition to the diners in tees and flip-flops, with bathing suits showing beneath their clothes, and a security guard of some sort, she noted a table of teens dressed in black, their hair dyed black. One girl had a ring through her nose and was sporting black lipstick. Goths. She'd seen a couple in Portsmouth. Apparently every town had them.

Ty slid into a booth, and she took the crackly fake leather bench seat across from him.

"Want a menu?" He offered her a laminated single page he plucked from behind a chrome napkin holder.

She dropped her purse beside her. "You don't need it?"

"Nope. I always get the same thing on burger night. Two quarter pounders with cheddar, pickles, ketchup, and mustard. No rabbit food. Side of boardwalk fries."

As she took the menu, her fingertips brushed his, and she felt a rush of warmth. She glanced up at him, her response surprising her. Not only had his touch not scared her, but it had felt good. He didn't seem to notice.

She pulled the menu from him, feeling silly. She didn't know exactly how old she was, but she knew she was too old for this kind of nonsense. She needed to get her hormones in check. "What are boardwalk fries?" she asked, reading the menu.

"I can tell you one thing, you're not from around here." He leaned back on the Naugahyde bench and stretched out a lean, tanned arm. "Just take my word for it. Order the boardwalk fries." He winked.

She tossed the menu on the table. "Okay, but I think one burger will be sufficient."

A college-age waitress in a pair of denim shorts and a tight-fitting white knit shirt approached the table. The only giveaway that she was a waitress was her sensible white sneakers, the straws sticking out of her pocket, and the notepad in her hand. "Hey," she said, grinning at Ty.

"Hey. You off soon?" Ty remained relaxed against the bench seat.

The cute, blond-haired, blue-eyed woman grimaced. "Not until ten. I have to work an extra hour to get Loretta through the after-movie crowd."

Ty motioned to the waitress. "This is Kristen Addison. My cousin. She's staying with us for the summer."

"I just couldn't go back to PA and suffer the summer with my parents again," she confessed.

"Kristen will be a senior at the University of Delaware this fall. She's going to be a nurse."

Jillian smiled. She liked Kristen immediately. She had that all-American freshly scrubbed look. She was beautiful without makeup. "Hi, I'm Jillian."

"I picked her up on the beach," Ty said.

Jillian laughed, feeling her cheeks grow warm.

Kristen just shook her head, seemingly used to Ty's humor. "Nice to meet you, Jillian. You visiting Albany Beach for the week?"

"I'm thinking about it."

"So what can I get you?" Kristen poised her pencil. "I already know what goof ball over here wants."

"I'll have a burger with cheddar, mustard, and relish. With the bunny food." She eyed Ty teasingly. "Boardwalk fries and a Coke."

"I'll get your order right in."

Kristen headed for the kitchen to place their order, and Ty began to systematically fold the paper placemat in front of him, advertising local business, into a paper airplane. "You serious about maybe sticking around a few days?" he asked.

"It seems nice here."

"You want me to see what I can find out about that cottage? I think it's for rent. It's owned by this old lady in town. It's been there forever."

"I don't know. It might be beyond my price range. I have to be careful with my money."

He halted the plane construction to meet her gaze across the table. "I could check. It might be nice to chill out in the same place for a few days. Get your bearings."

"It would be."

He slid off the bench. "Hang on. Let me go grab my cell; I guess I left it in my bag. I'll make a few phone calls. My dad knows this realtor. He's kind of a jerk, but he knows everybody in town." He dragged his fingertips along the table as he walked away. "Be right back."

A minute later, Kristen set two plastic cups of soda and straws on the table. "Burgers will be up in a couple of minutes."

"Thanks." Jillian picked up one of the straws and tore off the paper. As she dropped it into one of the sodas, the diner's door opened, and a very tall, slender woman in what she now recognized as a local police uniform walked in. Despite the uniform, blond hair tied back in a no-nonsense ponytail at the nape of her neck, and lack of makeup, the policewoman was what Jillian would have described as a gorgeous, willowy blonde. The officer stood in the doorway for a second, surveying the diners and then made a beeline toward the table of Goth teens.

"Get up, Ashley," she said to the girl with the black lipstick.

Jillian knew it was rude to eavesdrop, but she couldn't help herself. With no life of her own right now, other people's fascinated her.

One of the girl's companions snickered.

"Mom," the teen groaned, rolling her blue eyes lined thickly in black.

"Either you get up and walk out of here or I take you out," the policewoman threatened in a low voice that even Jillian could interpret as that she meant business.

Ashley, obviously the policewoman's daughter, pushed her soda aside and reached for her purse, managing to make each movement dramatic.

"You're still on restriction. You were supposed to go straight to your grandparents after work, so they could drive you home."

"I was on my way," the teen answered sourly. "I just stopped for a drink. Can't a person get something to drink if they're thirsty?"

"Yeah, can't a person stop for a drink if they're thirsty, *Chief Drummond?*"

The young man who spoke was tall and angular with the same shoe-polish black hair as his companions. He wore a ragged black T-shirt and a chain around his neck that appeared to come from a gate or a fence. The necklace was so ridiculous in appearance that it was laughable, but obviously from the young man's tone of voice, it made him think he was tough.

"A person certainly can," Chief Drummond answered, imitating the boy's tone of voice, "*Chain*—unless, of course, she's a minor and her parent has deemed that she may not stop for a drink, not even if she is dying of thirst."

The female companion again sniggered, but when the policewoman eyed her, she shut right up.

Jillian couldn't resist a smile as she sipped her Coke. Obviously the blond cop was a woman to be reckoned with, and Jillian immediately admired her.

The police chief stepped aside to allow her daughter

to exit the booth. "Be sure to say good-bye to your friends, Ashley. You won't be seeing them, or speaking with them on the phone or Internet, for another three days."

"Three days?"

The cop/mom crossed her arms over her chest. "The length of the extension of your restriction for this violation."

Again, the eye roll, but young Ashley climbed out of the booth, dragging her purse behind her. Her mother let her pass and then followed her out the door, where the two disappeared down the steps into the parking lot.

"Good news."

Jillian looked up to see Ty sliding into the seat across from her, setting down his cell phone.

"What's that?" she slid his straw to him.

"That house is for rent." He leaned forward as if he possessed a secret. "Cheap. Someone backed out of the lease for the month of July after paying half up front as security. I guess this whole mess with the serial killer spooked them. The owner just wants someone in the house, so she's willing to rent it for the balance of the rent. I warn you, it's basic. Small, no cable, no phone, and no air conditioning."

He named the price and Jillian found herself smiling back at him. That was doable. Very doable. "Two questions," she said as she leaned back to allow Kristen to slide her plate in front of her. "One, when can I move in?"

He reached for the bottle of ketchup and began to squirt it all over his fries and on the hamburger. "Tonight if you like. Key is hidden on the property, and I know the secret place. You can sign the contract in the morning." He put down the ketchup bottle and squashed the bun on top of the first burger. "And question number two?"

"I guess I'm asking these questions out of order," Jillian said, grabbing a fry that appeared to have been freshly cut with its skin still on. "But *what* serial killer?"

Chapter Two

Ty took a massive bite of his burger. "You haven't seen the papers? Watched the news? We're on national TV."

"No, I can't say that I have."

"Right. I guess you've been a little busy, huh?" He wiped his mouth with a paper napkin and took another bite. "We seem to have a slight serial killer problem in good old Albany Beach." He shook the burger at her. "Now, mind you, this is the first time ever. First homicides in like a hundred years or something."

Still watching him, she used her knife to cut the huge burger on her plate in half, then in more manageable quarters. "You said *serial* killer?"

He grimaced. "'Fraid so. Three women. No one's drawn any definite conclusions yet, tests still coming back from the lab on possible evidence, yada, yada, yada, but everyone's saying it's the same killer. The papers are calling him Bloody Bob or something asinine like that." Ty stuffed some fries in his mouth and reached for a squirt bottle beside the ketchup. "Vinegar. You have to try this on your fries. It's the best."

Jillian watched as he squirted the perfectly delicious

fries with the strong-smelling stuff. "I don't think so."
She popped a fry, minus the vinegar, into her mouth
thoughtfully. "You don't seem to be taking this serial
killer thing very seriously."

One-shouldered shrug. "I don't mean to make light
of the women's murders. I just think that if there is one
guy out there killing women, we shouldn't be plastering
it all over the newspapers, radio, and TV. It gives him
what he wants—notoriety."

"You think he's killing for the notoriety?"

"They all do, don't they?"

Jillian took a tentative bite of her burger; it was as
good as Ty had promised. "So what's the connection between the women?"

Ty shook his head. "That's the weird thing. So far,
nothing. You saw our police chief, Claire Drummond,
in here a minute ago, dragging off her derelict daughter? Well, it's no wonder she's in a pissy mood. She's in
charge of the investigation. So far, apparently, she has
almost nothing, and I hear the mayor is really putting it
to her. I guess revenue is already down, and this is our
first really busy week of the summer. People don't want
to vacation in a place where you can get murdered while
taking an evening walk. This town lives—or could die—
by the summer tourist population."

"Three dead women and the police have nothing?"
Jillian leaned over her glass to take a drink. "How's that
possible with all the techniques available to crime inves-
tigators these days?"

"Not TV, I guess. All the police know is that he picks
them up on the street after dark, kills them, and then
dumps them a day or two later." He finished off the last
of his first burger. "Oh, and the victims are always blond-
haired and blue-eyed."

She almost choked on a mouthful of soda. Without
thinking, her hand went to her own natural blond hair.
Blue eyes, too.

"Jillian," Ty said softly, leaning forward on the table. "I don't think you have to be afraid. I really don't. I mean, look around you. Look how many blond-haired, blue-eyed women there are in town. There's got to be something more with this nutball than just looks. And I really think Chief Drummond is going to nail the bastard soon."

"But you said the police had no leads."

He made a face and added ketchup beneath the second burger bun. "No leads that they're telling the public. If you were Chief Drummond and you were tracking down a guy who kills women by bleeding them to death, then tossing them in dumpsters, would you tell the papers what direction your investigation was taking or who your suspects were?"

Despite the humid warmth of the day, Jillian fought a shiver akin to the one she had felt a couple of times while still in the hospital. It was unbridled fear. "I suppose not."

He reached for his glass, but didn't drink. He shifted on the bench. "Listen, you should do what you want to. If you want to rent the cottage for the month, even for a week, that's cool. You've got a much better chance of dying by choking on one of those fries or by getting into a car accident a block from here than by running into a serial killer. But if you feel like you should move on"— he hesitated—"then you should trust your gut feeling."

And what if your gut feeling involved a thirty-something woman's attraction to a barely-of-legal-age man? Jillian wondered. Could she trust that?

She looked down at her burger, then up at Ty. "I think I'd like to take the place. For the week, at least, if that's okay?"

"Okay?" He reached for his burger. "That's great. After we're done here, I'll ride back with you, get the key the old lady keeps hidden, and help you get settled.

I know just the place we can snag some sheets and stuff. Rentals around here don't usually include that."

She smiled back. "That would be great."

The Bloodsucker pulled a white T-shirt from the dryer, still warm, and buried his face in it. It smelled "mountain fresh," like fabric softener, but there was another scent, one that was stronger and more primal. One most people couldn't detect. But then, he wasn't most people.

He inhaled deeply, letting his eyes drift shut and the power wash over him. *Blood.* He could smell *her* blood.

Phoebe Matthews had put up quite a fight in the very end. She had flung blood all over, making him thankful he was prepared with the new walls made with the plastic drop cloths to catch the spatter. He had bought them at the dollar store, and they were pretty decent for a buck. He'd have to get some more.

The Bloodsucker knew he had to be careful. Cops had ways of detecting blood. Luminol was one. When they sprayed it on a surface that appeared to be wiped clean, it would glow under blue light. He had seen it on TV. Of course, Albany Beach didn't have the budget to pay for such fancy technology.

He lifted the white T-shirt up to the light. Even though it had been bleached and he could no longer see the red droplets, he knew they were still there. In his mind's eye, he could see them, hear them, taste them on the very tip of his tongue.

The Bloodsucker shook out the shirt and began to fold it the way Granny had taught him. Nice and neat. Perfect square to add to an entire drawer of underwear folded in perfect squares. He could have gotten a job folding if he wanted to, in a Gap or a J. Crew at the outlets, his creases were so perfect. The shirt folded, he cradled his left forearm to his chest and pressed the shirt against it like a compress. He closed his eyes for a moment, feeling the healing power.

After a moment, he opened his eyes and added the shirt to the growing basket of clean clothes at his feet. He always washed his whites separately; he would never allow the dye from darks to bleed on his pristine clothes. As he fished two matching white athletic socks from the dryer and smoothed them out to roll them, he allowed his mind to drift to thoughts of the blonde he had seen today.

So pretty. So nice. Not like that Phoebe Matthews with her black, traitorous heart and foul mouth. He hadn't liked her. She had been rude and uncooperative when she realized he wasn't going to let her go. She had been a poor conversationalist who thought everything in the world revolved around her. And she hadn't even liked movies. He'd offered to try and hook the TV up in the barn so they could watch something together, but she had laughed at him. He'd almost been glad when she died.

But that was all done and over with, neatly tidied up. And conveniently, a new women had walked right into his life today.

The Bloodsucker knew, of course, that he couldn't pursue her right away. He would have to lay low and keep his distance for a few weeks . . . at least days. And then he would have to weigh his options. The police chief, Claire-Bear, was sniffing around a lot. He saw her looking at everyone she met, studying them, wondering if each familiar face she encountered could be a person capable of such heinous crimes.

She never suspected him, of course, because he didn't fit the type. And because he was smart. Granny said he was stupid, worthless. An idiot. But she was wrong and he was proving it, wasn't he? He was smarter than them all.

* * *

"You sure you're going to be okay here alone?" Ty carried her two small duffle bags to the larger of the two bedrooms, where Jillian was making the bed with sheets he had borrowed from his mother's linen closet. There were towels and washcloths in the bathroom now, too. Renters usually brought their own, he had explained, but there was no need for her to go out and buy anything, not when his mother possessed enough sheets to put everyone in Albany Beach to bed.

"I'll be fine." Jillian added the floral top sheet to the queen-sized bed and smoothed out the wrinkles. The sheets smelled of fabric softener and sunshine. She bet his mother still hung out laundry on a clothesline. She didn't think she had ever had a clothesline in a backyard, but the idea fascinated her. It was like bringing the sun into her bed, making it with these sheets that had hung outside. "I'm not afraid of the Boogey Man or your Bloody Bob."

Ty went to the other side of the bed and helped her spread the light summer quilt in blue and yellow that matched the sheets and the pale blue curtains hanging from heavy rods almost perfectly "I know. It's just got to be weird being alone in a house when you've been staying in a hotel full of people." He glanced up, grinning boyishly. "I could sleep on your couch, if you want. Or wherever."

She ignored the underlying suggestion. "I don't need a babysitter. Go home and get some sleep. You said you had to be on the beach at ten tomorrow morning."

The bed made, she walked out of the bedroom, down the short hallway past the full bath and smaller bedroom, to the living room and kitchen-dining room, which were really just one room. The cottage was tiny, as Ty had warned. It had no air-conditioning, but it did have running water, electricity, and a view of the Atlantic Ocean.

What else could a woman ask for—except maybe a phone, and then who would she call?

In the front of the house, Ty walked to the door. "Okay, I can see I'm being kicked out." He pressed one hand to his chest dramatically. "But I'm a man who can take it." He opened the door. "I'll stop by tomorrow after work, maybe even lunchtime when I get my break, to see how you're making out."

"That would be great. I need to get some blood tests done to satisfy my doctors in Virginia. I thought I might do that in the morning. Where's the closest lab?"

"Hospital. You should have seen it as you came into town."

She rested her hand on the old doorknob. "Great. Listen, I can't tell you how much I appreciate everything you've done for me today. You're a complete stranger and yet—"

"I'm not a stranger anymore." He stepped out onto the dark porch, holding open the screen. "See you tomorrow." He turned to go, then back around, touching the top of his head. "Sunglasses."

"Oh, on the table." She went back into the kitchen, grabbed his sunglasses off the table, and met him at the door. "'Night."

Jillian closed and locked the door behind Ty and then watched him cross the porch and disappear around the side of the cottage. Moments later, she heard his motorcycle start and then the sound of the engine until it died away down the street.

She stood at the door for a moment and surveyed her new surroundings. The cottage was really quite nice even though it could have used a paint touch-up here and there. It wasn't even hot. With the windows open in the back and the front, the way Ty had showed her, she got a cool breeze that bordered on chilly off the ocean.

Her gaze settled on the kitchen cabinets. Behind one glass door there were stacks of old flowered china. Something about the little blue and yellow flowers seemed so familiar. The cabinets with their little windows looking in at the old dishes seemed familiar. She felt as if she had been here before. Dried those dishes.

Which was silly, of course. She must have seen half the locals of Albany Beach while in the diner. Ty seemed to be friends with every one of them. No one recognized her.

Jillian checked her Timex on her wrist. It was only nine; too early to go to bed. She padded down the hall, the old linoleum cool on her bare feet, and retrieved a paperback book she'd bought in a drugstore in Virginia. She carried it into the living room thinking she would read for a while and then turn in. It was one of those espionage books with spies and double agents by an author she sensed she'd read before, and she hoped it would keep her mind occupied.

Jillian settled on one end of the almost-new couch Ty had removed the dust cover from, and she opened the book to the page she'd folded back. She read a page, glanced up, then read the same page again.

The house was so quiet. Yet it wasn't. If she listened carefully, she could hear the ticking of an old clock on the kitchen wall, complete with electric cord running down the wall to the outlet near the floor. She could hear the rustle of the curtains in the back bedroom where she would sleep. And the ocean. She could hear the water breaking on the beach as if she were on her own little island, surrounded by the incoming waves.

In a way, she supposed, she was.

Jillian took another look at the room around her. The glass-doored cabinets, the flowered dishes. She felt as if this had been a good decision, stopping here. And not just because of Ty who, in an instant, had become her new best friend, her only friend. There was something about this cottage that made her think the secret to her identity lay locked somewhere here. Maybe it wasn't the house; maybe it was the town. She didn't know. But when she considered the possibility, she felt a spark of hope. Maybe she wouldn't be Jillian Deere forever.

Claire, dressed in an old Delaware State Police Academy T-shirt and plain-Jane cotton panties, walked around the house in the dark, checking all the windows and doors. She glanced one last time at the security panel at the front entrance and then went back down the hall, past her daughter's closed door, the bathroom door, and the door that opened into the spare bedroom. She didn't need any lights to illuminate the way. The log cabin she shared with her teenage daughter was small, and she knew every inch of it, even in pitch blackness. Somehow that gave her a sense of security. That and the four thousand dollar alarm system. . . .

In her bedroom, she closed the door behind her and crossed the floor to flip on a bedside lamp. It was just after midnight. She knew she needed to get some sleep if she was going to be out of here by six, the same as every morning since Phoebe Matthews' body had been found in a Dumpster at a construction site.

The worst thing was that, in her gut, Claire thought the killer had meant to get Phoebe's twin sister, Marcy Edmond. Phoebe had borrowed her sister's car. Just been in the wrong place at the wrong time. For that reason, Claire thought Marcy and her husband were smart to take their family and get out of Dodge. They had left three days ago, right after the funeral, and were now headed for the Grand Canyon in a rented RV. Claire had never wanted to see the country by motor vehicle. Long car rides made her nauseous. She was a US Airways kind of gal all the way, but tonight, the RV and hot dogs cooked on a hibachi in a dusty, crowded RV campground actually sounded pretty appealing.

Claire sat on the edge of her bed and dropped her

head into her hands. She was exhausted. Jumpy, as if she had drunk way too much caffeine. She had, of course; coffee was all that kept a police investigation going some days. But mostly it was just lack sleep. How could she sleep, though, when the images of the three women's bodies flashed in her mind every time she closed her eyes?

Every time she closed her eyes, she could see them lying beside the trash can, behind the restaurant near the dumpster, at the construction site. Cold, lifeless, nearly bloodless bodies of women who had depended on her to keep them safe. Even the tourist, April Provost, whom Claire had never met before that hot night when she had studied her body sprawled on the pavement, had, in a way, trusted in the town's police chief. It was Claire's duty to protect these women. And now it was her *duty* to find their killer before he struck again.

She rose and began to pace. Despite the hum of the central air unit, it seemed stuffy in the bedroom. She wouldn't open the windows, of course. A breach of security. Sometimes visitors to the house asked her if she didn't feel confined locked up in her little cabin in the woods outside of town with her high-tech alarm system and lock-down at night. She didn't usually, and even on a night like tonight when she did, she knew it was worth the sacrifice to keep her daughter safe.

Claire halted in the middle of the bedroom floor, a rag rug her grandmother had made beneath her feet. She gazed at the Navajo patterned quilt on her bed and thought about Ashley asleep in the other room. Her fifteen-year-old daughter still slept with a Raggedy Ann doll she had received for a birthday gift when she was three. Each night, Ashley also filled a little ceramic dish she had made in art, on her nightstand, with silver rings embellished with bats and skulls.

The same sweet little Raggedy Ann girl was also dyeing her beautiful blond hair shoe-polish black and hanging out with kids who appeared to be ex-Ozzie Osbourne band members. Her new boyfriend, "Chain," was encouraging her to push the envelope of the household rules. At first he had brought her home right on time, then ten minutes late. Last week it had been a full hour, thus the restriction punishment. And now that Ashley had broken the rules of restriction today by stopping at the diner, it would be longer, torturing both her and Claire.

Ashley's father, now remarried with two children, had suggested that Claire consider sending their daughter to live with him for a year or so in Utah. Just to get her away from the crowd she had chosen to hang with, he said. Claire had outright refused. She told Tim it was because Ashley didn't want to go, didn't want to be a part of his new family with the cheeky wife and cheeky kids. Truth was, Claire couldn't stand to see Ashley go. Even being the pain in the ass that she was being right now, Claire's entire world revolved around her daughter.

And this crappy job that had been her dream job until a month ago, when waitress Patti Lorne's body had turned up.

Claire reached for the bottle of water she took to bed with her each night, then realized she'd forgotten it. Annoyed with herself, she opened her door and started back down the hall toward the kitchen. She passed Ashley's closed door, no light showing beneath it.

But she could have sworn she saw light as she opened her bedroom door. Claire had almost reached the kitchen when she caught the scent of something burning.

She cursed beneath her breath and stomped back down the hall. Without the courtesy of knocking, she grabbed the doorknob, twisted, and barged in.

Ashley was standing at the window in boxer briefs and a baby-doll tee. The room smelled of cigarettes, though there was no smoke to be seen by the dim light of the bedside lamp.

"You've been smoking again?"

"Mom—"

"Don't bother, Ashley," Claire interrupted, striding toward the window where the purple curtains were uncharacteristically drawn back. "You know I hate lying."

"You're supposed to knock." Ashley thrust one narrow hip out, offering her best belligerent teen tone. "I thought we agreed on each other's privacy, which includes knocking on the door before entering."

"And I thought we agreed you would not smoke." Claire reached out to check the lock on the window. Sure enough, it was open. It wasn't smoky in the room because Ashley had been enjoying her fag with the window open.

Claire twisted the lock on the window and yanked the drapes to cover the glass panes. "Were you trying to sneak out or just have a little cig break before you went to bed?"

"Sneak out? Where would I go?" Ashley crossed her arms over her small breasts and dropped onto her bed. "It's not like I would have any friends to go to. Not after the way you embarrassed me at the diner today."

"We lock the windows for a reason, Ashley. You know the reason."

"So serial killers don't sneak in and carry us away," her daughter mocked. As she spoke, the straight black hair that had once been duck-down blond brushed her shoulders.

"We lock the windows because it what all people with a lick of sense do." Claire thrust out her hand. "Now hand them over."

Ashley looked up at her mother, suddenly an innocent. "Hand over what?"

"You know what." Claire kept her hand extended. "You hear Grandpop wheeze. You see his oxygen backpack. Is that what you want? To slowly asphyxiate someday because, once upon a time, you wanted to smoke cigarettes and look cool? Or were you hoping for cancer? Lung, breast, tongue, take your pick."

"The nukes will probably kill me first." Ashley stared at her mother for a moment, and when she saw she wasn't going to back down, she pulled a pack of cigarettes and a lighter from under a Goth magazine spread on the messy bed. "Take 'em. They make my hair stink anyway."

Claire walked toward the door, circumnavigating a growing pile of clothes on the floor. "I thought you were going through your stuff. Bagging up clothes for the church yard sale."

"I am, obviously." The teen gestured to the clothes pile.

"I'd put you on restriction for this if you weren't already going to spend the rest of your life with no phone or Internet." Claire halted at the door and allowed herself a sigh. "Ashley, I don't understand why you have to be this way with me right now. I'm already at my wit's end with work. I could use a little support."

"Grandpop told me he caught you smoking in the woods behind their house when you were fourteen."

"Thanks, Dad," Claire muttered, rolling her eyes. "Yes," she admitted. "He did, after my girlfriend and I started a brush fire and the fire department had to be called. That was how I ended up with my first job." She crumpled the offending cigarette soft pack in her hand. "Dad got me a job with the park service."

"I know. Picking up butts." Ashley flung herself backward onto a stack of pillows on her bed.

Claire studied her daughter for a moment, trying to ignore the black poster of a man sticking a python's head into his mouth on the wall behind the bed. "I know I've said this a million times, Ash, but we're going to get through this, you and I. I swear we will."

"Yeah." Her daughter groaned, staring at the ceiling. "If we don't kill each other first."

Claire stepped into the hall. "I'll be gone by the time you get up in the morning. Grandmom or Grandpop will be here to get you in time for you to get to work.

How about if I pick you up at Stewart's when you get off?"

Ashley's blue eyes cut to her mother. "The nursery closes at five. You haven't been home that early in weeks."

"Well, I will be tomorrow. 'Night."

Ashley made no reply as Claire closed the bedroom door, but that was all right. Claire remembered being this age. She remembered how hard it had been. What idiots, she thought at the time, her parents were. All teenagers went through this. It was just a stage. She repeated the words like a mantra as she went back down the hall toward her bedroom.

"Just a stage. Just a stage." She shot the crumbled cigarette pack and lighter into the garbage can inside her bedroom door. "Lord, help me."

"May I help you?" A grandfatherly looking man in a light blue smock at the reception desk in the hospital's main lobby asked kindly.

"Yes." Jillian leaned on the counter, pushing some paperwork across the counter. "I'm from out of town, but my doctor in Virginia wants me to have these blood tests done. He said someone could call his office if need be."

The old man sported a name tag that said "Volunteer. Hi, I'm Randolph. May I help you?" Randolph was handwritten with a marker and there was barely room on the tag for the 'h'. "I don't think this will be a problem," he said cheerfully. "Someone in billing can straighten this out later, if necessary. Just fill this out." He slid a clipboard with a pen attached across the desk to her. "Then have a seat right here in the waiting room. Someone will call your name."

"Thanks." Jillian filled out the form, using the cottage's address and marked "temporary" on the margin.

She listed no phone number. For the insurance information, she fished a small card out of her wallet. The Amnesia Society offered a basic health insurance plan through the generosity of some apparently loaded benefactors.

Jillian rechecked the information she had written down, then handed the volunteer the clipboard. "Thanks."

"You're welcome"—he glanced down at the form—"Miss Deere. Have a seat and we'll be right with you."

Jillian took an end chair that looked just like the chairs in the hospital waiting room in Portsmouth. She wondered if every hospital in the U.S. had the same chairs. She picked up a magazine and flipped through the pages, glancing up occasionally as people came and went.

Two nurses dressed in white pants and bright smocks passed. A grandfatherly looking doctor on his cell. An elderly gentleman pushed a woman of the same age through the lobby in a wheelchair, talking softly to her as they went by. It was like a replay of the images she had seen in Portsmouth General. The only thing she spotted even slightly out of the ordinary was a heavy man in a Hawaiian shirt and a bad toupee who entered the automatic doors and marched up to Randolph's station.

"Can you get me in right now for these blood tests? I haven't got time to wait this morning, Randy," he said loudly, sliding a form across the desk. "City business to attend to."

"I'll see what I can do, Mayor," the elderly volunteer replied as he scurried through a door behind him.

While the mayor waited, he leaned against the counter and wiped his sweaty forehead with a folded white handkerchief. He caught Jillian's eye and smiled.

She gave a quick smile back and lowered her nose to the magazine, feeling silly for having been caught eavesdropping.

Randolph returned a minute later and ushered the mayor down the hall toward the outpatient area. The two disappeared into the bowels of the hospital, and the volunteer soon returned, minus the mayor, looking relieved.

Jillian hadn't waited five minutes longer when a young woman cheerfully called her name.

"Here." Jillian dropped the magazine and grabbed her purse.

"I'm Missy and I'll be taking care of you today," the bright-eyed, slightly plump hospital employee said from the outpatient services hallway.

Jillian noted that she wore a blue smock with yellow Spongebob characters all over it. Again, it struck that she recognized a kid's cartoon character, but she didn't know what her own occupation was. This morning it didn't upset her, though. This morning, it just seemed funny.

Missy led her down a wide corridor into a small lab where Jillian took a seat in a chair that resembled an old-fashioned school desk. She flipped the armrest down herself and offered her left arm.

"Randolph says you're just visiting us this week," Missy said cheerfully as she placed labels with Jillian's name and patient number on glass tubes.

"Yes. I rented a cottage on the ocean. Off Juniper."

"Ocean front. Great."

There was a knock on the open door, and a nice-looking man in his early to mid-thirties poked his head through the doorway. "Sorry," he apologized to Jillian before turning his attention to his co-worker. "Missy, can I grab a couple of syringes? I don't know who is stocking these rooms, but—"

". . . they ought to fire his or her butt," Missy finished for him. "Help yourself." She gestured to the counter. "This morning I didn't have a single cotton ball when I saw my first patient at six."

The lab technician took two white boxes from a stack on the counter and disappeared down the hall.

"Sorry about that." Missy tied Jillian's arm with a short length of rubber tubing.

"No problem." She glanced out the door, into the open hallway. "I've only been in town since yesterday, but everyone seems so nice."

"It's a great place to visit." The technician thumped the vein in the crook of Jillian's elbow. "A little stick, now." She eased the needle into the vein and popped a vial on the end of the syringe, removing the tourniquet. "Terrific place to raise children, too."

Jillian watched as the vial filled with blood.

"You have kids?" Missy asked. She removed the vial and snapped on another empty one.

"No." Jillian offered a quick smile. "But maybe someday." She didn't know what made her say that, but she sensed it was not the first time the words had come from her mouth.

"There. All done." Missy removed the needle and pressed a cotton ball to the tiny bubble of blood in the crook of Jillian's arm. "Just hold that up for a sec." She guided her arm in the air.

Missy dropped the vials of blood into a little tray and reached into a glass jar full of Band-Aids. "Let's see, Rugrats, Tweety, my favorite Spongebob." She plucked her smock. "Or boring old plain Band-Aids."

"Tweety," Jillian said.

Missy put the Band-Aid on Jillian's arm. "Okay, you can go. We'll have the results faxed to your doctor, oh . . . probably tomorrow." She turned to her. "So have a great day on the beach."

"Thanks." Jillian walked out of the lab, down the hall, and through the doors of the hospital, out into the parking lot. As she climbed into her car, she realized that if she was going to be at the beach for the week, she was going to need a bathing suit. She glanced up at the sky and squinted. "And suntan lotion and a pair of sunglasses," she told herself aloud.

Jillian stopped at a small shopping center she had passed on her way to the hospital this morning. She picked up the suntan lotion and a cute pair of ten-dollar sunglasses, but choosing a bathing suit took longer. As she held two suits up for inspection, she wondered what kind of woman she was. A one-piece or a two-piece? Trying them on behind a curtain in a makeshift fitting room in the back of the store, she decided she had a pretty nice body. No stretch marks. Pert breasts for a woman somewhere in her mid-thirties.

She went with the two-piece in navy. It was simple, but contemporary. She also grabbed a pair of rubber flip-flops printed in navy and white Hawaiian flowers. On her way through the checkout line, she picked up a striped white and blue beach towel, a six-pack of sodas, and two bags of pretzels. Two for the price of one. As she paid for her purchases, she thought that at the rate she was going through money, she was going to have to think about a job at some point. The question was, doing what?

In the parking lot, Jillian tossed her bags in the trunk. As she came around the side of the car, a man she recognized from the previous day approached her.

"So how's the old Williams' place?" Seth, the realtor, grinned like a used car salesman.

"Fine. Great." Feeling uncomfortable with the way he walked right up to her, getting into her personal space, she opened the car door, putting it between them. "How'd you know I was the person who took it?"

"Small town." He grinned. "I'm Seth Watkins."

"Yes, I know."

"You do?"

"Small town," she said. "And . . ." She pointed at his name badge.

He looked down at the tag on his madras plaid shirt, then up at her and laughed. "Yeah, right."

Jillian had fished her new sunglasses out of a bag before closing the trunk, and she now fiddled with the tag on the nosepiece.

"Well, if there's anything you need. Anything I can do. It's my listing," he explained. "Just call me at Waterfront Realty." He grabbed a lime-green pen from his pocket and offered it. "Number's right there."

"Thanks." She didn't really want the pen, but she took it and slid into the front seat. "Have a good day," she called before slamming the door.

Seth stood there for a second, then gave a wave and walked away, seeming to at last get the hint. Jillian tossed the pen on the seat and gave the price tag on the glasses a final tug. It came free and she pushed the glasses on before starting the engine. It was stifling in the car, but she didn't want to roll down the window. That guy gave her the creeps.

She made one more stop on the way back to the cottage. At a small grocery store, she bought lunch meat, wheat bread, cereal, milk, and half a watermelon. She had no idea how she was going to eat half a watermelon by herself, but it looked too tempting to turn down.

On the street beside the cottage, Jillian grabbed two bags and headed up the wooden walk. She'd have to go back for the others. As she came around the corner, she saw Ty sitting on the front steps.

"Hey," he called.

She found herself smiling. "You're just in time for lunch," she called to him, tossing her keys. "Bags are in the trunk."

He caught the keys in midair and passed her on the wooden walk. "You got it."

Chapter Three

"Thanks for the lunch, but I better get back on the stand so my relief can move down the beach. The watermelon was great." Ty trotted down the steps, lifting his hand in the universal peace sign.

Laughing, Jillian signed back. "Have a good afternoon."

"You, too." He turned and jogged backwards up the path, lifting his feet high in the hot sand. "Hey, my parents are having this annual barbeque thing tonight. Want to come?"

She hesitated. She felt uncomfortable in social groups. Not knowing who you were made you an outcast before you even walked into the party. But Angel had told her that one of the best ways to get back into sync with others was to spend time with them, chatting, having a cup of coffee. Jillian guessed that extended to backyard barbeques, too.

"Come on," Ty coaxed. "Just a few neighbors, friends, my family. My dad will be making his famous ribs, and there'll be plenty of cold brewskies."

"Maybe I'll stop by."

"Nope. You're not getting out of it that easily. I'll

come get you. That will give my Aunt Carmen something to gossip about besides my mom's lousy potato
salad. I'll probably go home and shower after work. Pick
you up at six-thirty?"

It sounded an awful lot like he was making a date
with her, and Jillian didn't know if she was ready for that.
He was, after all, barely more than a kid and she . . . she
was— "Ty," she called after him.

But it was too late. He had turned and run up the
sand dune, disappearing over the other side.

Jillian spent the rest of the afternoon cleaning out
the dish and food cupboards in the kitchen, wiping the
dust from the shelves and clearing the cobwebs. She
washed every dish with the tiny flower pattern and stacked
them neatly in their place. She didn't know if it was the
china itself, the kitchen, or just the dull routine of housekeeping, but somehow she found the simple domestic
tasks comforting.

At five-thirty, hot and sweaty from the work, she took
a shower and dressed in a pair of jean shorts, a white
tee, and her new flip-flops. Ready, she went out on the
front porch to wait for Ty. There was a cool breeze off
the ocean that blew through her still-damp hair, tick-
ling the back of her neck. Today while cleaning, her
hair had made her hot, and she had registered a mental
note to go tomorrow and find some elastics to put it up
in a ponytail. It was amazing how many things a woman
needed when she was starting out with nothing.

Jillian leaned on the front rail and stared out at the
waving dune grass. She wondered if somewhere, in some
bathroom, she kept a pack of elastics. It made sense,
considering the length of her hair. Somehow that made
her sad. What if she never made it back to the place that
had been her home, back to those hair elastics? What if
she never again saw her possessions? Rode in her own
car, slept in her own house? What if she never again ate

her favorite meal because she couldn't remember what it had been?

Jillian felt her chest tighten with anxiety, and she reined herself in before all the what-ifs overwhelmed her. She knew that she dwelled on these trivial things to keep from thinking about the bigger picture, but that bigger picture was what she knew she needed to consider.

What if she never discovered who she had been? What then? Even worse, what if she never found out how she ended up in the emergency room, dumped on the pavement? What if she never found out who had tried to kill her? Could she ever be safe, not knowing?

Jillian had left Virginia on the pretense of finding herself, discovering her identity. She told herself she came to Albany Beach simply because this was where the road led her. The truth was, she was hiding here. She just didn't know from whom.

The sound of an approaching motorcycle broke Jillian from her melancholic thoughts. She locked the cottage door behind her, let the screen door go, and went down the steps. She met Ty on the wooden walk alongside the cottage. He was wearing a pair of old shorts, a surfing tee, and his ever-present sunglasses. Under his arm was a motorcycle helmet.

"You came for me on the motorcycle?" she asked skeptically.

He tossed the helmet to her. It was the old style, without a Plexiglas shield. "Surely a woman who knows a '58 Chief likes riding motorcycles."

She followed him toward the street, pulling on the white helmet and fastening the chin strap. "I'm not so sure about this going to your parents' for dinner. Can't we just go grab a burger at the diner?"

Ty reached his bike and straddled it. "Nope. It's not Tuesday. Not burger night. Besides, I told Mom and

Dad all about you, and I want them to meet you. Hop on."

Jillian took a deep breath and climbed on behind Ty.

"Just hold on to me," he said, reaching behind to take her hands and wrap them around his waist. He had started the bike so he had to shout over the rumble of the old motor. "And if I lean, you lean. Ready?"

She tightened her arms around Ty's waist, thinking how good it felt to have the physical contact. Though it scared her, it was something she missed. When everyone was a stranger around you, there wasn't much touching, and when there was, it was only impersonal; doctor's exams, blood tests. Since she awoke in the hospital in the intensive care unit, no one had hugged her but Angel.

"I'm ready," she hollered.

The bike shot forward, and Jillian gave a little involuntary cry as she lifted her feet off the pavement to prop them on the footrests. She should have worn sneakers. But Ty was wearing flip-flops, too. And no helmet. She knew both were unsafe, and yet a part of her yearned for that indestructible feeling she knew went only with youth.

Ty picked up speed, and they flew around the corner out onto a broad, tree-lined street. Jillian could feel her hair whipping behind her and hear the wind whistling. There was something about the sensation of the speed on the back of the bike that made her smile. She felt, if just for a moment, that she was leaving the whole mess her life had become behind. She felt like she was flying.

They zoomed across town, through yellow lights, around tight corners, always just above the speed limit. Ty waved to other motorists, to a postman walking down a sidewalk with a mailbag on his shoulder, even to the cop she had seen at the diner the day before, who cruised by in one of the city's marked police cars. The ride was scary, but invigorating, and when he slowed, turned into a residential area, and pulled up in front of a two-story frame house complete with white picket fence and barking dog, it was too soon for Jillian for the ride to end.

She hopped off the bike, pulling the helmet off her head and shaking out her hair.

Ty was grinning as he climbed off.

"You're crazy, you know that?" she said.

He laughed and reached out to brush some hair off her face. An intimate gesture, as exhilarating as the ride had been. "True. But what's makes you say that?"

"Because you were speeding back there when you waved at that policeman."

"Him?" He gave a wave of dismissal. "That was Mc-Cormick, my sister's old boyfriend. He'd never dare give me a speeding ticket for eight over the limit. I caught him and my sister bare-assed on my parents' living room couch when I was fourteen. He's owed me ever since for not ratting on him."

Ty's grin was, once again, infectious. "Even so"—she laughed, propping the helmet on the bike's worn leather seat—"that will only keep you from getting a ticket. It won't keep you from being scraped off the pavement with a shovel when you hit a tree."

"I didn't hear you complaining on the ride over here," he teased, starting up the driveway.

"Only because I was too frightened for my life."

"Yeah, right." He reached back and grabbed her hand as if it was the most natural thing. "Come on and meet my folks before my dad gets too plastered and my mom starts threatening to leave him." He looked back at her over one shoulder. "Been happening every Fourth of July weekend since I was a kid. It's practically a family tradition."

Ty led Jillian through a screened-in breezeway, between the house and the garage, out into the fenced-in backyard where there was music coming from a boom box set up on a picnic table. The Rolling Stones; she knew the song. The yard was packed with people—adults, teens, kids, and at least two racing, barking mixed-breed dogs.

"You said just a few people," she whispered in Ty's ear, suddenly feeling very self-conscious. There had to be close to a hundred people crammed into the back-yard. The sound buzzed in her ears—voices of conversation, laughter, dogs barking, Mick Jagger crooning, and the occasional child's shriek of glee. For Jillian, it was almost overwhelming.

"Oh, this *is* a just a few people by my dad's standard. You ought to see the Christmas party. Mom says they're going to have to start renting the fire hall if he doesn't stop inviting people." He tightened his grip on her hand and led her around a clump of middle-aged men and women arguing over which episode of their favorite sitcom was the best.

"Dad," Ty called, weaving his way to a smoking stainless-steel grill on the far side of a cedar deck that extended out from French doors on the house. "I want you to meet Jillian."

She offered her free right hand, digging for Ty's last name. She knew he'd told her. "Mr. Addison, nice to meet you."

"Call me Dick." He pumped her hand like a high-powered executive. "It's not my name, but everyone does."

Ty grimaced. "Dad, that joke never went twenty years ago, I don't know why you're still trying it."

"Kids." Dick Addison gestured toward his son, who towered over him, with an expensive bottle of beer. "You send 'em to college and suddenly they think they're smarter than you," he said good-naturedly.

Ty glanced sideways to Jillian. "Okay, so if we wanted to catch him sober, we should have gotten here earlier."

Ty's father laughed heartily and patted him on the

back, sloshing beer on his shirt. "Get yourselves a plate. We'll have Dick's famous ribs coming off the grill any minute."

"Come on, I'll introduce you to his better half." Ty led her across the deck toward the house.

"Don't miss out on the ribs, Ty! My best batch yet."

Ty waved to his father over his head. "Be right back, Dad. Save me a side of pig." At the door, he stepped back to let Jillian pass.

She walked into an open, airy kitchen-dining room tastefully decorated and cooled by central air. The table, spread with a red, white, and blue tablecloth, was loaded with dishes of potato salad, pasta salad, macaroni salad, deviled eggs, and anything else a cook could think to make using mayonnaise.

"Mom?" Ty hollered.

"In here." A woman who appeared to be in her late forties popped up from behind the counter. "Good, it's you. I need you to pull the baked beans out before they burn. I've asked your father twice to come in and do it for me, but he started with the Molson's at noon."

"No problem." Ty released Jillian's hand and walked around the corner of the counter to don red bandana-print hot mitts. "Mom, this is Jillian. The friend I told you about." He opened the oven and slid an enormous baking pan from the rack. "You want this on the dining room table?"

"Yes, dear, you'll see where I set out the hot pads." Mrs. Addison wiped her hands on a red and white dish-towel on the counter and extended one hand. "It's nice to meet you, Jillian. I'm Alice."

Jillian shook her hand. Ty had her hazel eyes. Warm, genuine. "It's nice to meet you. Thanks for having me."

"Well, you're certainly welcome." She rattled around in a drawer and came up with a large serving spoon. "Although to tell you the truth, you could have come without an invitation and no one would have noticed. Dick has invited so many people that it might as well be the whole town."

"Baked beans have landed," Ty said, returning and tossing the hot mitts on the counter. "Anything else before we get in line at Dick's Grill? He's afraid he's going to run out before I get some."

"Run out? Jesus H. Christ, he ordered three pigs from the butcher shop. I'll be taking ribs in my lunch to work for the next six weeks."

"Mom's a nurse at the hospital," Ty explained to Jillian. He looked back to his mother. "You need anything else, you holler."

Alice waved her son away with a red hot mitt.

Ty grabbed Jillian's hand, and they made a break for the door. From a cooler leaning against the house outside, he retrieved two beers, opening first hers, then his own. "We can sit over here, out of the fray."

"That would be good." She followed him off the deck, across the freshly cut grass to a free-standing porch swing under a huge tree near the fence. It was hot out and muggy, and the beer was refreshingly cool in her hand.

Ty sat down, patting the spot beside him. Jillian eased down, and he gave the swing a push. "To crazy parents," he said, hitting his beer bottle to hers.

"Crazy parents," she murmured.

For the next hour, they sat on the swing, ate two plates full of food Ty had fetched for them, and talked. Ty got another beer; Jillian continued to nurse hers. They talked mostly about Ty's career plans, but he kept a running monologue going of the barbecue's attendees.

"You see *The Skipper* there?" Ty motioned to a big man in a shirt decorated with bright tropical flowers and parrots.

To her surprise, she recognized him. "You mean the mayor?"

He looked at her with exaggerated interest. "You know *The Skipper*?"

"I know the mayor. Well, I don't *know* him," she confessed. "He came in to the outpatient clinic at the hospital today while I was waiting to get my blood tests." She tilted her beer bottle to get the last swallow. "Why do you call him *The Skipper*?"

"Like on *Gilligan's Island*. Don't you think he looks just like Alan Hale Jr? Lots of people call him *The Rug Man*, but I like *The Skipper*."

She laughed because he did resemble the actor who had played the role. "*Gilligan's Island*? You're too young for that show. I'm too young."

"Nick at Night." He plucked her beer bottle from her hand and tossed it beside his two empties and their paper plates on the grass beside them. "A favorite pastime of college seniors cramming for exams."

She nodded. It was beginning to get dark outside. Someone had lit torches all over the yard, and there were lights along the back of the house, but the swing under the tree had fallen into the shadows. Ty slid his arm around the back of the swing to rest his hand on her far shoulder. "I know this is all kind of crazy, but I'm glad you came," he told her.

She looked at him. "Me, too."

Ty leaned forward to kiss her, and she didn't know what to do. The age difference between them, sitting in his parents' backyard—His mouth met hers before she had time to protest or duck. It was a quick kiss. Gentle. Sweet. He tasted like beer and the strangest sense of hope. . . .

Ty was smiling when she lifted her lashes to look into his hazel eyes again. He hadn't pulled back, so they were almost nose to nose. He seemed like the most incredible person to her, so different than the type A, conservative woman she sensed she was. She just felt drawn to him. Drawn to his sense of adventure and fun.

Ty brushed the back of his fingertips against her cheek. "I was thinking—"

"Ty!" Alice Addison's call broke the moment, and he sat up to look in the direction of the house, cursing under his breath.

Alice stood on the edge of the cedar deck, staring into the twilight. "Ty, honey, you still here?"

"Still here, Mom!" He hopped off the swing, sending it backward. "Sorry. Be right back," he told Jillian as he loped off.

Jillian let the swing go back and forth until it slowed of its own accord and then she stepped off. Retrieving the dirty paper plates and beer bottles from the grass, she cut across the lawn to the garbage cans lined up along the side of the yard. She dropped the plates into the closest can and was just about to release the bottles when a voice behind her startled her.

"Oops, those don't go in there."

She turned and, in the dim light, saw two men, similar in appearance in their early to mid-thirties, both with light brown hair, standing over one of the trash cans. She recognized one of them from somewhere. The diner, maybe? Or was it the grocery store?

"Recycling," he said, taking the three bottles from her. "They go here." He pointed to a different waste can.

"Thanks."

"Sure." He dropped the bottles into a can that, from the sound, contained more bottles. "Alan," he said, offering his hand. "I work with Alice at the hospital."

That was when she realized he was the man who had ducked in while she was having her blood taken today. "Jillian," she said. "A friend of Ty's."

"Nice to meet you." He smiled, not seeming to recognize her from earlier in the day. "This is Kevin James. He's an EMT for the county."

Kevin nodded shyly.

"Hi." She smiled. "Well, thanks for the recycling tip."

"You bet." The two men walked away. "Have a nice night," Kevin called to her.

"You, too."

Jillian stood for a moment in the dark beside the recycling bin, not sure where to go. What to do. She was beginning to feel a little claustrophobic. All these people. Everyone talking. Jimmy Buffett was singing now about that mythical place called Margaritaville.

She was ready to go home to the quiet of the cottage. To the relative safety she felt there. She cut across the lawn and entered the house through the same French doors Ty had taken her through before. No one was in the kitchen. It looked like wolves had been through the dining room, feeding on the great spread of food on the table. There was barely anything left but a few elbow macaroni noodles and a spoonful of baked beans. No Ty. Not even a sign of Mrs. Addison. Jillian would just go back outside and wait on the swing.

She turned to go when she heard his voice from down the dark hall that led off the dining room.

"Then, Mom, don't offer it," she heard him say, irritation in his voice. It was the first time Jillian had ever heard him annoyed. Granted, she had only known him a little more than twenty-four hours, but it added an interesting note to his personality. Even the happy-go-lucky Ty could get annoyed by his mother.

"I'm just saying, a woman her age—"

Jillian stiffened. They were talking about her.

"Her age?" Ty snapped. "I told you, she doesn't even *know* how old she is."

"Son, you can very well look at her and tell she's not still in college. She's a grown woman, for heaven's sake!"

"And I'm what? A Hostess Ho Ho?"

"Don't use that smart-ass tone with me. You do what you want."

"I will," he injected.

Jillian rested her hand on the handle of the French

door. She knew it was wrong to eavesdrop. It didn't matter that the conversation was about her; it was private between Ty and his mother. It wasn't any of her business.

She didn't move.

"I'm just telling you to be careful. Women her age shouldn't be interested in young men like you. It's suspicious, that's all."

"You think she's going to take advantage of me, Mom? What, take my money? I've got forty-two bucks in the bank and a 1958 motorcycle to my name." His voice grew closer. They were coming down the hall toward the kitchen. "Wait, I know! You're afraid she's going to take advantage of me sexually. Is that it? Steal my virginity from me—"

"Ty Addison—"

Jillian opened the door and slipped out into the semi-darkness. Her heart was pounding. She knew she shouldn't have come.

"Did you have some of my ribs, Jill?" Dick Addison asked her, approaching from the dark shadow of the grill.

She pressed her lips together, trying to keep it together. Feeling scared and silly at the same time. "Yes . . . yes, I did. Thanks so much. They were delicious," she said shakily. "It was all delicious."

The door opened behind her and Ty appeared at her side, her savior wearing wraparound sunglasses in the dark. "Ready to go?" he said under his breath.

She nodded.

"Ty, did you meet Nathan?" Dick Addison asked. "He's new on the block. An engineer at the plant."

Ty lifted a hand to the balding man standing beside his father. "Nice to meet you. I gotta go, Dad. Take Jillian home." He walked off, and she followed him.

Ty didn't say anything as they cut through the breezeway and walked down the driveway to his motorcycle.

He handed her the helmet. "Sorry, I didn't mean to let Dad corner you like that. Mom needed me to get some more ice out of the garage. She has a bad back and—"

The Bloodsucker stood in the breezeway, beer in hand, and watched Ty Addison walk Jillian down the sidewalk. He drew his tongue over the smooth, cool lip of the bottle, enjoying the pleasure of the moment—the taste of the beer, the feel of the breeze on the hot July night against the back of his neck, the sight of the lovely amnesia victim. . . .

The moment he saw her, he had known they were meant to be together. She was quiet, but kind. She had the personality of a person who had been through a war and survived, coming out a better person for it. He'd seen it happen in war movies. Vietnam, Desert Storm. She was a true heroine.

The Bloodsucker could only imagine the strength that had to be running through Jillian Deere's blood. He let his eyes drift shut, almost intoxicated by the thought.

Then he felt that hardness in his pants that plagued him. He knew what Granny thought about that. Knew the punishment. He squirmed, shoving her from his thoughts. It seemed as if she was there more these days than she used to be, and he didn't like it. Didn't like her interference.

The Bloodsucker saw Jillian and Ty halt beside the motorcycle. They were talking too quietly for him to hear, but he wished desperately that he could. He wished he could be a part of that intimate conversation. A part of her life. He had so many things to talk to her about. So many things he needed her to understand.

She turned her head toward him, almost as if sensing he was there, and he quickly lowered his head, reaching out to fondle the leaves of a potted plant on a stand beside him. The light was out on the breezeway, and a street-

light illuminated Ty and the bike and Jillian. The Bloodsucker knew she couldn't see him, but still . . . Out of
the corner of his eye, he stole one more look at her lovely
face and then headed back toward the party, whistling
beneath his breath.

Jillian glanced in the direction of the house, feeling
a little weird, almost as if someone was watching them
or listening in on their conversation. Just part of the recuperation, she reminded herself. She turned her attention back to Ty. "Ty, I heard what she said about
me," Jillian interrupted.

He ran his fingers through his blond hair. "I heard
the dining room door open when we were in the utility
room. I was afraid it might have been you. Look—"

"It's okay, Ty." She tucked the helmet under her arm.
"I mean, she's probably right. I am too old for you."

"Says who?" he demanded.

She shrugged. "I don't know. Society, I suppose."

"Then screw society." He swung a fist in the air. "I like
you, Jillian, and I think you like me. What anyone else
thinks is really irrelevant, don't you agree?"

She looked off into the dark toward the house. She
could still faintly hear the voices, the music. She looked
back at Ty. "I don't know what I think." She sighed. "How
can I?" There was a catch in her voice. "I don't know
who the heck I am."

He took a step toward her and slipped his arm around
her waist. "So let me you help you find out," he said quietly.

She met his gaze. This time she let him kiss her without
hesitation. It was long and slow and ended too soon.

"Come on," he murmured in her ear. "Let me take
you home."

The sound of the motorcycle prevented any more conversation until they reached the beach cottage. There,

he parked the bike, took her hand, and strolled in silence with her up the wooden walk. At the front porch, she slid down onto the step, moving over to make room beside her for him.

They were quiet for a long time. Then he slid his arm around her waist and turned to her, forcing her to look at him eye to eye. "Is it really that weird for you, me being younger?" he asked, pushing his glasses up on his head.

She pressed her lips together, thinking carefully. "Not as weird as I'm thinking it should be."

He grinned.

"But Ty. Don't you see my hesitation here? What if I'm married?"

He lifted her left hand and let it fall on her knee. "You said yourself, no ring."

"I know." She groaned. "But what if . . ." She didn't finish the sentence because she wasn't sure what she wanted to say.

"You're not married. If you were, he'd have found you weeks ago."

She knew he was right, but the idea that she really had no one still hurt a little. Somewhere in the back of her mind she'd been clinging to at least the possibility that someone out there loved her and was desperately searching for her.

"Look," Ty said. "This is the way I see it. You have two choices here. You can attempt to find out who you were and try to step right back into that life, or . . ." He hesitated. "You can make a new life for yourself. You can be who you want to be."

He made it sound so simple. Like the entire world was hers for the picking. Kind of like the world was when you were twenty-three and had a lifetime ahead of you.

"I just don't know, Ty."

He kissed her cheek. "I know. It's got to be scary as

hell. So let me hang out with you for a few days. A few weeks. Let me help you."

His offer was so genuine, so heartfelt, that a lump rose in her throat and she felt tears sting the backs of her eyelids. She closed her eyes and let him kiss her again. This time she slid her arms around his shoulders and kissed him back.

Ty drew his lips along the sensitive skin above her T-shirt at her collar bone and she sighed. She met his next kiss open-mouthed, hungry for the intensity of his feelings. His joy of life. Ty brought his hand up beneath one of her breasts, and she allowed herself a soft moan.

Suddenly the hair stood up on the back of Jillian's neck, and she looked up.

"What's the matter?" Ty murmured, planting little, fleeting kisses along her jawline.

Jillian stared into the darkness in the direction of the beach. Only a pale quarter moon hung in the sky, casting very little light. She couldn't see anything. Anyone. But she could sense something.

"There's someone out there," she whispered. Her heart was beating fast, but not for the same reason it had been moments before.

Ty let go of her and stood up, looking in the same direction. "Where?"

She rose, gripping the railing. "I . . . I'm not sure."

He glanced at her. "You saw someone?"

Jillian didn't want to admit the truth. Didn't want him to think she was a nut job. "Maybe." She chewed on her inner lip. "I don't know."

"I don't see anyone." He stood on his tiptoes on the top step. "There's not even anyone on the beach."

"Let's go inside." She went up the porch steps and fiddled in her pocket for the key as she held the screen door open with her hip. When she tried to unlock the inner wooden door with its glass windowpanes, she couldn't. The old lock could be temperamental.

Ty walked up behind her. She could smell the summer sun on his tanned skin. His presence calmed her.

"Let me." He reached over her shoulder, took the key from her trembling hand, and unlocked the door on the first try.

Inside, Jillian flipped on lights and pulled the shades down within an inch of the windowsills so that air could still pass through the open windows but, hopefully, no one could see inside.

Ty just stood at the door while she moved from window to window.

"You probably should go," she said. "I had a nice evening, but—"

"The mood's kind of shot at this point," he finished for her. His smile was lopsided. "That's okay." He leaned forward to kiss her a quick good-bye. "You sure you're going to be all right here alone?"

"Of course. There's no one out there." She opened the door to let him out. "I was just being, I don't know. Paranoid." She chuckled.

"If you want, I can stay. Sack out on your couch." He hooked his thumb in the direction of the chintz print furniture.

She managed a lopsided grin similar to his. "Good try, but no go." She pushed him playfully out the door. "Now go home before I let you strip me naked on the front porch and make crazy, mad love to me."

He laughed with her. On the bottom step of the porch, he turned and looked up. "I think you should stay the whole month. Take advantage of the good deal here." He motioned to the house. "Give you some time to figure out what you want to do."

She nodded. He was right. Whoever had tried to kill her couldn't possibly find her here. How could they when she herself hadn't known this was where she was going?

"I just might do that. But if I do, I need to find a job.

I'm not sure how long my money will hold out. But it needs to be mindless work. I don't think I'm ready to think yet."

"Albany Beach has plenty of jobs. What do you want to do?"

She opened arms. She had no clue.

"Check the boardwalk tomorrow. There's always someone advertising for help. Scooping ice cream is a pretty mindless job. It would give you time to think."

"I'll do that." She gave a wave. "'Night. And thanks again for the evening."

He raised his hand in his usual hippy salute and disappeared around the side of the house. Neither said anything about seeing each other again, but she knew he'd be back.

Inside, Jillian locked the door. Leaving her flip-flops there, she grabbed a glass of ice water and went down the hall. Changing into a sleep shirt, she climbed into bed to read. By eleven she was sleepy enough to turn out the light. In the dark, she lay beneath the sheet with the cool beach breeze ruffling the pale blue curtains, and drifted off to sleep.

Jillian was first aware of the bed. A big bed. King size. The rumpled sheets. A bedspread kicked off the bed and onto the floor.

The room was close. Hot. A musky redolence hung in the air the way it did just after sex.

She trembled. She didn't want to be here.

She heard the tick, tick, tick of a ceiling fan overhead. She felt the hot, moist air move.

She heard laughter. Female laughter. Thick. Throaty. Full of sexual implication.

The sound frightened her. She tried to back away. Escape. But she couldn't. She felt as if she were hover ing. Floating. It was as if she was a part of the bedroom and yet not.

Where was she? She didn't recognize the bedroom. It wasn't hers.

Or was it?

That was when Jillian realized she heard water running. A shower. Someone was taking a shower.

Light spilled from a door left ajar in the corner of the room. Steam fogged the sliver of the mirror she could see inside. It reflected a silhouette. A man.

Again, Jillian tried to back away. But she couldn't. She seemed to have no limbs. No means to escape. She was just . . . there. . . .

Then the falling water stopped suddenly. Someone had shut off the shower.

She felt as if she were going to be sick. She was afraid. But angry. So damned angry . . .

Then she saw him. Just a glimpse in the reflection in the steamy mirror. A man with dark, water-slicked hair. A slash of bare, muscular buttocks.

Jillian screamed.

The sound woke her, and she bolted upright in bed. A scream. But whose? She grabbed her chest and felt her pounding heart.

It was the first dream she had experienced since waking from the coma . . . and it had scared her half to death.

Jillian fumbled for the bedside lamp, found the switch, and twisted it. Low-wattage light encircled the bed with a sickly yellow glow. She slid across the mattress, throwing her bare feet over the side. Despite the chilly ocean breeze coming through the window, she was bathed in sweat. Her hair stuck to her forehead and cheek. Shoving it back, she climbed out of bed and crossed the room to slam the closest window shut. Then the other.

Still shaking, but awake now, Jillian went down the hall and closed every window in the front of the house, one by one. She pushed them down and twisted the locks. Then she double-checked the lock on the door. In the spare bedroom, where she knew she hadn't opened the windows, she checked the locks anyway. In the bathroom, she put down the toilet seat, stood on it, and checked the lock on the frosted window.

Back in the bedroom, she dropped onto the bed and reached for the glass on the nightstand. The water was tepid now. How long had she been asleep? She checked the glowing digital clock beside the bed. Two-forty a.m. She drank it anyway.

Her heart now beating at a semi-normal pace, Jillian lay back on the bed and stared up at the old-fashioned white tiled ceiling. That hadn't been a dream and she knew it. It was a memory. Just a shard of one. It made no sense at all. She didn't know the man. She didn't even know herself. She wasn't even sure she was actually in that room.

She closed her eyes. It was crazy. It didn't make any sense. Of course she had been in the room. How else would she have seen it? And she had recognized it. It had to be her bedroom.

She rolled onto her side and drew her legs up close to her chest. She laid there for a long time trying to set her mind free, not allowing herself to think about the dream. She listened to the ocean that she could hear even with the windows closed. She thought about the cold beer she and Ty had shared and his warm kiss. At last she drifted off to sleep with the light still on.

Chapter Four

Mid-morning the following day, Jillian walked down the boardwalk, peering into store windows in search of a "Help Wanted" sign. Despite her restless night and the frightening dream, she woke up with the idea that Ty was right. She should stay in Albany Beach a few weeks and take the time to figure out what she was doing, where she was going. If she didn't discover her identity in the next month or so, she needed a plan beyond driving all over the country hoping to bump into someone who knew her.

The little cottage with its haunting familiarity was as good a place as any to stay. This decision led her to her quest this morning. If she was going to stay, she needed a little income to supplement what the Amnesia Society had put in an account for her in Portsmouth. Besides, if she stayed the month, what was she going to do? Sit alone on the front porch feeling sorry for herself and wait for her memory to return?

Jillian spotted an orange sign in a window advertising that the business was hiring and excitedly peered through the glass to see what kind of store it was. The place was just opening up, and she spotted a face familiar from the diner. Chain, the police chief's daughter's boyfriend. She wouldn't forget that name. Her gaze fell to the items displayed in the window—incense, band decals, earrings, bars and studs for body piercing. She recoiled. A head shop.

At that moment, the young man in the Marylyn Manson T-shirt opened the door. "'Morning," he said, propping open the door with a cement block.

She felt as if she'd been caught doing something she shouldn't. "Good morning."

Chain thrust an "Open" flag on a pole into the bracket on the storefront, and the wind caught the fabric, whipping it over his head. "Looking for a new ring for your belly button?" he asked. "We got the best selection for twenty-five miles." His friendly demeanor didn't seem to match his appearance or the insolent man she had seen in the diner.

She laughed, still embarrassed. "No. No I was just . . . window shopping. Thanks."

He nodded, his crow-wing black hair falling forward over his face. She couldn't tell how old he was; he could have fourteen or twenty-four for all she knew. "Have a nice day," he said.

She hurried past the door. "You, too."

Jillian then continued her quest, checking out each storefront as she walked by. It was a nice boardwalk, clean, quaint. Bench seats ran along the ocean side with backs that could be flipped one way or the other so someone could sit facing the water or the boardwalk. She passed an ice cream shop, an old-fashioned five-and-dime with kids' colorful rafts and beach chairs displayed out front, and a pizza place. The boardwalk fries stand made her smile. She was sure she'd never had them before the other night at the diner, but right now, she might consider them her favorite food if asked. As she walked, families rode by on bicycles, kids on skateboards. Several older women passed her, power-walking in bright white sneakers, their thin arms pumping vigorously.

Ahead, Jillian spotted an elderly black man under the awning of a shop that appeared to sell art in various forms—pottery, paintings, jewelry. The old man sat on a big white plastic bucket, a paint brush in his hand. He was staring out at the ocean before them, brush poised over a canvas propped on an old easel. She stopped to study the painting. It was quite good.

"You're in my light," the old man grunted.

"Oh, sorry." She stepped back to stand beside him. "I just wanted to see what you were painting. It's beautiful."

He lifted his chin, shifting his attention to the canvas, and added a fleck of color to the contour of the sandy dune. "Thank you." He added another fleck of color. "Just passin' through?" He had a gravelly voice that seemed to speak silently of the rough life he had led.

She rested her hands on her hips, still studying the painting, fascinated that he could not only paint the sky and the water and the sand so realistically, but that he could paint the feeling of majesty it projected. "The month, at least. I've rented a cottage over on Spruce."

He nodded. "The Williams' place. I know it. Been there since the forties. Was a street back then, though. The ocean, she took the first street in Hazel in '54."

"Hazel?"

"Hurricane. Big one."

She looked out over the beach at the crashing blue-green water, finding it hard to believe such a beautiful thing could bring such devastation. "That's too bad."

"Called life." He wiped his brush on his worn pant leg that was streaked with days, weeks, perhaps months of oil paint. "The Lord giveth, the Lord taketh away."

She smiled at the old man's grumpiness that was somehow endearing. "Well, I should be on my way. I just wanted to tell you how nice your painting was." She started to walk away when he reached out and tapped her arm with the other end of his brush. "You huntin' for a job?"

His question startled her. He was still looking at his painting, not at her.

"Why do you ask?"

He gestured over his shoulder with the brush. "Millie's lookin' for help, not full-time, just when she's busy or she needs to run errands."

Jillian glanced at the store window behind him; *Silver & Things* was painted in gray on the glass. She saw a pottery lamp, a seascape on an easel, and several shelves of jewelry on black velvet display trays, but no "Help Wanted" sign. "Is she?"

"Go on in," he said. "Tell 'er Jenkins sent you. She'll hire you, all right."

She looked at the store apprehensively, then back at the painter. "Thank you, Mr. Jenkins." She set her jaw determinedly. "I think I will."

"Ain't *Mr.* Jenkins." He dipped his brush on a card of smeared oil paint and daubed at the blue sky on the canvas, adding swirls of white. "Just plain Jenkins."

Jillian nodded and pushed through the glass door, and a little bell overhead jingled.

"Good morning," a slender woman in her mid-sixties said from behind a glass counter.

"Good morning." Jillian smiled.

The shopkeeper, Millie, was an attractive woman for her age with white hair pulled back in a thick plait that ran down her back and a colorful gauze shirt. Long silver earrings that looked like wind chimes danced in her ears when she spoke. "Looking for anything in particular or just getting in out of the heat?"

"Actually, I was talking to Jenkins outside"—she pointed—"and he said you were looking for part-time help."

Millie had been polishing a piece of jewelry with a

green cloth, but she halted the motion to scrutinize Jillian. "Just moved to Albany Beach?"

"Sort of. I . . . it's a long story, but I've rented a place and I'll be staying the month at least. I don't know if you want to hire someone who—"

"You're that woman Alice Addison was telling me about." She waggled the polish cloth, her interest suddenly piqued. "The one Ty found on the beach with the amnesia."

Jillian chuckled, glancing at the indoor-outdoor carpet on the floor, suitable for sandy feet, then up at Millie. "Well, he didn't find me on the beach with amnesia; I've been like this for a while, but that's me. Word gets around fast here, doesn't it?"

She shrugged. "Those of us who live here year-round are a close-knit group. We talk a lot, especially with something terrible like what's going on right now."

"You mean the murders?" Jillian tucked a lock of hair behind her ear. "Ty told me."

"And you're not afraid?"

"Not really," she said with a practicality she seemed to have picked up from Ty. "Considering my situation, a serial killer stalking me seems the least of my worries."

Millie slipped the silver ring she had been polishing into the tray in front of her. "Can you run a cash register?"

Jillian glanced at the cash register on the end of the glass counter. "I don't think so. And to be honest, I don't think I know anything about art."

Millie hesitated for a minute, then broke into a grin. "What the hell, half the time I can't run this new-fangled register myself, and I certainly don't know anything about art. The place was my husband's, and when he died, it was easier to just keep opening the doors than to find a new way to make a living. You're hired."

Jillian grinned. "I am?"

"Sure. When can you start?"

"Well, now." Jillian lifted her hands and let them fall. "It's not like I have anything else to do."

"Then come on back." Millie gave a wave. "I'll show you the basics of the register, and you can start polishing these rings. You don't need to know who you are to polish silver."

The Bloodsucker sat at the lunch counter and stared at his uneaten BLT on toasted wheat in front of him. He took a potato chip off the Melmac plate and stuck it in his mouth. Chewed. Sipped his Coke. No ice. He jiggled his leg.

He was wired. He couldn't eat. Couldn't sleep. It was all he could do to keep up appearances at work.

It had only been a little more than a week since Phoebe Matthews. He could still smell the blood in the barn if he closed his eyes and breathed deeply. But already the power was waning. He could feel it seeping from his pores. Oozing out. And when it was gone, the last ounce spent, he knew he would feel worse than he had before. The blood had become like a drug . . . no, an elixir. It was the only thing that made him feel good.

"Need a refill, hon?"

The Bloodsucker looked up to see Loretta reaching for his glass, her large, pendulant breasts straining against the brightly colored apron. Fat, ugly Loretta. "No, thanks. I should get back to work."

She checked her watch. He'd seen it a million times before. It had a pink wristband and a Cinderella in the center of the dial. "I'd say so."

He hated that watch. What kind of woman her age wore a Disney timepiece? Looking up at her, smile on his face, he mused over the fact that fat people had a higher blood volume. If he killed her, there would be more blood. More for him. The only thing was, Loretta wasn't his type.

Against his will, the Bloodsucker's thoughts shifted to an image of a blonde. He played the image over and over again the way he could repeat a scene in a movie with his new DVD player. She had the prettiest smile. Blue eyes that had a look of confidence that he had never felt, but desperately wanted to possess. He had several women in mind right now, but she was the one who stood out. She was the one he thought about when he went to sleep at night. The one he thought about first thing in the morning. It was like she was calling him.

He rose from the lunch counter stool. He'd wrap the sandwich up. Take it home and eat it tonight. Share it with Max. Man's best friend. He didn't know who had coined that phrase, but it was true. Max really was his best friend.

His only real friend.

A familiar face walked behind the Bloodsucker and tapped him on the shoulder as he passed. "How are you, buddy?"

The Bloodsucker nodded. Smiled. "Good, good, and you? The family?"

"Great. Take it easy."

"You, too." The Bloodsucker almost forgot to leave a tip on the counter; how rude. He fished two dollars from his pocket for his three-fifty lunch special.

He thought about *her* again and the plan he was formulating in his head. He knew it was dangerous to take her so soon after Phoebe, but he wanted her. Needed her. And really, Phoebe didn't count because he had meant to take her twin sister Marcy.

No, Phoebe didn't really count at all, he reasoned excitedly. So, really, it wasn't too soon to take the one with the confident eyes.

Just the thought of her warm blood made him tremble inside.

And silly Claire-Bear, he continued to rationalize, was

no closer to him than she had been with Patti, and Patti had been dead more than a month now. Chief Drummond wouldn't catch him. The Albany Beach police wouldn't catch him. The State Police who kept threatening to enter the investigation wouldn't either. They could send in the FBI, the CIA, any initials they wanted to send to their sleepy little town. No one was going to catch him because he was too smart for them all.

Feeling good about her day at work, she walked down the boardwalk swinging her purse on her arm. She peered up at the night sky, where clouds were growing angrier by the moment. It looked like they were going to have a summer thunderstorm. The air was still thick, hot, and humid. Maybe some rain would cool things down a little.

A jagged light suddenly streaked across the sky, followed almost immediately by a crack of thunder. She could smell the impending rain now. She would have to make a run for it if she was going to make it back to the car before she got soaked.

Picking up her pace, she wished she'd thought to bring an umbrella. Like she owned one. She chuckled, taking a short cut down an alley between Tony's Pizza and the surf shop. Her car was just another street over. Raindrops began to fall and then, without warning, the sky seemed to open up.

She squealed, kicked off her flip-flops, scooped them up, and started to run.

"Wow, where did that come from?" The Bloodsucker popped his red and white golf umbrella over both their heads.

She glanced at him, obviously taken by surprise. She hadn't seen him waiting behind the dumpster. Had never suspected. And now it was too late.

"I . . . I don't know," she said with a little laugh. She had a nice laugh, full of youth and promise.

"I'm parked across the street from the mini-golf, so sorry, that's as far as this umbrella is going," he said, liking the weight of the umbrella in his hand. He thought about Gene Kelly in *Singing in the Rain*. He understood how rain like this could make a man want to dance, especially with such a pretty woman at his side.

Again the laugh. "That's okay. I'm parked there, too." She seemed to relax. She'd met him before; he was no longer considered a stranger, and therefore not suspect.

They walked around a white delivery van, skipping over a fast-growing puddle. He glanced behind them. Ahead. There was no one else in the alley. He could smell pizza through the rear screen kitchen door of Tony's. He wished he'd thought to grab a pie to take home. He'd be up all night and would need the nourishment, but he couldn't risk it now.

Lightning lit up the sky, and thunder cracked again. She gave a little yelp, and he lifted his arm as if to pull her closer, to protect her from the storm. She turned her face toward his as if suddenly suspecting something.

Women were funny that way. They seemed to have an intuition about danger. But it always came too late. And they were never very observant, not when they were worried about getting their new sandals wet, or finding a pack of cigarettes in their purse.

She never saw the latex gloves on his hands.

He clamped the square of chloroform-soaked gauze over her mouth and nose. Her clear, confident blue eyes grew round and clouded with fear, and then her eyelids fluttered as the chemical took effect. She fell into his arms, a rag doll, and he had to drop the umbrella to catch her. He only had to run a few feet to his car. He had lied to her, but just a little white lie. He hadn't been parked in the mini-golf lot at all. He was parked right here in the alley because he already knew where she had left her car. It was the same place she parked every day.

The Bloodsucker used the remote on his keychain to pop his trunk and dropped her inside with a thump. Then he ran back for his umbrella and to scoop up the flip-flops she had dropped. They were pretty. Pink paisley. As he threw them into the back seat and climbed behind the wheel to start the engine, he wondered what he would do with the flip-flops. He hesitated, breathed in the scent of her off them. He wanted to keep them, but he knew no trophies were allowed. That might give police a clue they could later connect to him, and he had no intention of giving them any help. If they wanted to catch him, they would have to outsmart him.

Maybe he would put the shoes back on her feet when he dropped her tomorrow or the next day. Maybe he would even leave the umbrella, too, if she was nice to him. The weather man said they could expect occasional thunder showers all week. He'd bought the cheap, generic umbrella at the Big Mart a town over. They probably sold millions a year, so it could never be traced to him. That way, if it was still raining tomorrow night, she wouldn't get too wet before they found her.

The Bloodsucker hated the thought of leaving such a nice girl in the rain. And Anne Hopkins was such a nice girl. Going to college, working full-time, making her widowed mother proud. It was a shame she wasn't more careful about walking in alleys alone after dark. He would have to speak to her about that.

Jillian stayed at *Silver & Things* until closing at ten and then raced down the boardwalk through the rain to her car thinking she needed to learn a shortcut. She had left parked in the mini-golf parking lot, where the attendant had promised she wouldn't be towed. She stopped at the grocery store for a couple of things, and by the time she reached the cottage she was sticky hot and her clothes were damp from the rain.

She found a note stuck in the screen door of the cottage, but she let herself in and locked the door behind her before reading it. Dropping her soggy bags on the kitchen table, she scanned the note.

J,
Just stopped by to see how you were.
Hope you found a job. Talk to you
soon.

It was signed "T" with a peace sign.

Jillian smiled, setting aside the note as she carried the bag of cold items to the refrigerator. She then went around the house and opened several windows to cool off the closed-up house.

She'd had a good day. She and Millie got along well. The fact that Jillian had no life she could recall beyond six weeks ago didn't seem to matter. They found plenty to talk about—lots of common ground. In the afternoon Jillian had gone out to get lunch for them and would have offered to bring Jenkins something too, but he had packed up his easel and gone. Millie said she never knew when he would turn up, but he always came back because she sold his paintings for him in her store.

When they closed the store, Millie invited Jillian out for a late supper, but Jillian declined. She was worn out from her whole day in public, smiling, pretending to have it all together. It was tiring. By six she had been ready to crawl back into the cottage where she felt safe and not so exposed, but Millie had been busy doing inventory, so Jillian had stayed to run the cash register and talk with customers.

Tomorrow, Millie wanted her to come in at three. Jillian thought maybe she would get some sun in the morning. Maybe find Ty on his lifeguard stand and just let him know she had found a job. After the kisses they had shared the other night, she really didn't know where their relationship was going. She didn't have any expectations, and she certainly didn't know where she wanted it to go, so she had decided to take Ty's relaxed attitude. Time would tell.

The groceries put away, Jillian changed into her sleep shirt, had a salad, and then climbed into bed with her book. Despite how tired she was, she read until almost one a.m. She was afraid to sleep. Afraid of what she might dream . . . remember. But at last, when she could no longer keep her eyes open, she had surrendered and fallen asleep in the cool breeze from the open window beside her bed.

"I don't understand why you're doing this," Anne sobbed, so terrified that she couldn't think. She didn't know where she was, or how much time had passed since he had taken her from the alley.

"I know, I know," the Bloodsucker soothed as he blotted her wrist with the towel. It blossomed with rich, red blood.

"Please, I'll give you anything you want." Tears ran down her face, making it hard to see. Snot ran from her nose. She sniffed. "I . . . I'll do anything you want," she said trying to think of what that might entail.

"Shhhhh." He stroked her hair with one glove-covered hand. She smelled like the sub shop where she worked. "There, there, it's all right, Anne. Don't cry."

"I just want to go home," she blubbered, shaking. She was cold now. Tired. She felt as if she had been there forever, tied, taped to this chair. Wherever here was. "I . . . I'm so afraid."

"I know. So why don't you tell me about your home? Maybe that will make you feel better." He lifted the towel and, satisfied that the bleeding had stopped, he stepped back. "You live in a blue house, don't you? A Cape Cod on Oak?"

Anne nodded. He knew where she lived. He knew where she ate her lunch, where she'd gone to dinner the other night with the new guy she was dating, Clark. He knew where she rented her videos. He'd been stalking her, and she'd not known. A sob wracked her body. She hadn't even known.

"Tell me," he whispered, gazing into her blue eyes that were not as brilliant as they had been. "You have a dog, don't you?"

She nodded, then let her head slump forward.

"A boy dog or a girl dog?" The Bloodsucker pressed, walking back to the picnic table. He folded the towel neatly and set it on the tray. The red and white umbrella, also on the table, caught his eyes and he smiled, thinking of himself walking through the rain with Anne under the umbrella. Just like Gene Kelly. "Tell me about you dog, Anne," he ordered sharply. "I told you, we can do this in a civilized manner or we can—"

"Okay, okay," she cried. "M-my dog is Pickles. She . . . she's a yellow lab."

His fingers closed over the cool steel of the scalpel, and he shut his eyes for a moment, enjoying the pleasure of the weight of it in his hand. "Is she a nice dog?" He turned to Anne, the blade of the scalpel glimmering in the lantern light.

She took one look at the scalpel and screamed.

"Anne . . . Anne," he tisked, drawing closer. "What did I tell you about screaming?"

Anne felt light-headed. She couldn't see through her tears, and she had to pee bad. "You . . . you . . ." She couldn't catch her breath. "You said d-don't."

"That's right," he breathed. "So let's practice, hmm?"

Anne watched, helpless, as he lowered the scalpel. She didn't even try to fight the bindings this time. She knew it was senseless. She felt the blade cut into her wrist again, more a burn or a sear than a cut, really.

All she could think about as the blood bubbled up was how devastated her mother would be.

Claire heard a tap on her office door and considered ignoring it. She was knee-deep in paperwork, had several calls to return, despite the holiday, and was expected to make an appearance in the town's annual Fourth of July parade this evening. She didn't have time to be riding in a parade, smiling, waving, and kissing babies, but considering how quickly her job was becoming precarious, she felt that she had to go.

She'd gotten a call an hour ago from Captain Kurt Gallagher, her ex-boyfriend from her state police days, giving her a heads-up that the state police had once again officially "offered" their help on her unsolved homicides. They, as well as the mayor, would be putting pressure on her to accept before it was forced upon the Albany Beach police department, but she was being stubborn. She knew this town better than anyone, knew the people of the town. The killer was somewhere here, somewhere among them, and she was going to find him.

She heard the tap again.

"Yes?" Claire bellowed. "Stop scratching at the door and come in."

The door swung in a little, and her best dispatcher, who also served as her personal receptionist, stuck her shaggy-cut brunet head through the door. "I'm out of here and you need to be in line for the parade in forty minutes, but there's something going on up front you might want to check on," Jewel said. She popped her gum.

"What's that?" Claire didn't look up. Jewel's gum popping made her crazy, but after hiring and firing three people for the job before she found someone bright enough to type out a form *and* speak clearly on the dispatch mike, she had decided she could put up with the gum.

"Detective Robinson's taken a missing persons statement. Anne Hopkins."

Claire felt the blood drain from her face. Anne had grown up in Albany Beach and was attending college somewhere; like many college students, she had returned home to work for the summer.

Claire glanced up, slowly lowering her pen to the desk. Her cool office suddenly felt warm. Close. "How long has she been missing?"

"I was listening through the door, so I didn't get too many details. You know how Robinson is—"

"How long?" Claire repeated.

"Apparently she left work last night about ten. The sub shop on the boardwalk. No one has seen her since."

"You son of a bitch," Claire muttered under breath.

"I thought you might want to talk to Mrs. Hopkins." Jewel hung on the door knob, showing a flash of pink bubble gum as she spoke. "She's pretty hysterical. Apparently, Anne told her mother yesterday morning that she was going out with a girlfriend last night after work and then probably staying with her overnight, so Mrs. Hopkins wasn't expecting her last night. She didn't know Anne was missing until she came home this afternoon to a message on her answering machine from the shop where Anne worked, looking for her. Apparently, she never showed up at ten this morning to open."

"When was she last seen?"

"Ten o'clock last night. Closed the shop with another employee."

Claire closed her eyes for a moment. Eighteen hours. Anne had been missing eighteen hours. Sour bile rose in her throat and she swallowed it, afraid for a moment that she might be sick. She knew Anne was already dead.

If she wasn't at another friend's house, sleeping off a night of partying too late, then he had gotten her. The killer had kidnapped her, and it was likely he had already killed her.

Claire rose from behind her desk, slowly, pressing her fingertips to the smooth surface. A part of her wanted to make a beeline for the door. She wanted to leave her resignation on a pad of paper, pick Ashley up from her parents' house, get in the car, and just start driving. Where didn't matter. Anywhere away from here. Away from this killer.

But running wasn't an option Chief Claire Drummond had. Her lids flickered. "Find McCormick," she ordered.

Jewel popped her gum, unfazed by Claire's abruptness. It was one of the young woman's best qualities. "He just got off."

"Then call him back in." Claire said it louder than she had intended; she didn't know if it was Jewel's damned gum popping or her fear that the killer had struck again that made her snap. She paused and took a shaky breath. Everyone here relied on her; they followed her lead. This was no time to crack. "Please tell him he needs to clock back in and take my place in the parade. There are boxes of the pencils and sticker giveaways in the storage room."

"I'll take care of it," Jewel said, but she made no move to go.

Claire looked up.

"You know, I always wanted to be blond," Jewel said, brushing her fingers through her short, fringed brown hair.

Her gaze met Claire's, and Claire saw fear in the young woman's blue eyes.

"Kind of makes me glad now that I'm not."

"Come on, it'll be fun." Ty held fast to Jillian's hand, leading her down the sidewalk. There were others on the sidewalk, too. Kids. Old folks, a family on bicycles. They were all headed to the old downtown area for the annual parade.

Jillian gazed up at the red, white, and blue ribbons tied on the lampposts. Somewhere in the distance she could hear a marching band warming up. There was the occasional bad note—the honk of a French horn, the squeak of untuned clarinet. Had to be a school band.

"Do you really think we ought to walking down the street holding hands?" She tried to wiggle free, but he held on to her hand tightly.

"If there's one thing you have to know about me, Jilly, it's that I don't give a crap about what anyone thinks. You don't like me the way I am, that's too bad."

She gazed up him, taking in his handsome schoolboy-crossed-with-beach bum good looks. The sun-bleached blond hair, the slight razor stubble, the clear, confident hazel eyes. She wanted to be more like Ty. More sure of herself. Something told her that in her past, even before the gunshot, she hadn't believed enough in herself. She had relied too much on others to define her self-worth.

Somewhere, illegal firecrackers popped and she flinched. Realizing what they were, she quickly recovered. "But your mom. It's disrespectful to throw it in her face."

He gave a wave. "Mom will get over it. She knows I'm going back to school next month. She knows you're just passing through. It's not like she has to worry that I'm going to move in with you or anything crazy like that. She just likes to worry." He lifted her hand and kissed the back of it. "Besides, it gives her and her girlfriends in the nurses' break room something to gossip about." He tugged on her hand. "Come on; it's already started. Here come the fire trucks. We have to hurry if we're going to get a good spot."

* * *

Claire parked her police cruiser in the grocery store parking lot and cut through the alley onto Main Street. She had made it in time for the parade, but she had no intention of joining in the festivities. She had come to check out those gathering to watch the Fourth of July parade.

"Evening, Chief Drummond," an elderly woman called from across the street.

Claire smiled, but she didn't stop. She wasn't in the mood to chitchat.

Firecrackers popped somewhere behind her. They were illegal in the state, but she didn't even turn around to see what kid was dumb enough to light a string with the chief of police so near.

Claire couldn't get Mrs. Hopkins' face out of her head. The woman had calmed down and repeated the story for Claire of how she hadn't realized Anne, her only child, was missing. But as she related the events of the last day, Claire saw the dread in the woman's dark eyes. There was something about the stricken look on Mrs. Hopkins' face that, as a mother, scared the hell out of Claire. It was a look of grief, as if Anne had already been found dead.

Claire strode down the brick sidewalk, well maintained in the old section of downtown. People nodded to her; some kids waved. Even tourists she didn't know said hello or smiled. She passed the empty lot on the corner of Main and Smith where the old bank used to be, filled with venders in booths, decorated in festive red, white, and blue. The air was thick with the scents of fries cooked in peanut oil, fresh funnel cakes, and coconut suntan lotion.

Ahead, an old-fashioned bandstand had been built on another empty lot. The local VFW put it up every year—red, white, and blue banners and festoons and all. There, she knew, the judges and some of the town's officials sat in folding chairs in the setting but still hot sun, sipping Mrs. Lafferty's homemade lemonade, hoping the parade wasn't any longer than the year before. Her father would be there, as the retired chief of police, his oxygen tank tucked beneath his chair. The mayor would be there, too, as well as members of the city council, representatives from the Daughters of the American Revolution, the VFW, and the local army reserves post.

Claire dodged a stroller with twins, flailing hands sticky with pink cotton candy. Ashley was here somewhere, no longer eating cotton candy as she once had, but dressed in black, wearing a belt made with chain suitable for securing a gate or a shed. She was off restriction and had begrudgingly been given permission by Claire to attend the parade with boyfriend, Chain, so long as she was home half an hour after the parade ended.

Claire thought of Anne Hopkins and searched the sea of faces around her. If she could have found Ashley right now, she probably would have made her join her grandfather on the bandstand, just so Claire would know she was safe. Claire could only begin to imagine how Mrs. Hopkins felt right now. No . . . no she could barely fathom it because when she tried, she became physically ill.

"There you are, Chief Drummond," a man bellowed.

Claire would know that grating voice anywhere. Mayor Morris Tugman. Morris who hadn't wanted to hire her in the first place because his loser nephew had applied for the police chief job, too. Morris who thought she couldn't handle a homicide investigation . . . multiple homicides. Morris who had atrocious taste in clothing.

"Claire!" he shouted when she pretended not to hear him. "Claire, it's urgent that I speak with you."

She glanced at him through her dark sunglasses. "Call Monday morning, Mayor. I'm sure Jewel can fit you in before noon." She turned her head, looking forward again as she strode past the bandstand. In the street, a group of senior citizens from the retirement home on the bay glided by on big Harley motorcycles. The men were all white-haired or bald, but every one sported a turquoise bandana tied biker style over their heads.

"Claire, listen to me," Morris shouted.

She continued up the sidewalk, weaving through the throng of sunburned, ice cream cone-licking vacationers. As she walked, she studied the crowd. Familiar faces were scattered everywhere. She saw Billy Trotter sitting on a mailbox, smoking a cigarette. His ex-girlfriend, Patti, had been the first woman to die a month ago. She saw Seth Watkins, a successful real estate salesman in town, sweet-talking a twenty-something chick in a blue crocheted bathing suit. She saw her mother, waving a tiny American flag, and Ralph, the dishwasher from the diner, leaning on a sapling recently planted by the local beautification committee. Beside him was Jose Sanchez, whom Loretta had recently hired to clean the restaurant a couple of days a week.

A police car siren sounded, and Claire glanced at the street. Jewel had apparently located McCormick. He drove by slowly, unsmiling, arm resting on the open window. Didn't he know it was okay to smile in a parade?

Spotting her, he saluted. She grimaced and walked on.

At the end of the block, where the crowd began to thin, Claire halted and edged out onto the curb. From behind her sunglasses she scanned the crowd again. Protocol for a missing person had already been initiated back at the station house. Ordinarily, a missing twenty-year-old in a beach town in mid-summer wouldn't have gotten more than a heads-up over the radio, but the State Police in Delaware and Maryland had already been notified. Leaflets with Anne's image were being copied by Jewel back at the station house right now.

Claire shifted her gaze slowly from face to face. He

was here. She knew the bastard was here. She could feel it the same way she could feel that Anne was already dead.

"Come out here, you son of a bitch," she whispered beneath her breath. "You want a blond-haired, blue-eyed woman? Why pick on a kid?" Instinctively, her hand went to the sidearm strapped on her hip, a Beretta Cougar given to her by her father when she took the job as police chief. "Why don't you come for me and see how you fare?"

The Bloodsucker gazed out on the crowd that surrounded him and was buoyed by all the smiles, the laughter. He liked parades. He liked the marching band and the girls who spun the banners in the colors of the local high school. He liked the gray-hairs on motorcycles, and the horses pulling the old-fashioned carriages. He liked the freshly spun cotton candy and the fried oyster sandwiches.

The Bloodsucker liked being a part of the celebration of the signing of the Declaration of Independence. He was proud to be an American. Proud to be a registered voter and a citizen of this fine town.

A burst of wind blew a lollypop wrapper past his face and, startled, he swiped at it. As he moved his hand across his face, he caught a scent of blood on his hand.

It was only imagined, of course. He knew that. He had been very careful with Anne. Latex gloves. Disposable suit. Those nice drop cloths from the dollar store. Two hours and he'd have the place clean as a whistle when he went home tonight.

He knew he should have cleaned up before he came. It was chancy leaving the barn the way he had. But he couldn't miss the parade! Besides, he had to come into town tonight, at some point anyway, to take care of the disposal.

He couldn't very well leave Anne's body in the trunk of his car all night. . . .

Chapter Five

"This way, Chief." Marsh, one of her officers, flashed a beam from his Maglight across the pavement. He was a retired marine, still sporting the shorn military-style haircut despite his thinning gray hair. He had worked for her father before her, and she had always felt like he was on her side.

It was almost two-thirty in the morning. After the parade, Claire had met with her officers on duty and a couple who had volunteered to come in and stay off the books to spare the force's budget. It was McCormick who had had the guts to speak up and suggest that as they patrolled in search of the missing college student, they begin searching Dumpsters easily accessible to the public.

The dreaded call that led Claire to the golf course had come in over the radio at two-seventeen. She had been cruising the side streets off the boardwalk near where Anne's car had been found parked. She had apparently never reached it. An interview with the girlfriend Anne was supposed to meet revealed she never made it there, either.

The radio call said that a female body had been located

by Patrolman Savage; he was a newbie on the force who had been riding with Jacobs, an older, seasonal officer. Claire didn't particularly like Savage, and his job performance was barely acceptable; she wasn't sure if he'd keep his job the whole summer. Savage had given Claire his report just a moment ago from the back seat of his cruiser. From the look on Jeff Savage's ashen face, it was obvious he had never seen a dead body before. Not like this.

"This is how Savage found her?" Claire questioned Marsh. "She hasn't been moved?" She wore her camera bag on her shoulder. Someone from the ME's office might take photos too, but she wanted her own.

"Savage checked for a pulse. Found she was cold and radioed in."

"Where was Jacobs while he was searching the dumpster?"

Marsh averted his gaze, concentrating on the beam of light they were following. "In the patrol car."

"Asleep," Claire muttered. "Perfect." She was firing his ass. Just not tonight. She looked up to see a tan police car parked cattycorner on the grass, its headlights illuminating a Dumpster behind the country club kitchen. Even from this distance, she could see the young woman's body sprawled on the ground. There was a long red and white object lying beside her.

The privately owned golf course and country club had just recently been annexed by the town, after a time-consuming debate in the city council. It had become part of the Albany Beach police's jurisdiction July first, and the killer was rubbing it in her face.

He was clever. He also knew the town well. This was no drifter as others had suggested, Claire thought. This girl's killer was one of Albany Beach's own.

Marsh led Claire down a slight embankment. "Medical examiner's on her way."

"What time did the club dining room close?" As Claire

approached, the smell of death filled her nostrils. In weather this hot, people didn't realize how fast a dead body began to decompose.

"They stopped serving at ten; the last person was out of here by eleven-thirty."

"What time—"

"Trash was dumped in this Dumpster around eleven-fifteen," Marsh continued. "No body there then."

So the body hadn't been here long, not long enough to begin to smell. The scent was all in Claire's head. She took a deep breath through her mouth as she walked down the slight embankment to the Dumpster. To Anne.

Once again, the body had simply been cruelly discarded. She lay haphazardly on her stomach, one knee caught under her, both arms flung outward. She was pale, waxen and very thin. Claire couldn't see her entire face—one cheek pressed into the loose gravel around the Dumpster—but there would be no need to ask Mrs. Hopkins to identify the body. Claire recognized immediately that it was Anne. Sweet, full of life Anne, who was no longer full of life.

Claire pulled on a pair of disposable latex gloves she had stuffed in her pocket before getting out of her car and walked around the body, the camera bag swinging on her shoulder. As she continued to breathe through her mouth, she reminded herself that the nauseating smell was in her head and that she needed to get a grip on herself.

As she stalled for time, waiting for the gag reflex to pass, she touched the white and red object she had noticed when she approached the scene. It was a cheap umbrella. Anne's? They'd had a downpour the previous night. Close to the time she had left work. It made sense she would have an umbrella . . . but it didn't look to Claire like the kind of umbrella a college kid would carry. It was one of those big ones, used by golfers. Was that a connection to the golf course?

"There've been no objects left with the bodies prior to this, other than purses," Marsh offered.

"I want it bagged when we're done with photos. Maybe we can get some prints off it. She didn't carry it here." Claire zeroed in on the small crocheted purse still looped over the girl's arm. "The purse, too." She glanced at the umbrella again, sensing it told her something about Anne's killer—she just didn't know what.

Claire took the heavy aluminum flashlight from Marsh's hand and crouched beside Savage, flashing the beam over the girl's body, hoping to find some clue as to who had done this to her. In the harsh white light, her skin seemed almost transparent. She, too, had been bled to death; Claire didn't need a medical examiner to tell her that.

An ambulance siren wailed in the distance.

"I've got the club manager here," someone called from behind.

Claire pulled her camera out of her bag and began to snap photos of Anne. They would get better pictures once she was taken to the morgue, but it was important that the scene be recorded just as the killer had left it.

"Chief—"

"Give me a minute," she snapped, rising from her knee. "And back up." She elbowed an officer behind her. "Give me some room." She took another photo, getting the umbrella in. "Savage?"

"Yes, Chief?"

She gestured slightly with her head for him to draw closer. She clicked off another picture. "You've done enough here tonight; you're relieved from this scene."

"I'm not off until seven, ma'am."

"I know; leave your partner here. You know where I live?" she whispered, clicking off another photo, forcing herself to focus on the crime scene in front of her. The dead girl sprawled on the gravel and not her teenage daughter, sprawled asleep on her bed at home.

"Sure."

"Go park in my driveway, lights off, and keep watch on my house. Keep your radio on." A waste of city funds? At this point she didn't give a crap. What was the city going to do? Fire her? How many applicants did they think they would get while there was a serial killer loose in their town? "We'll call if we need you dispatched elsewhere."

"What about Patrolman Jacobs?"

"I'll take care of him."

"Yes, Chief."

"And Savage—"

He turned back. "Chief?"

"You fall asleep and I'll have your balls in a Ziploc bag in my freezer next to the ice cream pops. You understand?"

"Yes, Chief."

The young police officer disappeared into the knot of men gathering at the scene, and Claire continued to take pictures. She had two rolls of film. She'd take all forty-eight shots, and then she had to go. She had a feeling Mrs. Watkins was waiting up for her.

"You read the paper this morning?" Jillian asked Millie as the store owner walked out front to say good morning. Jillian was dusting some hand-thrown pots she had found stacked in the store room.

"Didn't have to. Had breakfast at the diner. Everyone was talking about Anne."

"That poor girl's mother." Jillian carried one of the pots to the front window. She had seen some tropical plants marked down in the grocery store and thought she might get one, reasoning that if customers could see the piece being used as a planter, Millie might be able to move a couple of them. "The paper said she was a widow and that the girl was her only child."

"Anne grew up here in Albany Beach. We all knew her. Many of us saw her first communion, watched her cheer the football team on in her cute little rah-rah skirt, read about the scholarships she had gotten to go to college, and congratulated her in person."

"What kind of sick creep would do such a thing?" Jillian crouched and spun the pot around to show off what she thought was the best side. "The paper said she worked right on this boardwalk a couple of stores down from here—the sub shop."

Millie nodded, slipping change into the cash register for the day. "I spoke to her the day before she disappeared. She made me a spicy Italian. She always remembered I liked hot peppers, but not sweet."

Jillian caught movement outside the shop's front door and spotted Jenkins unfolding his easel. The bucket he sat on when he painted now served as a container to transport his supplies. "I'll be right back. I want to say hello to Jenkins."

"You just mind the counter this morning. I'll be in and out."

Jillian nodded as she pushed through the glass door, the brass bells jangling over her head. "Morning, Jenkins."

He didn't look over his shoulder at her, but continued to set up his easel. He had another seascape in progress. This one had some kind of stone turret Jillian had spotted along the beach as she drove into town, painted in the foreground. "Nice," she said. "I like the tower. It looks like a little lighthouse."

Jenkins tipped the white plastic bucket upside down and settled on top of it. "Built in World War II. Watch towers to look for German U-boats."

"Wow," she mused, taking a closer look.

"Weren't built to last beyond the war," he grunted. "Made mostly from sand. A little spit. After sixty years, they're falling apart. 'Nother sixty years, they'll all be gone." He reached for a tube of paint and squirted a dot of blue on a piece of cardboard that looked as if it had been ripped off a box. "The Lord giveth, He taketh away."

Jillian studied the old black man for a moment, suddenly getting the strangest feeling. He still hadn't looked at her. "I . . . just wanted to thank you for the lead on the job. Millie hired me."

"I know that." He squirted another gob of paint on the cardboard pallet. Yellow.

She looked at him, at the painting on the easel, at the ocean that stretched out before them beyond the boardwalk, and back at him again. What was it about him that was so strange? Not scary strange. Just . . . weird.

"Well, I better get to work."

He nodded. "You gettin' settled into the cottage?"

"Yeah. It's nice there. No air conditioning, so it's a little hot in the afternoons sometimes, but I get a nice breeze at night."

"Don't like air conditioning. Never had it," he grumbled. "Makes me cold to my bones." He had added other primary colors to his cardboard pallet and was now dabbing at the white with his brush.

Jillian grabbed the door handle to the shop. "If you need anything, a drink or something, give me a holler."

"Got my water bottle." He drew the paintbrush across his pant leg leaving a streak of white on the layers of other paint colors. "I freeze 'em at night. Stay cold all morning that way."

She smiled and went back inside. It wasn't until she reached the jewelry counter that she halted and looked back over her shoulder. "Oh, my God," she murmured. "He's blind."

"What?" Millie stood up from where she had been stooping behind the counter, pulling out a box of silver chains.

"Jenkins," Jillian said, pointing in the direction of the old man seated outside the shop door. "He's blind."

Millie pulled two chains from the box and returned it to its place under the counter. "So? He's been blind as long as I've lived here."

Jillian stared through the shop window glass, between the words "Come in, it's cool inside," at Jenkins' half-completed painting. "But the seascapes—"

"Memory, apparently." Millie stood up again. "You look close, you'll see they're all the same. He might throw in a seagull here, a crab there. It's why we only sell one at a time. People like the idea of owning one of a kind."

Jillian kept staring through the glass. "I'm so embarrassed."

"Why?" the older woman asked incredulously. "Because he's blind?"

"Because I didn't notice."

Millie chuckled. "My mama always said we've all got handicaps, some are just easier to see than others and those are usually the lucky ones. I'm going in the back for another cup of coffee and my morning constitution. Call if you get busy."

Millie disappeared into the back, and Jillian walked around the glass countertop to the stool where she could sit and wait for customers. She thought about what Millie had said about handicaps. Wasn't that the God's honest truth?

Look at her own predicament. Talk about a handicap.

Last night she had dreamed again. Almost the same dream. Everything seemed to come in a different order, but it was the same place. The same incident. She remembered the shower running. The close room. The cloistering, musky scent of sex. The rhythmic tick of a ceiling fan stirring the warm air.

Jillian sat down on the stool and closed her eyes. In that instant, she was in the bedroom again. It was hot, sticky. Someone needed to turn up the air conditioning. The bed sheets were rumpled. There was someone still there, long, bare limbs tangled in the sheets.

Jillian knew she shouldn't be there, but she couldn't help herself. Couldn't stop herself.

Then she heard the laughter again. Feminine laughter. Playful. Husky. Sexual. Jillian's eyes flew open.

She was breathing hard, her heart fluttering in her chest. Sweat had beaded above her upper lip. She slid off the stool and walked to the thermostat on the wall to check the temperature. It read seventy degrees. Plenty cool enough, but she turned the control down another notch anyway.

The bells rang behind Jillian and she jumped, startled. She spun around.

"A little too much java this morning?" Ty strolled through the door. He was dressed in a pair of ratty but clean jean shorts and a T-shirt that said ROOTS. A Canadian clothing company.

Jillian wondered how the hell she knew that.

"You just startled me. It's early for customers."

"You met Jenkins?" He hooked a thumb in the old man's direction.

She nodded, returning to her perch on the stool. She was still a little shaky. "The other day. He was the one who told me Millie might be hiring."

"You think *you've* got a whacked-out story. You should hear his." Ty leaned on the glass counter and pushed his sunglasses onto his head, taking blond hair back with it. "Get this. He served time in prison for killing his wife. Second, third wife, something like that. Stabbed her twenty-seven times."

"He murdered his wife?" Jillian breathed. It was hard to see the white-haired old man as a cold-blooded killer.

"Says he doesn't know. Drunk out of his head. Blacked out. He said it used to happen to him all the time when he drank heavily. There was another man there that night, apparently. Stepson or something. I heard talk over the years that the kid did it, and Jenkins went to jail to cover for him."

Jillian looked through the window at the old man. He was dotting streaks of color to the sand in the painting. He had added a seagull in the sky. It was hard to believe such an innocent-looking man could have ever done such a thing. And blind, too.

She glanced back at Ty. "He stabbed someone twenty-some times, blind?"

"Wasn't always blind, I guess. He's got health problems from the drinking. Diabetes or something took the eyesight. Since I was a little boy, the gossips have been saying he was on his last leg." Ty glanced over his shoulder. "He's looking a lot healthier these days than some of them. Outlived a fair number." He turned back to Jillian, slapping his hand on the counter. "I'm off today. Wanted to see if you wanted to hang out. I might do some surfing this afternoon if the waves are decent."

He made her feel like she was twenty again. The scary thing was, she liked it. She had a feeling she hadn't enjoyed twenty nearly as much as she should have. "I told Millie I would work until five. She has to go out to some Chamber of Commerce meeting later, or something."

"No problem. We can't surf until after lifeguard hours anyway. We'll be on Third Street. The city designates different streets for surfers each week." He lowered his sunglasses over his eyes. "Come on down. We'll grab something to eat afterwards."

Jillian knew all the reasons she shouldn't. "Sounds good. Maybe I will."

He lifted a shoulder and headed for the door. "If you don't feel like it, no worries." He pushed through the door, lifting his hand in peace.

Jillian signed back and then laughed at the absurdity of it. A thirty-something woman saying "Peace, man." She laughed all the way across the room to rearrange a display of silver toe rings.

*   *   *

"Martha? Claire Drummond." Claire sat on the edge of her desk, phone cradled to her ear, photos of a dead girl spread in front of her like some morbid collage. "I hate to be a pain in the butt, but do you have anything good for me on the autopsy of Anne Hopkins?" Claire held her breath, hoping the dead girl had left some lead.

"Like the sick son of a bitch's name who did it written across her belly?" Martha Pierre asked. She had a throaty voice like a middle-aged woman who smoked too much, drank too much. Which was entirely true. But who wouldn't in her line of work?

"Sorry," she said, sounding like she meant it. "No fingerprints. Again. He's wearing latex gloves, I'm sure of it now. I found a smudge of the powder that's inside some gloves to make them go on easier."

"Latex gloves, like surgical? The kind you would wear in a hospital?"

"Could be, but you can get them anywhere. When I had my father home just before he passed away, I bought them by the box at the Big Mart in town. Drugstores, grocery stores; everyone carries them."

Claire sighed. Generic. As generic as the red and white umbrella which also showed no fingerprints. The only clue there had been was that the lab she sent it to seemed to think it had been wiped down. And Anne's mother was sure her daughter didn't own an umbrella; she said it wasn't in her nature. So the generic umbrella had belonged to the killer, not the victim. It wasn't much, but it was something.

"She was bled to death like the others, too," Martha continued her oral report. "Again, he used something very sharp with a thin blade. Could be a scalpel. Like the latex gloves, you can get one anywhere. Hospital, doctor's office, school biology classroom. But this cutting is the creepiest damned thing I ever saw. Wrists slit again, as you already know. Not the ankles, though.

Guess that didn't work for him. As soon as the blood clotted, he'd cut her again. That's my guess. Must be why there were so many small cuts."

Claire heard the flick of a lighter. Martha breathed deeply as if inhaling on a cigarette.

"That's it?" Claire said after a moment. "That's all that's in your report?"

"All that's going to help you."

Claire exhaled in frustration. This guy was smart. He wasn't leaving her anything she could use to track him down. He didn't want to get caught. "Listen, Martha, thanks. I know you ran this through quickly for me, and I appreciate it."

"We want you to nail this son of a bitch, too. Never know when the guy will decide to move north above the canal to fresh hunting ground."

Claire didn't think the killer had any intention of going anywhere. He was too comfortable in Albany Beach. He was home. But she kept that thought to herself. "If you could fax copies of your report, that would be super."

"You bet. Check's in the mail."

Claire hung up the phone and glanced at the photos of Anne's body. She knew she had to find the connection between the college girl and the other murdered women, but what was it?

Claire groaned, leaned forward, and rested her forehead on the desk for a moment. What possible connection could there be between these women who were both locals and outsiders? Anne had only been here a few weeks, home on summer break. April had been on vacation, here less than a week when she was killed. Phoebe and Patti had lived here on and off their entire lives.

Think. Think. Think.

She had already come to the conclusion that some of the women didn't know each other at all. Some in passing. Her gut feeling was that they were not associated

with each other. The killer was singling them out somewhere in town. The link was the *place*, not the women.
Where? was the question. Where could all of these women
have gone where a man might have been waiting? Watching. Choosing his next victim. Claire had been reading
up on serial killers who killed in one location, and she
knew that was how they worked. First they watched
women, then they made their selection and watched
her some more. Part of the process was the *chase*. What
was really frightening was that from what Claire read,
she could safely assume that with Anne dead, the killer
already had his next victim picked out.

Claire was so frustrated, she could have screamed.
She flipped though the legal pad where she kept her
notes to a blank page and began to make columns with
each dead woman's name as a heading.

If she could figure out where he was choosing them,
she was sure she would be taking a step in the right direction. And since April was the one who had been here
the shortest time, that was where she needed to begin.

Claire wrote below each woman's name where she
had disappeared from, or at least as close as they could
figure. Then she reached for the phone. She would re-
interview all the families, co-workers, and friends, starting with April's. Maybe if she could figure out where
these women had all been, she would know where to
find the killer.

The Bloodsucker carried the morning paper to the
kitchen table. Having the paper delivered was a luxury.
Growing up, Granny had never allowed him to read the
paper. He couldn't watch the news, either. The only thing
they ever watched on the old TV that had gotten bad reception because she refused to waste her money on cable,
was religious shows. The kind with women with piles of
white hair on their head, fake eyelashes, and black mas-

cara that always ran in rivers down their faces halfway through the show.

As God-happy as the old bitch had been, they had never gone to church. The Bloodsucker would have loved to have gone church. He would have liked to see others dressed in their Sunday best. Gone to Sunday school, maybe attended a church supper. But that would have meant contact with others, and Granny hated people. Hated him most of all.

The Bloodsucker placed the newspaper, open, on the table and smoothed out the fold in the center. There he was, on the front page again. After nearly a week, he thought he would have moved to the local section. The paper came out of Wilmington. Most days, it barely even mentioned what was going on below the canal in the two lower counties. But he was big news.

No Leads Leave a Small Beach Town Terrified, the headline read.

He liked the sounds of the words as he read it aloud. He liked alliteration. He checked the byline. Lewis Carson. He liked Lewis. Liked how clever he was with his article titles. It wasn't exactly about the Bloodsucker today; it was about Albany Beach and its citizens. But that was okay. Lewis was just trying to make a buck, climb the newsroom ladder, and it looked like he was doing well. It was his fifth front-page article in a little more than a week, and he had the Bloodsucker to thank.

"You're welcome," he said aloud to Lewis. "Any time, buddy."

At the sound of the Bloodsucker's voice, his dog, Max, lifted his head in interest. Sometimes the Bloodsucker called him buddy, too.

"I'm not talking to you, boy, silly boy." He crossed to the stove to turn his sizzling scrapple. Growing up with Granny, scrapple had only been for Sundays, then just one piece. A half pound lasted weeks, until it was nearly rancid in her refrigerator. Now he ate it twice a week, al-

ways on Mondays and Fridays. Who said scrapple was
only for Sundays? He never ate it on Sundays now.
Sundays he had hotcakes and as many link sausages as
he wanted. Tuesdays and Thursdays he always ate at the
diner. Loretta had good specials those days.

The Bloodsucker flipped the rectangular pieces of
scrapple carefully. The trick with scrapple was to never
turn it over too soon. It had to be crispy before you
flipped it.

Max caught the scent of the frying meat and got up
off the floor to trot over to his master. The dog didn't
beg, though. He was too well-mannered.

The Bloodsucker set the spatula on the plate he had
taken out of the cupboard for just that purpose. This
way he wouldn't have to scrub the whole counter down
with a bleach wash; you had to be careful with raw pork
products. He crouched down to get eye level with Max
and scratched behind his ears.

"You waiting for your breakfast, boy?" he said. "What
a nice boy to wait so patiently." He drew his hand down
the dog's back and not a single hair was shed. The
Bloodsucker had just brushed him on the porch last
night. Brushed him until his coat shone. Granny had
never let him have a pet because she said they were a
big responsibility, and he was too lazy, too stupid to care
for one.

The Bloodsucker took good care of Max. He took
him to the vet every year for his checkup and never
missed his monthly heartworm pill. He had even read
last year about the dangers of the West Nile virus with
pets and gone back to the vet to get a new product to
keep fleas, ticks, and mosquitoes off Max. If he was
going to have a pet, he knew he had to give him the best
care. It was his responsibility.

"Okay, now go lay down. First my breakfast, then
your kibble. I wouldn't want you to burn your tongue
on the hot scrapple." The Bloodsucker pointed, and

Max obediently lumbered over and lay back down in his favorite spot again.

At the sink, the Bloodsucker washed his hands carefully with bacterial soup and dried them with a paper towel. You always had to be careful when handling food.

He drained the piece of scrapple on a plate of paper towels and fried two eggs perfectly, sunny-side up. Not runny. Never runny. Granny made her eggs runny.

He carried his plate, fork, and knife to the table, where he had already put down a placemat and a glass of orange juice.

Now he was ready to enjoy his breakfast before work and read the article about how the town was terrified. Terrified of him.

The thought made him smile.

The bells on the front door of the shop jangled, and Jillian looked up from the cash register as she counted out the change for her customer. "That's eighteen, nineteen, and twenty." She handed her the small white bag. "Thanks so much. Come again."

Jillian recognized the person walking through the door, even without her police uniform. It was Chief Claire Drummond. "Good morning," Jillian called. Millie wouldn't be in until the afternoon; Jillian was on her own.

The chief smiled. She was a beautiful, tall—close to six feet—slender woman with blond hair cut in a shoulder-length shaggy style that made her look even younger then she had to be. She was dressed casually, like everyone else who came into the shop off the boardwalk, in shorts and a tee. Only as she drew closer, Jillian saw that she was wearing a New York City Police shirt with a precinct number embroidered on the left side.

Jillian's mouth went dry, and she felt the hair rise on the nape of her neck. She couldn't take her eyes off the shirt. There was something hauntingly familiar it. Something that spooked her.

"A friend gave it to me after nine-eleven," Claire said, touching her hand to her left breast. "My daughter said I shouldn't be caught dead in it. She says it's like announcing *narc* to everyone I pass on the street." She wrinkled her nose as she leaned on the jewelry counter. "Scary thing is, my daughter thinks she's being nice when she offers this kind of advice." She offered her hand. "I'm Claire Drummond."

Jillian shook it. The anxiety she had felt over the shirt was fading, leaving her with nothing but an eerie sense of déjà vu. "Jillian Deere."

"I know. Amnesia victim come to town to find herself and stalk cute college guys." Claire laughed when Jillian looked surprised. "Chief of police. Kind of my job to know who's who."

Jillian could feel her face growing warm with embarrassment. "Don't tell me you've been talking to Mrs. Addison."

"Actually, Penny, the girl who cuts my hair, who also cuts Alice's." The police woman flicked her fingers through her blond hair. "Just got it cut this morning. Feels like Penny did a real hack job, but I always feel a little naked when I get my hair cut. I think all women do."

Jillian covered her eyes with her hand for a moment. The hairdressers in town were talking about her? Now she was mortified. "So, Chief Drummond, did you come in here to round me up and run me out of town?" she asked, realizing how foolish a grown woman looked hiding behind her hand. She lowered it.

To Jillian's surprise, the police chief burst into laughter. It was an easy, bubbly laughter that was contagious.

Jillian couldn't resist a chuckle.

"It's Claire, please. And, actually, I came in to get my mom a gift. Sixty-seventh birthday." She shook her finger. "But from what I hear, Mrs. Addison would have you run out on a rail if she had her way, you sly older woman you, taking advantage of her little boy."

Jillian thought she should have been offended by the stranger coming right out and saying such a thing, but she wasn't. She liked Claire Drummond. Liked her directness. And who could not like a woman with enough guts to drag a teenager from a public place?

"I don't know what to say," Jillian confessed. "Except that he hit on me first."

Claire grinned. "That's my boy, Ty." She leaned forward, as if bringing Jillian into her confidence. "And let me tell you, had I not been his baby-sitter once upon a time, I might be pursuing him, too. I love the motorcycle."

Claire had Jillian chuckling again. "What can I help you with? Anything in particular your mom might like?"

The police woman tapped on the glass. "I need a silver charm for a bracelet, the sand dollar is the newest one in the series, I think." She glanced up; she had such an expressive face. "I'm boring. I bought my mom and my daughter the silver charm bracelet two years ago. I get them charms for every occasion. Of course, these days, my daughter prefers bats and skulls over horseshoe crabs and lighthouses."

She wrinkled her lightly freckled nose. "I've got the bracelet in my jewelry box for safe keeping right now. I know you were in the diner the evening I yanked her butt out of there; you saw what she looks like. I just keep praying this Goth thing she's into is just a passing phase."

Jillian laid the silver charm in the shape of a sand dollar on a black velvet tray for Claire's inspection.

"That's perfect. Could you wrap it?" Claire asked. "That and a year's subscription to *People* magazine, and I've got Mom's birthday wrapped up for another year."

"No problem." Jillian grabbed a gift box from under the counter. Millie pre-cut silver and white wrapping paper to fit the jewelry boxes, so it would only take her a minute.

Claire fingered a silver chain hanging from a display rack. "Listen, I don't want to start a panic in the town or anything"—she started out casually, but as she spoke, her voice became keener—"I know you know what's going in our town. The women who have been murdered."

Jillian glanced up as she reached for a strip of tape from the weighted dispenser.

"I don't know if you know all the women who've been murdered were blond-haired and blue-eyed."

"Like me," Jillian said softly.

"And me, and my daughter before she dyed her hair Death Valley black, and twenty percent of all the women in this town . . ." She let the words hang in the air for a moment. "I'm not saying you're at more risk than any woman is in any town in this country, but I just want you to be careful. I want every woman in this town to be careful." There was hint of emotion in her last words.

"I am," Jillian said lightly. "Besides, I know martial arts. Someone comes after me, I'll hi-karate them." She ducked under the counter to grab a silver foil bow.

"You do? Take classes?"

Realizing what she had just said, Jillian slowly stood up, shifting her gaze to the floor, but not focusing on it. "I have no idea." Her mind was completely blank on the subject. She had no clue how she had learned the art of self-defense. She just knew she knew it.

Claire slid her credit card across the counter. "So you really do have amnesia, and not just about your assault?"

Suddenly feeling self-conscious, Jillian carried the credit card to the cash register to scan it and make the sale. "I don't really know how to explain it. I know how to do everyday things, but it's almost as if my personality is gone."

She glanced up, meeting Claire's attentive blue-eyed gaze. "I don't have any idea what I did for a living. I remember no one. No places. No familiar landmarks. It's erased clean." She slid the charge slip, along with a pen, to Claire. "It's the strangest feeling."

"Well, I wish you the best of luck." She signed the slip, tucked her credit card into her wallet, and reached for the bag. "And please do be careful. Lock your doors and windows. Check the backseats of cars before you get in. You know, common-sense things."

Jillian thought of the cottage and its lack of air conditioning. She kept the front and back doors locked all the time, but she had to leave windows open; otherwise she'd smother. But she didn't want to bother the police chief with silly details like that. "I will. Thanks." She pressed her lips together. "And listen, about Ty. We're really just friends. I think Alice Addison is making way too big a deal out of—"

Claire raised her hand. "You really don't have to explain anything to me. You're both consenting adults, and he really is a nice guy." She shrugged. "So enjoy it while it lasts." She drew her hand down in a wave. "Have a good day."

"You, too." Jillian watched her go out the door and turn at the end of the building to leave the boardwalk, headed for the street. She stared at the New York City Police logo on the back of Claire's shirt and wondered what the connection was to her past.

Chapter Six

"It was the strangest feeling," Jillian explained to Ty as they walked along the water's edge. "Seeing that T-shirt scared the daylights out of me, and I have no idea why."

The sun had set over the ocean, but it was still twilight, that eerie time between day and night that seemed to distort ordinary images. The ocean tide was coming in, washing cold white foam over their bare feet as they walked south toward the cottage. After he got off work and grabbed a shower, they had followed the beach all the way to the boardwalk, more than half a mile, and gotten a piece of pizza and a frozen lemonade.

Ty caught her hand in his. "You think you're from New York City? Maybe you're a cop."

She laughed. "I don't think so. I don't know what it was about the shirt, but I know it has something to do with me. With how I got this way."

"You should start writing all this stuff down," he said thoughtfully. "I mean, it might seem haphazard or meaningless to you right now, but as time passes, and you remember more stuff, something might begin to come together."

She nodded, squeezing his hand. His touch was comforting; she didn't feel quite so all alone in the world with Ty beside her. "Oh, and there was something else."

She halted on the beach. Across the sand, beyond the dune and the gently swaying sea grass, she could see the outline of her cottage in the fast-fading light. "Claire was saying something about how I need to be careful with this crazy guy on the loose. You know, not me in particular, but women need to be careful, and I told her not to worry, that I knew martial arts. I've had self-defense classes."

"You're kidding me! He let go of her hand and stepped back to study her. "So show me a move."

She laughed. He was so spontaneous. So unencumbered in life by things that dragged other people down. Things they couldn't even remember. "No," she said.

"Oh, come on." He moved his hands as if he were in a bad martial arts movie. "Pretend I'm the nutjob. You're walking down the beach and I come at you."

She laughed shaking her head, glancing away. "No, that's silly. How would I know you were the killer? What if you just wanted to ask me the time, or directions to the best pizza place in town?"

"I don't know." He gestured excitedly. "Wait! I'm wearing a T-shirt. It's got, you know, like a count of how many women I've killed." He drew his hand across his pale blue, garment-dyed shirt, nearly white with wear. "I've got this permanent marker in my hand, ready to mark off my next victim."

Jillian held up both hands and Ty came at her. Without thinking, she lowered herself into a defensive position and fended off his playful attack.

He moved toward her again, this time faster. "Leaping Dragon, Flitting Fly," he taunted.

Jillian felt her body spring forward, but she didn't feel as if she was in control. Without conscious thought of what she was doing, she grabbed Ty and threw him to the wet sand, pinning him down so that he was unable to move.

"Damn."

She looked down at Ty, forty pounds heavier than she was, trapped beneath her. She was as surprised as he was.

"How did you do that?"

"I don't know," she whispered, shaken. She let go of his arms and stood up. What kind of woman could do that to a young man Ty's age and size? she wondered, walking away. "And the movie was called *Crouching Tiger, Hidden Dragon.*"

"Wait," Ty called after her.

All Jillian could think of was that she could have hurt Ty. Throwing someone around was dangerous. She had no right to do that, to him or anyone else.

"Jilly, wait." Ty came after her, throwing sand as he ran.

She kept her gaze fixed ahead, cutting across the beach to the crossover in the dunes in front of the cottage. "I'm sorry," she said, still shaken. "I didn't mean to hurt you."

"You didn't hurt me." He grabbed her hand.

She pulled away.

"Jilly, would you listen to me?" He caught both her hands this time, forcibly stopping her. He made her turn to face him. "I'm not hurt," he said quietly. "I asked you if you could defend yourself. You showed me you could." He broke into a grin. "You kicked my ass."

Something about the way he said it made her laugh.

"I love women who can kick my ass," he whispered, wrapping her in his arms.

Ty lowered his mouth to hers, and Jillian accepted it greedily. She didn't know what was wrong her. Suddenly every nerve in her body was alive and trembling. Those dreams about sex. The bed. The tangled sheets and the naked man coming out of the shower. They must have made her horny.

Ty thrust his tongue between her lips, lifting his hand

beneath her breast, and she moaned. There was something about the taste of him. The smell of him. The feel of his skin beneath her fingertips. Ty made her feel that she could survive this nightmare. As if she could, somehow, come out of it a whole person.

Jillian pressed her hips to his and smiled against his mouth. She could feel his desire for her, hard against her thigh. She molded her body to his, letting him kiss her breathless again. He was a good kisser, attentive. Giving.

She knew she shouldn't be doing this but . . . his touch, his taste made her feel so alive.

Ty slid his hand into her gym shorts and cupped one cheek with his hand. "Mmmm, no panties," he whispered huskily in her ear.

She chuckled, but it didn't sound like her own voice. It was deeper. Throaty. "Wash day."

He nipped her earlobe with his teeth. "Okay by me if every day is wash day."

Jillian dug her fingernails into Ty's back and dragged them downward. At the waistband of his board shorts, she hesitated. She felt as if she were on the precipice of a cliff. Did she have the nerve to step over the edge?

But his gentle kisses urged her on. She was trembling from the tips of her bare, wet, sandy toes to the ends of the strands of hair on her head. What had the police chief said to her today? Something about them both being consenting adults?

She felt her knees grow weak and she leaned against Ty's sturdy body for support as she stroked his warm skin along the waistband of his shorts. She wanted to slide down into the sand in his arms, wanted to make love with him.

He covered her mouth with his again and she closed her eyes, surrendering to this desire that she didn't understand for this kid. Didn't care at this moment if she understood. She let him lift her shirt over her head and drop it to the sand at their feet. Next came her bikini top. Her nipples hardened as the cool ocean air and his fingertips brushed against them.

Smiling, she reached out and tugged his shirt over his head, letting it fall behind him. They kissed again as he stroked her breast with an unhurried hand.

Then suddenly, the strange feeling came over Jillian again. She tore her mouth from his, tightening her arms around him, pressing her breasts to his bare chest. She scanned the beach. It was dark now, and silent except for the crash of the waves washing up on the shore behind Ty.

"What is it?" he whispered. "What's wrong, Jilly?" He brushed her hair from her face. "I don't want to push you, but you know it's what we both want."

She shook her head. "That's not it." Her gaze darted across the dark beach that stretched in every direction around them. Engulfed them. There was someone out there. Someone watching them. "Let's go up to the house," she breathed, almost afraid to let go of him.

"Here's okay, you know," he whispered, stroking her bare back beneath her shirt, ever so gently. "No one can see us this far from the water. Too dark, now."

"No." Her tone was emphatic, bordering on frantic. "Let's just go up to the cottage." She gazed into the darkness, unable to see anyone or anything, but knowing he was there. "I don't want you to leave," she whispered in his ear, her arms still tight around his neck. "I just want to go inside."

He picked up their clothes, and hand in hand they ran across the sand, over the dune and onto the front porch. Shivering from fear rather than cold, she fell to her knees in front of a pile of seashells she had collected, covering her bare breasts with one arm. The key was hidden in one of the bigger ones; she had started leaving it there when she went for walks, for fear of losing it in the sand.

Where is it? Where is it? Her mind screamed as she turned

over shells, sending some skittering over the edge of
the porch into the sand. Her hand, at last, found the
cool metal of the key, and she leaped up, jerking open
the screen door. Her hand was shaking, though; she
couldn't turn the old lock.

Ty reached over her shoulder and turned it with one
click. Inside, she closed the door behind him, locked it,
and then threw herself into his arms. Here, she felt safe.

Jillian threaded her fingers through Ty's hair and
pulled his head down over hers. She didn't care what
his mother thought, or Penny who cut hair, or anyone
in this town. All she cared about was the ache in her
body almost as great as the one in her heart.

"Ty," she murmured, tears filling her eyes. "Make love
to me."

"Ah, sweetie, it's all right," he soothed, caressing her
bare back. "Don't cry."

She lifted her chin, looking up into his hazel eyes as
she drew his mouth over hers, kissing him hungrily.

It was as if all the fears, all the pent-up energy of the
last few weeks was suddenly channeled into this one
kiss. He caressed her bare breast with his hand, brushing his thumb rhythmically across her nipple. She slid
her hand down below the waistband of his board shorts
and cupped one muscular cheek, than dragged her fingernails over his skin.

"Mmmm," he groaned.

She pulled her mouth away from his, panting hard,
and took a breath and kissed him again. Touching Ty
like this, kissing him, feeling his hard, muscular frame
against hers felt so familiar in the world of unfamiliar
she now lived in. It felt so good to know what to do, how
to react. *He* felt so good.

Jillian hooked her thumbs into his board shorts and
pulled them down. Ty's hazel eyes were heavy-lidded;
he was smiling. He stepped out of his shorts and grabbed
hers. They stood naked, barefoot on the hardwood floor

in the middle of the living room, kissing again. She loved the taste of him, the feel of his arms around her.

"Come here," Ty whispered, turning to sit on the couch and pulling her with him.

She sat on his lap, straddling him, looping her arms around his neck. There was no way to deny his desire for her now. She pressed her groin to his, enjoying the prickly sensation of his pale, crisp hair against her skin.

Ty slipped his hands down onto her buttocks and she lifted upward, using her hand to guide him into her. Jillian closed her eyes, throwing her head back in the sweet sensation of the moment. She slid her arms around him, rested her head on his shoulder, and began to move slowly, stroking him, pleasuring herself at the same time.

He nipped at her neck and earlobe, whispering sweet, silly things in her ear. He drew his tongue over her lips . . . her eyelids.

She smiled. Laughed, drunk with sensation. A part of her wanted to stay like this forever, drifting in the pleasure, in the sanctuary of his arms. But deeper urges pressed her onward. She was overcome by the heat of the hot, humid evening and of their lovemaking, and she pushed her damp hair off her forehead.

She moved faster, grasping the back of the couch with both hands, straining against him one moment, moving with him the next.

Too soon, she felt that tightening sensation deep inside. Her muscles contracted and she threw back her head, crying out as the orgasm swept over her. Ty moved slower, then faster, coming inside her as the last ripples of pleasure washed through her.

"Oh," Jillian moaned, relaxing her head on Ty's shoulder, her arms wrapped tightly around him. "I think I needed that."

She laughed, and he laughed with her, pushing her backward until he was looking into her eyes. "Just glad I could help you out, ma'am."

Laughing, she gave him a shove and climbed off his lap. "Don't call me that. You make me feel like I'm robbing the cradle or something."

He flopped down on the couch and caught her wrist, dragging her down on top of him. Stretched over him, Jillian rested her head on his shoulder and, for a moment, lay there listening to the sound of the waves breaking on the beach. Then she sighed loudly.

"So, now what am I going to do?" she asked, feigning distress.

"About what?"

"You. Me. I just told the police chief this morning that there was nothing sexual going on between me and Mrs. Addison's son."

Ty kissed her temple, chuckling. "You're sweet, Jilly," he whispered. And then he sang in her ear, "*Sweet as Tupelo honey.*"

She laughed. "What?"

He tucked one hand behind his head. "It's a song. Van Morrison. *She's as sweet, as Tupelo honey,*" he sang, smoothing her cheek with her palm. "Even if you can kick my ass," he finished matter-of-factly.

She laughed and tried to get up, but he caught her around the waist. "Where are you going?" he asked.

"To the bathroom and then to get us a beer."

He let go of her so quickly that she almost rolled off him, onto the floor. "Well, why didn't you say so in the first place?" He watched her walk out of the living room. "Just so you don't have ideas about putting your clothes back on."

"Nah," she answered over her shoulder, smiling. "I'll be right back, sans clothes."

Tonight she didn't want to be alone.

The Bloodsucker stood barefoot in the cool sand, his hands in his shorts pockets, watching the cottage in the darkness. Jillian had closed the curtains the moment she and Ty had gone inside, but he had been able to see their silhouettes because the light in the living room had been on and he had been here in the dark.

He had watched them kiss on the beach. Seen Ty take her T-shirt off and drop it in the sand. His, too. Had she also taken off her bikini top? He had been too far away to tell, but he didn't think so. Jillian wasn't like that. Not his sweet, lost Jillian.

After they had kissed, she had said something to Ty. She had looked around as if she knew the Bloodsucker was there. She must have felt his presence the same way he felt hers. She was beginning to feel the connection between them, and that thought excited him.

The Bloodsucker had been very disappointed when they had run across the sand, over the dune, and into the cottage. He had liked watching them kiss, though it was a little embarrassing. It made him feel funny. Squirmy. But he liked it because if he was very still, if he breathed evenly and shallowly, he could imagine what it was like to have Jillian kiss him.

Now she and the college boy were inside, behind the drawn curtains. When they had first gone in and closed the curtains, he had been able to see them because they'd been standing in front of the windows. He had watched them hug and kiss, but then they must have sat down. To watch TV maybe? No, the cottage had no TV. No air conditioning. Best of all, no phone.

The Bloodsucker hadn't meant to follow Ty and Jillian tonight. Certainly not when they went back to the cottage. He had intended to just go for a walk on the beach and then go home to clean out the refrigerator. He always kept detailed records of house maintenance and upkeep and it was definitely "clean the refrigerator" night.

But there was something about Jillian, about her lovely

blond hair, her delicate oval face, and her tragic circumstances that he couldn't resist. He had followed her across
the beach—unseen, of course—and over the dunes. Now
he just stood in front of the cottage, watching the living
room window, imagining what it would be like to be Ty,
to be inside with her.

In the living room, on the couch, he knew they had
to be talking. He was good at conversation. He liked to
talk. And there were so many things he wanted to say to
Jillian. So many things they needed to discuss.

The Bloodsucker slid a bare foot forward, toward the
porch, yearning to draw closer. To look in the window.
Just a peek.

But the steps creaked. What if they heard him? Would
Ty come outside? Would he holler at the Bloodsucker?

No. The Bloodsucker could come up with a logical
explanation as to why he was on the porch. He was
good at explanations. Good at making things up that
people would believe. They believed because they wanted
to. Because they wanted to believe in good people like
him. Like themselves.

The Bloodsucker clasped the rail and slowly lowered
one foot onto the step. The wood groaned, and it
sounded loud in his ears . . . but not so loud that they
would hear inside, he thought.

He took the next step up. Then the next, each time
pausing. Waiting. He couldn't hear Ty and Jillian talking right now, but maybe it was because she had the fan
going. He knew she had bought an old-fashioned box
fan; he'd seen her at the store. And they could be so
noisy.

Reaching the porch, the Bloodsucker paused for a
minute and took a deep breath. He placed his hand on
his breast pocket and felt the ridge of the photo. He
didn't have to take it out. Just knowing it was there was
enough.

Another deep cleansing breath and he slid his bare foot across the uneven floorboards that were badly in need of some paint. Another two steps and—

A shadow rose up suddenly in front of the curtained window, and the Bloodsucker held his breath. He heard Jillian laugh. It was low, sexy laugh . . . like Marlene Dietrich's in her movies. He didn't like Jillian laughing like that, not with Ty, at least. He wanted that laughter to be his and only his.

He heard Jillian's voice again. Ty's lower rumble. She had gotten up off the couch, stood there for a moment to say something, and now she was walking away. Down the hall maybe?

The Bloodsucker slid one foot behind him, then the next, backing toward the step. He didn't want to go, but he knew he had to. To be caught here now would complicate things and he wanted no complications. Another night he would come for Jillian, just not tonight.

Another night maybe he would even come for her here. . . .

Monday at one, Jillian walked out of the shop to take her lunch break. Jenkins was still there, finishing a seascape he intended to leave to replace one she had sold out of the window Saturday. She stood beside him, studying his latest artwork. "You want some lunch?" she asked. "I packed an extra turkey sandwich. Plenty of sweet tea."

The old man sighed and got to his feet slowly, as if every bone ached. He set his brush on the easel, his hand unfaltering, and then reached for the arm she offered. She hadn't mentioned his blindness, but he knew she had figured it out.

She headed for a bench across the boardwalk in front of the store that was shaded by a wooden slatted awning built by a Boy Scout troop. There were only a few of them, and older folks were known to get into fights over them. The other day Millie had threatened to call the police on two women if they didn't stop shaking their fists at each other over who had dibs on the covered bench.

"Business has been good today," Jillian said, making conversation. She flipped the back of the seat so they could face the ocean while they ate and she sat down, touching Jenkins's sleeve to indicate he could sit.

"I know that," he grumbled. "Blessed bells been ringing all morning. Disturbing my concentration."

She opened the small insulated lunch bag she had purchased at the drugstore and unzipped a sandwich baggie. She set the sandwich on a napkin and handed it to him. "How can the bells disturb you?" she teased, unfazed by his grumbling. She'd known him long enough to realize it was just his way. "You can't see the ocean anyway."

He took a bite of the sandwich and chomped on it noisily, the way only old people seemed to do. "I see it in my head, girl!" He took another bite. "Now what's this I hear about you runnin' some kid? Where's that tea you promised me? I'm not sittin' here getting any younger."

Here's your tea." She pushed a plastic cup from the sub shop into his hand with tea she had poured from a small plastic container kept cold in Millie's refrigerator. "And where did you hear such a thing? You know you shouldn't be listening to gossip like that."

"Not gossip if it's true." Mayonnaise oozed from the corners of his mouth.

She pushed a napkin into his hand and gazed out over the sunbathers to the blue ocean that stretched out before them, looking as if it went on forever. "Ty Addison. You know him?"

"I know him. Sassy mouth. Smart boy."

She smiled as she reached for her tea. She made it herself with tea bags and fresh lemons and sugar. It was too sweet for sassy-mouthed Ty, but she craved it. "You know," she said indignantly, "I don't know how old I am."

"You know you're old enough to be too old for him." He looked down between them as if he could see into her lunch bag. "You bring any fruit? A man my age needs fruit, every meal."

She popped open a recycled Chinese food container and set it between them.

Jenkins wiggled his nose that was so big it looked as if it took up half his face. "Cantaloupe. Good. I like cantaloupe." He reached in with his painted-stained fingers. "It better be ripe."

"It's ripe and you know it is because you can smell it." She took the last bite of half her sandwich. "Just for the record, I didn't set out to 'run' with Ty or any other man. It just happened." She looked at him. "I mean, it's not as if I have anywhere to go. Anyone to go to."

He popped a piece of cantaloupe into his mouth, his unseeing dark eyes staring out at the ocean. "There's one thing I've learned in life, girl, it's that you got to look forward. No sense dwelling on what bad things have happened to you. It'll just hold you back—keep you from being what you were meant to be. Drag you down, it you're not careful."

She thought about what Ty had said about Jenkins. He obviously hadn't had an easy life. The drinking, the loss of his wife, the jail time. Now his health. He certainly had the right to dwell on the past if anyone did.

"But I don't even know what happened to me," she said in frustration. "How do I move on if I don't know where I started from?"

He popped another piece of melon into his mouth and sucked nosily. "Start here."

She put the second half of her sandwich back in the baggie for later. "What?"

He pointed to his feet. "You start here."

She squeezed her eyes shut behind her sunglasses.

"That's what Ty says, too. That I can just start new here. Go wherever I want to go. Be whoever I want to be." She dropped the sandwich into the lunch bag. "Pretty easy to say when you're twenty-three and the whole world is laid out for you."

"What other choice you got?"

Jenkins was looking at her, and though she knew he couldn't see more than a few shadows, she felt as if he could see her. Perhaps better than she could see herself.

"Jenkins, someone tried to kill me. That's how I ended up with the amnesia. A bullet wound in my neck sent a blood clot to my brain."

"Didn't hear that."

She stared at her hands on her lap. She was beginning to tan; her skin had gone from deathly pale to a warm brown. "I hadn't told anyone."

Oddly enough, Ty had never asked, not even when he found the bullet wound scar on her neck. Jenkins was the first person she had told. And now that she had said it aloud, it seemed all the more real.

Someone had tried to kill her.

So, the weird feeling she got in the cottage sometimes—that she was being watched—might not be her imagination. The other night on the beach with Ty. She had been sure someone was watching her then. Was it whoever had tried to kill her? Was he coming back for her? If so, why was he trying to kill her? She knew it had to have something to do with the nightmare, but how?

To Jillian's surprise, she felt Jenkins's touch. She looked down to see the huge black hand, wrinkled, liver-spotted, and stained with paint contrasted against her much fairer, smaller hand. "Nobody has all the answers. Me least of all. You just don't want to ruin the possibilities you got coming to you, over things that already happened. That's all I'm saying." He let go over her hand and got up. "Thanks for the sandwich, girlie. I got to get home. My soap'll be coming on before long and I got to feed my fish."

She watched him walk back across the boardwalk to his easel, a slight limp making the going slow.

"See you tomorrow," she called after him.

He didn't look back. "Lord willin' and the creeks don't rise."

Two nights later, Jillian sat on the steps of the cottage front porch. It was already dark out, but still warm and humid. It had been a hot day. She'd had it off, so she had spent the morning on the beach near Ty's lifeguard stand, reading a new book she'd picked up at a used place off the boardwalk. When she got too hot, she'd taken a dip in the water. To her surprise, she discovered she was a strong swimmer and knew several strokes. Ty had told her it didn't surprise him. Kung Fu chicks always knew how to swim, he said. It was the only way they got the parts in the movies.

Jillian heard the now-familiar sound of the Chief motorcycle approach, and a minute later Ty sauntered up the wooden sidewalk, barefoot, still wearing sunglasses despite the fact that it was after eight and there was no sun.

"You shouldn't go barefoot on that bike. You're going to get hurt," she said.

"Yes, Mother." He walked up the steps, planted a kiss on her lips, and continued into the house. "Got a beer?"

"You left most of a case in there last night."

He came back out carrying three bottles. He twisted the top off one and handed it to her. Settling on the step beside her, he twisted off another bottle top and took a drink.

She eyed the extra beer on the step between his bare, sandy feet.

"Spare." He winked and took another swig from the bottle in his hand.

She sipped the beer and deliberated on how good it was. Cold. Sharp. Ty had good taste in beer. He said that was why he never had any money. She turned to him. "You know, considering the circumstances, that's not funny."

He propped his elbows on the porch landing and leaned back, his hip pressed against hers. "What?"

"Calling me your mother."

"So don't act like it." Despite his words, he didn't sound the least bit upset. "You ready to go?" He jumped up and offered his hand to pull her to her feet.

"Just let me lock up." She reached through the doorway, flipped off the kitchen light, and then turned the lock on the doorknob and pulled the door shut. The screen door slammed behind her as she ran down the steps.

Ty tucked his spare beer in his shorts pocket and took her hand in his. They walked over the dune and down to the waterline, heading north up the beach.

"You sure this is okay, bringing me?" Jillian asked, swinging his hand as they walked.

"It's cool. I'm telling you, no one cares about how old people are except old people." He cut his eyes at her and she laughed.

"Your mom still upset that you didn't come home the other night?"

"I moved out of the house four years ago. She knows she's not my keeper."

She studied the imprints her feet were making in the wet sand as she walked, and took a drink from her beer bottle. "She's your mother. It's her job to worry about you."

He gave her a look that was all too easy to read.

"I can't say that either?"

He shook his head.

"Makes me sound old?"

He lifted the green bottle to his lips. "Yup."

"For a guy with no rules, you have quite a few."

He laughed and shrugged. "Seriously. Don't worry about Alice. She's doing that menopause thing. Dad says we're just to ignore her any time she goes off the deep end. He always reels her back in." He pointed with his beer. "Up there. See the fire?"

One of Ty's friends had gotten a permit to build a bonfire on the beach in front of the house that he and twenty or so of his best friends had rented for the summer. At first, Jillian had been uncomfortable with the idea of meeting Ty's friends. She knew she wouldn't fit in. But now that she was sleeping with the guy, she decided so what if she didn't fit in? They probably wouldn't fit in with her friends, either. If she knew who they were . . .

"Jason," Ty called as they cut across the beach toward the dune.

"Hey, man." Jason looked like a duplicate of Ty except his hair was darker and he wasn't nearly as good-looking.

The two shook hands, fingers clasped, thumbs up the way only those born after 1980 did.

"Jason." Ty pointed to his buddy in introduction. "Jilly." He hooked his thumb in her direction.

Jason tipped an imaginary hat. "Hey."

She nodded. "Hey."

"So come on up." Jason motioned, walking up the beach toward the bonfire. "We've clams we baked in the sand. Joey swears they won't poison us. Drinks in coolers. Just be cool about the beer. We're not really supposed to have it on the beach, so use a cup and get rid of those." Jason pointed toward the beer bottles Ty and Jillian were holding. "McCormick catches me with beer on the beach again, and he swears I'll spend the night in the clink."

Jason wandered away, and Ty turned to her. "You want to try some clams?"

"Sure."

For the next two hours, Ty and Jillian wandered around the bonfire, talked, laughed, and listened to the music blaring from the front porch of the old house Jason and his friends were staying in. She recognized some of the music—Marley, the Stones—and some she didn't. She had three or four beers which, she decided when she sat down in the sand in front of the fire, was at least one too many.

Sitting alone while Ty left her to wander off into the dune grass to pee, a guy about his age plopped down beside her.

"Someone said you don't know you are," he said, taking a sip from the plastic cup in his hand. He'd been smoking marijuana, or *weed*, as Ty called it. She could smell the sweet scent.

She laughed. "That's pretty accurate."

"Cool." He nodded thoughtfully. "So you could be like the president, or that crazy Arab king everyone keeps trying to assassinate?'

She laughed again. "I don't think either of them is missing."

He nodded again. "But if they were."

She motioned with one hand with amusement. "Could very well be me."

Again, the nod. "So, you still here with Ty?"

She glanced at the young man, even more amused now. "Yeah. He'll be back in a second."

"Okay. Hey, that's cool." He sipped from his cup. "Just asking."

"Hey." Ty walked up behind her.

There was just enough light from the bonfire for her to notice how sexy he was when he was covered in sand, had had way too many beers, and needed to brush his hair. "Hey." Jillian leaned back against his hairy shins and looked up at him. "This guy here is asking me if I'm still with you. Am I?" she teased.

Ty glared at the young man seated beside her in the sand. "You hitting on my girl, Jones?"

"No, man." He looked at Jillian, then up at Ty. "Just making conversation, that's all."

Several guys with their girls across the bonfire must have overheard the conversation. Most of them were snickering. Someone was laughing pretty loud.

"Get lost, Jones," Ty ordered.

"Hey, it's cool. It's cool." But as Jones spoke of how cool the situation was, he scrambled up and walked away. "Nice talking to you, Mr. President."

Jillian laughed and Ty kneaded her shoulders and leaned over to kiss her. "What's so funny?" he asked against her lips.

"Nothing."

He grabbed her arm and pulled her to her feet, swinging her into his arms. "I can't believe Jones was hitting on my girl. He's got nerve."

He had called her his girl. That was a pretty big commitment for a guy his age. She wrapped her arms around his neck, flattered, and leaned against him. She knew she was going to have a headache in the morning. She'd be sure to take some ibuprofen before she went to bed and drink a couple of glasses of water to rehydrate.

"So what you want to do now?" Ty nibbled on the corner of her mouth.

"I don't know." She teased his lower lip with her tongue. "What do you want to do?"

"I'm twenty-three and male, what do you think?"

She tipped her head back and laughed. "I'm not doing that in the sand with your friends watching. Besides, you know what sand can do to a woman's plumbing?"

Laughing, he took hand and led her into the dark, scooping up someone's beach towel. "So how about a little grope session, instead?"

On her feet and walking, she was pleasantly dizzy. Someone had brought an acoustic guitar down to the campfire, and he was playing a fair rendition of a song she thought was familiar. "What's that—" She pointed in the direction of the fire.

"Jack Johnston. You know it?"

"Vaguely," she mused.

"And the doctors are sure you're over thirty?"

Far enough away that she knew those gathered around the fire couldn't see her in the dark, she grabbed the towel from him and shook it out. They both dropped onto it, laughing, and he pushed her back into the sand and kissed her. He tasted delicious; beer and hope.

Ty came up for air and kissed her again. He stroked her breast, and she wriggled under him. "I told you—"

"I know," he whispered in her ear. "I just want to keep your motor running 'til we get back to your place, that's all."

She laughed and lifted her head to meet his lips with hers. "Oh, my motor's already running. Have no fear of that."

As Ty, lying on his side beside her, lowered his head over hers again, Jillian caught a glimpse of motion. Something . . . someone was in the dark. She turned her head, grabbing his shoulder. She was suddenly completely sober. "Ty," she whispered.

"Yeah?" He tried to nuzzle her neck.

She nearly felt incapacitated, she was suddenly so inexplicably afraid. "Ty, there's someone out there."

"Just one of the boys takin' a piss."

She squeezed both his forearms. "No, there in the dunes," she breathed.

He picked up his head. "Where?"

She started to turn her head and point when Ty leaped off the towel and took off running across the beach.

"Ty!" Jillian called.

"What the hell do you think you're doing, you pervert asshole?" Ty shouted into the darkness.

Jillian sat up, then came to her feet. She didn't want to be alone. Didn't want Ty to leave her. "Ty, come back!"

He disappeared over the far side of the dune. Several girls and guys from the bonfire came running toward Jillian. They must have heard her cry out.

"You all right?" someone asked.

The first face she recognized was the kid who had tried to hit on her. Jones. "There was someone watching us from the dunes," Jillian said. "Ty went after him."

Jones ran his hand over her arm. "You okay?"

She nodded.

He picked up the towel, shook the sand from it, and handed it to her. Despite the condition he had appeared to be in only a short time ago, he, too, seemed to have sobered up. "Go on back to the bonfire with the others. Jason and I will check it out."

Everyone was talking at once. As they walked back toward the bonfire, a girl the same age as the guys offered Jillian the joint she was smoking, but Jillian shook her head.

This was not her imagination this time; someone had been watching her. Ty had seen him, too. He had to have. You couldn't chase someone's imagination.

At the bonfire, Jillian sat down and pulled the towel around her shoulders. Someone brought her a bottle of water. The CD player on the porch came back on, but the music was quieter, mellower. It was a full ten minutes before Ty reappeared.

Jillian got up, the towel still around her shoulders, and went to him. He put one arm around her. "You all right?"

She nodded. "I just want to go home," she whispered.

"Okay. That's cool. We'll go."

"You didn't see who it was, did you?" She pressed her cheek to his chest.

"No."

"But there was someone there?"

"Yeah. Someone who ran like hell. I lost him over a fence around a condo pool down a couple of blocks. We ran into McCormick on our way back." Ty was now speaking to the entire crowd. "Sorry, guys, but he'll probably be by. You better take the coolers up to the house."

Someone muttered a half-hearted protest, but no one seemed particularly upset. A couple of guys grabbed each end of the coolers and headed up the path to the house.

"We're going to take off," Ty called to Jason.

"You want to borrow my car so you don't have to walk back?"

"No, we're fine." Ty looked down to Jillian. "Unless you want to?"

She shook her head, her voice barely a whisper. "Let's just go."

They walked along the water back to the cottage in silence. On the porch, Ty found the key under the seashell and opened the door. He flipped on the kitchen light for her before stepping aside to let her in.

"You want me to stay a while?"

"Nah," she said, trying to be brave. In the light of the bright yellow kitchen, the darkness, the mysterious Peeping Tom, or whatever the hell he was, seemed far less dangerous. More a nuisance than a threat. "I'll be fine." She went to the refrigerator to get a bottle of water for each of them, turning her back to Ty. "Go home and appease your mother. She—"

Jillian turned from the refrigerator, a cold bottle of water in each hand, and froze suddenly. The refrigerator door swung shut, smacking her on the hip. She stared at the kitchen table. "Someone's been in here," she whispered.

Chapter Seven

Ty reached for one of the bottles of water in her hand, glancing around the kitchen. "What do you mean?"

"Someone's been in here," she repeated, her gaze darting from one object in the kitchen to the next. Everything looked the same; the flowered china behind the glass panes, the kitchen towel hanging from the closed utensil drawer, the roll of paper towels hanging from below a cabinet, even the peanut butter jar that now served as a vase, filled with flowers Ty had picked for her from his parents' yard. Even Ty's cell phone that she knew he had left in the kitchen looked right, and yet she knew something was different. "I'm not crazy. Someone's been in here since we left."

"Nobody said you were crazy."

Ty twisted the top off the water bottle, the sound deafening in Jillian's ears.

"What makes you think someone's been in here?" He continued to glance around as he sipped the water. "Nothing looks messed up to me."

"The list." She zeroed in on the table. "When you came in for the beer and to leave your phone, did you move it?"

He glanced at her grocery list written on the back of a receipt from a previous trip to the store. It read, *mustard, lemons, dish detergent*. He shook his head, still sipping from the water bottle. "No."

She stared at the simple objects, almost afraid to touch them. "The notepad was turned at an angle when I left it. The pen was *beside* the list, not *above* it."

Ty made a face. "You're sure? How can you remember something like that?"

Jillian, realizing she had been holding her breath, exhaled heavily. She was dizzy, but she didn't know if it was from all the beer, her fear, or lack of oxygen. She took a deep breath, exhaling again, forcing herself to be calm. There was something inside her, though just a glimmer, that told her she had to fight this time.

This time? What did that mean?

"I know because I always write at an angle," Jillian told Ty firmly. "I like objects at angles, not perpendicular."

"Now you are beginning to sound a little crazy. How many beers did—"

"Ty, listen to me," she snapped, dropping her bottle on the table. She grabbed her grocery list and shook it at him. "I'm telling you, someone was in here. He read, then straightened my list, and put the pen above it." She turned around toward the sink. "And that magazine, open to the recipe for crab cakes. I was going to try and make some. It's been straightened, too."

He stared at the magazine. "You think it was my mom, come to tidy up the love nest?"

"This isn't funny," she snapped.

His demeanor changed at once. "You're right. I'm sorry." He put down his bottle, coming to her to pull her into his arms. "Why don't you let me walk around the house, look under the beds, in the closets and shit. You wait here."

She pressed her cheek to his chest. His T-shirt smelled

of beer and the beach. "You can look, but he isn't here," she murmured. "I would know if he was here."

He closed his arms tighter around her and smoothed her tangled hair. "Want me to call the police? I'm sure McCormick could swing by and—"

"And tell them what? Someone broke into my house, moved my grocery list, and then let himself back out again?" She squeezed her eyes shut. She was caught between the feeling she was unraveling and that fierce stubbornness that she hadn't seen in herself before tonight. "No, thank you. People around here are already offering me a spot in the freak show at the carnival next month. I don't think I want anyone thinking I'm crazier than they already think I am."

He chuckled, but tenderly. "Ah, sweetie, nobody thinks you're crazy."

She held on to him tightly, as if the sheer strength of his young body could shield her from the world beyond the cottage walls. "No? Your friend Jones asked me if I thought I was the president of the United States."

"He was wasted."

She looked at him, into his blue-green eyes. "I hate to ask, considering Alice's position on this, but do you think you could stay tonight? I feel like such a baby, but—"

"Shhh," he hushed, hugging her against him. "Of course I'm going to stay. And if Alice doesn't like it, she's just going to have to have herself another hot flash."

Jillian laughed, though she knew it wasn't funny. Ty really wasn't being very understanding of his mother's position. It was subjects like this that reminded her that she really was much older than him, more mature. He had the selfish rashness of a young man who had not yet had his fair share of lumps in life, or known real responsibility. It was a wedge she knew would eventually drive them apart, but she didn't want to think about it. Not right now.

"I'll call home," he said. "At least she can't say she was up all night waiting to hear from the morgue. Why don't you get a shower?"

She nodded and lifted her chin to let him kiss her. It was a warm, loving kiss, not of sexual desire, but a different kind of intimacy she desperately needed right now. He made her feel like he cared.

Ty scooped up his cell phone from the counter and flipped it open. He punched the buttons as he went down the short hall in front of her, flipping light switches. "I'm still checking under the beds and in the closets," he told her. "Just to be sure."

"Mom?" he said into the phone. "What are you doing up so late?"

Jillian heard Ty pause as she stepped into the bathroom.

"Mom, we talked about this before. I don't think the morgue calls directly. I think a cop or priest or someone comes to the door to tell you your kid is dead and has been scraped off the road with a shovel."

Jillian managed a grim smile as she lowered herself to the toilet and peed, not caring if the bathroom door was open and Ty saw her. She was still too shaky to be closing any doors between them yet. She then stripped out of her sandy clothes, leaving them on the pink tile floor, and turned the shower head on over the old bathtub that was easily big enough for two. Turning the cantankerous knobs until she got pleasantly cool water, she stepped in and pulled the plastic shower curtain shut to keep water off the floor.

Jillian lathered her head with shampoo, rinsed, added conditioner to the ends, and then reached for a disposable razor in the soap dish. The routine of her shower calmed her. She wasn't crazy. She had seen the man on the beach tonight. Someone had been in the cottage.

She heard Ty come into the bathroom, pee a stream only a twenty-three-year old male could produce, then flush and drop the toilet seat with a bang. When she stepped out of the shower, he was seated there waiting for her, a towel from his mother's linen closet on his lap. He stood and opened the towel, wrapping it around her wet body. He handed her a smaller towel.

"For your hair," he said.

She smiled as she took it and leaned over to wrap her wet hair up, turban-style. "You act like you've done this before."

He offered a boyish, *I'm-not-kissing-and-telling* grin.

She leaned over the sink, gazing into the steamy mirror to wipe away any mascara smudged under her eyes. "Come on, tell the truth," she coaxed. "I know very well you were no virgin there the other night, Ty."

"Why do women always want to know about the other women you've slept with?" he asked, moving to the doorway to give her some room.

She glanced at his refection in the mirror as she reached for a tube of moisturizer. "Hon, I've got bigger matters to be concerned with than who you've slept with or even who you'll sleep with when I'm gone." She applied the moisturizer to her face, then propped one foot up on the toilet lid to smooth it over her legs.

"I went out with the same girl for almost two years sophomore and junior year in college. Thought I was in love."

She met his gaze in the mirror again as she switched legs. "Or at least in lust?'

He leaned lazily in the doorway. "Definitely in lust."

"What happened?"

"You know. The usual college romance bullshit. She didn't want me hanging with the guys anymore. She wanted a commitment. So on, so forth." He paused, his eyes getting a distant look. "Sounds clichéd, but I miss her."

"You think you'll ever get back together?"

He frowned. "Nah, I pretty much screwed those

chances up." He crossed his arms over his chest. "I think I'll hop in, too, if you don't mind."

"No, go ahead." She tried to duck under his arm to leave the bathroom, but he caught her. The towel tucked under her armpits fell away as he pulled her naked and wet into his arms.

"Jilly, I didn't mean what I said in there about you being crazy."

She looked up. "I know."

"You sure you don't want me to call the police?"

She shook her head. "Maybe you were right. Maybe I did move the pad of paper—the magazine."

"Don't do that." He lowered his head, brushing his beard-stubbled cheek against her smooth one.

"Don't do what?"

"Doubt yourself."

She drew back to meet his gaze again.

"Did you leave that list on the table like that?" he asked.

She shook her head.

"Then someone moved it. But that doesn't mean Jack the Ripper is after you. Who knows who could have done it? There must be two dozen realtors in town who have access to keys of rental properties. Some kid could have found the key or climbed through the living room window. The summer I was fourteen, a couple of friends and I were the terrors of our neighborhood. We'd climb through open windows and leave tomatoes from my mom's garden on people's pillows. Chief Drummond—the one before Claire, her dad—was going crazy trying to figure out who was doing it."

She laughed. "Why tomatoes?"

He laughed with her. "Who knows?" He kissed her, grabbed the towel she'd dropped off the floor, and handed it to her. "I'll be in in a minute."

She wrapped the towel around her again as she went down the hall toward the bedroom. Behind her she could see that Ty had shut off the kitchen and living room lights. "You tell Alice you were staying the night?"

"Yup."

She heard the shower come on.

"What did she say?"

"Have fun."

"Yeah, right," Jillian laughed, pulling the towel off her head. "I'll believe that one right after the 'you were still a virgin' story.

By the time Ty had showered and entered the bedroom, Jillian had taken her ibuprofen, finished the water bottle, and pulled on a pair of clean panties and a T-shirt. She left her hair to air-dry; it would be a frizzy mess in the morning, but she didn't care.

He slid into bed beneath the faded yellow top sheet, naked. "What's with girls and clothes in bed, anyway?" he asked, punching his pillow.

She turned off the light and rolled onto her side, against him. He wrapped his arm around her so that she could rest her cheek on his shoulder. "I don't know," she asked rhetorically. "What *is* it with girls and clothes in bed?"

He kissed her forehead and then lay back and relaxed. Suddenly, Jillian was so tired that she couldn't keep her eyes open. Within minutes, she drifted off to sleep.

The Bloodsucker stood barefoot on the cool tile of the bathroom and buttoned up his pajama top.

He had been very naughty tonight. Done something he knew he should not have done and he was ashamed. Instinctively, he wrapped his arms around his waist to protect himself, then remembered he no longer had to.

Mistakes like tonight were stupid. Mistakes like that would get him caught.

He reached for his toothbrush and squeezed a long worm of blue gel toothpaste on it.

He didn't know what had made him go to her house tonight. He hadn't meant to. He was getting everything out of order. Getting confused.

He continued to brush, up and down, never back and forth.

You don't go into their houses. Not even wearing gloves. It was too easy to leave evidence behind. Something physical. Something about himself. He had to remember it was a small town. So many people knew him . . . or thought they did.

And he had to stay in order. He couldn't hop around the board no matter how excited he got about a new prospect. No matter how excited she made him. It was too easy to make a mistake.

He picked up the plastic cup on the edge of the sink, filled it with water, and rinsed his mouth. Then he used mouthwash. One cap. He put everything back in its place, adjusted the angle of his toothbrush so that it hung properly in its holder, and then he was ready for bed.

Shutting off the light in the bathroom, he went down the hall toward his bedroom.

Tonight had been strange. He had been himself and yet he had not felt like himself. It was almost as if he had been watching a movie and he was the main character. He got gas in the car. Checked the oil level. He knew they did it in the shop where the car was serviced regularly, but he liked to double-check it anyway. Then he parked a couple of streets off the boardwalk. It was a nice evening there, hot but not too hot. Lots of girls, young women in skimpy tank tops. Lots of blondes.

He had had a piece of cheese pizza and a Coke. Several people stopped to speak to him. They smiled. He smiled. Chatted. Even flirted with a couple of tourists hanging around outside one of the few bars on the boardwalk. Then he went for a walk. The next thing he knew, he was there, standing in front of the cottage.

Out of order, he remembered telling himself. *Out of order.*

He barely remembered climbing through the window, walking through the house in the dark. He looked at her things. The bed where she slept. The hairbrush she used on all that pretty blond hair. He saw a magazine on the kitchen counter; the recipe looked like one he might want to try sometime. She was out of lemons.

The next thing he knew, he was on the beach, in the dunes. Hidden by the sea grass.

She had gone to a party. Young people drinking beer. Singing. Laughing. He had never been allowed to go to those kinds of parties when it had mattered the most.

The next thing The Bloodsucker knew, he was running. Someone was chasing him. Ty. Other college boys.

The next thing he knew, he was back in his car, driving slowly down the street as if nothing had happened.

Ty had actually spoken to him as he drove by. Silly boy.

Jillian saw the rumpled bed sheets first. Same sheets. Same bed. Again, the room was hot and stuffy. She heard the click of the ceiling fan, felt the warm air stir without offering any relief.

She heard the shower running. Water splashing against the side of the shower stall. Then it stopped.

Jillian couldn't quite place herself. It was as if she were hovering above the bed, the room. Drifting. She was in the bedroom, yet she wasn't.

She saw the steam-fogged mirror inside the bathroom door. Saw the man step out again and reach for a white towel.

She knew the man. Knew his compact, muscular body. The dark, prickly hair on his legs and chest.

Her heart began to race. Her mouth went dry.

She didn't belong here. Shouldn't be here.

The next thing she knew, she was in the bed. Naked. He was there beside her, their limbs entwined.

Jillian couldn't breathe. There was something wrong about the scene. She shouldn't be here. She was afraid. But she was also angry.

This was wrong. *Wrong.*

She heard the feminine laugher again, reverberating off the shadowed walls that seemed to have no shape or form. She recognized the sexual undertone of the laughter.

But who was laughing? Was that her?

The man rolled over, reached out to her. She felt his fingertips brush against her bare belly. She knew him. Knew his touch. She felt that flutter of sexual desire deep in the pit of her stomach, but she resisted. She had the distinct feeling that this was a clandestine meeting. No one could know.

It was wrong.

Jillian bolted upright in the bed and clutched her chest. She could feel her heart racing. Her breath short, labored. She glanced over in the bed at Ty, sound asleep on his back.

She took a deep, shuddering breath and climbed out of bed. Without turning on any lights, her eyes accustomed to the dark, she went to the kitchen for a bottle of water.

She was not afraid now of the dream, but shocked. Appalled. Her dream. She had been the one in bed with the man. In bed where she didn't belong. Having sex with a man she should not have been having sex with.

Since Jillian woke from the coma, she had been focused on figuring out who she was. She had been intent on finding herself so that she could return to the life she had once possessed, become the person she had once been. But one thought had never occurred to her until this moment.

She opened the refrigerator, and the stark, blinding light made her recoil.

What if she found out who she was and then was sorry she had asked?

"One box," Claire said, leaning on the shopping cart. She was dead tired. It was after eight and she had gone to work at six this morning. She had picked up Ashley at her parents' house, intending to go straight home, but her daughter had reminded her that it had been more than two weeks since they'd been to the grocery store. They were out of everything.

"Mom."

"You heard me." Claire tossed a box of granola bars into the cart. "Only one box of Toastie Sweetie Peeps, which disguises itself as a breakfast cereal and probably causes cancer in lab animals."

"But I'll need more than one box if you're not going to go to the grocery store for another year," Ashley whined.

"So get a box of something else." It took a great deal of effort for Claire to push the half-loaded cart forward. "How about Cheerios? I like Cheerios."

Ashley made a gagging motion with her finger in her mouth, complete with sound effects. "I'd rather eat Styrofoam packing chips."

"Then do." Claire offered a quick, motherly, *don't mess with me tonight* smile and turned the corner to go down the paper goods aisle.

"We forgot hot dog rolls," Ashley called.

"Be my guest. Back on the first aisle." Claire raised her hand and let it fall in surrender. She stopped in front of the paper plates and grabbed a stack. Depositing them in the cart, she scanned the shelves for paper cups. All she saw was plastic. Ashley insisted plastic was bad for the environment, or whales or something. She wouldn't drink from plastic. Unless, of course, it came from a fast food place with biggie fries. Claire chose to pick her battles carefully.

"Look at her."

An elderly woman's voice penetrated Claire's cup-search daze.

"Who does she think she is, shopping in here?"

"I don't know, Mary Lou," came another crotchety voice. "I just don't know."

Claire spotted the cups Ashley preferred and grabbed them.

"A killer on the loose, stalking our streets, and look at her, doing her shopping, just as you please."

Realizing the old bats were talking about her, Claire snapped her head around to see who it was. Mary Lou Joseph and Betty Friegle. They both attended church with her. They were friends with her mother and played cards on Tuesdays with her. They didn't seem to notice that Claire had noticed them . . . or that she could hear them. Both apparently needed to have their hearing aids adjusted because they were talking loud enough for everyone in the store to hear them.

"Well, I spoke with Mayor Tugman this morning, and he says the city council is about to convene over this matter. She refuses anyone's help with this investigation and then look at her." Mary Lou dared a glance over her osteoporosis-hunched shoulder, then back at Betty again.

Apparently she needed a prescription change with the glasses, too. She still didn't notice Claire coming right for her, pushing the shopping cart.

"You know, when they hired her, I said this isn't a job for a woman," Mary Lou continued. "I don't care if her father was the chief of police for forty years or not. Of course, I would never say so to Marlene."

"Of course not," Betty echoed.

Claire resisted the temptation to just release the cart. All the momentum she had going, she could probably take out both blue-hairs and still catch up to make the turn and head down the dairy aisle.

"Of course not," Claire mocked, halting inches from

Mary Lou's well-padded behind, covered in an orange flowered housecoat.

Mary Lou turned around, looked stunned for an instant, then rebounded with a great big denture smile. "Claire, how are you, dear?" she asked sweetly.

"I have to eat," Claire said.

"Excuse me." Mary Lou leaned over, continuing with the sweet old lady shtick. "What's that, dear?"

"I said, I have to eat!" Claire snatched a bag of napkins from above Betty's head. "Serial killer or not, I'm still permitted to eat, right? Feed my child? Everyone has to eat." Claire was angry. Frustrated and angry. Angry with these old biddies, with herself. With *him*.

"Of course, dear," Betty offered.

Claire steered the cart around them both. "And next time you speak to Mayor Tugman, Mary Lou . . ."

"Yes?"

"Tell him that if he has something to say, he should have the balls to come say it to my face." Claire turned the corner to the next aisle and pushed right past the skim milk.

"You go, Mom," Ashley breathed from behind Claire.

Claire glanced over her shoulder. "You heard that? I'm sorry. It was completely uncalled for." She pointed back to the milk case.

"No, Mom, that was way cool." Ashley grabbed a cardboard milk container. "Nobody stands up to Mary Lou Who. She's the biggest gossipmonger in the county."

Claire looked at her daughter's grinning face and thought to herself how pretty she had become, black eye pencil and all. "Go find the syrup, light, and you can get one more box of Toastie Sweetie Peeps. I'll meet you in the checkout line."

"Thanks, Mom." Ashley darted down the aisle as if she were a carefree kid again, instead of the moody teenager she had become.

"You're welcome," Claire whispered with a bittersweet smile. If only her other problems were solved so easily.

That night Claire lay in bed on top of the Navajo patterned bedspread. Ashley was already asleep and the house was quiet.

Claire had to get up in less than five hours, but she couldn't sleep. Couldn't turn her mind off long enough to surrender to sleep.

She'd been doing phone and personal interviews for days. She had officers who could do them for her, but she felt as if it was important that she hear what each friend or family member of the victims had to say. There might be something, some tiny thread of a clue that had been lost in the stacks of already recorded interviews.

And Claire thought about the old ladies in the grocery store. She knew they were harmless. She even knew that for the most part they liked her and supported her in her position, even if they didn't like to admit it.

Maybe they were right. Maybe she needed to hand the investigation of the homicides over to the state police. But she knew what they would do. Take over her office. Order her employees around. Bad-mouth her to her officers behind her back.

Just because she hadn't caught the killer yet didn't mean she was running a poor investigation. It didn't mean she wasn't doing her job. Serial killers were almost never found quickly. These were not random acts of passion or stupidity killings, and this killer was not a random or stupid man. She had to outsmart him. And she would. She knew she would. It just might take a little time.

Claire stared at the turning ceiling fan over her head. So to hell with Mary Lou and Betty and anyone who claimed she couldn't do her job. And to hell with them criticizing her for going grocery shopping after pulling a thirteen-hour day and charging the city for eight. Everyone had to eat.

Everyone had to eat. . . .

Claire bolted upright in bed. "Everyone has to eat," she repeated, this time aloud.

She scrambled out of bed, jerked open her door, and ran down the dark hallway to the dining room where she had left her now numerous legal pads of notes.

Everyone had to eat. Of course! That was the connection.

She turned on the wrought-iron chandelier over the dining room table and began to sort through the legal pads. She had one just for April, and that was where she had to start. April had only been in town four days when she was abducted.

It didn't matter how long a person had been in Albany Beach. It didn't matter if she was here for a week of a lifetime. She had to eat.

"Where did you go, April?" Claire whispered. She knelt on a dining room chair and shoved her reading glasses on. "Where did you eat?"

She flipped through her pages of notes on April. "Arrived Saturday," she read. She reached for a brand-new pad of paper, fresh out of the six-pack she had bought. "Went grocery shopping."

Where? Claire scrawled across the page with a big question mark. She would have to call April's husband yet again. But she would wait until a decent time of day. She checked her watch. 12:45 a.m. It was going to be a long night. This was going to take a while, maybe days, but Claire knew she was on to something. She could feel it in her bones.

Chapter Eight

Jillian sat on the boardwalk bench, too tired to eat her lunch, and sipped her sweet tea. She stared out at the crashing waves as if the Atlantic would somehow offer a solution to her predicament that seemed without a solution. Angel had told her that often amnesia victims had to be treated for depression. The two had laughed at the time, Jillian remarking who *wouldn't* be depressed with this diagnosis.

She wasn't laughing now. She had discovered that knowing something of her past could be worse than knowing nothing. Her returning memory was tearing her apart. She had to determine how to get this craziness out of her head. She couldn't live this way the rest of her life.

Jillian felt like a condemned prisoner, night after night. She went to bed afraid she would have the dream. Knowing it was coming. No matter how late she stayed up or what kind of nighttime cold medicine she took, the dream always came back.

"Dead man walking" was what she thought they called it. She remembered seeing a documentary or a movie on it once. She had given up trying to figure out the particulars of such memories. The piece she had seen had been about the journey a condemned man or woman made to the execution chamber. They called out "Dead man walking" as the prisoner passed through the corridors.

Each night Jillian felt as if she were walking the same corridor.

She would enter the bedroom. She would hear her own laughter. See the naked man beside her in bed. Smell his sweat on her skin. She would know she didn't belong there. Know that the man was not her husband, but someone else's. She would know in her heart of hearts that she was betraying someone very close to her and she would wake up each morning hating herself for it.

The latest development in the ever-expanding dream sequence was the addition of a third person in the room.

The person would turn, just about to reveal himself— or herself. Then, at the last minute, just when she thought she was on the verge of making sense of all the nonsense—the turning ceiling fan, the water running in the shower, the other person in the room—she would suddenly be jerked back. She would be torn from the dream to wake in a cold sweat, only to walk the journey again the next night.

"Use a little company?"

Jillian looked up to see Jenkins. He was so big that when he came around the boardwalk bench, he blocked part of the summer afternoon glare of the sun.

"Sure." She scooted over.

He lowered his age-ravaged body beside her, and she poured him a cup of icy sweet tea and handed it to him. They were like an old married couple these days. Often they sat together and didn't talk at all, both lost in their own worlds of regret and longing.

"Millie says you ain't sleeping," Jenkins grunted after taking a long drink of tea.

She glanced at him. Apparently today was a talking day, whether she wanted it to be or not. She continued to look out over the beach. A toddler playing with a beach ball caught her eye, and she watched her tumble laughing into the sand with the ball. She wondered if she would have a child. For the first time she realized she wanted one, had wanted one for a long time

"Bad dreams," Jillian said, not sure she wanted to talk about it. She'd been pretty close-lipped with Ty about her nightmares, and he seemed to be okay with that. He said she would tell him when she was ready . . . or not. Either way, it was cool with him.

A part of Jillian wished he wasn't. She wanted him to want to know, to be more demanding. Make her tell him. But it wasn't in Ty's nature, and she wasn't going to change that.

"You remembering things?" Jenkins asked. He stared straight ahead at the beach she knew he could not see dotted with colorful beach umbrellas and sunburned sunbathers. Where he couldn't see the immense ocean.

Jillian studied the sandals on her feet. "I think so."

"I'm guessin' from the what you're dog-hangin' your head, they ain't good memories."

His apropos phrase made her smile. "You know," she said, thoughtfully. "It never occurred to me I might not like what I found. I mean, I know I was shot, I know I was somehow involved in something that couldn't have been good, but . . ." She exhaled and started again. It was difficult to express what she was thinking aloud. She felt the threat of tears sting the backs of her eyelids. "But it never occurred to me that I might have somehow been at fault. I never thought I might have hurt someone or done something wrong."

"You think you were in a shooting match with someone?"

She dropped her head to her hands. "No. But I have a feeling I might have been cheating on someone. That's part of the problem; nothing makes any sense. The more time that passes, the surer I am that I wasn't married, and yet . . ." She paused, waiting to gain control of her emotion again. "Yet I *feel* like I was cheating on my husband. *Betraying* him. Betraying someone else close to me."

"Maybe this man you remember was cheating on his wife, and you just got dragged down with him. Men can be sly as foxes. They can be such liars when it comes to wanting to get a pretty woman into their bed." He chuckled, but it was a dry, humorless laugh, filled with regret. "I ought to know, I was good at it once."

She studied Jenkins's ebony, liver-spotted face and tried to imagine him young, handsome, picking up women in bars. Pursuing women he had no right to be pursuing. "Maybe."

"The real question is, what you going to do about it?"

"Do about it?" She looked at him. "How can I do anything about it if I don't know what *it* is? I can't remember anything that makes any sense!" Her words came out harsher than she had intended. She didn't mean to take her frustration out on Jenkins. He had been a good friend these last two weeks.

He drained his plastic cup, unaffected by her outburst. "You really want to know what you did? Who you were?"

"Of course."

"Because some people, they don't want to fess up to what they done. I know I didn't. I went years blaming this one and that one." He pointed a finger one direction and then another.

"Jenkins." She dropped her head to her hands again. "You don't understand."

"I do," he said firmly. "I messed up so many different ways in my life that I ain't got enough days in this world left to tell you 'bout 'em. The one thing I finally learned is that you got to look yourself in the mirror and make the best of what you got left."

"Make the best of what I've got left," she whispered. "I don't have anything."

"Sure you do. You got brains. You got your youth."

She laughed bitterly.

"Don't be laughin' at me, girlie." He rose slowly from the bench. "When you're ninety-one, somebody in their thirties, that's a babe."

"You're ninety-one?" Jillian asked in amazement. She leaned over the back of the bench to watch him walk slowly back across the boardwalk.

"You tell anyone and I'll call you a liar," he threatened.

She laughed at him. At herself. It felt good.

"Why did you drag me here?" Ashley moaned. She didn't touch the menu in front of her.

Claire had carefully chosen a booth in the back of the diner where she could watch everyone who came in or out. She'd been here a thousand times in her life. She knew the menus by heart and the trick to getting the ladies' room door unlocked when it trapped you inside. She knew every employee, local customer, and most of the delivery men who came to the back door. Now suddenly she was forced to look at what seemed like the heart of the town in a different light.

It had taken her a day and half to gather the information, but Claire thought she knew where the killer was finding his victims. Right here. The diner. She didn't know why she hadn't thought of it sooner. Patti had been a waitress here. The twin sisters had eaten here regularly. Anne, like the other locals, had frequented the diner often when she was home from college. Most importantly, April Provost, the woman who had only been in town four days when she was kidnapped, had eaten here the first night she and her husband were in town. And they had eaten breakfast with her in-laws in the diner the morning of her disappearance.

Claire was so excited that she might be on to something that she felt as is she were going to jump out of her skin. So maybe it was the nine cups of coffee she had today.

"Hi, Chief, what can I get you?" Kristen, the new waitress Loretta had hired the previous month to replace Patti, smiled. She was Ty Addison's cousin from somewhere north, New Jersey or Pennsylvania. Like many college kids, she had come to the beach for a job; she was staying with the Addison family for the summer.

"I'll have the fried shrimp, coleslaw, no fries, and a glass of water with lemon."

The blonde scribbled on her notepad. "And what can I get for you?" She glanced down at Ashley, who had laid her head on the table between her hands.

When Ashley didn't respond, Claire looked up and smiled apologetically. "She'll have the chicken fried steak with sawmill gravy—"

"Gross," Ashley moaned.

"Mashed potatoes and fried okra."

"I'm not eating that," Ashley snapped, lifting her head from the table. She looked to Kristen. "A Coke, no ice, fries, no gravy." She gave her mother the evil eye. "And a crab cake. No roll."

"You got it." Kristen hit her order pad with the point of her pencil in emphasis. "Be right back with your drinks."

Ashley lowered her head again, but this time just to her hand, elbow propped on the table. "So why are we here? We never eat dinner here in the summer. You said—"

"Shhh," Claire murmured. She was trying to take notes on her legal pad beside her on the fake leather bench. She was writing down the name of every male she could identify who came through the diner door.

Ashley studied her mother across the table. "Does this have anything to do with the sicko murderer?"

"Keep your voice down."

Ashley glanced over her shoulder. It was six o'clock, and the place was busy. There was already a line beginning to form at the door and into the parking lot. Loretta didn't take reservations or names at the door. It was first come, first serve, and you waited in line until a table opened up.

"Isn't it like illegal to take a minor with you on a police stakeout?"

"Not if you're the police chief, and you've got a mouthy teenage daughter," Claire muttered.

She was jotting down men's names as fast as she could. Dr. Gordon from the hospital was having the chicken basket with Dr. Larson. Billy, Patti's old ex who worked at a bar in town, sat alone at the counter eating the fried clam basket. Three of her father's old cronies, all widowers, waited for their meals and argued over the best antacid tablets. She was tempted to scratch them off the list. They could barely walk thorough the door under their own power. They weren't kidnapping young women late at night, or any other time of day. But she was trying to keep an open mind. She added to her list Ralph, the dishwasher, and Pedro, the eighteen-year-old Mexican kid Loretta had hired to clean the place.

"Mom," Ashley said, leaning over the table. "What's going on?"

Claire glanced at her across the table, added another name. The mayor was at the cash register picking up take-out. His wife had been out of town for weeks, visiting an ailing sister in Florida, apparently. Claire had never taken into consideration the take-out business Loretta did. "You can't say a word."

"I won't."

"I'm not kidding," Claire threatened. "We're talking about a multiple homicide case here."

"Mom, I'm better at keeping secrets than you are."

Claire met her daughter's blue-eyed gaze. "What about Chain? You two don't talk?"

Ashley lifted the eyebrow Claire knew she was dying to have pierced. "You think Chain wants to talk about my mom the cop?"

She had a good point.

"I think the killer is finding the women here."

Ashley looked around. "Here?" she breathed.

"It's the way these guys do this kind of thing," Claire explained.

"You mean how serial killers choose their victims?"

Claire nodded, thinking how worldly her daughter was at this age, compared to what she had been. She jotted down two more names. She also kept a tally of how many unidentified males she saw. Tourists. She doubted that would play into her investigation, but she was trying to think outside the box. It was the only way she was going to catch him.

"You think he's from Albany Beach?"

Again, Claire nodded.

"And he's picking out his women while he's here?"

"All four dead women were here at least twice in the weeks prior to their kidnapping and murder."

"Coke, no ice, and water with lemon." Kristen appeared at the end of the table and slid their glasses to them. She reached into her apron for straws. "Sorry it took so long. We're really jammed up."

"No hurry," Claire called after the waitress as she hustled down the aisle to refill the doctors' iced-tea glasses.

"Wow," Ashley breathed, ripping the paper off her straw and dunking it into her glass. "That means everyone in town is a suspect. All the men, at least."

Claire lifted her pencil from the paper, her daughter's words sinking in. "Shit," she whispered, then glanced up apologetically.

"Shit is right," Ashley agreed. "Think about it. Everyone coming in here. Every man we see in a day is a suspect. The mailman, Pastor Jack, Grandpop—"

"Chief."

Claire looked up to see Officer Savage approaching the table. He had just come on at three and was probably picking up dinner for himself. "Hey, Jeff. How are you tonight?"

"I'm good. You, Chief?"

"About the same as I was when we had our briefing a couple of hours ago." She smirked.

He smiled back, looked away. Claire had feeling he had a thing for her. She wasn't interested. He was too young. Besides, she'd already gone down that path with Kurt, dating a fellow police officer, and it had been a disaster.

"Well, I better pick up the sandwiches. See you tomorrow, Chief."

She nodded. "Patrolman."

"He's got the hots for you," Ashley said, barely giving him time to walk away from the table.

"Oh, he does not." Claire dropped the pencil and reached for her water.

"He does too, and he's also a suspect." Ashley stirred her coke with her straw. "Put him on your list."

"He's a police officer, Ash. One of *my* officers."

"So?" She pressed her gray lips together. The black lipstick was fading as she drank her soda. "You said yourself, all males are suspect. Just because you're a cop doesn't mean you can't be a sicko creep. Personally, I think it ups the ante."

Claire frowned, but she knew the teen was right. She had been so buoyed by the idea that she had this clue. This possible link to the killer. Now, as she looked out at the sea of familiar faces, she realized he could be any one of them. Now the task of finding him seemed even more daunting.

"Jilly. Jilly, wake up."

Jillian became aware of Ty leaning over her in her

bed, shaking her. Her heart was pounding, and she had that dry taste of fear in her mouth. She blinked her eyes open. "What? What's wrong?" She was sweaty and trembling all over.

"You were having a nightmare." He sat down on the edge of the bed, and she realized he was dressed to go home.

She grabbed his arm. "I . . . I heard someone scream."

He brushed her damp hair, plastered to her head, from her face. "I think it was you."

She sat up. She was naked. They had had dinner together, played Frisbee on the beach. They'd made love on the bed, and then she must have fallen asleep. She had told him he didn't need to stay the night. "I was screaming?" she whispered, her pulse beginning to slow to a normal rate.

"Not really screaming. Just one scream."

"Oh, Ty." She fell back on her pillow, covering her face with her hands.

He was quiet for a minute before he spoke. "Listen, I told you I didn't need to know anything you didn't want to tell me, but . . . maybe you need to talk about it? I know you're having these dreams, memories. Something. Maybe if you tell me about it, it might make things better. You know, kind of like facing your greatest fears."

She gave a laugh that came out something close to a sob. It was the dream, but it was getting worse. But this time, first she heard a crunching sound, like rocks in a driveway beneath car tires. Then the same scenario. The bed, the ceiling fan, the shower. But this time there had been a gunshot. She had smelled the gunpowder.

That was when she screamed.

Ty continued to stroke her hair. "You want to tell me?"

Miserably, she shook her head no, then nodded yes. She couldn't look him in the eye. She didn't want him to know what a terrible person she must have been. She didn't want to lose him. Of course, she knew she would lose him, eventually. In a few short weeks he would be returning to Penn State. Her lease on the cottage would be up. They would go their separate ways, as they had known from the beginning they would. But that wasn't for two or three weeks. She needed him now.

A shudder went through her as she fought tears.

"Jilly, what is it, huh?" He lowered himself to his knees on the floor and leaned over her, continuing to stroke her hair. "Whatever it is, you can tell me."

"I'm afraid," she whispered.

"Of who?"

She shook her head and swallowed. "Afraid if you know—"

"I'm not telling anyone. You have any secrets, they're safe with me. I'm not the narc type."

"It's not prosecution I'm worried about," she whispered. "It's what you'll think of me."

He chuckled. "Jilly, sweetie, whatever it is, it's not going to change how I feel about you. I'd think you know me well enough by now to realize that."

When she lifted her lashes, he was gazing into her eyes.

"Just tell me. You'll feel better; I know you will."

Her lower lip trembled as she slowly revealed to him what happened in the dreams and what she thought it all meant. She told him about her conversation with Jenkins, too, and how he thought she needed to confront her past and own up to the wrongs she had committed.

Ty turned the light on beside the bed, got her a bottle of water, and then climbed in beside her, still dressed in shorts and his wrinkled tee, she still naked.

"Jilly, I don't know why you didn't tell me this crap sooner. I can't believe you've been holding this all inside you."

She was still trembling, but she felt better. Stronger. "And you don't hate me?"

"Sweetie, I don't care what you did."

"But, Ty, I told you, I think he was my best friend's husband. You don't care if I was screwing my best friend's husband?"

"That's not you," he answered calmly.

"But it was me."

"Nope. This is Jillian Deere." He drew a finger between her breasts. "Jillian who works at a funky art shop on the boardwalk and likes vintage motorcycles. Jilly who can swim half a mile in the ocean and not get tired. Jilly who can kung fu my ass to the ground any time. Jilly who's *as sweet as Tupelo honey,*" he crooned.

She laughed, and a tear ran down her cheek. She wiped it away. "You don't even care that I was such an evil, conniving bitch that someone shot me?"

"Not really, but you don't know that that's what happened."

She looked up at him.

"You don't," he said, gesturing with one hand.

She slid over to lie in his lap between his legs with him resting against the old headboard and her resting against his chest.

"Look, you said the doctors told you that the mind as a weird thing. That you had to be careful about what you interpreted as memory when it first started coming back."

"I know it's real. The details never change."

"But what if this memory is all something you saw in a movie sometime?" He kissed her bare shoulder. "What if it's something that happened to someone you knew?"

"Ty—"

"Jilly, the fact is, this is just silly. Whoever you were, whatever you did, it doesn't matter anymore. You're not that person anymore. Why not just forget it? The board is wiped clean. Talk about second chances. You've sure got one here."

She pressed her lips together, closed her eyes. "You think I should just forget it all? Stop trying to figure out who I am? Who I hurt?"

"Hey, you were the one with the gunshot wound, the one who ended up in the hospital in a coma."

When she didn't respond, he went on. "Look, you want to know what I think? I think you need to do what you want to do. Not what I think or Jenkins thinks, or anyone else. We can tell you what we would do, but we're not you. Our experiences haven't been yours so we have no way to judge what you should do."

Jillian didn't really need to think about it. She already knew her decision. "I need to know," she whispered. "Whatever wrongs I've committed, I feel like I need to face them."

As he exhaled, she felt his chest rise and then fall. "You're sure?"

"Yeah."

"You want my help?"

She turned in his arms to look up at him. "Your help? How are you going to help me?"

"I don't know. Go on the Internet and start looking at missing persons lists?"

"Angel said no one on the lists fit me."

"So a few weeks have passed and the lists have changed. Besides, you know more now."

"Know more?" She turned on the bed, kneeling between his legs to face him. "Ty, my dreams are all in that same nameless bedroom. I think it might even be a hotel room. I don't know anything."

"Sure you do. You know you're a kung fu expert and you don't like vinegar on your fries."

She couldn't *not* laugh. "Talk about crazy."

He raised one shoulder. "It's a place to start."

She glanced away, then back him. "My doctor is having my records faxed to the hospital. I thought I should have them in case I don't go back to Virginia. I never really looked at them. You think there could be anything in there?"

"Might be."

She slipped her hands over his shoulders. "It's late. You should go home."

"I don't have to."

"I ran into your cousin Kristen on the boardwalk today. She said your mom is really angry with you about spending so much time here with me."

He gave a wave. "Kristen exaggerates."

"I don't think so," she whispered as she brushed her lips across his. "I mean it—go home, Ty."

"Now?"

"Yes, now," she breathed.

He met her lips as he drew both hands over the bare cheeks of her derriere, stroking her. "Right now?"

"Okay," she conceded, parting her legs and scooting forward to wrap them around his waist. "Maybe in a few minutes."

"Hey, I don't want to force my affections upon anyone who doesn't want them." Ty released her bare bottom and lifted both hands up in the air. "Let no one say—"

Jillian grabbed the collar of his T-shirt with both hands and pulled him toward her, covering his mouth with hers.

"That I, Ty Addison . . ." he mumbled against her lips.

She thrust her tongue into his mouth, drawing her hand down over his bare chest to caress one nipple. That shut him up.

Ty slid his hand over her shoulder and down her back, drawing his fingers slowly downward, sending little shivers of pleasure through her. He was such an attentive lover, especially for his age. He understood that a woman's body wasn't just about boobs.

Breathless, Jillian drew her mouth away from Ty's, across his cheek to nibble his earlobe.

"She's as sweet as Tupelo honey," he sang softly.

Already heavy-lidded with desire, Jillian gazed down at him as she grabbed the hem of his wrinkled T-shirt and pulled it over his head. "I'm going to have to get that CD." She tossed his shirt over her shoulder.

He nuzzled her neck, pressing light, teasing kisses across her collarbone. "Soon as you get a CD player."

She laughed, grabbing his shoulders and arching her back, still seated on his lap, her legs wrapped around his waist.

Ty accepted her invitation, greedily taking her nipple in his mouth. Jillian groaned, moving on his lap, grinding her hips against his.

"This would be better without the shorts," she murmured.

"She's an angel, of the first degree."

"Enough with the singing, Van." She slid off his lap and grabbed the hem of his shorts, tugging hard.

Grasping her shoulders, he stood up on the bed, letting her pull down his board shorts. She glanced up at him, to see him grinning. She couldn't resist a smile as she tossed the last vestige of clothing over her head. Then she grasped his erection in her palm and closed her eyes. *"He's an angel,"* she sang.

Ty groaned and swayed on his feet, gripping her shoulders for balance as she closed her mouth over him. "Gotta get you a CD player," he muttered. "Van really does something for you."

A minute later, Ty tightened his grip on her shoulders and lowered himself to his knees in front of her. She rested one hand over his shoulder, using the other to guide him as she settled on his lap.

"Baby," he whispered in her ear.

Keeping her eyes open, gazing into his, she moved rhythmically. The best part about making love with Ty, besides the great orgasms, was the fact that time always seemed to stand still. For these few moments, Jillian had no past and no unknown future. It was just she and Ty and the sweet sensations that rippled through her body.

As always, she tried to hold back, tried to make the moment last, but she was already too far gone. Jillian cried out, closing her eyes, resting her head on Ty's shoulder, as every muscle in her body seemed to contract and then release in pleasure.

"Jilly, I'm going to have to put a muzzle on you," Ty moaned. "You know I can't stand it when you're loud."

She laughed, lifting up, lowering herself over him, and he came with a loud groan. Still laughing, Jillian eased off his lap and flung herself backward. Ty fell on the pillow, wiping the perspiration on his forehead with his hand.

"So can I go home now?" he demanded indignantly.

She grabbed a pillow that had, somehow, wound up on the foot of the bed and threw it at him, hitting him square in the face.

The following day, Jillian locked the cottage up, taking care to be sure the windows were closed and locked and the doors were locked. She took the key with her. She had had no further indication that anyone had been in the cottage, and she hadn't even gotten the feeling for a couple of days that she was being watched. Any one of Ty's explanations became more logical with each passing day. She didn't dwell on the break-in because right now it seemed like the least of her problems.

Sitting on the front porch this morning alone, enjoying the solitude of the beach and her first cup of coffee, she had reaffirmed in her mind the need to try to figure out who she had been and what she had done. While she appreciated Ty's youthful idea of simply moving forward and being the best person she could be from this day forth, she knew that, as Jenkins had suggested, she had to face what she had done. It would be the only way she could forgive herself and truly move on.

She pulled into the lot of Albany Beach Community Hospital and parked under a shady tree. According to the weather reports she'd heard on the little radio Ty had given her, the Delaware beaches were expecting record highs today. The cottage would be stifling by midday, especially with the windows and doors locked tightly, so she intended to spend part of the day running errands for herself and Millie, the rest of it on the beach reading and swimming.

In the parking lot, several people waved to her, called out to say hello, or just nodded in greeting. It seemed that word had got around who she was, and she was now a bit of a celebrity in town.

Just inside the revolving doors of the outpatient wing, she nearly bumped right into Seth Watkins, the skeezy real estate guy. The morning he was wearing a puke-green blazer that was close to hideous. "How's the place?" he asked, his smile way too toothy.

"Hot," she said and laughed.

He laughed, though she wasn't sure he got her reference to the lack of air conditioning.

"There's a possibility it might be available next month, too." He gestured with his hand as if drawing a pistol. "Interested?"

"Maybe." She kept walking. "Can I let you know?"

Again, the drawn finger pistol. "You bet," he called as he pushed through the revolving doors.

At the front desk, Jillian spoke with a pleasant volunteer who directed her to records on the third floor. She hadn't realized the hospital was big enough to have three floors. She rode up in the elevator with a guy she thought she recognized from the diner. He was in his mid-twenties, a little scruffy, wearing a T-shirt that advertised a bar in town. His eyes were bloodshot, and he didn't look like he was quite awake.

"Somebody screwed up my blood test," he said conversationally. He was holding an unlit cigarette.

She looked at him but didn't say anything.

"Checked positive instead of negative on my hepatitis test." He gestured with the cigarette. "Got to have a negative to work with food. I have to get it straightened out. Thinking about moving from the bar into the kitchen."

She nodded. Smiled. "Just picking up some records," she said, not really wanting to get into a conversation with him, but not wanting to seem impolite, either. The guy didn't really scare her, but she was glad when the elevator stopped and the doors opened. He stepped back to let her pass first.

Jillian stopped at the water fountain outside the elevator bay, giving the hepatitis guy a chance to pass her and go into the records office first. Wiping water from her mouth, she walked slowly down the corridor. There was a bay of windows to her left, and behind the glass was a large rectangular room filled with wheelchairs, exercise equipment, low beds, and other interesting paraphernalia. There were only two people inside—a man in his mid-thirties in a white coat and an elderly man seated in a wheelchair. The man in the white coat was lifting the older man's leg, bending it.

The strangest feeling passed over Jillian as she halted and watched in fascination as the therapist worked the old man's leg. The elderly gentleman was getting physical therapy for his recent knee surgery. He had had his knee joint replaced with an artificial one. The latest implants were made of titanium and would last the gentleman the rest of his life. Recovery time would be faster, too. With the proper care and regular physical therapy, he'd be as good as new. Better, within a year.

How could she have known all that?

Jillian brushed her fingertip against the words painted in gold on the glass, realizing she was on the brink of a major revelation.

Physical therapy.

She knew this room. She recognized the equipment. She knew what every piece was for and for the recuperation of what injuries. She had worn a white coat just like the one the physical therapist was wearing now.

She pressed her fingertips to her lips, dizzy with excitement. It was if she had opened a door in her mind and all the information was tumbling out. Physiology. Diagnoses. She even vaguely recalled a couple of patients—not their names, just their faces. Their injuries.

Tears filled Jillian's eyes as she started back down the hall toward the records office. She had been a physical therapist! That meant that eventually, she could get a decent job and not be forced to rely on the good will of people like Angel. She might even eventually be in the position to help someone else who had suffered her same fate.

She wiped at the first tears of joy she experienced since she'd woken from her coma. She was foolish enough to think this would solve all of her problems. She knew the process to begin work again would be complicated. If she never found out who she was, she wouldn't be able to prove she'd been licensed, but surely there were exams that could be taken? Surely there was some way she could prove she was an experienced physical therapist. A damned good one, she thought to herself with a smile.

She pushed open glass doors to the records office. The scruffy guy was gone.

"May I help you?" A woman peered from behind half glasses.

Jillian stepped up to the desk with a smile, feeling like she was somehow headed in the right direction.

Chapter Nine

Jillian glanced at her watch as she dropped a bag of items that she had picked up for Millie at the local craft store into her trunk. It was noon; Ty had his lunch break from twelve-thirty to one. If she hurried, she could catch him as he was climbing off his lifeguard stand. The guards switched stands weekly, so he was blocks from the cottage this week, but if she took him lunch, she knew they could sit out of the sun under one of the umbrellas at the rental stand nearby and eat lunch together.

It was Ty's parents' anniversary, and he, his cousin Kristen, and Ty's sister, who was flying in from Texas, would be taking them out to dinner, so Jillian wouldn't see him tonight. She didn't think she could wait until tomorrow to tell him what she had discovered while picking her medical records up at the hospital.

She pulled out of the strip mall parking lot and zipped down the street. Ty wasn't into fast food, but the diner was only two blocks away. It was two-for-one burger day. She'd eat half a burger, he'd eat one and a half, and they'd share the large boardwalk fries. Jillian was feeling so good about herself that she thought she just might even give the vinegar a try.

Inside the diner, Ralph took her order. He wanted to linger at the lunch counter, stare at her breasts and chat with her, but a kid in the back unknowingly rescued her when he announced that there was a delivery out back to be checked in. While Jillian waited for her burgers and fries, she sat at the lunch counter and sipped her Coke in a to-go Styrofoam cup.

When she glanced around, she noted several people she recognized, and that felt good. She no longer felt so alone in the world. The mayor, in a green and yellow palm tree shirt, was at the register picking up take-out. He nodded pleasantly. A middle-aged couple who had bought one of Jenkins's paintings the day before was there. They waved. A guy in his early thirties who had been hitting on her in line on the boardwalk for ice cream yesterday was there, too—with his toddler and a woman who appeared to be his wife. He did not wave.

There was also a table of hospital employees, including the woman who had taken Jillian's blood and one of the men she'd met at Ty's parents' party. They were laughing, having a good time. In the very back, Jillian spotted the guy from the head shop down the boardwalk from Millie's store; he was with the police chief's daughter again. They were checking out their bill, each adding crumpled dollars to a pile on the table.

"'Afternoon."

Jillian looked over to see one of Albany Beach's policemen sliding onto the stool beside her. He had been two seats down, waiting for take-out, too, apparently, with the cop on the end who was reading a paper.

"Hi." She half smiled. It was Ryan McCormick, the one who had once dated Ty's sister. She tried not to think about what Ty had caught McCormick and his sister doing on his parents' couch.

"You waiting on lunch?" He was so close to her that the pressed long sleeve of his khaki uniform shirt brushed her bare arm.

"Um, yes." She avoided eye contact. "I'm grabbing lunch to have with a friend."

To her surprise, he frowned, the corner of his mouth turning down in almost a sneer. "Ty Addison? He's a kid." He cut his eyes at her. He gave her the impression he thought he was good-looking and assumed she thought the same. "What you need is a night with a *man*. A man who can show you a thing or two in the sack."

She glanced away, unable to believe that an on-duty police officer had just said such a thing to her. Ty said she was naïve in the ways of the world, especially when it came to men and women. She guessed he was right.

Jillian debated how to respond to McCormick's inappropriate remark. A week ago, she might have ignored him. Maybe risen, pretending she thought her order was up, and walked away. But her memories, as much they were scaring her, were also empowering her. She wasn't going to live the rest of her life a meek mouse, and she didn't have to put up with this kind of crap. Certainly not from cops.

Jillian turned slowly to Patrolman McCormick, offering a sassy smile as she lowered her voice until she knew it was sexy. "You know what I really need?" she whispered, breathy. "Right now?"

He puffed up like a toad; she could smell the testosterone rising off him like heat off a pavement.

He cut his eyes, checking to be sure no one in the diner was listening, then leaned closer. "Tell me," he murmured.

"For you to get lost! You ought to be ashamed of yourself," she lit into him, standing up so she could look him eye to eye. "You're in uniform. You ought to have a little more respect for your position and for women in general."

The cop a couple of stools down snickered. "Strike three! I think you're out, buddy."

"Shut up, Savage."

The other cop got up from his stool, leaving the paper. "Come on, order's up." He tapped McCormick on the shoulder as he passed.

Patrolman McCormick got up quickly, obviously embarrassed by Jillian's outburst and having it overheard by so many, including a colleague. Apparently he wasn't used to being taken down a notch. "You shouldn't have done that," he bit under his breath as he brushed past her.

Jillian stared at the cop's broad back as he retreated. *Had he just threatened her?*

The guy in black from the head shop passed behind her, right behind the cops, a look of amusement on his face. He'd obviously overheard. He raised one fist in salute to Jillian as he passed.

To Jillian's surprise, his teenage female companion, walking behind him, stopped and spoke. "I thought every woman between twelve and seventy was going to stand up and clap," she whispered with amusement.

Jillian glanced at the cash register. McCormick had left his partner to pick up the food and pay the bill and strode out the door. She'd been scared there for a moment, afraid she'd made a mistake and pushed it too far. Right now, the last thing she needed was to have the cops in town pissed off at her. But watching him go, she knew she was just overreacting. Men like him needed to put in their place once in a while.

Jillian turned her attention to the teenager. "I just can't stand that type."

The teen girl, dressed in black jeans with hanging suspenders, a tight black T-shirt, and leather straps with studs around her neck and waist, propped one hand on a jutting hip. "Me either. Guys like him, they like think they're all that and a bag of chips."

Jillian chuckled. Despite the dyed black hair and hideous black lipstick and eye liner, she was quite pretty. "Ashley, right," she said, pointing her finger.

Ashley gave a suspicious nod. "Right, how do you know that?"

"I know your mom—sort of."

She rolled her expressive blue eyes. "Criminy, everyone knows my mother. It's like this curse. Damned to ever walk in the footsteps of the mighty Claire Drummond, second generation police chief." She took a jerky Frankenstein step forward, arms raised, then relaxed. "Anyway." She brushed her hair from her face, moving from comically animated young woman back to sulky teen mode. "I just want to tell you that you made my day. McCormick hits on everyone, but he acts like such a super robo cop that nobody realizes what a creep he is. Even our *police chief*."

Jillian couldn't resist a grin. Despite the teen's choice of fashion, she liked her immediately. She had her mother's same penetrating gaze, same forwardness that was refreshing. "Well, thanks. Glad I could make your day."

"You comin'?" her boyfriend grunted from the door.

Ashley glanced at him, then back at Jillian. "I have to go back to work, and if you run into my mother, *I was not here.*" She started to walk away, then glanced back. "That Styrofoam cup." She pointed to Jillian's drink on the counter. "Do you have any idea how long that takes to disintegrate? Like a couple million years." She cupped one hand around her mouth so no one else would hear her. "Ask for a paper cup next time. Loretta's got them in the back. She's just too cheap to use them; you have to ask."

Jillian nodded thoughtfully. "Thanks, I'll keep that in mind." She lifted her hand. "Have a good day."

"You, too. Come by Stewart's Lawn and Garden and get a plant to brighten up the cottage. Just ask for me. I work there almost every day."

"I just might do that." Jillian spotted Loretta lifting a bag and got up from her stool. "See you," she told Ashley.

She grabbed her nonbiodegradable cup of Coke and walked to the register.

"Got your two Cokes, large cup ice water, two burgers and large fries with vinegar and ketchup." Loretta punched the register keys with gusto; Jillian noticed that she seemed to do everything that way. "Anything else?"

"That'll be it." Jillian paid and headed out. She managed to find a parking space only a block from the street where Ty was life guarding. Her timing was perfect, and she met him halfway between his guard stand and the street.

"I've got lunch. Want to sit in the shade?" She lifted the two paper bags and indicated the umbrella sales stand behind her.

"You're the best." He grinned, pulling his shirt over his suntanned bare chest.

They spoke to the guy who manned the umbrellas. He knew Ty; of course, everyone in town knew and liked him.

They chose a bright blue umbrella already open and lodged in the hot sand, and Jillian let Ty spread out the beach towel she had brought with her from the car.

"Burgers, fries and Coke. Oh, and ice water," she said, sitting down cross-legged. "Sorry, I didn't have time to stop for any fruit."

"No, this is fine. It's so cool. Thanks." He took a drink of Coke and unwrapped one of the burgers. "You have a good morning?"

"The best." She set out the little plastic containers of ketchup, mustard, and vinegar and grabbed a fry. "My records had been faxed here. It's like a book this thick." She indicated the thickness of a dictionary with her finger and thumb.

"That's cool. Maybe we'll find something in there that will help give us some clues where to start looking for you."

"That's not the best part." She used a plastic knife to

cut the second burger in half. "I had another memory. Well, not memory." She took half the burger and slid the other half toward him. "A recollection, sort of. And it had nothing to do with the dream for once."

"You're shittin' me!" He fixed his blue-green gaze on her as if she were the only person on earth.

"I think I was a physical therapist," she said softly, almost afraid to say it aloud for fear it would make it untrue. Then she went on excitedly. "It was the weirdest thing. I walked by the physical therapy department in the hospital on my way to records, and when I looked through the windows, I knew what every piece of equipment was. Just like that." She snapped her fingers. "It was like all this technical stuff came flooding back. "Types of injuries, length of time of recuperation after surgery. I don't remember anything specifically about where I worked or anything, but I even got some flashes of the faces of people I must have worked on." She took a big bite of burger. "That's got to mean something, right? That things might start coming back faster now. Maybe clearer."

"Yeah, oh, yeah." He chomped on his burger enthusiastically. "I started doing a little research last night on the Internet. There are sites with bulletins about who's missing. They're a mess to try to get through, but I might get lucky and find a physical therapist missing in Butte."

She laughed. "And her name will be Buffy, with my luck."

He laughed with her. "Buffy Bigsby."

"From Butte," she finished, still laughing, not sure why she thought it was so funny.

Ty took another swig of soda and rested his hand casually on her shoulder. "That's great, Jilly. It really is. I think this is going to work. We're going to find you."

She met his gaze and a chill of fear rippled through

her. She didn't say anything, but all she could think of
was—would she be sorry when she did?

Claire glanced at the index card at the top of the pile
on the car seat beside her and signaled to turn onto
Dogwood Avenue. It was one of the oldest streets in the
town that had been established in the 1890s. It still
sported a red brick walk and lovely old elm and maple
trees on both sides of the street.

Most of the original Victorian houses had been torn
down to make way for modern beach houses; there were
a couple of upscale townhouses farther down the block.
Original land plots had been divided, sometimes three
or four times, to make the best return on beach real estate when prices skyrocketed a few years ago. Just one of
the old properties remained, looking completely out of
place with more than an acre of land and a three-story
white clapboard Victorian house, complete with full
wraparound porch.

Claire approached the house slowly; if there was car
in the driveway, she'd cruise by, but otherwise, she wanted
to have a quick look.

She glanced at the name on the card, almost feeling
a little silly. But she had taken what Ashley had said to
heart. Every man in Albany Beach was a suspect. That
included Mayor Morris Tugman, aka *The Rug Man*.

No white Cadillac in the driveway.

Claire pulled over to the side and stared through the
passenger side window at the house. The wooden exte-
rior was sorely in need of scraping and painting. The
louvered shutters needed repair, and the iron fence
and gate that ran the length of the property was beginning to look beyond outdated. Of course, there was always someone in town making a snide remark about
believing their mayor should live in a nice house, but

apparently Morris had no intention of ever selling. He had inherited the place from his grandmother or something.

And honestly, the place didn't look that bad. Claire thought it was actually kind of charming. The lawn was always well manicured, and Claire liked the old-fashioned lilac bushes and magnolia trees. She heard a dog bark and looked up to see if she'd been spotted by the mayor, but the sound was coming from the backyard near the old barn that really *was* falling down.

Claire glanced down at her index card. Morris had been in the diner five times in the last three days, according to Ralph. Apparently he wasn't much of a cook. Claire also learned that there might be something more to Mrs. Tugman's extended stay in Florida with her sister. Loretta said the rumor she'd heard was that the missus had left the mayor. She'd been gone since the week before Memorial Day. Since before the killings began.

Claire glanced up at the shuttered windows in the big house that looked a little bit like eyes. The house seemed to watching her.

She groaned at her own inanity, shifted the police car into drive, and eased away from the curb. She'd been staying up too late, watching too many old Alfred Hitchcock movies with Ashley. There was nothing about the old Victorian house that looked sinister or even remotely spooky, and it certainly gave no indication that a serial killer lived there.

This was probably all a waste of time. She glanced in her rearview mirror and pulled onto the street. She didn't have time to do this. She needed to get back to the office and do some real police work like reviewing the victims' lists of personal effects; she'd been meaning to do it all week.

Morris didn't seem to her to fit the profile of a serial killer, but that didn't mean he wasn't one. His index card had moved to the top of the pile because she had begun quietly running background checks on all the men in town, and his had been one of the first to come back with information warranting her attention. It seemed Morris Tugman had a little run-in with the Florida police a few years back, before he was mayor. While vacationing in sunny Orlando, he'd been arrested on one count of invasion of privacy and another misdemeanor count of public indecency, which she knew translated to a peeping Tom jacking off in a flower bed. The case had been dismissed due to a court or county law enforcement error, but Claire had managed to speak with the arresting officer. He still remembered the case because they'd gotten three calls from the hotel before he was able to catch the Peeper in action. It appeared that Mayor Tugman had been creeping around the motel he was staying out, peering in the windows of vacationing coeds, and if he saw something he liked, getting his jollies off.

Claire didn't know she if should laugh or be disgusted. She'd always known Morris was a creep. This just confirmed it.

But Morris wasn't the only man in town with a criminal record. Her father had always told her that everyone had something to hide. That everyone had a past. And he was right. In a way, she wished she hadn't been forced to run so many of the townspeople's records. There were too many men she would now look at in a different light. True, it was all in the past, sometimes ancient past. And it wasn't fair. But she was only human.

Claire turned the corner, glancing at the index cards that slid. She caught them just before they shot off the edge of car seat into the passenger side door.

All the reports weren't back yet, but Claire had already learned that both Billy Trotter and Ty Addison had been busted for marijuana possession in the last four years. No surprise with Billy. No big surprise with Ty. He seemed like a good kid, but they all screwed up once in a while. He'd probably just gotten unlucky and gotten caught. Joe Climber from down the street from her parents had an assault charge against him a couple of years back and realtor Seth Watkins—now this one was bizarre—had been charged with invasion of privacy for audio taping women urinating in a public bathroom.

The incident had taken place in a restroom on a conference floor at a hotel in Reno where he'd been staying for a realtors' convention. Apparently taping hadn't been enough. He'd then proceeded to play the audio tape in a local bar to anyone willing to buy him a drink. Someone called the cops, and the tape recorder was recovered from the restroom. It appeared that Mr. Captain High School Football Team Seth had gone all out and bought two recorder/players so as not to miss out on any of the fun. He'd been put on probation for the little stunt.

Claire wasn't really concerned with the drug charges of the men in town, or even the assault charges she had discovered. One had been at an Eagles game in Philly. Another of Albany Beach's fine citizens had caught his wife in bed with another man and punched him.

What did worry her was the Peeping Tom crap and the pee taping. Both were bizarre, as well as sexual. Although the killer wasn't raping the women or having any sexual contact that the ME's office could find proof of, with serial killers, on some level, it was almost always about sex. It was about degrading women.

Claire didn't care for Seth or Morris, but she didn't see them as killers. She just wanted to be sure she was seeing them accurately. She was going to call both of them in just as soon as she got her notes together and planned how the interviews would go. She thought she might even call her old beau from the Delaware State Police, now a captain, to ask his opinion on the information she'd obtained and how he thought she should proceed. It might get some people who were upset that she hadn't let other agencies take over her investigation off her back. She also thought he might be able to offer some unbiased observations she might have missed. She'd known Seth and Morris for years. She wanted to be sure she didn't allow that to affect her investigation.

Claire turned onto the street that ran behind the boardwalk, thinking she would take a quick cruise along the street just to see what was going on before she headed back to her office. As she turned onto the boulevard, she spotted a familiar face. Actually, it was a back. All dressed in black, today sporting a leather belt studded with silver metal spikes.

Setting her jaw, Claire slowed down, putting down the electric window. "Need a ride?"

Ashley turned, paled a shade whiter, and then thrust out her jaw, her expression very close to Claire's. "No," she said flatly. "We don't need a ride."

Claire nodded to Chain, acknowledging his presence. He lifted one finger in response. At least it wasn't his middle finger.

"I thought you were at work," Claire hollered above the rumble of a motorcycle passing.

"I was." Ashley kept walking.

Claire kept driving. It was tricky because there were cars parked along the street. She didn't want to have to call in an accident caused by her own negligence while stalking her daughter. The paperwork for a single-car accident involving a police car was mind-boggling. "You're a long way from work," she remarked.

Ashley shrugged one shoulder. "Not that far. Mr. Stewart gives me a long lunch. I was just walking Chain back to work."

"You'd think he'd walk you back, being the gentleman he obviously is. The nursery must be a mile from here."

Ashley turned to her mother and rolled her eyes as if Claire were the stupidest person on earth. "*I told you,* Mr. Stewart gives me a long lunch. Chain only has an hour." She flipped her hair, teenager style. "I don't mind walking."

Claire nodded. "Well, I tell you what. You might not mind, but I do. So jump in and I'll give you a ride back to work, sweetie. It's awfully hot to be walking so far in those dark clothes with a serial killer stalking our streets."

"I'm not hot, and I'm with Chain."

"Get in the car." It was a cross between an order and threat.

Ashley halted and looked at Chain, her body language a myriad of markers, all pointing toward one obvious message. The teen hated her mother's guts.

Ashley said something under her breath that Claire couldn't catch. He answered. The two teens met lip to lip like pecking chickens, and then Ashley cut between two cars and jerked open the police cruiser door. "Call me," she hollered.

Again, the finger wave from Chain.

Claire put up the electric window on Ashley's side and speeded up, leaving Chain behind. "I don't know why you do this," she said.

Ashley clicked on her safety belt and then slouched in the seat, gazing out the window. "Do what?"

"Worry me unnecessarily. I think you're at work, safe and sound, and you're running the roads with Mr. Chain Link Fence."

"I'm not *running the roads*. We went to lunch. Since when am I not allowed to eat lunch? Last week you were harping about how I didn't eat enough."

"You didn't tell me you were meeting Chain for lunch."

"I didn't know. He called. I met him at the diner. Sheesh, Mom." Ashley glanced at Claire, then out the window again. "Why don't you just lock me up in prison now and get it over with."

She eyed her daughter. "Don't think I haven't contemplated that."

They didn't say any more until Claire pulled up in

Stewart's Lawn and Garden gravel parking lot. "Your grandfather will pick you up after work."

The slam of the car door was the only response Claire received. "Have a nice day," she called cheerfully. Then under her breath, "And thanks again for another day's worth of gray hairs."

The Bloodsucker sat alone in the dark in the barn on the end of the picnic table bench and breathed deeply. He was trying to find his center. Trying to calm his pounding heart. With his eyes closed, he could still see Anne seated in the chair in front of him. He could hear her whimper. Smell her blood, wet, cloying. It seemed like there had been a lot of blood; he was getting better. It was a good thing the barn was so old, that it had a dirt floor that had been covered in sawdust on and off for years. Sawdust was so easy to rake up. To burn in the old trash barrel out back. It was so easy to replace without drawing any suspicion.

He opened his eyes. He used to be afraid of the dark. Afraid of this barn. He absently rubbed his forearm through the long sleeves of his chambray shirt.

He wasn't afraid anymore. No need to be. The nightmares of Granny coming into his room were just the bad dreams of a little boy who was now all grown up. A little boy gone forever. A little boy who could never be hurt again.

He listened to the flutter of wings and the coo of pigeons nesting high in the rafters above him. This barn comforted him, now. It offered him strength.

It gave him a place to hide. To hide with the women he brought here. To get a chance to talk alone with them, uninterrupted.

He closed his eyes again and thought about Anne. He tried to conjure up the feeling he had when she'd been here with him. It had been so wonderful. Exciting.

Scary. Like riding a roller coaster. But those feelings were fading, fading faster than before. The power, the blood, it was so sweet, yet the feeling so fleeting.

That was why he had come here tonight. To prepare. To be sure everything was ready. He rose from the bench and lifted the clean kitchen towel from the tray. Without gloves he didn't dare touch the neatly folded white hand towel, the stack of sterile gauze or the gleaming handle of the scalpel. That didn't mean he couldn't look. Couldn't fantasize . . .

The Bloodsucker trembled in the glory of the moment as images of Anne were replaced with those of the stranger. He'd seen her again today. Beautiful. Aloof.

He wanted her. Had to have her. Already, in his mind, the plan was forming. He opened his eyes, carefully covering the tray. Patience and planning, he reminded himself. Success was all about patience and planning.

Chapter Ten

On the front porch, Jillian kicked off her sandy flip-flops and let herself into the cottage. Just inside the door, she dropped her canvas beach bag and made a beeline for the living room windows. Despite the hour, just after eight in the evening, the little house was stifling.

She gave the first window a shove; it groaned and slowly rose upward, rewarding her with a rush of much cooler night air. She pushed the faded cotton drapes aside and opened the next window. Right now, she didn't care if a serial killer or the mysterious man from her past came in the window and killed her. In this heat, she'd die anyway.

Jillian backtracked and closed and locked the front door, her one concession to the any madmen who might be in her life. There was probably no need to leave the door open for him. If he was going to get her, the very least she could make him do was climb through a window.

In the kitchen, she leaned over the sink and opened the window. She breathed in the sweet aroma of a fallen magnolia blossom that she had found behind the cottage the day before and stuck in a glass of water. The magnolia tree was actually on her neighbor's property, but she knew they wouldn't mind. Mrs. and Mrs. Collins had both stopped by the first week she was there and had been very friendly. They always waved to her whenever they saw her getting into her car or elsewhere in town.

Jillian brushed her fingertips across the delicate white blossom of the magnolia, thinking it looked too beautiful to be real. She groaned, realizing that any movement of her arms now brought stinging pain. She'd used suntan lotion, but she could tell she had still burned.

She went back to her bedroom, pushed open the faded blue drapes, and opened the window before going into the bathroom for a shower. After dawdling under the heavenly cool water until her sunburned skin began to prune, she reluctantly stepped out of the old tub. She patted her smarting skin gingerly and pulled a flimsy white nightgown she'd just bought over her head. She had liked it because it reminded her of the old-fashioned nightgowns women used to wear, white with little blue, green, and yellow flowers. It was thin and pretty transparent, but what did she care? She wasn't wearing it to work.

After towel-drying her hair, Jillian wandered back down the hall to find something for dinner. Her first thought was that a bag of microwave popcorn and a cold beer would be great. She really missed the new microwave she'd bought. Small, stainless steel door, high powered enough to nuke any dinner selection in less than three minutes.

She smiled to herself. This was beginning to happen more often now. Flashes of her past were coming to her; sometimes it was feelings rather than specific memories, but they were no less real or important. She didn't actually remember buying the microwave, not from where or from whom, but she knew she'd had one and sensed that, in time, she would remember such details along with all the other puzzle pieces in her life.

Instead of microwave popcorn, since she had no microwave, Jillian settled for a ham sandwich and a cold beer. As she padded barefoot toward the couch to enjoy her dinner with her book, her new nightgown fluttering at her knees, she halted. Suddenly, she had the strangest sensation of doing this very thing before.

The hair rose on her neck beneath her damp hair. She felt dizzy and disoriented as she recalled the cold, wet feeling of a drink in her right hand, the flowered plate with a sandwich in her left. Only before it had been lemonade and peanut-butter-and-jelly. And the nightgown. She knew the sensation of cool, airy cotton against her sunburned knees.

Still dizzy, she looked down at the ancient linoleum floor and stared at her bare feet. For a split second, they were much smaller. A child's bare feet.

Jillian didn't breathe. She had been here before as a child. She knew this cottage. The dishes. The linoleum.

Someone called her name. It was only a whisper on the cool, salty breeze that fluttered the old chintz curtains, but she heard it and turned her head to look down the hall.

No one was there, of course. And she didn't hear the actual name that was spoken; at least it didn't register in her mind. But she knew someone had called her. It was her own name she heard in her head.

Then, as quickly as the moment was upon Jillian, it was gone. The earth seemed to spin once again on its axis at a reasonable pace, and she came back to reality.

She exhaled loudly. "Wow," she muttered. "Freaky." It was one of Ty's words.

She walked slowly to the couch, set the beer bottle and plate on the coffee table littered with old magazines Millie had given her, and sat down. She studied the fluttering curtains on the far side of the living room. She looked at the faded carpet, the walls, with their faded paint and small cracks in the plastering, hoping for another glimpse of what she knew must be her past.

"Come on, come on," she breathed, concentrating on the objects that seemed so familiar.

But nothing else came to her. Once again she was only person she knew. Jane Doe. Jillian Deere.

She ate her sandwich and sipped her beer, listening to the silence of the house and the rhythmic sounds of the ocean that filtered through the open windows.

In the last couple of days, she had vacillated, not knowing if she really wanted to find her past. Ty's suggestion of just moving forward, becoming a new person, was tempting, yet she felt as if there was some reason she had to go back.

The word *justice* floated in her head, and she lowered her gaze to the floor again. A feeling of shame overcame her, though she could put no specific event to the feeling, no recollection. All she knew was that she had done something terrible. The thought even crossed her mind that maybe she had deserved to be shot. What if she had a robbed a bank or something? It didn't really fit into the bedroom scene she continually dreamed, but who knew?

She put her dirty plate in the sink and leaned over to rinse out the beer bottle before she put it into a paper bag she would take to the recycling center when it was full. A sound on the front porch caught her attention, and she glanced toward the front door.

In an instant, her heart was pounding. Her mouth was dry. She shut off the noisy faucet, but didn't move from the sink. She stared at the door. She could have sworn she heard the white glass knob rattle.

Ty?

No, it couldn't be. He was out celebrating his parents' anniversary. Besides, she had gone to the hardware store and had a copy of the key made for him. He could let himself in; there was no need to rattle the doorknob.

She waited for what seemed an eternity.

Ty had suggested she should get a cell phone. He said he worried about her here alone at night. She had made light of his concern, saying the Collinses were barely a scream away. What she hadn't told him was that they had noisy room air conditioners in their closed windows and that they would never hear her.

Jillian slowly stood up from where she had leaned on the sink. She stared at the curtains and wondered if that was a shadow she saw coming from the porch, or just her imagination.

For the first time today, she wished she had taken Ty up on his offer to be his date at the anniversary party. Right now, she could be at some nice restaurant eating a piece of key lime cheesecake and pretending to not know that his mother disapproved of her.

She darted suddenly for the window, slammed it down, twisted the lock, and shut the other just as quickly. She ran across the cool linoleum and closed the window of the sink. Leaving the lights on, she hurried down the hallway and closed the bedroom window.

The house was locked up tightly now. No one could get in easily.

She dropped onto the bed. It would get hot inside soon, and all she had was the one box fan she had bought at the Big Mart. She stared at the fan near the bed. She'd never get any sleep, as hot as it got in here.

Like she was going to be able to sleep now, anyway.

Claire sat at her desk methodically running her finger down the list of personal effects found in Patti's denim purse, left with her body. This was the third time she had read through it, and she knew there was nothing there. Nothing there that could lead her to a killer. Half a pack of cigarettes and a lighter, a wallet with a driver's license, blood bank card, and seven dollars and forty-eight cents in it. A pack of matches from Calloway's

Bar. No fingerprints that weren't her own; she had a record for shoplifting and had been printed.

Claire contemplated the matchbook for a moment. The local bar and restaurant was where Patti's ex worked, but it was also the bar all the locals hung out in. And they did have cool matchbooks. Claire didn't even smoke, and she knew there were a couple of Calloway's matchbooks in her junk drawer in the kitchen. Other items in Patti's purse was girly stuff—pink lipgloss, aspirin, tampon, blue nail polish. A couple of receipts from stores in town, but nothing that indicated who she had hitched a ride home with the night she died.

Claire set the sheet of paper aside and glanced at April's personal effects list. She'd had nothing on her, poor thing. She'd walked out of the rented condo that night to cool off and take her mother-in-law's dog for a walk after a family fight. No identification, no money, not even a roll of breath mints.

Phoebe Matthews. She'd had a purse too. The killer had also slipped hers over her shoulder before dumping her near a dumpster at a construction site. Conscientious son of a bitch, wasn't he?

Phoebe's list of stuff was more interesting than Patti's. She had a cell phone, turned off. Claire suspected Phoebe had been talking to her twin sister when the killer had picked her up. He had thoughtfully turned it off to save her battery; no fingerprints, of course, because of the latex gloves the ME said he wore. Along with the usual stuff like a wallet and make-up and pens, Phoebe also had a joint, three "lubricated for her pleasure" condoms, a pair of dice, and a page ripped from a magazine advertising for mail order brides in Alaska. Interesting, but none of the stuff was a lead in any particular direction or toward anyone on her index cards.

Claire glanced away, then looked at the list again, realizing something had caught her eye. A pen from Waterfront Realty.

She dropped the list on her desk and scrambled through a pile of manila envelopes with photographs from each crime scene. Also included were photographs of each victim's personal effects. She located the one with Phoebe's name on it at last and jerked the 8 1/2 by 11 inch photos of her dead body out. At the very bottom of the pile was the photograph she was looking for.

There was the pen! The photograph had been taken by one of her detectives. It wasn't as high a quality as she would have liked, but there was definitely writing on the pen. She squinted. Still couldn't read it.

She jerked open the middle drawer of her desk and ran her hand over the paper clips, rubber bands, spare pens and pencils. She found a school photograph of Ashley from two years ago, numerous pizza coupons, and a toothbrush, but no magnifying glass.

Claire left the photo on her desk and hurried out of her office and down the hall. She found her gum-popping assistant, sitting at her desk in the glass office in the front of the building. She was painting her nails.

Claire punched in the security number that would allow her through the fishbowl door.

"Sorry, things are a little slow today," Jewel said, quickly screwing the top on her glitter nail polish.

"Do you have a magnifying glass?"

Jewel got up, carefully keeping her hands in the air, fingers spread so as not to smudge her nails. "What? No."

"I need a magnifying glass. I know we have one somewhere," Claire said impatiently. "I thought it was in my desk, but it's not."

Jewel snapped her fingers together, then checked her polish job for damage. "Check the break room," she told Claire. "Somebody had a splinter in his hand the other day."

Claire hurried out of the office.

"You have a splinter, boss?" Jewel called after her.

Claire pushed through the swinging door that led into the break room. It smelled of burnt coffee, stale pastries, and men. She really needed to get some women on the force.

Beside an empty pizza box on the small kitchenette countertop, she spotted the magnifying glass. "Gotcha!"

Back in her office, Claire slammed her door and dropped into her chair. She pulled the photograph beneath the magnifying glass, gripped the handle, and looked closer.

"I'll be damned," she whispered, dropping the cheap plastic magnifying glass.

Seth Watkins, the pen read. There was no mistaking it. His name, the realty company's phone number, and his personal cell number. Seth was always passing those pens out. A pen in Phoebe's purse meant it was very likely she had had contact with him recently.

Claire jotted his cell number on a clean yellow legal pad and wrote his name above it in big bold letters, followed by a question mark.

Could Seth Watkins be a serial killer? He didn't strike her as the killer type. Maybe he was a little too pushy sometimes, a little too used-car-salesman-like. But a killer?

Of course, if you'd ask her two days ago if she thought he could be capable of recording women peeing in a pubic restaurant and then playing the tape for others' enjoyment, she wouldn't have thought that of him either.

She sat back in her chair and glanced at the phone. Hesitated, then dialed the number she had dialed hundreds of times in her previous life as Kurt Gallagher's lover.

"Captain Gallagher," he barked into the phone, picking up his extension on the first ring.

She almost wished she hadn't called. Where was her confidence in herself? If Watkins might be her man, why did she need Kurt to confirm her suspicions?

"Hello?"

"Kurt, it's Claire."

"One little, two little, three little bodies, four little—"

"Shut up and listen to me."

"Sorry, that wasn't funny," he said, reasonably contrite.

"No, it wasn't. I think I've got a serious lead."

"Good thing. Word upstate is that there's talk of a task force convening to take care of Albany Beach's little serial killer problem. People are beginning to worry the tourists will stay away from our beaches. We need their revenue."

"Perfect," she groaned. "I wondered what had held them back this long."

"Same old, same old. Money for overtime. Manpower."

Claire closed her eyes for a moment. This could mean the end of her short-lived career as the police chief of Albany Beach. She could wind up working for some chicken plant as the security officer keeping the county's chickens safe from animal activists bent on setting the oppressed free, and the occasional fox. But she couldn't think about that right now.

"I've got this lead," she repeated, "on a guy I kind of liked to begin with. But I need you to think this through with me. Help me steer clear of meaningless crap."

"You want me to cut out of here early? Come to your office?"

She checked the clock on her wall. It was her father's retirement clock given to him by the city; he'd "loaned" it to her when she'd been hired for his position. "No. Come to my place? I'll throw some steaks on the grill. We can go over notes."

"And have some reindeer games, just for old times?"

"Not hardly. See you at seven. Bring wine." She hung up on him, realizing she was still a little hung up on him.

"Ty, this is silly." Jillian followed him through his parents' dark laundry room. The dryer was tumbling and the warm room smelled of detergent, fabric softener, and dog food. "Why don't we just walk in the front door? You say 'Hi, Mom, hi, Dad, I'm taking my friend the older woman up to my room.'? Then we go upstairs to the computer."

"Because Mom will start giving Dad the look she gives him, she'll start to hyperventilate and need a vodka on the rocks to settle down, and Dad will be in the doghouse for a week for *letting me* take women to my room. And just for the record—" He glanced over his shoulder at her in the shadowed hallway. "You'd probably be classified as my fuck-buddy, not my friend."

She could hear the TV blaring in the front of the house. "Your what?" she whispered.

He chuckled. "Well, we're not really boyfriend and girlfriend."

"I'm a little old for that."

"Exactly. And we really are friends. But we do"—he raised and lowered his eyebrows comically—"You know. So—"

"So I'm your fuck-buddy," she repeated, not sure if she was horrified or amused.

He grinned and beckoned with his finger. "Come on, the back staircase is here. Mom and Dad have the TV up so loud, they'll never hear us. We could probably" — again, the eyebrow waggle—"in my room and they'd never hear us."

"Fat chance of that." She gave him a playful push forward. "Come on, let's go if we're going. This is ridiculous. I feel like I'm sneaking into a frat house after hours."

He started up the narrow back staircase. "You did that?"

She thought for a moment. "Actually, I think I did."

"Cool." Ty jogged up the stairs, suntanned arms pumping.

In the long, carpeted upstairs hallway, they bumped

into his cousin Kristen, wrapped in a green towel, another towel tied in a turban around her head. She was just coming out of the bathroom.

"Hey," Ty said, opening a door to what was apparently his bedroom.

Kristen lifted her hand in greeting. "Hey." She smiled at Jillian. "Hi there."

"Hi." Jillian followed Ty into his bedroom, closed the door behind her, and leaned against it. "She's not going to—"

"Say anything to Mom? Nah. I've got almost as much on Kristen as I do on my sister." He sat down at a desk and flipped open a laptop. "Computer's my dad's," he explained as it booted up, various Microsoft screens flitting by. "I left mine at a buddy's house with all my other stuff. Seemed silly to haul it all here, then back to PA in a few weeks."

Ty's casual explanation was a stark reminder to Jillian that he would be leaving soon. He would be returning to his graduate program at Penn State and she would be on her own again. She needed to let the skeezy realtor guy know if she was staying in Albany Beach at the cottage or moving on. She didn't know yet; maybe she and Ty would find something on the Internet tonight that would help her make that decision.

"There are all these lists of missing people. Networks set up to find them. But I haven't found any central location to look at names, so this may take a while. I mean like days. Weeks," Ty explained. "You know, it's amazing to me how many people in this country are missing. Not just kids. Adults. Some are dead, I guess. Some maybe in circumstances like yours. But did you know there's a trend of adults just getting up, walking away from their lives, and starting new ones?" He punched a couple of keys on the laptop and it squealed as it made the Internet connection. "I was reading about it this morning before I went to work. They leave jobs, wives, husbands, kids."

Jillian shook her head, checking out his room. It was interesting, definitely masculine with dark walls and bookcases lined with books. The faded posters were of surfers and musicians, left up from his high school days, she supposed. "I can't imagine leaving your life behind like that," she mused aloud.

"I don't know. I mean, I would never do it, but you can see a forty-something guy just sick of his life walking away from it all. I mean, imagine a nagging wife, snotty, ungrateful kids, going-nowhere job."

She dropped onto his rumpled, denim duvet-covered bed. It smelled like him. "I suppose a woman could feel the same way. Unsupportive husband. Trying to work full-time, but still expected to keep the house clean, make gourmet meals—" Jillian halted in mid-sentence, that weird feeling she had remembered something coming over her again.

Ty glanced over his shoulder.

She met his gaze.

"You think—"

"Nah, I didn't shoot myself so I could get away from anything. But," she said thoughtfully, "there's something about what I just said that means something."

He waited for a moment and when she didn't elaborate, he returned his attention to the computer screen. "I saved a couple of sites that looked interesting. Come sit here and tell if any of these names or places sound familiar. They've actually got photos of some people." He patted his knee.

Jillian rose from the bed and dragged a chair over to the desk to sit beside Ty. She lifted her gaze to the computer screen, not entirely sure she was ready for this. What if she recognized her own name? What if she didn't?

"I thought it would make sense to start from where you were found and then fan out. The sites seemed to be organized by the state the missing person was last seen in." He clicked on North America and scrolled down past names, physical descriptions, sometimes photos. The heading for the state of Virginia floated by. "This site doesn't organize people by year, but I thought we'd just skim through the pages looking for this year, and if nothing comes up, maybe look back later."

"I think it's pretty safe to assume I disappeared about the time I was shot. I arrived at the hospital in Portsmouth on May eleventh."

"I know, I'm just saying, we need to stay open about the particulars. It's always possible you've been missing for a while." He kept scrolling downward.

"How?"

He shrugged. "I don't know. Kidnapped, held prisoner, maybe?"

She frowned, images of the naked man in her bed flashing in her mind. The sound of her drunken laughter. She had definitely been there of her own free will. "I don't think I was held captive," she said dryly.

"Here goes."

Jillian held her breath for a moment and then exhaled slowly.

At first, the names and places Ty scrolled through were just a blur, but as her eyes focused, they began to register. Only the women's names caught her attention; she just let the men's names pass. Marie Adams, Bristol, 1998. Desiree Smith, Danville, 1977. Patricia Eckard, Charlottesville, 2001. "So many," she whispered.

"Listen to this one. Anna Preston, last seen in Richmond, January 21, 2004," he read aloud. "Age twenty-seven. Red hair, green eyes. Went out to buy a pack of cigarettes and never returned. Her husband and daughter miss her. Someone must know something. Someone must have seen her." The listing gave a contact name and e-mail address.

Jillian shook her head. "It's not me. Too young. Doctors said I've never given birth."

"I know." He scrolled downward and more names, a few faces passed on the screen.

An elderly woman named Mae, who wandered from her granddaughter's house. A forty-one-year-old housewife who worked her shift at a paper cup plant, left to go home to put her daughter on the school bus and never made it home. The photo of a twenty-year-old girl, blond, smiling, dressing in a soccer uniform, holding a big trophy.

It was heartbreaking.

"Anything look familiar?" Ty asked after a few minutes. He had paused at several names of missing women in their thirties; none had disappeared in May of that year.

"No," she said, staring at the screen but no longer seeing the names or faces that scrolled by. She put her arm around Ty. "Listen, this is really nice of you to do, but talk about a needle in a haystack. How—"

"I know, Jilly. It's probably a wild shot, but maybe you're here somewhere and I just have to find you." His voice held enthusiasm for the impossible task that only a twenty-three-year-old could possess. "I've got another five or six websites bookmarked. And some states have hotlines you can call."

"Ty, you don't want to spend your last two weeks at home sitting in front of this computer looking through hundreds, thousand of names. I might not even recognize my name if I see it." She squeezed his shoulder and got up from the chair. "You mind if I call it a night?"

"No, not at all. You don't need to be here for me to do this. I just thought you might want to see what I found." He looked away from the computer screen. "You want me to go home with you?"

She had driven herself and then parked half a block and walked up to the house. "I'll be fine."

"Want me to walk you down?" His attention was on the computer screen again. He had gone to another website and had popped a CD into the CD player. Some hip band she didn't recognize.

"Nah." She rested her hand on the doorknob. "I'll just put on my stealth cloaking device and slip out of the house, undetected by man or dog. Good night."

He didn't look up from the screen. "'Night. I'll let you know if I find anything."

Jillian slipped out the door, closing it behind her and headed down the dark hall. Halfway to the staircase, she heard a bedroom door open and for a moment, she froze. Then she realized it was the same door Kristen had disappeared into a little while ago. She was dressed in short shorts and a cute gauze top, purse slung over her shoulder.

Kristen smiled when she saw Jillian. Like Ty, she had that kind of all-America good looks. Straight blond hair, perfect teeth, slim, athletic body.

"Going out?" Jillian asked.

She nodded. "Some friends. I'm not really into drinking, but I like to dance. Fake ID," she whispered, sheepishly.

"You know that nut case is killing blondes with blue eyes. You need to be careful," Jillian warned.

"Sure. I always am. You want me to go ahead?" She swept her long hair off her shoulder. "Run lookout for you?"

"That would be great."

The two women made it safely out the back of the house and then walked together through the backyard and out front to the sidewalk.

"I'm just parked down there," Jillian said, pointing.

"See you." Kristen walked toward a car in the driveway.

* * *

The Bloodsucker watched the two women appear from the side of the house, blond heads close together, whispering as if they were sisters . . . or maybe sorority sisters. He had never known any sorority sisters, but he had seen enough made-for-TV movies to recognize the friendly familiarity.

They were pretty, the both of them. Smart. He liked them both, although Jillian was a little reserved for his taste. He guessed she would warm up a bit, once they had a chance to really sit and talk in the barn where he would have her undivided attention.

He watched as the two women parted company on the sidewalk, Kristen climbing into her car in the driveway, Jillian heading down the street where she had parked her car earlier. The Bloodsucker had watched her and Ty sneaking into the backyard and then, he guessed, into the house. He wasn't sure what was going on there. He knew the rumors. He had seen them together, but he sensed they weren't really a couple. Not in love or anything. He would have to ask her.

He glanced in his side-view mirror as Jillian passed his car, but on the far side of the street. She checked over her shoulder as if she feared someone was watching her. How did she know? He tensed, perspiration gathering on his upper lip. Who was she looking for? Him?

He slid down at little in the seat of his car, forcing himself to relax. Anxiety could be controlled; it was all about heart rate and the adrenaline that drove it. Anxiety had no place in what he did. He had to stay calm. Calm and composed. His anxiety, of course, was simply a reaction in his brain to what he was doing. This was dangerous sitting here like this, even in the cover of darkness. What if someone saw him, casually asked him what he was doing here this time of night?

The Bloodsucker heard the engine of the Honda start

in the Addisons' driveway, and his attention returned to the college student.

Kristen wanted to be a nurse like her Aunt Alice. Such a noble profession. And she would be good at it. So compassionate, so tender. She always had a moment to spare for anyone; it was an admirable trait in someone so young.

The car's headlights flashed on, and Kristen gunned the engine of the little car. She was in a hurry to get somewhere. Meeting friends at a bar, maybe? He knew she used a fake ID to get into the bars in town where the bouncers didn't know her. He had seen her use it. Someone probably needed to speak to the young woman about the dangers of underage drinking. Besides the reprisals by the law, all sorts of terrible things could happen to a pretty girl under the influence of alcohol. Men could take advantage of her . . . worse.

The two-door Honda seemed to shudder as she threw the gear shift from reverse into drive, and the Bloodsucker glanced in the side-view mirror once more at Jillian. Lovely, mysterious Jillian. She was the talk of the town. Word had gotten around about her amnesia. One gossip had said someone had tried to murder Jillian by slitting her throat with a knife. He didn't think that was true, though. He'd seen no scar on her slender neck, not the kind such an attack would have produced.

Jillian was now in her car; her face under the streetlamp looked harsh. She was upset about something. Nervous. He watched with fascination as she looked over her shoulder, down the dark street. Once again, he got the feeling it was him she was looking for. It was that instinct many women seemed to have, and it fascinated him. It could be so reliable, yet most women ignored it.

Jillian started down the sidewalk, heard Kristen start her car and then back out of the driveway. Uncomfortable, she glanced up and down the street. Suddenly she felt as if someone was watching her. But who? From where?

Her gaze darted from the street to the house and back to the street, where there cars were parked on each side. She quickened her pace.

In the middle of the street, Kristen shifted her car into drive and whizzed past, waving as she went by. Jillian reached her car, climbed in, and locked the doors. She checked the rearview mirror and again the street. She saw no one. Heard a dog bark in the distance and saw Kristen pull away from the stop sign at the end of the street.

Her imagination? Or was someone watching her again?

Kristen shot by in her little car, and the Bloodsucker started his engine. He was letting his mind wander, and that wasn't how he operated. He had a plan, and plans were meant to be followed.

His heart fluttered in his chest. But he was so tempted . . .

Was it really necessary to keep the women in order in the line? Did he dare switch one for the other? Simply speed up the plan for B, while temporarily postponing the plan for A?

He shifted his car into gear, not turning on his headlights. He would wait until he was down half a block or so and then turn them on, looking surprised as though he had forgotten, in case anyone was watching.

The women were headed in opposite directions from each other. Wouldn't it be fun if they were both going in the same direction? Then he could follow both. Delay his decision another moment or so.

But the Bloodsucker was only daydreaming. He already knew whose blood would be next. He could smell its essence. Taste the saltiness. Feel its all-encompassing warmth. Its power.

Chapter Eleven

"Great meal."

Kurt handed Claire the plate he had just scraped and rinsed off, so that she could put it in the dishwasher. Which she found interesting, since she never recalled him ever rinsing a plate in his kitchen or hers in the two years they had dated.

"You want some dessert?" she asked.

They had enjoyed a leisurely meal outside on the redwood deck; Ashley had even joined them and had actually been pleasant. After dinner she had retreated to her room, and now Claire and Kurt were dawdling in the kitchen, delaying what he was there for.

"My mom sent a couple of pieces of her homemade key lime pie home with Ashley tonight," Claire said. "She specifically stated it was for you."

Claire had let it slip to her mother that Kurt was coming over, and even when she tried to backtrack and warn her it was for work, Janine hadn't been interested in the details. She loved Kurt, more than Claire had ever loved him, for sure. Janine had wanted her daughter to marry him; the fact that he didn't want to was a detail she ignored.

"Key lime pie?" Kurt perked up. "Janine sent me key lime pie? God, I love that woman."

"Dowry, I think. You take me off her hands, and she'll provide you with a lifetime supply of key lime pie," Claire joked caustically as she closed up the dishwasher and hit the rinse and wash button.

"Claire . . ." Kurt brushed her jawline with his fingertips. "Don't you think we should—"

She ducked away and walked toward the better lit dining room. "We should what? Talk about it? I don't think so. Water under the bridge."

She slid into one of the rustic birch wood chairs she loved. The handmade table and chairs shipped from Montana had been a gift to herself when she broke up with Kurt, knowing the relationship would never go anywhere beyond the bedroom. When she divorced her husband, Tim, she'd bought a new combination clock radio and sound machine.

Claire wondered if there was some significance to the amount of the expenditure. Had Tim, the father of her only child, really meant so little to her? More disturbing, had Kurt meant that much?

"First I need you to take a look at the crime scene photos. Then pie. I know you've seen a few of these," Claire said, dealing out the glossy eight-by-tens as if they were cards, "but I want you to look at them side by side. Give me your first impression. Instant cop gut intuition."

He walked up to the dining room table, standing back a little. "White, male."

"Duh. Killers rarely go outside their ethnicity."

"He's educated, college maybe."

"Definitely smart. But you're still not wowing me. White collar or blue?"

"Probably white. Some sort of professional even, maybe." He touched the photo of Anne sprawled beside the dumpster behind the country club kitchen.

"Now, for all the money *and* the car," Claire said after

a moment, "what's different from the others about this photo?"

"Do I get the girl?" He didn't look up.

Kurt was looking good tonight. Past good. Downright delicious. He'd changed after work. Arrived in a pair of stylishly wrinkled khaki shorts and a plum-colored pique polo, his full head of dark hair, slightly shaggy, falling over one eye. It would be so easy to fall into bed with him.

Claire resisted. She wasn't completely against good sex for the sake of good sex, but not with Kurt. That emotional territory was just too dangerous. "Nope, you don't get this girl." She hooked a thumb in her direction and hopped down off the chair to pad barefoot to his side of the dining table. "Come on, come on, what's different?"

He barely skipped a beat. "Umbrella."

"I have never liked you," she muttered, snatching the photo out from under his hand. "What's really remarkable is that I think it's his, not hers."

He hooked his thumb in his shorts pocket, thoughtfully. "He left nothing at any of the other scenes?"

"Nope."

"He killed her, but then left her *an umbrella?*"

"It had been raining the night before when she was kidnapped. Rain still in the forecast the night he dumped her." She shrugged. "He left it for her in case another storm came through?"

"Sick fuck."

She exhaled. "Amen to that." She walked back to her chair and patted the one around the corner. "Now, sit down here and listen to what I have on one of my potential suspects. Tell me if I'm getting off track, because I desperately need someone to point my finger at."

Kurt listened attentively to her explanation of her conclusion that the killer was picking out his victims from the diner. She then proceeded to go through the top suspects. He never lifted a brow when she brought up the mayor's police record. The man had never had much respect for authority.

"But Seth Watkins is who I think I like." She slid a copy of his criminal record faxed to her from Nevada. "He's single, so he lives alone. He's a realtor, so not only is he constantly meeting people, but he has access to vacant properties. He lives in a condo, but maybe he's not killing them at home. Maybe he's taking them somewhere else."

Kurt read the police report of the pee incident, slowly, his mind obviously at work. "Could be," he said.

She let her arms fall to her sides in exasperation. "Could be? You should meet this guy. There's something definitely slimy about him. He was born and raised here. A big star of the high school football team. One of those people that high school was the highlight of his life. And he's big on the dating scene in town. He's seen in all the bars all the time. And . . ." She slid a photo of the contents of Phoebe's purse to him. "The pièce de résistance—Phoebe Matthews had a pen in her purse with his name on it."

He glanced at the photo. "I thought you said you believed he meant to kill the other sister. The one who was in that accident and had the plastic surgery."

"I did. I still do," she corrected herself. "But Phoebe was living with her sister. They both knew him. Either one would have accepted a ride from him in a minute. And he was the realtor the sister was using to look for property for a restaurant. She bought a place and intends to open up next spring."

Kurt glanced up, brown eyes unreadable. "Have you talked to her?"

"Can't really. She and her family went on an extended vacation—and I think it was smart."

"If sick boy missed her the first time—"

"He might try again," she finished for him.

Kurt shuffled through the other police reports she had on the citizens of her hometown. He read a couple, went back once to reread something. After a long silence, he pushed the paperwork away from him. "I think you've got some good ideas here, Claire."

"But you don't think Seth Watkins is my man?"

"I'd bring him in. Better yet, go see him. Make a house call. See if there's anything that strikes you as odd at his place. But I'd interview the others, too."

"I want to keep this quiet. You have no idea how fast stuff spreads in this town. The flu and information," she said wryly.

"Well, this kind of killer has to know you're looking for him. He might want to talk to you. It might add to the whole thrill of stalking and killing these women."

She nodded, considering his words. "Could be, because I keep getting this feeling it's something about outsmarting us. Not just the women, but the whole town." She rested her forehead on her hand for a moment, letting her guard down slightly. "It's awful, Kurt. Everywhere I go in town, I'm looking for him. I'm looking into the faces of men I've known my whole life and wondering if I'm looking into the face of a killer. Even my officers could be suspects."

"Could be." He frowned. "But cops usually leave certain telltale signs that scream law enforcement gone bad. You know what kind of macho son-of-a-bitches they can be."

She chuckled, cutting her eyes at him. "Do I ever. The thing is, though, if you were killing women and you didn't want to get caught, wouldn't you be careful not to leave any signs you're a cop with predictable cop ways?"

"Probably," he agreed, meeting her gaze.

There was something about the way he was looking at her. Something he knew that he wasn't telling. She let her hand fall. "Okay, so out with it."

"Out with what?"

"Whatever it is you aren't telling me, Captain Kurt Gallagher."

He glanced away, then back at her. "The task force."

"I know, you already told me it was only a matter of time. That's why I've got to hurry up and figure this out. Well, not just for that reason," she backtracked. "This isn't about my career; I don't want to see another woman die."

"Claire, the wheels have already begun to turn."

"What wheels?"

"You know what wheels."

She slapped her hands on the table and half rose from her chair. "A couple of hours ago I talked to you and you acted as if it was some nebulous thing." She put out her hands, palms down, shifting them one way and then another. "Could be, possibly—"

"The call came after I spoke to you."

"What kind of call?" She stared at him, knowing very well what he meant, but she wanted to make him say it.

He was looking at her notes in front of him. Or maybe his fingernails.

"Don't tell me they're convening this task force—"

"Claire, this should have been taken over by the state police as soon as you found the first dead woman—"

"Don't tell me they're putting you in charge of my case!"

"It was unfair of anyone to expect you and your force"—he stood up—"to handle this kind of—"

"You son of a bitch." She slapped the table again with one hand. "Get out." She pointed to the front door. "You came here anyway, knowing you were taking over my case? You came here pretending you were helping me when you were trying to find what direction I was going." She was definitely screaming now.

"Claire, please. It could be weeks before this comes to fruition. There's got to be money allocated, people—"

"Get out!"

"Mom?" Ashley peeked around the corner of the dining room. "You all right?"

Kurt glanced at Ashley. "She's fine. We're just having a difference of opinion." He tried to smile. "You know how it's always been between the two of us."

Ashley thrust out her lower jaw. "Want me to call the cops, Mom?"

"I am the cops," he said indignantly.

Claire marched out of the dining room into the front hall. "No need to call, he was just going." She unlocked the deadbolt and jerked open the door. "Weren't you, Kurt?"

He had followed her to the hall. He had that look on his face men got sometimes. Like they had no idea how they had arrived in the position they were currently in. "What about my key lime pie?"

Claire stared him down, her arms crossed over her chest. "No pie."

He stood there for a second, as if in indecision, and then, wisely, seemed to draw the conclusion that the best way to save face and his ass was to get out. "I'll be getting in touch."

Claire slammed the door behind him and threw the dead bolt. "I bet you will."

As she punched the keypad on the house alarm to set it, Ashley came closer. She didn't actually put her arm around her mother, but she brushed back and shoulder. "You sure you're okay?"

Claire nodded.

Ashley glanced at the curtained window that showed a flash of headlights as Kurt backed up and pulled out. "That's kind of too bad he left like that. When he showed up tonight, I kind of thought maybe the two of you—"

"Not a chance," Claire said, closing the door on the alarm box. "But what do you care? You never liked him anyway."

"Sure I did. He was nice to me." She shrugged. "To you."

Claire stared at her daughter in surprise. "When we were dating, you acted like you hated his guts."

"Not any more than I would have hated anyone who loved you," Ashley said matter-of-factly. She turned away. "I'm eating the pie. You want some?" She disappeared into the kitchen.

Claire couldn't resist a chuckle. Her whole life was falling apart and she was laughing. She threw up her hands and followed her daughter into the kitchen. "Sure. Why not? And I want Kurt's piece. The big one."

Tonight, Jillian didn't fight the dream. Tonight she was ready for it. She went to bed early. No allergy medicine to help her sleep. No alcoholic beverages. As she drifted off, she thought about the bedroom, the man in the shower. She willed him to come to her bed.

And he did.

Jillian got out of a car. Not her own. A rental, maybe? She heard the gravel crunch beneath her feet. She was wearing sandals. The ones she had been wearing when she was left at the hospital. Some nurse had bagged them up for her. Jillian had thrown them in the trash along with the jean skirt and the white T-shirt. They were too bloody to be salvaged.

Only now in the dream, they weren't bloody at all. They were new and a soft butternut brown. And she liked them. She thought they made her feet look small.

She remembered seeing a car she recognized in the driveway. Whose driveway? Whose car? She didn't know.

She walked up to the door. Knocked maybe?

But if he was expecting her, why did she knock?

Tonight the dream seemed to come to Jillian on more than one level. She was seeing it as she must have seen it that night, but also, she was thinking through it, not as the woman in the dream, but Jillian. As Jillian who had been shot by someone inside.

The dream seemed to skip forward then, as if she had hit the scene skip with the remote to her new DVD player.

She had a new DVD player?

Her mind flitted from the dream to a shiny new piece of electronics. She remembered being so proud for buying it herself, hooking it up to the cable box and the TV all by herself without his help.

Whose help?

Suddenly she was in the bedroom again. Transported forward in time and space. Only now her heart was pounding and she was afraid.

Why? Her lover was expecting her, wasn't he?

All over again, she heard the shower running, the fan ticking. The air was humid, hot. Steamy from the shower. She could smell the sex on the air, the musky scent of exchanged body fluids. And alcohol.

Some had spilled. She could almost taste the bite of the Scotch. She saw the sweaty glass on the nightstand, the melted ice cubes in the bottom, the ring of water beneath it.

Now she was in the bed, her naked legs tangled in the hot sheets. She heard the drunken laughter. Her own. She was calling to him. He was just stepping out of the shower.

That was when Jillian saw the pistol on the nightstand beside the bottle of Scotch.

She screamed as she saw it rise, seemingly of its own accord. Saw the gun barrel pointed at her.

Light travels faster than sound.

She saw the flash, then heard the shot. She opened her mouth to scream, but no sound came out as the pain exploded in her neck.

Jillian woke from the dream, shaking but in control of herself. She flipped on the light in the stifling bedroom and reached for her glass of water. The sweat on the glass from the melted ice reminded her of the glass of Scotch on the nightstand.

Why had she been drinking Scotch? She hated Scotch. It tasted medicinal. Like drain cleaner, she remembered telling *him.*

Jillian finished the glass of water and lay back on her sweat-soaked pillow to stare at the stained white ceiling. Instead of making more sense, the more details she remembered, the less she understood.

"You're not going to believe this." Jewel popped her gum enthusiastically as she approached Claire's desk. "I know I'm not supposed to be really be looking at this stuff, but . . ." She didn't bother to make an excuse. Another reason why Claire liked her. "It just came over the wire. Ralph's got himself an alias," she sang.

Claire looked up from her notes on Seth and snatched the paper from Jewel's hand. "You're kidding me."

She shook her head. She was wearing bright blue, metallic eye shadow à la the seventies. The funny thing was, it worked with her. "His name's not Ralph Jones; it's James Claus. Known as Jimmy Claus. He's wanted for assault and battery and attempted murder of a woman he met in some bar in Jersey."

"Eleven years ago," Claire said, scanning the report quickly. "I'll be damned."

"Picked her up after she left the bar and slit her throat with a box cutter after he beat her up. Left her to die in the alley behind the bar," Jewel offered.

Claire glanced up, eyeing her. She wanted to read the report on her own. She didn't need Jewel to relay the information. She looked at the printout again.

"Sorry," Jewel squeaked. "I'll just be going back to the fishbowl." She backed her way out the office. "Give me a holler if you need me. Nails are already done."

Claire read the report, then read it again. Was Ralph her man? Good old, slightly rumpled Ralph? It was certainly possible. He was on her list of suspects because of his proximity to the victims.

She'd run into Seth this morning in the diner. She was getting coffee. He was having the number two special—hotcakes, sausage, and biscuit—and flirting with a young woman who appeared to be just getting in after a night of partying, rather than just getting up.

Claire had sat and chatted with Seth for several minutes. He hadn't seemed nervous in the least, even when she'd asked him where he'd been the other night when Anne had disappeared from the boardwalk. He apparently hadn't made the connection between the date she provided and Anne's disappearance. He thought it was about some woman who hadn't paid her rent and his company was evicting her. He'd been quite charming in his own used-car-salesman kind of way. Claire could have sworn he thought she was hitting on him. She had walked out of the diner with her coffee and donuts thinking her gut instinct told her Seth was not her man.

And now this criminal report on Ralph, aka Jimmy Claus. Talk about a gift from God. Claire reached for the phone to dial the number of the police department in New Jersey that had put out the warrant for Ralph's arrest. Hopefully someone was still around who remembered him. She needed details on the incident before she went by the diner to pick him up.

"Please God," she mouthed as she waited for the call to go through. "Let this be my lucky day."

Chapter Twelve

The silver bells on the door of the shop jangled and Ty burst in. "You're not going to believe this," he declared.

Jillian glanced up from the cash register where she was running a charge for a customer. Another lady was checking out the artwork on some easels up front.

Jillian eyed Ty and held up one finger for him to wait. She finished the credit card transaction, then handed the elderly woman her bag. "Thanks. Enjoy your last day in town and come see us next summer."

Ty took the customer's place at the counter. "I think I found you!"

"What?" Jillian glanced at the tourist who was now looking her way with interest. "Shhh," she whispered to Ty. "I'm not sure I want to share."

He rolled his eyes, obviously thinking she had no reason to care who heard, but he lowered his voice. "I think I might have found you." He slapped his hand on the glass jewelry case.

"Aren't you supposed to be on the stand?" She checked her watch. "Didn't your lunch break get over more than an hour ago?"

"I took the afternoon off. Not feeling well." He faked a cough. "Now, are you going to listen or not?"

She met Ty's gaze. He was as excited as a boy on Christmas morning. He didn't seem to realize the impact of what he was saying. It was as if "finding her" was just a game. And he always loved to win at games.

"I'm listening," she said quietly.

"Laura Simpson. Dr. Laura Simpson." He grinned.

She stared at him for a moment. The name meant nothing to her. Absolutely nothing. "Ty, I wasn't a doctor."

"Orthopedics." He pulled his sunglasses off and set them on the glass countertop. "A bone doctor. Atlanta, Georgia."

She crossed her arms over her chest protectively. The lady was headed out the door. "Have a great day," Jillian called after her. She looked to Ty again, her voice a little shaky. "I said maybe I was a physical therapist, not a doctor."

"An orthopedic doctor with some sports medicine group in Atlanta," he went on, ignoring her. "She went away on vacation for a week, the middle of May, and never returned. One of her partners called it in."

Jillian knew it wasn't her. She didn't look like a Laura. Didn't feel like one. And she certainly was no bone doctor. But against her will, her interest was piqued. "Is she married?"

"Divorced or in the process of divorcing, for some reason it wasn't clear. Blond hair, blue eyes. Five-foot-seven, one hundred and thirty-five pounds."

She flinched. "If it is me, you didn't need to know that."

He chuckled, and then grew serious. They were both leaning on the glass counter, face to face, foreheads nearly touching. "I really think this could be you, Jilly."

She pressed her lips together. This was it, her chance to just walk away, if she was going to do it. She glanced over his shoulder at the striped awning over the shop and the place where Jenkins sat on his bucket to paint. He wasn't there now; he'd gone home to watch his soaps more than an hour ago. But in her mind's eye she could see him sitting there, hear him say that everyone needed to make amends with their past to find their future.

She shifted her gaze to Ty. "Was there a contact number?"

"Yup. Atlanta police. I hope you don't mind. I already called. Talked to a Detective Whitby or Whitley."

Jillian wanted to chastise him for contacting the police without coming to her first, but she had asked him to help her and she would have told him to go ahead, anyway. "What did he say?"

"You know, the usual cop run-around. I think he was a little busy."

"He doesn't think I could be Dr. Laura Simpson," she said, surprised by how disappointed she was.

"He said something about the disappearance of the doctor was suspect. I got the idea they thought maybe she was dead. But hey, how do they know?" He stood up. "Anyway, I asked him to fax a photo to my dad's office. He wasn't sure he could. He said he might have to fax it to the police station here in town, but I told him that was cool." He shrugged. "I figured you wouldn't mind. I told him to send it to Ryan McCormick's attention. You know, because I know him."

She grimaced. "You told him to fax it to McCormick?"

"Yeah, sure, why?"

Recalling the incident in the diner the other day, she shook her head with a sigh. "Nothing. Doesn't matter. Either it's me or it's not, and it's probably not." She began to tidy up around the cash register, so disappointed she could cry, and she wasn't even sure why.

"Well, I'm going to go." He hooked his thumb in the direction of the door. "Jason got the new Play Station II game last night. Hot off the presses."

"You're not going back to work?"

"Can't." He started for the door. "Sick. Remember?" Again, the fake cough into his hand.

She couldn't help laughing. "You're going to lose your job," she called after him, picking up his sunglasses and waving them at him.

"So." He flashed that grin and stepped back to take his glasses. "Quitting in a week, anyway. Might stop by tonight." He lifted his hand in the customary peace sign and then he was gone.

Jillian grasped the round pedestal mirror customers used to try on necklaces and studied her face for a moment. "Laura Simpson," she murmured. "Dr. Laura Simpson."

The name didn't seem to fit the face that looked back at her. It didn't taste familiar on the end of her tongue. As far as she knew, she had never heard the name before Ty walked into the store.

The bells over the door rang and she pushed the mirror away, dismissing Dr. Laura Simpson from Atlanta. Of course she wasn't a doctor, and she certainly wasn't from Georgia. She didn't have a Southern accent. "Hi," she said, putting a smile on her face. "Let me know if there's anything I can help you with."

"I'm telling you, I didn't kill those girls," Ralph repeated miserably, twisting his red, dish soap-chafed hands.

Claire had arrested him more than six hours ago, and she'd been interrogating him on and off for the last four. So far, he hadn't budged, and Claire was getting a feeling she didn't like at all. He just sounded so hurt that she would accuse him of such a thing as killing Anne, or Patti, or any of the women who'd been murdered. And the officers she had sent to inspect his place the minute she'd wrangled a search warrant out of Judge Collier had turned up nothing even remotely damaging except for a laundry basket of women's clothing.

"Ralph, come on. You lied to me about being Jimmy Claus. What would make me think you're not lying to me now?"

McCormick paced behind Ralph's chair. Claire knew he was making Ralph nervous because he was making her nervous. He kept punching his hand with his fist, saying she needed to let him take over the interrogation, that he could get a confession out of the dishwasher. It was a side of McCormick she had never seen before; a side she wasn't sure she liked.

Ralph was leaning forward, elbows on his knees, face cradled in his hands. He glanced up at Claire across the table from him, his eyes watery. "All that other stuff, it was a long time ago, Chief. You got to believe me."

"So you're saying you did try to kill Kissy McGee in Trenton, New Jersey, in February of '93?"

"I'm not sayin' nothing like that until I get to talk to a lawyer, but you got to believe me when I tell you, I didn't kill those women." He wiped his runny nose with the back of his hand. "Chief, you know me. I flirt a little, but I'm harmless. Just Ralph, Loretta's harmless right-hand man."

"Maybe we ought to ask Kissy McGee how harmless you are, huh?" McCormick struck the back of Ralph's chair and the poor man jumped up, slamming his knee on the table as he tried to get away from the officer.

"McCormick," Claire snapped with irritation. "Take a break." She nodded in the direction of the door.

"I don't know if I should leave you alone with him," McCormick said.

Claire flashed him a warning glare. "I'll be fine," she said dryly. "He gives me any trouble, I've got my side arm." She patted her pistol on her hip.

Ralph stared at the pistol, gulped, and sat down again.

Claire waited until she heard the door close and lock behind her before she returned her attention to Ralph. She sat back in her chair and sipped some of the bad, lukewarm coffee from a Styrofoam cup from the break room. Ashley would kill her if she knew her mother was drinking from Styrofoam. "You want something to eat, Ralph? Maybe something to drink? We've got some of those chocolate-covered donuts in the other room. I know you like those."

"What I'd like is to talk to my lawyer."

"I know, I know. But everyone's on vacation. End of July. You know how that is. And we're going to have to extradite you to New Jersey anyway. They've got good lawyers in New Jersey."

He looked at her, then away. He was jiggling one knee. "I have to go there?"

"I'm afraid so." She hesitated. Set the coffee cup down. Drinking the grounds would have tasted better. "Unless there's something else you want to talk to me about." She lifted her shoulder and let it fall casually.

She always liked to play her interviews as the accuser's buddy. It worked for her. Kurt had always said it was the shaggy blond hair and to-die-for blue eyes. She liked to think it was her technique. "Maybe you'd like to talk about something you might have done in this town that you're sorry for now. Something I might need to keep you for questioning about."

He sniffed. Wiped his nose again. "I didn't kill those women, Chief. I might . . . might have done something to Kissy. It was so long ago, and she was such a little c—" He bit back a vicious word and exhaled before he met her gaze. "I didn't kill 'em, Claire. I just didn't."

She almost felt sorry for him. He seemed so lost, so scared in the small, overly warm interrogation room that was sorely in need of a coat of paint. Of course, this was what interrogation rooms were supposed to be. They were supposed to be confining and stuffy. They were supposed to be used as a technique to squeeze confessions out of criminals.

Ralph was a criminal, all right. She just wasn't sure he was the one she was looking for.

Claire rose, pressing her fingertips to the tabletop. "I'm going to send someone in to transfer you to a holding cell."

"Not McCormick," he said shakily.

She shook her head. "Savage is here. How about if I send him in? You like him, don't you?"

Ralph half smiled, seeming very juvenile all of a sudden. It was funny the kind of behavior you got out of people when you cornered them.

"I like Savage," he said. "He's nice."

"I don't know if you'll be here the night or if we'll send you up to Georgetown."

"I'd rather stay here with you," he said, his thin hair falling over his eye. He needed a haircut badly. She hoped someone would take care of that before he went before the judge in Jersey.

"I'll see what I can do. Now, you think of anything you need to tell me, you get one of my officers to come get me. Middle of the night." She shook her head, waving her hand. "I don't care, Ralph. Because I want to help you with this. I just need you to help me."

He leaned forward on the table, meeting her gaze yet again. Murderers didn't look their accusers in the eye this way, did they?

"I want to. God knows I do, I just don't know anything about who killed those girls. I just don't."

Claire knocked on the door and it opened from the outside. "Savage will be right in," she told Ralph.

"Move him to a cell," she told Savage. She walked past McCormick, heading for her office.

He followed her down the hall. "You want me to take a stab at it, Chief?"

Considering the weapon Ralph/Jimmy allegedly used in Jersey, his choice of words didn't amuse her. "No, McCormick. Go shuffle some papers or something."

"Chief, there's a lot of different ways to interrogate a prisoner. Maybe a different approach—"

She whipped around. "Officer McCormick, I'm well aware of the processes of interviewing of a prisoner and I don't need you, *Patrolman First Class*"—she pointed at his insignia—"to tell me, a *Chief of Police*, how I should be interviewing anyone. I don't approve of the style I'm guessing you prefer, and I'm warning you." She brought her finger up beneath his chin. "There's so much as scrape or a bump on Ralph when he leaves this station, I'll have your ass and your badge." She narrowed her eyes dangerously. "Do we understand each other?"

A look flashed across his face that made Claire think he was calling her bluff. It was just there for an instant, then gone so fast she wondered if she had imagined it. He took a step back, lowering his gaze subserviently. "Yes, Chief Drummond. We understand each other."

She walked into her office and closed the door behind her. "Ass," she muttered. In her chair, she pulled open a drawer and reached for a bottle of Excedrin Migraine. The phone rang. It was Jewel.

"Yup?" Claire took two capsules with a swallow of water from a half empty bottle on her desk.

"Captain Kirk of the Enterprise is on line two."

"Very funny," she muttered. "You're not even old enough to have watched that show."

"Reruns on the Sci Fi Channel," the dispatcher came back.

Claire punched two phone buttons, the first to cut Jewel off, the second to pick up Kurt on line two. She knew there was no sense in trying to avoid him forever. She'd made a fool of herself the other night, and there was no way of getting around it.

"Drummond," she said, pretending she didn't know who the call was from.

"It's Kurt." His voice was all warm and fuzzy. "I just wanted to call and congratulate you."

"For what? Powerball hasn't been drawn this week yet. I still have to get my ticket."

"Word is you've picked up a suspect who looks good for your killer."

She groaned. "How the heck—" She stopped, took a breath, another swallow of water, and started again. "I'm holding a guy wanted in Jersey for attempted murder which, on the surface, looks close to how our girls died."

"That's what I—"

"Eleven years ago, Kurt. And it's not him."

He was quiet for a moment. "You don't know that. How long have you talked to him? These kinds of interviews can take days."

"I know very well how these interviews can go. I don't want anyone else telling me I don't know what I'm doing," she said irritably.

"Look, I don't care what you think," he snapped back. "I'm not the enemy here. I took up for you. I've put a drag on this whole task force thing from the beginning to save your lovely ass, so don't get premenstrual with me."

Claire gripped the phone until her knuckles went white. When men said things like that, it made her want to rip their guts out.

Maybe she was premenstrual . . .

"And in light of this arrest," Kurt continued, "I intend to suggest the Attorney General hold off a little longer. We'll save the state a hell of a lot of money and time if we've got our man."

How the killer had become Kurt's man, she didn't know. She was the one who couldn't sleep at night out of guilt for the women who had died. She was the one who had cried silently behind her sunglasses at each and every funeral. She was the one who checked and rechecked the locks on her doors every night, fearing a madman might come for her daughter.

"Look," she said coolly. "I'm following every rule of procedure by the book. If Ralph is the killer, we'll find out sooner or later." She hesitated, wondering if it was wise to go on, but she couldn't stop herself. "But we've got no evidence. No one should have leaked we were questioning him for anything but the New Jersey gig."

"You know how these things get out, Claire. And as hard as you may find to believe it, there's a lot of people rooting for you all over the state. We want to see you get this guy."

Claire leaned forward on her desk, pressing her forehead to her hand as she cradled the phone in the other hand. "Kurt, you're the one who always told me to go on gut feeling, and my gut feeling is—"

"Sometimes it's wrong."

"For once, I hope you're right," she said, and then she hung up.

"So I guess you heard the news, even on your day off," Millie said. She sat on one of the chairs she and Jillian had dragged out onto the porch and rocked back to prop her feet on the rail. They'd had dinner together and were now just relaxing before Millie headed home for the night.

"People were actually talking about it on the beach today." Jillian followed Millie's lead, leaning back and propping her bare feet on the worn white rail. "Not just locals. Tourists. A lady from western Maryland on the towel next to me was telling this other lady about how she'd met Ralph at the diner the other night and how he was the *nicest man*," she mimicked. "She just knew he couldn't have killed anyone."

Millie gave a snort. "Like she would know. Of course, there are some women who like that kind of man. You read about it all the time. Women writing to, visiting, even marrying men on death row who they never laid eyes on before the men went to jail. It gives these women some kind of kick, I guess." She waved her hand in dismissal. "World's full of all kinds, I suppose."

"The Wilmington paper said Ralph would be extradited to New Jersey, where he's wanted for trying to kill that woman." Jillian tucked her hair behind her ears so that it wouldn't blow in her eyes. There was a nice breeze coming off the bay tonight, whipping around the porch. She was hoping it would cool the house down nicely before she had to batten down the hatches after Millie went home.

"I guess they have to take one matter at a time," Millie mused.

Jillian glanced at the older woman. "Like they have dibs or something?"

Millie chuckled. "Something like that, I suppose."

Jillian stared out over the waving beach grass. She could no longer see the ocean over the dune when she sat down; in the time she had been here, almost a month, the grass had grown too high. But she didn't mind; she knew the Atlantic was there, right on her doorstep. She could hear it. Feel it. And all she had to do was stand up and its vastness was hers again.

"The paper wasn't really clear on what kind of evidence they had on Ralph," Jillian continued. "I mean, it sounds like they're pretty sure he tried to kill that other woman by slitting her throat, but I don't think there's been any real evidence that points to him in these killings."

"Circumstantial, Bill Knowles says."

Millie reached for her glass of mint iced tea. She'd made it fresh for Jillian to try, and while Jillian liked it, it still wasn't her sweet tea.

"Like what?"

"All four women had been in the diner in the last week before they were killed. He spoke to all of them."

Jillian lifted a brow. "So did half the people in the town. I met Anne the first day I was in town."

"I'm just telling you what Bill Knowles said, sweetie." Millie patted Jillian's hand. "Apparently, when they searched his trailer, they found some women's clothing. *Young* women's clothing. Patti's T-shirt, specifically. I heard Loretta told the police that Patti had left it accidentally at work one night, in the back where they keep their stuff. The next day when she came back for it, it was gone. Apparently she made a big fuss about it. Was her favorite shirt or something."

"That's weird," Jillian agreed, "but that doesn't make him a killer either. It just makes him a thief."

"And you know how he flirted with women. Everyone said he was half in love with Patti. Always offering to marry her and save her from all the young jerks she dated."

"Again, that does not a killer make."

Millie turned to Jillian. "What are you, the Ralph the dishwasher fan club?"

"No. I'll tell you right up front, he creeped me out. He was always looking at my boobs when I went into the diner." She slapped a mosquito on her calf. "But that's just a man."

Millie rattled the ice cubes in her glass. "Well, I don't know what all else they've found, but if Claire Drummond thinks he did it, he did it. She's one smart cookie, that girl. And they haven't actually charged Ralph with anything. "Excuse me, *Jimmy*," she corrected herself. "But everyone says he did it. The whole town's pretty relieved."

Jillian stared out into the darkness, mulling over Millie's words. If the killer had been arrested, she could leave her windows open tonight, couldn't she? With Ralph safely tucked away in the Albany Beach jail in the basement of the police station or en route to New Jersey, she should feel safe here in her little cottage.

So why did Jillian still feel like someone was watching her?

She reached for her glass of mint iced tea on the porch floor and lifted it to her lips. She didn't care what Millie said about Ralph being the killer. Tonight she would sleep with the windows closed and locked. Otherwise she wouldn't sleep at all.

Chapter Thirteen

After Millie went home around eleven, Jillian put away the dinner dishes they had washed and dried. She refilled all the plastic ice cube trays in the freezer, thinking how she yearned for her automatic icemaker in the new stainless steel refrigerator she had somewhere.

She smiled to herself as she stacked the ice cube trays. Her memory was coming back to her like that now, in little dribs and drabs. Sometimes it was a just a flash of recollection—like an old photo appearing on a movie screen in her head. Other times, she would remember a texture, a smell, an emotion. This morning she remembered where she left her favorite running shoes. By the back door. That bit of her past not only surprised her but amused her because not only hadn't she known she was a runner, she wasn't sure she had any desire to be one again.

Though the memories had still not become significant, Jillian realized these little details that continued to pop up in her head were slowly filling in the huge gaps in her life. The stainless steel refrigerator and the sound of the ice cubes dropping into her glass on command and the recollection of the sneakers by the door were just two more insignificant details that were making her feel whole again.

After closing and locking all the windows and doors in the front of the cottage, Jillian retreated to the bedroom to read for a little while before she went to sleep. Mrs. Jargon at the Albany Beach Public Library had turned her on to a techno-thriller author, and she was devouring the third book in a series. She'd left the hero about to be caught by an international spy ring, and she was anxious to see how he would escape this time.

Changing into her sleep shirt, Jillian went to the bedroom window to double-check the lock, and when she pulled the curtains back, dust filled the air. It tickled her nose and she sneezed. The thin, pale blue cotton curtains were filthy and needed to be washed, but there was no washing machine or dryer in the cottage. She'd have to take them to the laundromat next time she washed her clothes.

Jillian rubbed her nose and stared in indecision at the dusty curtains for a moment, then walked through the dark house to the kitchen, grabbed a sturdy wooden chair, and brought it back to the bedroom. She knew it was a little late at night for housekeeping, but she just couldn't stand the thought of those dirty curtains hanging there any longer. She climbed up on the chair to try to dislodge the massive wooden curtain rod, similar to the ones in the living room, so she could slide the curtains off.

With a tug, she jerked the rod upward. It came loose suddenly and she almost lost her balance on the chair. "Whoa!" She caught the back of the chair with one hand while holding on to the dangling rod with the other. "Now, won't I feel stupid if I break my leg and have to crawl for help," she muttered.

Jillian climbed carefully off the chair, holding the rod up in the air as high as she could so as not to tear the other bracket free from the wall. With her other hand, she dragged the chair to the far side of the window and climbed up again.

She pushed the rod up to slide it out of its bracket, but it seemed to be stuck by layers of dust, or maybe old paint. With a grunt, she shoved it upward.

A tap on the window startled her, and she turned her head to see if she had inadvertently struck the glass with the other end of the cumbersome rod. All she needed was a busted window; then she'd have to talk to Seth.

Realizing that she hadn't hit the glass, she looked at the window, divided into eight large panes, top and bottom. She saw a hazy reflection of herself in the white T-shirt that fell to her mid-thigh.

But behind the reflection, she caught a glimpse of something solid. Dark. At the same instant, there was another tap on the window and she realized someone was out there.

Giving a little cry of fear, she leaped off the chair, pulling the curtain rod down with her and ripping the wooden bracket off the wall.

"Jilly! It's Ty. Let me in."

The voice cut through her panic as the tap came again. "Ty?" She dropped the wooden rod, stepped over the crumpled mess of dirty curtains, twisted the lock on the window, and slid it open. "What the hell are you doing out there? You scared me half to death."

"Did you realize the screen fell out of this window again?" he asked, holding it up before lowering it into the darkness.

"No, I did not realize the screen had fallen out again," she said irritably. "Why didn't you knock on the front door, use your key, something?"

He raised his leg, throwing it over the window sill that was only waist high. His sandal dangled on the end of his foot for a moment and then tumbled inside. "I was walking up the side of the house and saw that the only light on was here in the bedroom." He pulled himself through the window and landed on the blue curtains on the floor.

"Get off the curtains." She jerked her thumb in the direction of the bed.

"Sorry." He stepped gingerly over the rod.

Jillian picked up his flip-flop, tossed it over her shoulder in his general direction, and picked up the curtain rod to slip the dirty curtains off.

"You want me to go?" he asked.

"No, of course not. I was kind of hoping you would come." She got the first panel off and tossed it aside. "You just scared me. That's all."

He dropped onto the edge of the queen-sized bed. "Why's everything locked up? Everyone says the police have the serial killer. I still can't believe it's old Ralph, but you never know, do you?"

"I guess not." She tossed the second panel into the pile and peered up at the wall where she'd torn the bracket loose. What a mess.

"I can bring some spackle over, fix that right up," Ty said. "It won't be any problem to screw that thing back into the wall."

Jillian leaned the painted white rod against the wall and turned to him, unable to resist a smile. He was just so darned cute. His hair was even blonder than it had been when she met him, and his skin had tanned to a such a dark hue that he could have claimed some European or Islander ethnicity rather than his Caucasian Irish heritage.

"How about me?" she asked, walking toward him. "Any problem screwing me?"

He laughed and put out his arms out to her. She walked into them and brought his head to her breasts, stroking his silky hair. Jillian knew that in a week Ty would be gone from her life, probably forever. She was going to miss him. She'd known from the beginning that this relationship they had, whatever it was, wouldn't last long. But Ty had been a good friend to her when she had desperately needed one, and she would never forget him.

He lifted his head to look up at her, and she covered his mouth with hers. He slid his hand up the back of her thigh, higher, until he cupped one bare cheek of her rear. She pushed on his shoulders and they tumbled back onto the bed laughing.

She landed straddling him, pinning him to the bed with his legs dangling over the side. "Now you're at my mercy," she teased.

He flung his arms over his head in surrender. "I guess you'll just have to have your way with me."

"Guess I will." She leaned over him, covering his mouth with hers.

Ty threaded his fingers through her hair, caressing her breast through her T-shirt and, for the moment, the broken curtain bracket, the unidentified man in the shower, and Jillian's past were forgotten. For a short while, she took on Ty's attitude of living in the moment.

Ty caught the hem of her T-shirt and pulled it over her head, tossing it on the floor. She stretched her body out over his, molding her hips to his, pressing her breasts against his chest. She threaded her fingers through his and pushed his hands over his head again.

"I'm your prisoner," he whispered against her lips. "Do what you will with me, just promise you'll be gentle."

Laughing, she released his hands and grabbed the hem of his surf shirt. She pushed the thin yellow fabric upward and leaned down to catch his nipple between her teeth.

"Unfair," Ty groaned.

"It's not." She tongued his nipple, shifting her gaze to look at him. "But maybe this is." Still keep eye contact, she slid down his body, dragging her tongue over his skin.

"Cruel and unusual punishment for sure," he moaned, rolling his head back, closing his eyes.

At the waistband of his board shorts, she licked the line of suntanned flesh just above the flowered fabric, slowly lowering them. She slid them lower and lower until he sprang free and she drew her tongue upward, closing her mouth over him.

"Okay!" he cried, kicking off his shorts and grasping her arms to lift her head and draw her toward him. "That's enough of that."

"But what if I'm not done?" she teased.

"Oh, you're closer to being done than you realize." Laughing with her, he rolled her onto her back and buried his face between her breasts. Stroking one nipple with his tongue, he caught the waistband of her pink bikini panties with his finger and slid them down, running the palm of his hand between her thighs.

"Now that's definitely cheating," she whispered, fingering his wind-tousled hair.

"It's not." He stretched out over her. "But maybe this is," he whispered, nuzzling her neck.

She parted her thighs, already wet and aching for him, and he took her with one stroke. She moaned in relief, drawing her knees up to cradle his body. The rhythm of his thrusts, the oneness of their lovemaking, lifted Jillian even further from the realities of her life. For a short time she drifted in the pleasure of the moment, living in only that pleasure.

They came almost simultaneously, wrapped in each other's arms, bathing in mutual admiration, need, fondness, if not true love. And afterward, Ty held her, seeming to know, without the words being expressed, how thankful she was to have him in her life right now.

Someone's going to see you walking around buck naked," she said, pointing to the still open window. "No curtains."

He lifted one shoulder in a shrug. "Mr. and Mrs.

Collins have been asleep for hours." He flipped the wall switch off anyway, leaving Jillian in the quiet darkness.

She scooted up in the bed to rest her head on the pillow, not bothering to put her night shirt back on. Knowing Ty, they'd make love again. A definite advantage to a barely-of-legal-age lover, she thought, chuckling to herself. She listened to him go into the bathroom, pee, then go down the hall to the kitchen. A feeble light fell across the hallway for a moment. She heard the click of glass bottles and then the light went out.

Ty entered the bedroom with two bottles of beer and a bottle of spring water. He tossed her the water, set the bottles on his side of the bed, and plopped in beside her. "Almost out of beer."

She twisted the top off the plastic bottle and took a drink. "You should watch your drinking. You're going through a lot of beer a week here. I can't imagine how many you're actually drinking."

He twisted off the beer bottle top and it made a satisfying hiss. He tipped it back, downing half the contents in one swallow. "I'm a growing boy. It's what growing boys use for fuel," he explained.

She chuckled and took another sip of water. "I know, breakfast of champions, and so on."

Ty rolled onto his side and drew the cold bottle across her bare belly.

She laughed, flinched, and pushed him away.

"You know," he said, sipping. "I haven't heard from that cop in Atlanta. Dad hasn't received the fax he promised, and it didn't come into the police station. I checked."

"It's not me, Ty. The guy's busy chasing bank robbers and giving out parking tickets. Police don't have time to correspond with everyone who contacts them looking for their long-lost friends or relatives."

"He said he'd fax me the photo and information." Ty tipped back the brown bottle, finishing off the first beer.

"You say you're going to do something. You do it." He set the empty bottle down on the nightstand and reached for his second beer. "I'm calling him again tomorrow, and I'm going to keep calling until I get that fax."

"I wish you wouldn't."

He twisted the top off his beer, looking at her in the darkness. "Why? Changed your mind and don't want to know? Because if that's the case, hey"—he gestured with the bottle—"you know that's cool with me."

Still holding the water bottle, she rested her forearm on her forehead. "No, it's not that, it's just . . ." She sighed, not knowing just what it was. "Okay" she said. "Go ahead. You keep bugging Detective Whitby—"

"Whitley," he corrected.

She glanced at him. "You said you didn't know."

"Whoever."

"You keep bugging him, he'll fax the photo just to get rid of you." She leaned over to set her bottle on the nightstand and then rolled onto her side to face him. She took his beer bottle from him, still half full, and pressed her mouth to his. "I know you should probably go," she whispered against his mouth, tugging on his lower lip playfully with her teeth. "But you think you could stay a few more minutes?"

He slid his hand up her thigh, and over her hip to grab her around the waist and pull her closer. "I think that be arranged, Doctor."

She laughed and gave him a push. "Don't call me that."

"I don't know," he teased, rolling her onto her back and climbing astride her, spraying beer as he went. "It might be kind of fun. You could be my doctor and I could be your patient."

Jillian laughed, stretching to set the bottle on her nightstand. "I was thinking I could be the doctor and *you* could be the nurse."

"We could do that, too," he teased, leaning over to catch one of her nipples between his lips.

Jillian let her head fall back on the pillow as ripples of pleasure began to wash over her again. The sensation of Ty's mouth on her breast mingled with the feel of the cool breeze coming in through the open window to caress her hot, sweaty skin, and she let go of all thought to drift on Ty's "no worries, mon, it will all work out" attitude.

"So, you want to come back to my place? See our condo?" the guy named Chase asked.

The bar was so crowded that there was no place to sit. Kristen was standing near the end of the bar, waiting for her girlfriends to come off the dance floor. As soon as Amy and Sarah turned up, Kristen was out of there. They had been the ones who met Chase and his two buddies at the surf shop today. They'd told the guys to meet them here and brought Kristen along to make an even three on three. The only thing was, Chase was a jerk.

"So, you want to?" the guy repeated, stepping closer, accidentally bumping into her breast.

Only Kristen wasn't so sure it was accidental. "I don't think so," she said, beginning to get annoyed. Not just with this bozo, but with her friends, too. So what if they met some guys they liked? They should have checked out the friend before getting her involved.

Chase said something else, but Kristen didn't catch it. "What?" The music was so loud and there were so many people. Her head was beginning to hurt. She'd only had two drinks, but she was beginning to think it had been two too many. "What did you say?" she repeated, leaning closer.

He cupped his hand and leaned to speak, but instead of repeating himself, he stuck his wet tongue right in her ear.

"Gross," she groaned, giving him a push. "I'm out of here. Tell Amy and Sarah I went home."

"Kristen," Chase called after her.

She ignored him, bobbing and weaving her way through the crowd, purse slung over her shoulder. It was hot in the bar, and there were too many people. The drinks had made her queasy. No, it was probably Chase from Pennsylvania who was making her sick to her stomach.

The Bloodsucker watched Kristen give the guy a shove and then walk off. The boy had been making the Bloodsucker angry all evening. The way he was bragging drunkenly, trying to impress Kristen. And the way he kept trying to touch her inappropriately. It made the Bloodsucker want to hurt him. He wasn't tempted by the jerk's blood, but the idea of making him dead, smashing his head against something hard until gray brain matter oozed out did interest him.

Kristen crossed the crowded dance floor, not seeming to realize that the guy was only a couple of feet behind her. The Bloodsucker followed, concerned that she might go out into the dark parking lot, still not realizing he was there. Didn't these young women understand the dangers in public parking lots?

"Kristen, wait," the guy shouted.

"Take a hike, Chase," she shouted back, walking past the hostess and out the door.

The Bloodsucker had to walk around people, duck. He craned his neck, watching Kristen, trying to hurry, but not wanting to draw any attention to himself. Of course there were so many people, no one would notice him. No one ever noticed him.

By the time the Bloodsucker got out the door, Kristen was halfway across the parking lot. She had parked out on the corner of the lot, but at least under a security light. He'd parked right next to her.

"Didn't you hear me?" Kristen said, turning around

to face the college boy. "I said, I'm not interested. What part of that did you not understand?"

"You're not going to do this to me," the boy sneered. "Act all slutty in there, act like you're interested and then tell me to take off." He reached out to grab her arm, and Kristen jerked back.

"Is there a problem here?" the Bloodsucker asked, cutting between two cars, headed straight for them. There was no one else in the parking lot.

"No one was talking you," the boy said, a nasty tone in his voice.

This close, the Bloodsucker could tell he was pretty drunk. So drunk that he'd probably not remember any of this in the morning. The Bloodsucker's heart began to beat a little faster. Kristen looked so pretty tonight. So sweet.

"Would you like me to walk you to your car?" the Bloodsucker asked her.

"Who do you think you are—"

The Bloodsucker turned to the drunk, looking right into his eyes. "Go back inside or I'm calling the police." He said it softly under his breath, but his tone must have scared the kid.

"Fine," he grunted, swinging his fist and walking away. "Bitch," he muttered under his breath.

The Bloodsucker turned angrily toward him, ready to defend Kristen's honor, but she grabbed his hand. She touched him. . . .

She touched him and then he knew that tonight she would be his.

"He's not worth it," she said, letting go of his hand. "But it would be nice if you'd walk me to my car. It's just over there." She pointed.

The Bloodsucker smiled.

*   *   *

Kristen woke groggy and confused. It was like she was dreaming and fighting to wake up, only she couldn't quite come to.

She smelled the fumes of exhaust. Felt something bump beneath her. When she opened her eyes, she saw nothing but darkness. There was something all around her, a box. A coffin? She tried to scream out in terror, beginning to realize this wasn't a dream, but she couldn't scream because there was something covering her mouth. Tape. She could smell the adhesive, feel the stickiness on her mouth.

Then she realized where she was and she tried to scream again. She was in the trunk of a car. She could hear the radio now, feel the bumps in the road.

Oh, God. Oh, God! her mind screamed.

How had this happened?

She was dizzy and sick to her stomach, and for a moment she was afraid she was going to throw up. If she threw up, she might aspirate on her own vomit.

She willed herself to calm down, swallowing her sour bile again and again.

Her head was pounding. Not as fast as her heart, though.

She tried to think back to the last thing she remembered happening. Memories came back in a flood, a little out of sync. She remembered cleaning up after work. Showering. Telling Aunt Alice she didn't want any dinner. She'd run into Ty in the hall. He was going out with friends. He had told her that maybe he'd head to Jilly's for a while. She'd teased him about being an old lady's old man and he had laughed.

She had been going to Calloway's out on the ocean. Into the bar. She used the fake ID she'd bought at school. Billy Trotter had been behind the bar; he knew very well she wasn't twenty-one, but he'd been cool about it. Even given her a free drink when the bartender wasn't looking.

Kristen remembered that she had gone to the bar to meet Amy and Sarah and a couple of cute guys from Pennsylvania that they had met at work today. The one guy who was supposed to be her date turned out to be a jerk. She'd only had a couple of drinks so she walked out, thinking she'd just go home. She remembered being in the parking lot. One of the guys. Chase was it? He followed her out. He was pretty wasted. Hollering at her. Accusing her of being a tease.

Someone had told him to take a hike. Someone she knew. Then he'd been nice enough to walk her to her car.

Kristen began to shake all over as she fought tears and nausea. How had she gotten in the trunk of this car? Had Chase put her in his trunk? Where was he taking her?

No, no she didn't need to think about that. What she needed to think about was how to get out of here. She racked her fuzzy brain. Maybe she'd had more to drink than she thought. Nothing was processing smoothly. Her head was full of random thoughts.

How to get out of the trunk of a car.

She'd seen it on a talk show once. Someone, Oprah maybe, had had guests who had escaped train wrecks, plane crashes, and kidnappings. Make noise. Get someone's attention.

She tried to scream. She lifted her feet that were tied together somehow at the ankles and tried to hit the lid of the trunk above her. Her arms were taped painfully behind her, so on her back, they were under her. She managed to bang on the lid several times.

The radio got louder. It was a local rock station. The Beach.

And the car was moving. Fast. How would anyone hear her?

Then she remembered the story about the taillights. It *was* Oprah. A woman had been kidnapped by her ex-husband and she got another motorist's attention by kicking the taillight out and sticking her hand or fingers or something though the hole.

Kristen rolled onto her side and wiggled forward, trying to figure out in the dark where the taillights must be. Something crackled under her— some kind of plastic. She drew back her feet and kicked hard. She thought maybe she heard something snap. She kicked again.

The car slowed and she began to panic. She kicked hard, again and again, tears running down her face. Her makeup stung her eyes, and something in the trunk was jabbing into her side. "Please, please," she cried silently.

The car slowed further. Turned. The surface changed. It wasn't smooth any more. It was bumpy. So bumpy that she was thrown almost onto her stomach, then onto her side again.

Kristen thought she heard a dog bark as the car rolled to a stop. She knew she couldn't really scream, but she did it anyway.

The engine cut off along with the radio.

It was definitely a dog she heard. Then a man's voice. He was talking to the dog in a nice voice. Friendly. Calling him "buddy."

Maybe he would be nice to her?

Kristen heard the trunk lock pop and she instinctively kicked hard, pushing herself as far into the trunk away from him as she could. No light came on in the trunk; it was so dark out that she couldn't see him. Just his form.

"Hmmm. Now, what do we have here? Awake, are we?"

It was the same male voice she remembered in the parking lot. Chase. No, not Chase. The other voice. The man who had come to her rescue. Been so nice to her.

A flashlight clicked on and she recoiled at the bright light that burned her eyes. In just that instant, before he fixed the beam on her, she saw his face. Recognized him.

Then she realized this wasn't a horny guy, kidnapping her to rape her. She knew who he was. Knew she wouldn't live.

From the bathroom, Jillian heard banging on the door. "Jilly!"

It was Ty and she could tell immediately that something was way wrong. In bra and panties, toothbrush in her mouth, she hurried to the front door. Ty hadn't left until two in the morning, and he had to be on the beach to lifeguard by ten. She knew he wouldn't be up at eight in the morning if he didn't have to be.

She unlocked the door and opened it. "What's wrong?" she asked, her words garbled by the toothbrush still in her mouth.

His hair was rumpled, his face still sleepy. He was wearing the same clothes he'd worn the night before, now wrinkled as if they had been slept in. "Kristen never came home last night."

Jillian walked to the kitchen sink to rinse her mouth. "At a girlfriend's maybe?"

"Mom doesn't think so. She's always good about coming in at night. Letting my parents know she's home. If she had stayed at a girlfriend's, she would have called."

Jillian splashed water on her face and then tapped the wet toothbrush on the rim of the old stainless steel sink. "Maybe she went out drinking with friends, had a little too much, and was embarrassed—"

"Mom's afraid she's been kidnapped. You know, by the killer."

Jillian turned to look at him. "I thought everyone thinks it was Ralph. That he's been arrested and hauled off so women are safe again in Albany Beach."

Ty brushed his bed-rumpled hair out of his face, his concern obvious. "What if they're wrong?"

His simple statement of fact was enough. Jillian went down the hallway. "Did you call the police?"

"Not yet." He followed her to the bedroom. "Mom and Dad are driving around looking for her car, just in case she is at a girlfriend's or something. I'm supposed to be looking, too."

"Her cell phone?"

"Turned off. Which isn't like her, either."

Jillian pulled on her shorts and reached for the sleeveless button-up shirt she'd left on the bed before taking her shower. "Ty, we need to call the police, now."

"You think so?" He began to pace in front of the window he'd climbed through the night before. "I thought so maybe, too. But I wasn't sure. She's going to be pissed if she's sleeping off a drunk on a friend's couch." He pushed his hair back again. "Or some guy's place. And we call out the cavalry."

"You got your cell phone?" She dropped to the floor to find her sandals under the bed.

"Yeah."

"Call the police, then call your parents and tell them you've contacted them."

He hesitated.

"Do it now, Ty. The women who were kidnapped were always missing twenty-four hours before they were found. If this nut did kidnap Kristen, she might still be alive." Locating her sandals at last, she got up and dropped them to the floor to slip into them.

Ty pulled his phone from his pocket and punched numbers.

"I'll be ready to go with you in just a second," she said. "If she's in town, we'll find her."

"Don't you have to get to work this morning?" he called down the hallway.

She stepped into the bathroom to run a brush through her wet hair and twist it up on her head. "Millie will understand. Call the police."

"Where are they now?" Claire cradled the phone with her shoulder as she hopped on one foot to pull on her uniform trousers.

"Here in the station," Officer Marsh said quietly.

"You know what information we need." Claire fastened her pants and ripped the dry-cleaning bag off her shirt hanging on the closest door.

"Yes, Chief."

"Keep them calm, and don't you dare let on like this is any more than a girl sleeping off too many frozen frufru drinks on somebody's couch."

"I understand, Chief."

"In the meantime"—she punched one fist into her shirt and then the other—"you call everyone in. Everyone. I want Jerry and Al on their bicycles. I want every car we have on the road."

"We offering time and a half? It's a Sunday, Chief."

"We're offering whatever it takes to get everyone on the force who's not out of state or drunk on a Sunday morning on the road looking for this girl."

"You coming in now?"

"Give me fifteen minutes, twenty tops." She hurried to the small safe in her closet where she kept her service revolver.

Claire heard a female voice in the background, then Marsh spoke into the phone again. "Jillian Deere is here with the Addisons. You know who she is—"

"I know her." She turned the dial on the combination lock, missed her mark, cursed under her breath, and tried again. "What's she saying?"

"She says to tell you this is a not a young woman who

would take off without telling anyone. She and the Addison boy found her car in Calloway's parking lot."

"That's where she was last seen?" Claire finally got the safe open and grabbed her revolver.

"They don't know. She was out with girlfriends last night. Probably underage drinking."

"Time to crack down on Calloway's again," Claire muttered, hurrying down the hall, trying to strap on the holster for her gun.

"I've got Mrs. Addison and her son making a list of the other girls Kristen might have gone out with last night," Marsh said. "And I got a call in to the manager at Calloway's. I'll see who we can talk to who might have seen her last night. Bartenders, waitresses. Maybe regulars."

"Good work, Marsh." Claire hurried down the hall, slipping her feet into her shoes as she went. She'd tie them when she got to the car. "I'll see you in a few minutes."

Hanging up the phone, Claire walked past Ashley's door, then backed up. Hesitated. The teen would be furious with her mother if she woke her this early on a Sunday morning, but Claire couldn't help herself. Another young blond woman missing? It scared her to death, and her first instinct was to be sure her daughter was all right.

Claire quietly opened the bedroom door to see Ashley sprawled in her bed asleep, her dyed black hair spilling across the blue cloud pillowcase. Claire hated the dyed hair, the black makeup, the skull T-shirts, but this morning, she was almost glad her daughter wasn't a pretty blond.

Taking one last look at Ashley, she backed out of the room, closing the door quietly behind her. She scribbled a quick note for her daughter to call her when she rose at the crack of noon, and then set the house alarm locking Ashley safely inside. As Claire hurried out into the muggy summer morning, she prayed the body of Kristen Addison wasn't waiting in some Dumpster for her today.

"Please," Kristen whispered. She barely had the strength to speak now. Her head was too heavy to hold up any longer. It hung, putting painful pressure on her neck.

"What do you need?" he asked, almost tenderly. "Some more ice chips?"

She managed to shake her head no, then let it fall back, loose like a rag doll's. Water, at this point, she reasoned, might just prolong the inevitable.

Kristen wasn't afraid anymore. The worst was over. Her hands were now numb, taped down for so long. She couldn't really feel her feet anymore, though if she opened her eyes, she could see them there on the blood-stained sawdust floor of the old barn.

She knew she was going to die. Was resigned to it. And she knew that when she did die, she would go to heaven. It was her parents she was so upset about. And Aunt Alice and Uncle Richard. Her cousin Ty.

"Kristen," her captor said softly. "Try to drink a little." He lifted a cup to her lips, but she refused.

"No. I'm not thirsty."

He brushed her hair off her face and she flinched, trying to get away from him. She couldn't, of course, and the energy it took to move was only wasted.

"Sleepy," she murmured.

"I know. But don't go to sleep. Not yet. Please?"

His last word was almost desperate and she was surprised that she felt a twinge of pity for him.

Early on, when she'd still had the strength, she'd asked him why he was doing this to her, to any woman.

Why was he kidnapping women . . . killing them this way?

He wouldn't tell her. Instead he'd wanted to talk about other things.

Now she didn't care why. It didn't really matter anymore.

Kristen saw a flutter of white wings out of the corner of her eye, and they drew her attention. What on earth was that? *Angels?*

Her mother liked angels. She collected them. Glass ones, ceramic ones. Even little wooden cut-out ones. Last Christmas Kristen had given her a little silver angel on a chain to wear around her neck. Her mother wore it all the time.

There were more wings now. All around her. Kristen could hear them fluttering.

"Kristen? Kristen? You can't go to sleep yet," her captor ordered. He grabbed her T-shirt and shook her, but she didn't move. She was too fascinated by the flickering angel wings around her.

"Kristen!" His voice barely penetrated her mind now.

"Kristen?" This time it was her grandma's voice she heard.

She had loved her grandmother so much. Had been so sad when she passed away last year. Now Grandma was here, here in the old barn with that . . . that sick bastard who she'd actually been nice to the other day. Her eyelids flickered, and she saw his face again. He was calling her name, trying to get her to answer

"Kristen, don't worry about him," her grandmother said gently, drawing Kristen's attention back to her again with a brush of her fingertips on her granddaughter's chin. "He'll get his in due time. Have no fear of that." Grandma laughed, as if she had a private secret, and then began to magically pull away the duct tape that held Kristen to the old wooden chair.

"Grandma, I didn't know you were here," Kirsten said, feeling oddly stronger now.

"I just arrived in town." She was smiling as she stooped to remove the tape from Kristen's ankles. She was still wearing one of those silly flowered housecoats she liked. And the thin pink slippers. But she seemed so much more agile than Kristen remembered her. And her mind was sharp again. As sharp as a tack.

"You hungry, sweetie?" Grandma asked.

Kristen rubbed her ankles where they were sore and stood up. The blood that had pooled in the sawdust was gone. Her captor was gone; she wondered where. Only the dog was still there. Watching her curiously.

"Sorry, old boy," Kristen told the dog, giving him a pat on the head.

He whined.

"I have to go," she told him.

He looked at her with big, sad brown eyes and whined again.

Kristen looked to her grandmother, who was already on her way across the barn floor, headed for the door. "Grandma, do I have to leave him?"

"Sorry, sweetie, you know your grandfather won't want another dog. We've got seven . . . or is it eight?" she chuckled.

Kristen hesitated, feeling bad that she had to leave the nice dog behind with that son of a bitch who had done this to her. But she understood that her grandparents couldn't take in every stray dog she felt sorry for.

"Kristen, come on," her grandmother urged. "It's almost time to eat."

Kristen looked up. "I am hungry. Did you make fried chicken?" she asked as she hurried after her, leaving the whining dog behind.

"Of course I made chicken. I know it's your favorite."

Grandma opened the barn door and bright white ligh spilled in. Kristen knew that morning had come . . maybe even afternoon, but the sunlight seemed ever more brilliant.

Grandma reached back with one hand, and Kristen took it.

"We have to hurry," Grandma insisted, "else we'll be late for supper."

As Kristen stepped out of the barn, into the light, she heard her captor behind her, calling her name. He wa crying. Sobbing. But the frying chicken smelled too good, and her grandmother's hand was too comforting in hers, for Kristen to look back.

"Kristen," the Bloodsucker said softly. Then louder "Kristen!" He reached out with one shaky hand. He touched her cheek, wishing he didn't have the latex o the glove between them. She was still warm, but her chest wasn't rising and falling anymore. "Kristen," he wailed, pressing his fingertips to the artery in her neck The one that should have been pulsing . . .

"No." He shook his head. "No, not yet. Not yet!" he screamed at her, kicking the chair.

Her body moved. Her head rolled, but he knew she was dead. Dead and gone. She had left him!

"You weren't supposed to die," he shouted at her "Not yet! Didn't you hear what I told you? Didn't you! He kicked Kristen's chair so hard that it tipped on tw legs, hitting the plastic table beside it and knocking over before settling upright again. Kristen's head rolle like a rag doll's.

The plastic table hit the makeshift wall he had bui of plastic sheeting and two-by-fours, sending the cup c ice flying. The Bloodsucker gave the table a vicious kic and it flew out into the barn.

The table skittered across the hard-packed dirt floor and Max gave a yip of fright and took off.

"Not yet. Don't leave me!" the Bloodsucker howled, falling to his knees in the damp, dark sawdust. He rested his cheek on Kristen's knee and felt her warmth as tears ran down his cheeks. "Don't leave me," he whispered, rocking side to side.

He lay there another minute, sniffling, and then took a deep breath. Another. He was still shaking, but not so badly. He had to pull himself together. He knew that.

Slowly he got to his feet, brushed the blood-soaked sawdust off his plastic-covered knees, and turned toward the picnic table. To his horror, Max was cowering beneath it.

"Oh, Max. I'm sorry," he whispered. "I didn't mean to scare you. You all right, boy?"

The dog gave a pathetic whine.

"Ah, poor doggy," the Bloodsucker said. He knelt in front of the picnic table and peered between the bench and the table. Slowly he slid his hand toward the dog. "It's okay," he crooned. "It's okay, Max. I would never hurt you. You know that."

The dog whined again, then twisted his head to let his master pet him.

"That's a good boy. Good Max." He scratched behind the dog's ear. "Would you like a treat? How about a treat for such a good boy?" He reached above him to the table and picked up a half-eaten bologna sandwich he had tried to get Kristen to share with him earlier. "Some of this?" He tore a piece off, not too big, though. He wouldn't want Max to choke.

The dog took the bread and meat from his hand.

"That's such a good boy," the Bloodsucker cooed. "Bad old Kristen. She left, didn't she? But Max will never leave. No he won't."

Chapter Fourteen

Claire glanced at the green digital clock on th
cruiser's dashboard and ran her hand over her face. I
was two-twenty in the morning, and she was gettin;
dopey. Her contacts were dry in her eyes, and she had
kink in her neck. She stretched her head left, the
right, trying to relieve some of the tension.

She'd left the house just before eight this morning
Seventeen hours was too long a day. It was time to g
home, and she knew it. She'd read the studies on polic
officers' work schedules. It didn't matter how good
cop she was. After this long at it, her reaction time wa
slowed, her judgment impaired. She needed to go home
get some sleep, and let the next shift do the job the
were trained to do.

But Kristen Addison had not been found and Clair
felt responsible. She needed to find the girl, or he
body. It was a morbid thought, but she knew from pa
experience that the worst thing for the family of victim
was the waiting. The not knowing.

Kristen Addison was just gone. Gone right off th
face of the earth as if she'd been beamed off by alien

s Marsh had guessed, the previous night, Kristen had
een at Calloway's drinking at the bar. All day long,
laire had conducted interviews right in the bar that
ie manager had so graciously offered, probably hop-
ig to keep from getting busted for serving alcohol to
n underage college student. Claire spoke to every em-
loyee or customer she could track down who could
ossibly have come in contact with Kristen.

She talked to the bartender who had served her.
fter swearing on his grandmother's grave that her fake
river's license looked authentic, he had been able to
ive the most details of Kristen's evening. He remem-
ered she was wearing white shorts and a pink T-shirt
nd that her hair had been in a ponytail. He knew where
ie worked and the names of the girls she'd come with.
alking to Kristen's friends, Amy and Sarah, Claire
earned that they had met some guys from Pennsylvania
t the bar. No last names, of course, but they were cer-
in that Kristen had left alone because the guy she had
een with, Chase, passed on the message that she had
one home, and Chase had left with another coed more
ian an hour after Kristen was seen by the hostess leav-
ig Calloway's.

Claire also talked to Billy Trotter, who still worked at
ie bar in the restaurant. He, too, recalled seeing Kristen
t the bar, confirming what the bartender said—that
ie had left alone sometime between eleven and eleven-
iirty. He also confirmed that the guy he'd seen her with,
iis Chase apparently, had left with another blonde just
efore the bar announced last call.

While both the bartender and Billy's stories collabo-
ited, Claire had made a mental note to look into Billy's
ory if Kristen turned up dead. He had, after all, known
atti, could well have known the other women, and he
ad a record. His index card sat toward the top of the
ack on her desk right now.

Claire signaled, turning onto a dark street. Some thing white blew across the road in front of her, star tling her, and she hit her brakes. A cat?

Just a paper napkin.

She hit the accelerator with her foot, feeling foolish for being so jumpy. It was time to give in, give up for the night and go home.

But what if Kristen was out there somewhere alive?

Kristen's two girlfriends had been very little help They had been drinking heavily, apparently, and invited their "dates" back to their places. Due to their consump tion of alcohol, they were able to provide fewer details of the evening than the bar's employees. Kristen was just gone.

Claire signaled again and turned into a wide alley that ran behind a strip shopping center. The alley was dark with only a couple of security lamps at the rear de livery entrances to the stores. To her surprise, she saw red and white taillights light up ahead of her.

She'd been cruising the garbage Dumpsters in town for hours and had seen very few cars since around one thirty. The bars and restaurants were all closed by one everyone was tucked in for the night by one-thirty.

Curious, she sped up a little. To her left was a tall chain link fence, to her right, the rear of the stores, each marked with plain signs. She spotted the row of Dumpsters and her heart gave a little trip.

She gazed up. The car was still ahead of her, red tail lights tiny beacons in the darkness. She hadn't caught any tag numbers; she wasn't even positive she had seen a license plate. Maybe the light was out. She considered catching up to the car, pulling the driver over just to be sure he or she hadn't been drinking and had just parked behind the strip mall to sleep it off.

But if she pursued the taillights, then she would have to go around the block to get back to the Dumpsters The alley only ran one way. Of course, she was the chief

f police. Who was going to say anything about her dri-
ing the wrong way down a one-way street at two-thirty
n the morning while looking for the body of a girl that
he didn't even know was dead?

With her luck, Mary Lou Joseph and Betty Friegle
vould be hiding behind the Dumpsters, just waiting to
atch her. Claire would be the talk of the over-sixty gos-
ip mill by morning.

The car ahead of her reached the end of the alley
nd turned left. Claire tapped her brake in indecision,
hen pressed it down, bringing her police cruiser to a
top. Leaving the engine running, headlights on, she
rabbed her issued Maglight off the seat beside her and
limbed out. She'd check these Dumpsters, then call in
nd head home. Ashley had ended up going to a girl-
riend's to spend the night so the house would be empty,
ut at this point, Claire was too tired to care.

The alley wasn't what she would call well lit, but be-
ween her headlights and a security lamp at the back door
f Pat's Pets, she could see well enough. She flicked on
he heavy flashlight in her hand and moved the beam of
ght back and forth in front of the Dumpsters. Nothing.

She heaved a sigh of relief.

Maybe she was wrong. Maybe Kristen was just hiding
ut at some guy's house. Or maybe she had taken a road
rip with people she had met at Calloway's. It sounded
razy, but sometimes college kids did crazy things. And
aybe Ralph had killed those women; maybe the Sussex
Tounty Correctional Center that was holding Ralph
ntil the extradition hearing did have Albany Beach's
erial killer under lock and key.

Claire drew the flashlight beam along the edge of the
Jumpsters again. Nothing. Just the huge green metal
ontainers and a couple of paper cups that hadn't made
heir way inside. There was nothing here. Nothing but . . .

Something pale on the dark pavement passed through
he beam of light. Claire reversed the path of the beam.

Squinted. What was that? A crumpled piece of paper? Had that napkin that had blown across the street and startled her come back to haunt her?

She held the flashlight on the object, taking a step closer. It seemed to be wedged between the two large green industrial-sized Dumpsters. The shape seemed familiar, but in the shadows that ranged from black to gray, she couldn't identify it. She was so tired that those synapses in her brain weren't firing too rapidly. She was five or six feet away when it registered in her mind what she was looking at.

A hand.

Claire halted for a moment, a death grip on her Maglight. "No," she whispered as tears filled her eyes.

Then her cop instinct kicked in. With one hand, she unsnapped the leather strap that kept her Beretta secured in its holster. With the other, she held the flashlight beam steady on the hand.

Looking one way, then the other down the alley and seeing no one, hearing nothing, Claire took a step forward and went down on one knee. She directed the flashlight beam between the two dumpsters to a body on the pavement. She couldn't see the face for the wave of long blond hair covering it, but she knew who it was. White shorts. Pink top.

Claire picked up the slender, feminine hand. It was cool to the touch. There was no need to check for a pulse where the girl's wrist had been slashed repeatedly. She checked anyway.

Kristen Addison was dead.

Claire's tears spilled over and ran down her cheeks. She took a breath, trying to stifle a sob, and rose, releasing Kristen's hand. As an afterthought, she realized she should have put on gloves before touching her.

She took a moment to regain her composure and then touched her chin to the radio fastened to the shoulder of her uniform. "Unit one-o-one," she managed.

"Unit one-o-one, go ahead," came across the slightly static voice of the night dispatcher.

"This is unit one-o-one," Claire said, enunciating carefully to keep the emotion out of her voice. "Requesting backup in the alley behind the Johnson Center on Poplar between Pine and Oak."

"Ten-four, unit one-o-one. Copy that." Static. "What's the nature of this response?"

Claire pressed her lips together. She knew the dispatch codes by heart; many were universal in the world of police lingo. But she couldn't recall the code for a dead body. A possible homicide. Like there was any *possible* to it. A lump rose in her throat and she swallowed against it, fearing for a moment she might throw up.

"Unit one-o-one, I repeat, what's the nature of your request?"

"Code thirty," she choked. Then, without regard to proper procedure, she spoke again. "I found her."

"Ten-one, one-o-one."

"I said I found her." Claire's voice cracked, but it was stronger when she spoke again. She had a job to do now. This was no place for emotions or tears. "Send all available units. That's an eleven-forty-four. Coroner requested."

"ETA of first unit to assist, four minutes," the dispatcher said.

"Ten-four." Claire released the transmitter on her radio and walked to her car to turn on the flashing blue lights so her officers could easily locate her. Then she turned off the Maglight and walked back to the Dumpsters. She didn't need the flashlight to find her way.

As she crossed the narrow alley that now seemed a mile wide, she glanced in the direction the red taillights had gone only moments ago. Somehow, deep in the pit of her stomach, she knew it was him. She'd been a hundred yards from the killer, and he'd gotten away.

Now she was pissed. She latched on to her anger and

held it tightly in her fist. He thought he was clever, didn't
he? With Ralph arrested for his crimes, he'd struck again.
Gotten away with it again. What the bastard didn't realize was that she was going to catch him. She'd catch him
if it killed her.

Taking a deep breath, Claire tugged on her freshly
dry-cleaned uniform pants and squatted down to wait
in the darkness with Kristen.

Fearing she wouldn't be able to stand it another moment, Jillian scooped up the nearly empty ice bucket
and hurried from the Addisons' family room for the relative sanctuary of the kitchen. This afternoon she had
attended Kristen's funeral with Ty and his family, and
now family and friends had gathered at the Addison
home to share memories of Kristen, eat plates of cold
ham and macaroni salad, and begin the process of mourn-
ing.

Ty had asked Jillian to attend the funeral with him
and then come back to the house. She'd tried to get out
of the wake. She knew she really wasn't welcome in the
Addison home, and she hadn't known Kristen very well.
But Ty had insisted he wanted Jillian there. He said he
needed her, and there was no way she could deny him.
He'd been there for her since the day she arrived in
Albany Beach.

But now that Jillian was here, the situation was worse
than she even imagined. There were several camps in
the house now. A group of women on the couch in the
family room surrounded Kristen's mother, crying together, taking turns hugging her.

A group of older women stood together near the
buffet table, heads down, whispering. The were making
comments about where the young woman had been
when she'd been kidnapped and how bad ends always
came to girls like that. Then there were a group of men

standing on the back deck drinking beer, talking about fishing, the weather, and how poorly the Baltimore Orioles baseball team was playing. The group that had really set Jillian's nerves on edge were the men and women in the front foyer right now hotly discussing the Albany Beach police force's failure to catch the serial killer before he struck again. Some were the same folks Jillian had overheard only days ago insisting that all along they had suspected the dishwasher, Ralph, had been the killer. They were the ones who had sent her retreating to the kitchen.

Jillian pushed through the swinging louvered doors; Ty's mother was there, preparing more food to place on the buffet table already groaning with casseroles, lunchmeat, and various desserts. "I thought I'd refill the ice bucket," she told Alice, feeling a little uncomfortable to be alone in the room with her. Jillian knew the older woman didn't approve of her relationship with her son, and truthfully, Jillian couldn't really blame her.

"Oh, thank you." Alice turned from the counter, slipping on the red hot mitts Jillian remembered from the Fourth of July picnic.

It was hard to believe that had only been a month ago. It seemed like a lifetime.

"I put another pan of macaroni and cheese and baked ziti in the oven to heat up," Alice continued, sounding a little befuddled. "People seem to like pasta."

Jillian stood at the refrigerator, letting the ice bucket hang from her hand. She felt so sorry for Alice. For the entire Addison family. She had no way to express her sadness for them. She could only imagine how horrible it must be to lose a loved one so young, so full of life. No one in the family had really slept in days. It was beginning to show on Ty. It was definitely showing in Alice's face.

"You're right, people do like pasta," Jillian remarked, knowing that what she said wasn't really important right now. All Alice needed was a little kindness. "And you have so much. Everyone has been so generous. Kristen was well loved."

"A small town is like that, you know." Alice went to the oven and rested one hand on the door, turning to Jillian. "You won't see that in a big city. That's why Connie and Ash decided to have her buried here in her father's hometown instead of in Harrisburg. Because everyone's so warm here. So welcoming. You should really consider settling down in a small town like Albany Beach."

"I just may do that. I like it here. People have been very kind."

"Well, these young kids, they say there's nothing here for them." Alice turned back to the oven, waving in dismissal with her hot mitt. "But what do they know? Ty needs to live away to find out just how nice home is. That's what I say." She opened the oven and reached in. "And I don't mean college. Everyone knows very well that's not the real world. But you can't tell these young men—ouch!" Alice jerked her hands out of the oven and one of the glass casserole dishes clattered loudly on the oven rack.

"You all right?" Jillian dropped the ice bucket on the counter and hurried over to Alice.

"Burned my hand somehow," Alice said, close to tears. She tried to pull off one hot mitt, fumbling with the other still on her hand.

"Let me do that for you." Jillian eased both quilted mitts off the older woman's hands.

"Must be getting thin," she muttered. "Need to pick up some new ones."

Jillian turned Alice's hand in her own and found two raised red welts, one on her thumb and the other on the index finger of her right hand. "Why don't you sit down and let me get you some ice for this."

"Oh, no. I'm fine," Alice protested, but she allowed Jillian to lead her to a kitchen stool.

Jillian let go of Alice's hand and hurried to the ice bucket. She scooped a couple of half-melted ice cubes from the cold water and dropped them into a hand towel she grabbed off the counter. She twisted the towel into an ice pack and went back to Alice. "Try this."

Jillian gently guided the lump of ice to Alice's burned fingers.

"The ziti." Alice lifted her hands in the direction of the oven. "It'll burn."

"I'll get it." Jillian didn't bother to try the faulty mitts. Instead, she grabbed a folded bath towel left on the counter by someone who had dropped off hot food. She opened the towel and used it to gingerly remove the macaroni and cheese and the baked ziti.

"Jillian," Alice said from behind her. "I haven't meant to be unkind to you."

"You haven't been unkind." Jillian set the towel down and dug through the clean utensils in the dish rack to find two serving spoons.

"I have. If not unkind, at the very least, rude. I know Ty really cares for you, it's only that—"

"It's only that he's twenty-three. A kid. And I'm . . . I'm a bit older." She laughed and stuck a spoon into the ziti; steam rose from the pasta and sauce with a heavenly aroma. "And you don't want him to either be taken advantage of or hurt. I understand completely."

Alice shifted the homemade ice pack in her hand. "Ty tells me he might have found some information on who you might be. He says you might be a physician."

"Ty's mistaken." Jillian turned around to lean against the counter. "But it's very sweet of him to be trying so hard to help me. I know he's leaving in a couple of days to go back to school to start his graduate program; he must have better ways to spend his last few days at home."

"I think he's worried about you, dear. That's all. He wants to be sure you'll be all right when he goes."

"I'll be fine." She said it so convincingly that she almost believed herself.

"Right in here, Miss Ruth," Jillian heard Ty say loudly from the other side of the swinging kitchen door.

The door swung in, and an elderly woman with an osteoporosis hump on her back hobbled in carrying a small casserole dish. She was wearing her Sunday best, a rose-colored dress with a smart patent white clutch purse on her elbow.

"Ty, carry that to the counter for Miss Ruth," Alice said, rising from her chair as she fell into the role of hostess again.

"Tried to." Ty swung a beer bottle between his fingers. "She almost bit my head off. I think she thought I was going to steal it or something."

"Tyler Addison," Alice snapped. "How rude of you to speak that way to Miss Ruth."

Jillian turned to look at Ty and mouthed "Tyler?"

He gave a playful shrug and glanced back at his mother. "It's not like she can hear anything I say."

"What's that?" Ruth Williams demanded loudly.

"Thank you so much, Ruth," Alice said, matching the old woman's volume. "You really didn't need to bring anything."

"Blueberry buckle," Ruth shouted, her voice scratchy with age. "My older sister Elsie's recipe. Always did make a better buckle than I did, little witch."

Jillian pressed her lips together to keep from laughing out loud.

"If Ruth's the younger sister, how old do you think Elsie must be?" Ty asked. "A hundred. Hundred and ten? She's out parking that boat of a Buick they drive."

Jillian snatched Ty's beer from his hand and took a sip to keep from laughing out loud.

"Looks delicious!" Alice said as she accepted the casserole dish.

The old woman brushed her hands together as if they were dirty, or maybe still had flour on them from making the homemade sugar crust. "I wouldn't put it out if I were you. Save it for yourself and your family. Go to waste on most of that bunch out there!" She turned suddenly to stare at Jillian. "I know you?" she asked.

Jillian was surprised by the woman's unexpected question. She'd never seen Ruth Williams in her life, as far as she knew. "I . . . I've been staying here in Albany Beach for a few weeks. I live in the Williams' cottage." It wasn't until she said it aloud that she realized the last name was the same. She glanced at Ty, who nodded.

"Ruth and Elsie's family built the place over a hundred years ago," Alice explained.

Ruth took a wobbly step closer to Jillian, her purse swinging on her elbow. "But do I know you?" she demanded, shaking a wrinkled, skinny finger.

"I . . . I don't think so." Jillian had to fight the urge to take a step back. "But maybe we've run into each other at the diner or the grocery store."

"I don't eat in the diner; knew Loretta Jean's mother, and she was nothing but trash. And Elsie does the shopping." She scrutinized Jillian from behind wire-frame glasses. "You're Lori, right?"

"Jillian, Jillian Deere." She offered her hand, unsure what else to do.

The old lady's touch was cool, her grasp surprisingly firm. "Jillian!" she shouted. "That doesn't sound right. It's Lori or something like that. Don't tell me it isn't because I'm good with names and faces. Ask Elsie."

Jillian blanched. Laura was the name of the physician missing in Atlanta. She knew it wasn't her. Ruth was old. Obviously a little confused.

"Came here as a girl, didn't you?" Ruth demanded loudly. She snapped her finger. "Used to take the whole month of August every summer. From Jersey, right?"

Ty looked at Jillian, his eyes wide with excitement. He turned to Ruth. "You know her, Miss Ruth? You recognize her?"

"I said I never forget a face. You hard of hearing, boy?" She waggled her finger, still studying Jillian as she spoke. "She was shorter then, of course. Just a kid. Hair all wild like her sister's."

Ty darted forward, grabbing Ruth's hand and talking loudly. "You said her name was Lori or Laurie. Do you remember her last name?"

Ruth stared at Ty. "Well, doesn't *she* know her name?"

"Miss Ruth, it's a long story. Just tell me, are you sure this is who you think it is? Do you possibly remember her name?"

"Long time ago," Ruth mused aloud. She scrutinized Jillian again. "Seventies, I think. Don't remember the family's name. Just the blond hair." She touched her shoulder. "They always paid in advance. Good renters. People today, they want to back out of obligations. They think they can—"

"You said her family rented your cottage every August," Ty interrupted. "Would you have kept any records?"

Ruth tilted her chin upward, thinking. "Can't say I did. That was before Waterfront started taking care of the rental. They're not as good as everyone says they are, you know."

Ty squeezed the old woman's hand. "Isn't there anything else you can remember about Lori, Miss Ruth?"

She thought again for a minute, then shook her head.

Ty let go of her hand, obviously disappointed.

"It's all right," Jillian told him softly. She reached out to rub his shoulder. He was going through enough today; he didn't need to be worrying about her.

"Where do you think Elsie got to?" Ruth demanded, shuffling toward the kitchen door. "She hits another parked car this week, I'm taking her license. Swear on Papa's grave, I am!"

Ty, Alice, and Jillian watched the old woman push through the swinging doors and disappear into the hall.

"This might be something," Ty told Jillian.

She nodded. "Maybe." Then she looked to Alice. "Is there anything else we can do, Mrs. Addison? I can wash dishes for you if you like." She pointed to the couple of dirty bowls in the sink.

"I'm fine. And please, it's Alice." She waved them both away and stepped up to the sink, reaching for the plastic bottle of dish detergent. "Let me do this. I need to keep my hands busy today."

Ty walked up behind his mother and put his arms around her in a hug. "Love you, Mom," was all he said, but his simple words made Jillian tear up. He was going to make a great husband and partner to some woman some day.

"I love you, too, Ty," Alice answered, patting his arm. "Now why don't you two get out of here. I would think you've had enough of this by now."

"I think I will go home," Jillian said. "Thank you, Alice. This was very nice today."

She turned and smiled sadly. "Thank you, Jillian. If you decide to leave town, please come by and say good-bye."

"I will. Thank you."

Ty took Jillian home on the back of his Chief. It was twilight by the time they reached her cottage. They both sat down on the front steps, and Jillian removed her sandals. Ty kicked off his flip-flops, and they buried their feet in the warm sand.

"I think you're her," he said quietly, after a while. "I mean what are the chances this could be just a coincidence, Ruth knowing your name."

"She said Lori. You said the physician in Atlanta was Laura."

"Close enough and you know it." He turned to look at her, forcing her to meet his gaze. "I'm calling that cop again tomorrow. And I'm going to keep calling until he faxes me that photo."

Jillian looped her arm through Ty's and leaned her head on his shoulder. "You're a good man, Charlie Brown."

The Bloodsucker stood in the barn motionless, leaning on the shovel. It was growing dark quickly. The shadows were lengthening, and he could feel the darkness closing in on him.

He had everything cleaned up here. He had burned his plastic clothing and the latex gloves in the pile of bloody sawdust out back. He'd also burned the sheet of plastic he'd used to line the trunk of his car; you could never be too careful with trace evidence. He had just shoveled a couple of wheelbarrows of fresh sawdust on the barn's dirt floor and returned the plastic chair to the workshop. He'd even tipped it upside down and thrown some musty feed sacks on top just for good measure. It had been years since there had been animals in this barn, since before he had come here, but the sacks were still around. He didn't know why.

The Bloodsucker stared at the place where Kristen Addison had sat with him only four days ago. He had felt so good when she was here, talking to him. She had been just what he had dreamed up. She was good at conversation; she told him about her classes in college and about wanting to be a nurse. She was a good listener, too.

What a sweet night they had spent together. As the blood had seeped from her body, he had been filled with her life's blood. Embodied by it. But the joy had been too short. It had all happened too quickly.

That was why he had lost it for a minute, there. That

was why he'd been so upset. Kristen didn't hold up her end. She didn't stay with him like she should have. It was her fault.

He rested his chin on his hand, leaning on the shovel. What he wondered now was why he was not still experiencing that euphoria he had felt when Kristen had been with him. After all, she was what he had imagined she would be. She was all of it and more. So why was the feeling gone . . . drained from him the same way Kristen's blood was drained from her? Why, in place of the euphoria he had experienced, was there an overwhelming heaviness? A desperate sadness?

He dropped down onto the bench seat of the old one-piece picnic table where he sat when he talked to the women. Sometimes had a little snack here or even read the paper to them.

The Bloodsucker felt so bad that he wanted to cry. So lonely. He leaned on the table, resting his forehead on his hands. Why hadn't his joy with Kristen lasted longer? It couldn't have been her. She was perfect.

Was it him?

Stupid. Lazy. Worthless. Leech.

Granny's words buzzed around his head like an angry bee, and he tried to swat them away.

"No, it wasn't me. It was her," he said aloud, pushing Granny out of his head. "It was all her fault!"

Max, who waited by the barn door, lifted his head at the sound of his master's voice.

"It wasn't me," he repeated. "It was her. I thought she was right. But maybe she wasn't." He rose, gesturing with both hands. "She just wasn't."

Then he thought about Jillian and the night he had seen both her and Kristen in the Addisons' yard. He had contemplated moving Jillian ahead in the line and then decided against it because changes in plans were always dangerous.

But maybe he needed to be more flexible.

The Bloodsucker felt a little flutter of excitement in his chest. Maybe that was what was wrong. It wasn't that Kristen's blood was bad. It was just the wrong blood. That night, it must have been his instinct that told him to take Jillian next. Lovely, distant Jillian, who did not know her real name.

So maybe that was all he needed to lift his spirits. He needed Jillian.

But this was too soon. Claire-Bear was about to be usurped by some task force organized by the Attorney General. She was angry, everyone said. Determined now to find the killer. Hunt him down. She'd been interviewing people, sneaky like. People he knew. People she should never have considered suspects, yet obviously did.

It was only a matter of time before she interviewed him. His heart began to pound in his chest. What would he say?

The Bloodsucker knew he needed to lay low for a while. A few weeks at least. He lifted his head to stare at the empty place where the chair had been. But he needed Jillian, he thought desperately. He needed her strength.

So it was decided. He could hold off a few days, but Jillian would be next.

Chapter Fifteen

Jillian made herself a grilled cheese sandwich for a late dinner and then went out to sit on the rail of the front porch so she could see the ocean while she dined. The moon was big and full tonight, so close and magical that it seemed as if she could reach out and touch it.

She was in a quirky mood tonight. Ty had gone out with friends. He had said he might stop by later, might not. They had left it at that, already beginning the process of going their separate ways. She didn't mind being alone, but she found she was restless. She was ready to move on, not sure where to go. Not even sure she should go at all, but Ty was leaving in two days, and her month's rental of the cottage would be up then, too. She needed to make up her mind.

She had run into sleazy Seth at the mini-mart this morning, and he told her that, so far, no one had rented the cottage for the month of August so it was open, for the same discounted price, if she was interested. He said that not only were tourists not coming to Albany Beach in the numbers they usually did, but that he'd had multiple cancellations this week after news of Kristen's murder was spread in local and national newspapers and on all the news broadcasts.

The town, dependent upon the tourist trade to survive, was heading for serious financial trouble. A town meeting was being called by the city council next week to discuss their situation. By then, the state's task force would be set up to catch the killer. He said everyone was counting on the state police being sent to accomplish what their local police had not—catching the killer.

Jillian sipped her water bottle thinking about what a raw deal Claire Drummond was getting. She'd run into her several times in the last couple of days, and it was obvious not only that the police chief was working hard to solve the case, but that she was taking these women's death personally. Jillian couldn't help thinking that if this were a male chief of police, the state wouldn't be so quick to jump in and take over. And she didn't care what Seth said about this experienced team of law enforcement officers coming into town to catch the killer; she was laying her bets on Claire.

Jillian peeled the crust off one half of her sandwich and munched on it, her thoughts straying back to her own woes. Ty had called the Atlanta cop again the day after Kristen's funeral to ask about the photo being faxed again as it had never arrived at his father's or the police station. He had been furious to discover that Detective Whitley was off for the week and would not return until the following Monday. Ty insisted he wasn't going to give up; he was going to have that photo of Dr. Laura Simpson if he had to ride his motorcycle to Atlanta to get it.

Jillian smiled to herself at the thought of his youthful indignanation. She really was going to miss him. She wished he didn't have to go so soon. But he did, and that meant it was time for her to make a decision as to what she was going to do. Where she was going to go.

One of her options was to stay at the cottage another

month and work for Millie through Labor Day, but then what? After the first week of September, the shop would only be open on weekends; her friend wouldn't have the income to continue paying an employee. And was staying another month just delaying having to make a decision as to what would come next?

She was considering going to New Jersey. A part of her knew that Miss Ruth Williams, who would ninety-seven on her next birthday, couldn't possibly be right about Jillian being this Lori or Laurie from Jersey who had stayed at the cottage as a child. But a tiny part of her wondered if it could possibly be true.

In a way, it would make sense. And make her feel a little saner. From the first day, Jillian had had the feeling she had been in this cottage before. Even though the name of the town, the name of the street, didn't jog any memories, it was the little things that made her almost certain she had been here. Things like the pattern on the old china dishes and the layout of the kitchen and dining room that gave her that hair-raising sense of déjà vu.

As for being from Atlanta, but not actually *from* there, that made sense, too. Jillian had learned that sweet tea was a favorite drink among Southerners; drinking it was practically a pastime. A transplant from New Jersey who had lived in Atlanta for years would certainly have accepted such a practice, but she would not necessarily have picked up the accent of the region. The idea that she might be a physician still seemed pretty far-fetched, but so was waking up in a hospital having no idea who you were or how you got there. And then how unbelievable was driving into a town where there was a serial killer on the loose, killing blond-haired, blue-eyed women like yourself?

Talk about fact being stranger than fiction.

The possibility that Jillian might be this Dr. Laura Simpson forced her to extrapolate even further. If she was Laura, what had she done to cause someone to shoot at her? Had she threatened someone? Tried to shoot someone? Was she wanted?

The detective had not said anything to Ty about Dr. Laura Simpson being wanted, so she doubted she had committed any crimes. But if her recollection was accurate, she was certainly an adulteress. That wasn't the kind of person Jillian would even want to be friends with. How could she accept that she could be that kind of person?

Jillian heard Ty's Chief rumble up the street and smiled to herself. A minute later, he strolled around the corner of the house, barefoot.

He climbed up onto the railing beside her. "Hey."

"Hey, yourself," she said.

His brow knitted as he stared out over the dunes. "Seen my sunglasses?"

She grinned. "Yup. On my kitchen table."

"Cool."

Then the two just sat in comfortable silence, staring out at the ocean bathed in moonlight.

The Bloodsucker walked the beach in his bare feet, enjoying the cool sand between his toes and the rush of water that was pleasantly startling each time it washed ashore. He wondered why he didn't spend more time on the beach than he did. He liked it here. It was peaceful and yet exhilarating at the same time.

Granny had hated the beach, and even though they had lived so close to it, he only remembered coming a handful of times and that had been on school trips.

He turned to look up toward the beach. Over the dunes, through the grass, he could see the tiny white dilapidated cottage and the silhouette of a woman sitting beside a man on the porch rail.

The moon was big and full tonight. Not a good night to be here. To be watching . . .

When the Bloodsucker left his house, he had not intended to come to the beach. His intention had been to go for a walk on the boardwalk. In an effort to draw some business from neighboring beach communities, the city council had sponsored a "Battle of the Bands" tonight. In a large, stage-like gazebo, different local bands were playing for the crowd. Blue grass. Country and Western. Some good old-fashioned rock.

He had thought he would go listen for a while, just to get out, see some familiar faces, maybe have a piece of pizza or an ice cream cone. He thought getting out might break him out of the funk he was experiencing. It wasn't depression; he refused to use that word.

But before he realized what he was doing, like the night he had gone into the cottage, he found himself, not on the busy boardwalk, but in Jillian's quiet neighborhood. He found himself on the beach, in shorts but long sleeves. Always long sleeves. Watching her.

He glanced at Jillian and Ty perched on the porch rail and wondered if they would take a walk. He looked up and down the beach, which was fairly empty tonight due to the entertainment on the boardwalk. If they walked out on the beach, he might approach her. Maybe say hello, ask them why they weren't on the boardwalk tonight, listening to the bands. Would Jillian smile shyly, laugh, or would he get that look of disapproval he sometimes saw on her face? Would Ty say something about this being one of his last nights in Albany Beach before returning to Penn State, and wanting to be alone with Jillian?

How would the Bloodsucker respond? Would he give a casual wave, tell them to have a nice evening, and walk away? Or would he . . .

His pulse quickened.

The Bloodsucker had no real interest in the young man, but he wondered if it might be fun to kill him. Just to see if he could.

His mind raced forward, trying to catch up to his pulse.

How on earth would he manage two of them? He would have to be very clever.

But he was.

He could wait until they both fell asleep in her bed and then sneak into the house. He could slip the plastic Ziploc bag with the chloroform-soaked cloth from his pocket and cover his mouth and nose with it, then hers. But would there be enough chloroform? Maybe he'd have to save the chloroform for Jillian and just kill the young man in the bed.

But with what? Guns were too easy to trace. And then you had to worry about gunpowder residue, stuff like that. Maybe a simple household item? Then there was the blood issue. There was always the blood issue.

But if he did kill Ty there at the cottage, he could just leave him behind. He could carry Jillian to his car, parked only a block from her house, in his arms, her beautiful blond hair falling over his arms. Or he could hope there was enough chloroform and take them both with him. That might be fun, too.

The Bloodsucker trembled with excitement.

He halted on the edge the water and turned to face the cottage, staring brazenly. Jillian's silhouette was so perfect in the moonlight. Of all the women, she was the closest to the old photo.

He slipped his hand into the breast pocket of his shirt and removed the photograph he always carried with him. Always. Even in the moonlight he could see her image. The exquisite blond hair, the slightly upturned nose, the blue eyes that could look right through you to your soul.

He pushed the photo back into his pocket. He had

to be careful with it; it was the only one he possessed. To lose it would be to lose himself.

The photo safe once more, he glanced up at the cottage. He walked up the beach toward the dunes, his hands thrust casually into his khaki shorts pockets. Still no one on the beach either north or south of him for more than a block.

He lost sight of Jillian and Ty for a moment, but closer to the dunes, he could see them again. They were talking quietly, but their voices didn't carry on the slight breeze. He wondered what they were saying.

Then she looked out over the dunes right at him, and the Bloodsucker froze. Thinking quickly, he leaned over and pretended to pick something up. A pretty shell, maybe. He scuffed his bare foot in the sand the way he saw others do, then walked on as if just out for a solitary evening stroll on the beach.

He kept walking.

"Where?" Ty asked, craning his neck. "I don't see anyone."

Jillian climbed off the porch rail, chilled despite the warm, muggy night. "There in the dunes. Didn't you see him?"

Ty leaped off the porch rail, still staring into the darkness. "Jilly, I don't see anyone. Want me to run down and have a look?"

She grabbed his arm, leaning against him. Her heart was pounding, her hands shaking, and she had no idea why. "No," she whispered. She could have sworn the man was in sand camouflage, long sleeves, and long pants, but she kept it to herself, knowing how crazy that sounded on a warm night like tonight. "Let's just go inside."

* * *

The Bloodsucker walked a good distance down the beach before turning back to look at the cottage again. He knew he should go home. She had seen him. He might not have the same element of surprise. Besides, now she was inside. With him. Doors locked. Windows closed.

Of course there were ways to get indoors. Easy enough when you had a copy of the key. He chuckled at his cleverness. His forethought.

It would be foolishly dangerous to go inside for Jillian. Especially with Ty there. It would be so easy to make a mistake, leave some sort of evidence behind. But he had outsmarted the cops so far, hadn't he? Even the cleverest of all, Claire-Bear. Granny had been so wrong. They were the ones who were idiots, worthless, stupid idiots. He was the smart one.

He could prove it.

After they made love, Jillian lay on her stomach against Ty, her cheek pressed to his heart. She listened to the slow, steady beat, wishing she could be him. So relaxed and calm. He was still so young, his life had so many possibilities.

But maybe hers did, too.

"I've been thinking about leaving when my lease is up," she said quietly.

He rubbed her bare back. "Don't you think you should wait until I hear from Detective Twit in Atlanta?"

"But the possibility that could be me is so far-fetched," she said. "I'd feel silly waiting around for weeks only to find it isn't me."

He smoothed her hair at her temple, kissed the top of her head. "I don't think we're talking about weeks. I'm telling you, I'll get the picture. But where would you go?"

"New Jersey maybe?"

He caught her chin between his thumb and forefinger and lifted until she met his gaze. "You think there can be any truth to what Ruth Williams said? She's crazy, you know."

"Not crazy, just getting up there in years."

Ty chuckled. "Almost a hundred, yeah, I'd say so."

"I was just thinking that if the little girl she remembered from the cottage was me, maybe something in New Jersey would look familiar. I mean, I was drawn here. If it is me Ruth remembered, somewhere in my head I know who I am, where I came from. Maybe we should be checking missing persons in New Jersey."

"I did that this morning." His tone told her he'd found nothing.

"No thirtysomething blondes with blue eyes missing, huh?"

He kissed her forehead. "'Fraid not."

She laid her head on his shoulder again. "You should go home."

"I'd rather stay here with you. Tomorrow night's my last night. I thought we could spend tomorrow together."

"Your mother's been through a lot in the last week." She sat up, making no effort to cover her nakedness despite the window still without curtains. With the funeral and all, she hadn't had time to get to the laundromat, but she was going tomorrow for sure.

She looked down at him. "You should go home. Otherwise, she'll sit up all night waiting for you to come in."

"You're right." He sat up with a groan. "But I wish you weren't." He gave her a quick kiss and then got up to get dressed. "You want to meet me in the morning for breakfast, like ten, and then we'll go to the beach?"

"Millie already gave me the day off, so that would be nice."

He stepped into his board shorts and pulled them over his narrow hips. "Then I thought maybe we'd go out tomorrow night for something to eat—like in a real restaurant. I got paid, so I could actually buy you more than one of Loretta's cheeseburgers."

"I don't know, one of Loretta's cheeseburgers might be good." She laughed. "I've gotten pretty hooked on them, you know."

He dropped his white Green Day T-shirt over his head and leaned over and kissed her again, this time full on the mouth. "I'm going to miss you."

She closed her eyes for a moment, emotion welling up inside. She stroked his cheek; he needed a shave. "Hey," she whispered, barely trusting her own voice. "No mushy stuff. We promised each other, right?"

"No mushy stuff," he repeated gently. He pulled away. "So I'll see you in the morning?"

She dropped back on the bed, head on her pillow. "You bet."

Ty went down the dark hallway, grabbed his sunglasses off the table, and let himself out the front door, making sure it locked behind him. As he went down the steps, he pushed his sunglasses onto his head.

Ty followed the wooden plank sidewalk around the front of the house and made the turn to go along the side. As he came around the corner, he tripped on something that hadn't been there earlier and went down hard, his glasses flying off his head and landing somewhere in the sand.

"What the—"

Before he could get the words out, something hard struck the back of his head. It felt as if his brain was exploding, and then everything went black. As he fell face forward, off the plank sidewalk, all he could think of was his new sunglasses and how the sand would scratch them.

* * *

After Ty had gone, Jillian got up and went to the bathroom, then back in the bedroom, and pulled one of his surf shirts that she had commandeered over her head before climbing into bed. She was worn out, but there were so many things going on in her head right now that she didn't know how she would sleep.

She thought about Jenkins and what the old man had said about having to confront the past to make a future. Then she thought about Ty, whose attitude it was to just move on, forget the past and make the best of the day. They seemed like opposing philosophies and yet, she wondered if they really were. Maybe she could confront her past as Jenkins had confronted his, then leave it behind the way Ty left his sunglasses everywhere.

She rolled onto her side, studying the pattern of light and dark cast by the moonlight on the hardwood floor. Jenkins had confronted his past, but in many ways, it seemed to her that that confrontation had left him a broken man. Could she use her past, the mistakes she had made, to make herself stronger? Could she forgive herself for betraying those she sensed had been close to her heart, and then move on?

And then, where would she move on to? How would she support herself? What kind of life did she want?

The thoughts, the questions, all tumbled in her head. The clock beside the bed ticked, and she began to get drowsy.

A sound in the direction of the kitchen made Jillian roll over and look toward the bedroom door. What was that? Ty coming back in? She didn't remember hearing his motorcycle, but she could have drifted off for a minute.

Had he forgotten his glasses yet again?

She waited for what seemed an eternity, but heard nothing. Then, just as she relaxed on her pillow, she heard it again.

The front door.

At once, Jillian's pulse was racing. "Ty?" she called.

Again, silence.

Jillian took a shuddering breath, not sure what to do.

The house remained silent, except for the tick of the old clock in the hall and her own breathing.

Then again, just when she thought her imagination was playing tricks on her, she heard the sound again. It was the front door creaking. The old house made lots of noises. There were moans and groans from the pipes. The ancient shutters on the windows scraped at night, sometimes. An old TV antenna wire sometimes snapped against the side of the house on windy nights. But the door hinges did not creak of their own accord.

Heart pounding in her chest, Jillian climbed noiselessly out of the old bed.

Someone was in the house, and it wasn't Ty. She could feel his presence now. Feel her fear of him.

As she stood there, time seemed to slow down. Lag. The thoughts that ran through Jillian's head were now jagged. Disjointed.

Was Kristen's killer in the house? Had he come for her?

She had no phone, no way to call for help. And to scream would do no good. Her elderly neighbors would never hear her.

Jillian looked frantically around the dark bedroom, searching for a weapon to defend herself. All she could think of was, he might take her, but not without a fight.

Of course she had no weapon. No gun. She hated guns. No knife or other sharp object. All she had was . . . Her gaze settled on the silhouette of an object leaning against the wall. A wooden curtain rod.

Jillian reached out, ear still turned to the door, and grabbed the heavy rod.

No sound came from the front of the house.

It was her imagination. All her imagination.

She glanced at the window. Ty had climbed in it. She could climb out. Run for help.

Help for what? A creaky house?

There was no sound now. If someone was in the house, wouldn't he be moving around? Either gathering whatever he'd come to steal or coming down the hall for her, if that was why he was here?

Jillian took a step toward the door, sliding her bare foot soundlessly. She knew which floorboards creaked and which didn't. If it was Ty into the kitchen trying to scare her, she was going to whack him over the head with the curtain rod anyway.

She took another step, then another, breathing easier with each.

There was no one in the kitchen. The man she had seen on the beach tonight—or imagined she had seen—had just spooked her. This whole idea that someone was following her was probably just her conscience. No one was after her. She just felt guilty for what she had done, sleeping with the man she should not have been sleeping with. With her best friend's husband.

The realization that had just gone through her head halted her mid-step.

The man in the shower. He had been her best friend's husband? How could she have done such a thing?

She took another step, almost a stagger. The more she remembered, the more she wondered if she really wanted to know.

Then Jillian heard another sound in the kitchen.

Her head snapped up. Was someone really there?

She slid her bare foot along the smooth wooden floor, easing into the hallway. In the moonlight, she could see the front door ajar. Had Ty left it open?

No.

She slid her foot forward again, easing farther down the hall. She could still not see anyone.

A part of her still assured herself this was all her

imagination. This kind of stuff didn't really happen.
She'd felt spooked ever since she woke up in that hospital. She'd been imagining someone watching her for
weeks. A woman who had been cheating on her best
friend probably would be looking over her shoulder.

Jillian took another step, curtain rod still in her
hand, raised above her head to strike. Another step and
the kitchen would be in view.

She held her breath. Slid her bare foot forward.

For a moment, she didn't believe her own eyes. A
man was standing in the dark, back to her. A real man,
not a figment of her imagination. In sand-colored camouflage.

And it wasn't Ty. This man was too big. Too brawny.

Jillian couldn't breathe. Her heart was pounding.
Her pulse racing. It was all the same feelings she remembered from the bedroom in her dreams. Suddenly
she felt dizzy. Somewhere in her head she could hear
the shower running. The fan ticking overhead.

But this had nothing to do with her dream. She had
to think clearly. This was an intruder. Possibly even the
man who had killed Kristen and the others.

Jillian had to get out of the house.

Had to get back to the bedroom. No. The bathroom
was closer. She could lock herself in there. Break the
window. Climb out.

She started to slide one foot back and then he turned.

"Where do you think you're going?" he said in a cool,
impersonal voice that was more frightening than his actual presence.

A voice she knew.

Jillian suddenly felt as if she were being sucked backwards into some science fiction vortex. For an instant,
lights seemed to flash in her head, and she felt as if she
were falling.

The male voice triggered a flood of memories all at
once. Memories piled on memories. Overlapping. The

emotions hit her like his fists as she saw pictures of herself . . . of him . . . flash through her head.

Tears. Screaming, shouting matches. Him pushing her. Slapping her. A trip to the hospital for a fractured tibia. A laceration over her eye that had to be stitched.

The embarrassment. The feeling of guilt that it was all her fault.

A lump rose in Jillian's throat as her tears clouded her vision. Slowly she lowered the curtain rod, not having the strength to hold it up.

"I've been looking for you, Laurie."

His voice penetrated the very essence of her being.

It was Michael who had stepped out of the shower in her dream. In that bedroom that night.

Michael, her husband. No. Not her husband any more. Separated. The divorce final by now.

Another sob rose in Jillian's throat. She choked. Gasped as the painful memories surrounded her, engulfed her until she felt as if she were drowning in them. Suffocating under their weight.

Michael, her husband, stepping out of the shower. His muscular bare back slick with water. Her drunken laughter.

But it wasn't Jillian naked in the bed. She'd had the dream all wrong. It wasn't *her* laughter. *She* wasn't the one who was drunk.

Jillian lifted her lashes that glistened with tears as she realized what had really happened. "My best friend," she murmured. "You were sleeping with my friend. Maggie." The name came out of her throat in a gasp.

Maggie whom she loved. Maggie, a fellow physician whom she had been friends with since medical school. They'd done their residency together. Found jobs in Atlanta together. It was Maggie who had introduced Jillian to Michael.

Jillian loved Maggie like a sister. Like Lynn, her sister who lived in California.

The memories were coming back so fast that Jillian was overwhelmed. Lynn. Lynn had to be so worried. And Mom and Dad. Getting on in years. Living on the golf course in the retirement community in Florida, begging her to leave Atlanta, leave Michael and start a new practice in sunny Fernandina Beach.

Jillian stumbled forward, dizzy, fearing she might faint. She caught the wall with her hand to keep from going down.

Michael turned toward her. Michael, her cop. Michael who was divorcing her before she had the chance to divorce him.

He had a gun in his hand.

She hated guns, and he had so many. A collector.

He was dressed in camouflage and boots as if he was going hunting, only the camo wasn't the kind you wore in the woods. The colors were all wrong.

There was sand on the floor. Sand he had brought in when he'd approached from the beach. It hadn't been her imagination tonight when she thought she'd seen a man behind the dune. It had been Michael watching her.

Jillian slowly lifted her gaze from the pistol at his side to his face. "Maggie shot me when I walked in on you."

"She didn't mean to," he said, easing a step toward her. "She was drunk. High. You know she has that little problem."

Jillian hadn't known.

She stared at Michael's handsome, rugged face, not sure if she was more shocked by the memories or by him standing in front her now with the gun. Laura had never thought he would really try to hurt her. He just had a bad temper. She made him angry. She pushed his buttons. All they needed was some counseling. He needed to work through his anger. His job. There was so much stress . . .

Bullshit, Jillian thought, pushing Laura aside. "I came

to tell you that night that I didn't want the divorce," she said. "That I wanted to give our marriage one more chance." She almost chuckled, remembering clearly now. What could she have been thinking? She should have taken the divorce settlement and run.

"You startled her." He took another step toward her, his tone still calm, so matter-of-fact. "She thought someone had broken in. She grabbed my sidearm before I could stop her."

Jillian heard the tick, tick, tick of the fan overhead. Saw the glass of Scotch. The line of coke beside it.

The place hadn't been a hotel room. It had been a rented condo. A condo her husband and her best friend had rented. He was supposed to be at a police officers' conference in Portsmouth. Work for the new anti-crime division he would be heading up. Maggie's husband thought she was visiting her sister in Florida.

"She shot me," Jillian repeated. "Maggie shot me."

Against her will, her vision blurred with tears again. "And you left me to die on that street corner," she accused him, bitter anger bubbling up inside her.

"We didn't know what to do." He took another step, his tone still cool. Businesslike.

Instinctively, Jillian tightened her grip on the curtain rod, lifting it up a little.

"You were barely breathing. She thought for sure you would die."

"A physician high on coke, drunk. I'd certainly rely on her medical advice," Jillian bit out.

"Laura, you don't understand. This got out, Maggie would lose her medical license. I'd lose my badge. The promotion. I've worked my whole life for this promotion. You know how badly I've always wanted to work undercover."

"You cheated on me with my best friend, let her shoot me, and then you left me for dead, you son of a bitch!"

In the moonlight she saw him twitch. She saw his face change. She'd pushed a button. Now he was angry.

"It was all a mistake," he said through clenched teeth. "All a big mistake. Bad luck. No one was supposed to find you so soon. Then they said you would die in surgery. Maggie checked on you. When you came out, they said you wouldn't recover." He rubbed the barrel of the pistol against his pant leg. "You weren't supposed to wake up from the coma, Laurie," he grunted.

Once she would have flinched at the sound of his raised voice. Maybe even cowered. She didn't know what had happened to her brain in the time she'd been unconscious. Maybe she'd just had some good sense knocked in her. All she knew was that today she was not the woman she had been then.

"So when I did make that mistake and survive, you couldn't just let me go?"

"There was too great a chance your memory might come back. Maggie talked to your doctor in Portsmouth. Pretended to have heard about you case, pretended she was treating a similar one. Your physician thought your memory might return, and we couldn't have that. Not after we left you like that."

"So you followed me here? You've been watching me all these weeks?"

He shook his head. "We went back to Atlanta. We had to. And when you woke up with the amnesia, I got Maggie to file the missing persons report. I couldn't let anyone know I knew where you were."

"Because you would lose your big promotion," she said with biting sarcasm. "How'd you find me?"

"The kid who called. I couldn't believe my luck. I just happened to pick up the phone in the bullpen."

Her gaze fell to the pistol again. "And now you're here to finish me off? Clean up your *mistakes*? Your *bad luck*?"

He took another step toward her, and as he moved, she caught the flash of a knife blade in his other hand.

Suddenly afraid again, she looked up at him.

"The serial killer," he said quietly. He was calm again. Confident again. "Another stroke of luck. This one good. At least for us. All those poor girls with those slit wrists. And now one more."

"Guess you are a lucky man," she murmured.

That was when she realized he wasn't going to kill her without a fight. She was done with the shame of his abuse. The shame of the divorce. The guilt that what he said was true, that her dedication to her career had gotten in the way of the marriage.

"Laurie, honey," he said. It was that pleading voice she knew too well. The voice that made her think it was her fault he had hit her. Her fault they couldn't have children. Her fault he had been forced into affairs with other women. The voice he used when he was trying to make amends. Convincing her not to go to the police and turn him in.

"Don't you *Laurie, honey* me!" Jillian lunged forward and swung the heavy curtain rod around with surprising nimbleness.

Taking him by complete surprise with her offensive move, she struck Michael hard in the side, knocking the knife out of his hand.

He sprang sideways, grunting angrily. Cursing. He was pissed that she was going to make this difficult for him.

Jillian swung again. Higher this time, even harder, and struck him with such force in the side of the head that she thought she heard his jawbone crack.

Michael growled as he threw his bulky, iron-pumped body into hers, knocking the curtain rod from her hand. He slammed her head against the kitchen wall, rattling her teeth.

Jillian screamed. She knew no one could hear her. She screamed anyway and not so much out of fear as anger. All these years she'd let him hurt her. Not just physically, but emotionally. He'd taken from her her self-confidence, her positive attitude, her belief that the world was a good place. He'd stolen from her the concept that her life could have meaning.

Jillian fought wildly. She fought for the person she had been who couldn't fight back. For the person she was now. She had too much to live for to let this sick son of a bitch kill her.

She wrenched one hand free and balled it into a fist remembering her self-defense classes. She threw it upward, knocking him in the chin, and then dragged her fingernails down his face, clawing his flesh.

Michael cursed in pain as he tried to turn his face away, yet still held her against the wall, still hung on to the pistol.

Jillian panted to try to catch her breath. She was dizzy. Disoriented. The weight of his body against hers against the wall was crushing her. She felt him lift his hand. Felt the cold barrel of the pistol catch on the hem of Ty's T-shirt. Brush her bare thigh.

He was going to shoot her. It wouldn't look like the serial killer had done it, but she'd be just as dead. And Michael would be on his way home to Atlanta and Maggie. No one would ever know what had happened to Dr. Laura Simpson.

Not if she could help it.

Jillian jerked her knee upward and at the same time threw her head forward and swung her free hand, attempting to knock the pistol out of his hand.

The sound of the gun wasn't loud. Just a pop, really.

The gunshot startled the Bloodsucker and he let go of Ty's unconscious body, dropping him into the weedy mpty lot behind the cottage. He looked back toward he source of the sound.

What was going in inside the cottage? That had ounded like a gunshot. Had Jillian committed suicide?

All that wasted blood, he thought, horrified by the possibility. All that strength spilled onto the floor. Wasted.

A dog barked on the street, and he jumped in his kin. Suddenly he was afraid. Fear had no place here. People who were afraid made mistakes. There could be no mistakes.

The Bloodsucker thought he heard a shout. From he street? The beach?

He looked down at Ty, lying unconscious in the spiky grass. Dark clouds had drifted across the full moon. He could barely see the young man's face and the blood natted in his hair. He would sleep a while. The Blood-ucker had used a little of the chloroform, just for good measure.

He glanced at his car pulled up to the curb. Contemplated finishing his task. At least he would have Ty.

Then he heard the voice again. Footsteps pounding on the pavement. Coming from the condos on the other ide of the street, toward the cottage. Toward him. Some-one else had heard the gunshot, too.

The Bloodsucker ran for the driver's-side door. Jumped n. He started the car, shifted into gear, and sped down he street, headlights off, leaving Ty Addison uncon-cious in the weeds and sand behind the cottage.

Chapter Sixteen

The sound of the gunshot wasn't what Jillian expected. It was almost anticlimactic after the violent struggle.

Again, time seemed to lag. Almost stand still.

She felt the warm blood run down her leg. Smelled it. She vaguely thought of the OR. The bright lights. The music piped in. She liked Jimmy Buffett, and her favorite assist team hated his music. She saw herself in scrubs. Felt the weight of the scalpel in her hand. But she wasn't in the OR right now, and Dr. Laura Simpson seemed like another person she only vaguely knew.

Dazed, still pressed against the wall by Michael's weight, Jillian looked down at the floor. Blood pooled on the old boards in a patch of moonlight. Dark. Congealing.

She felt no pain. Not yet. Not like at the condo when Maggie shot her in the neck and there had been blinding, searing pain. She just felt the dead weight of Michael's body against hers and smelled his musky cologne.

Michael.

She looked into his large, round, frightened brown eyes and realized that he had been shot not her. She pushed against his chest and he swayed; his knees buckled.

She watched him fall. Watched him reach out to her.

The pistol hit the wooden floor. Skidded away. Under the table? The couch?

She stared at Michael at her feet. The pool of blood in the moonlight was growing bigger by the second. It was amazing how much blood a man could lose before he became unconscious.

Michael must have hit a main artery when he accidentally shot himself. Her gaze swept his body. One leg of his camo pants was shaded a differently color. His leg. Thigh. That was the source of the blood. He had apparently hit his femoral artery.

"Help me," he whispered, his voice rough. He sounded scared.

Jillian didn't think she had ever seen Michael afraid.

He'd be dead in a matter of minutes, she thought matter-of-factly. Blood loss. There would be nothing anyone could do for him in the ER by the time the ambulance got him. Transported him. Started the transfusions.

He deserved it, she thought.

But then Jillian . . . Laura . . . remembered her Hippocratic oath. The promise she had made years ago. The responsibility she had accepted when she became a physician.

She could save this man who had beaten her, abused her emotionally. Cheated on her. Lied to her. Let his girlfriend shoot her.

Jillian reached behind her and flipped on the hall light. The living room lamp. She took her time, walking to the kitchen counter. She opened a drawer and pulled out a handful of old flowered dishtowels. As she walked back toward Michael, she heard a dog barking. She heard a man shout.

Someone else must have heard the gunshot.

She stepped over Michael's prone body, squatted, and pressed the pile of towels to his thigh where blood was gushing out. She grabbed his hand and moved it over the pile of towels turning red with blood. "Hold that."

Michael muttered something. He was slipping into unconsciousness. Blood loss did that.

She ignored him. Got to her feet. Went down the hall. She picked up her new white leather belt. Walked back down the hall realizing she had stepped in the blood and left footprints with her bare feet. She'd have to buy a mop for sure now.

Jillian crouched over Michael and made the tourniquet. She was just tightening the belt to put pressure on the femoral artery when someone pounded on the door frame. A young man she recognized from the new beach condos across the street from the cottage opened the screen door and stuck his head through the open door.

"You all right?" he called.

"I need an ambulance," she said. "There's no phone here."

He took one look at Jillian drenched in blood, at Michael on the floor, and ran. "I'll call from my place," he shouted.

She gave the tourniquet another yank.

Michael grunted.

"Take your time," she told the kid who had already gone for help. "The son of a bitch will live." She met Michael's gaze and smirked. "He'll be as good as new by the time he and Maggie go to trial."

"You sure you don't want me to stay another day or two?" Ty asked. "I don't mind. I'm already registered for classes. No one will even notice if I show up a couple of days late."

He and Jillian were sitting on rail of the front porch of the cottage each sipping a beer. She could tell it had been a hot day because even though the sun was beginning to set, she could still see the waves of heat rising off the sand on the beach over the dunes.

Jillian had spent most of her day in air conditioning. After her neighbor called 911 and the ambulances and police cars arrived, she was transported to the hospital to get checked. When an officer found Ty in the backyard of the cottage, just coming to, he'd been transported there, as well. It was after four in the morning before they left together, him with seven stitches in his "dome," as he called it, her with a clean bill of health. They went directly to the police station and talked with Claire for hours.

Jillian told the police chief exactly how things had unfolded that night in the cottage. As implausible as it all sounded, Claire seemed to believe every word. Claire spoke to Michael's precinct captain in Atlanta and confirmed both his and Jillian's identity and got the full story of her alleged disappearance.

Apparently, when Maggie and Michael returned to Georgia and found out Laura might live, she filed a missing persons report. When he was questioned, he said Laura had decided on the spur of the moment to drive to her parents' place in Florida. Because he had filed for divorce and was moving out, and the couple weren't getting along well, he said he didn't check to be sure she had arrived safely in Florida. It was only more than a week later when her office called saying she'd not returned to work after suddenly taking the week off, that he said he became worried.

Though Michael had gone to surgery and was unable to be interviewed yet, by noon, between what Jillian knew and what the Atlanta police had to say, Claire had put the whole shocking story together.

After dumping Jillian's body, Michael must have hid-

den her car, run it into a lake or something, and then
he and Maggie—Dr. Margaret DiStefano—returned to
Atlanta as if nothing had happened. When they later
discovered through Maggie's inquiries that Jillian had
been found alive and taken to the Portsmouth hospital,
they went on with the farce that Dr. Laura Simpson had
gone missing while traveling to her parents' house in
Florida. Michael hadn't known where his wife went
after being released from the hospital until Ty accidentally spoke with him while trying to find Jillian's true
identity.

Michael had apparently taken a few days off immediately to drive to Delaware and finish the job he had
started to cover his and his lover's tracks. And almost
succeeded.

Jillian tilted the green bottle back, enjoying the slightly
bitter, cold taste of the beer Ty had brought with him.
"You might as well go back to school," she told him. "My
sister will be arriving from California tonight, and we're
going to drive back to Virginia together to return the
car to the Amnesia Society and see Angel. Then I think
we'll fly down to visit with Mom and Dad before I go
back to Atlanta to testify. Michael should be able to be
transported by then."

"Then what?" Ty asked.

She lifted her shoulder, imitating one of his carefree
shrugs. "I'm on a leave of absence at the hospital in
Atlanta right now, but I pretty sure I won't go back into
practice there. Mom and Dad want me to come to Florida.
Lynn thinks I should join her and her family in the Napa
Valley. I don't know what I want to do yet. Maybe neither."

He nodded. "You should take your time. Go to both
places once the crap in Atlanta is over. Decide where
you like it better."

"Well, Mom and Dad don't live far from the beach."
She brushed some sand of her calf. "I think I'd like to

live on the beach." She gazed out over the ribbons of dark clouds hanging over the ocean's horizon. "At least near it."

"Florida's cool. I could come see you spring break. Bring my surfboard. I never did get a chance to teach you how to surf."

She turned to him. "I'd like that."

He tipped his bottle, finished off the beer, and set it on the rail. "Guess I better hit the road. Mom and Dad want to follow me up on my bike." He rolled his eyes. "Like a few lousy stitches are going to bother me?"

She laughed. They still weren't sure why Michael had attacked Ty coming out of her cottage, but it would be a while before they knew because he had refused to speak without his attorney present.

Jillian smiled, sad and happy at the same time. She hated to see Ty go, but she was so thankful for the time they had spent together. Thirteen years her junior or not, he'd been her lifeline for a month. But from the day they'd met, she'd known they were only passing through each other's lives.

Ty leaned over and kissed her. "See ya."

"See ya," she breathed, keeping her eyes closed for a moment.

He jumped down off the railing into the sand and turned to go.

"Ty," she called.

He spun around. "Yeah?"

She held up his sunglasses that he'd left on the railing.

He reached out and then stood on the wooden plank sidewalk and slid them on. Then he raised his hand in a peace sign. "No worries."

Afraid she might cry, Jillian didn't say anything. She just lifted her hand, copying his motion. She watched him disappear around the corner of the old cottage. Then taking a deep breath of the salty ocean air, she smiled, jumped down off the rail, and took the first eager step into her new life.

The Bloodsucker squirted ketchup on his cheese-burger, then all over his basket of fries. He glanced up as he returned the plastic bottle to its place beside the napkin dispenser.

The diner was busy this evening; he'd had to wait until the booth here in the back was vacated by a bunch of people from the hospital. They'd invited him to join them, but he'd politely declined. He had a book with him, just so no one would think it was odd that he was here alone.

The Bloodsucker took a bite of his burger. Everyone in the diner was buzzing with the news. As he chewed, he listened to them speaking Jillian's name, calling her Dr. Simpson now, as if they had known her their whole lives, instead of a month. Everyone was talking about her and the incredible story that had unfolded in Albany Beach the day before, bringing the small town to national attention once again. She was gone now. His Jillian. Gone for good. He had accepted that. He had lost his chance.

What he didn't like was they way she and her story had taken precedence over his. She was the one on the front page of the morning paper, a professional photo from her hospital in Atlanta, apparently because she refused to allow the news reporters to photograph her. She hadn't given any interviews either. And now she was gone. Back to Atlanta, somewhere. He was mad at her. Mad at Claire-Bear, too.

The police chief hadn't figured out that it wasn't Jillian's crazy husband who had hit Ty Addison on the head, knocked him out, dragged him behind the cottage. Claire had let the reporters say it was the cop. She hadn't figured out it was him. Hadn't figured out what a crazy coincidence had been happening that night. Two men after the same woman. How stupid was Claire-Bear that she didn't know it was him?

The Bloodsucker frowned and stuck a fry in his mouth. His gaze shifted to the lunch counter, and a young woman caught his eye. She was drinking from a paper cup. Pretty. Blonde.

He chewed thoughtfully. He had an ache inside him. An ache that he had intended to fill with Jillian's blood, but now he knew he would have to lay low for a few days. Be patient. With the whole Albany Beach police force stirred up like bees in a hive, he would have to be careful. He would have to watch out for the queen bee, his own Claire-Bear.

He could almost hear her buzzing in his ear the way he heard Granny sometimes. He pushed thoughts of both of them aside.

He knew he'd made some mistakes with Jillian, but they were mistakes he could learn from. *Had* learned from. He watched the blonde walk up to the cash register, her hips swinging as she went.

It was the first of August, the busiest week for the tourist trade in Albany Beach. And there were so many blond-haired, blue-eyed women. He had only to choose who would be next. . . .

Her days are numbered . . .

. . . by a sadistic madman who calls himself the Bloodsucker. All summer, he's been preying on blond-haired, blue-eyed women in the small resort town of Albany Beach—abducting them, then draining them of their blood.

Women are dying—drop by drop . . .

Business is down. Suspicion is up. And fear runs rampant. With people's livelihoods—and lives—at stake, police chief Claire Drummond has her work cut out for her. A single mom with a rebellious teen daughter, she finds herself leaning on councilman Graham Simpson for support. But it's hard to trust her own heart when everyone is a suspect.

Meanwhile, the Bloodsucker spins a web to reel in his next victim. He has set his sights high—on Claire. And he knows the perfect way to get to her . . . *through her daughter. . . .*

Please turn the page for an exciting sneak peek of

Hunter Morgan's

SHE'LL NEVER LIVE

coming in September 2004!

Chapter One

The Bloodsucker sat on the bar stool and smiled and listened attentively as the blonde twirled a strand of over-processed hair around her finger. She lowered her head next to his so that he could hear her above the blasting music and the voices of the Sunday night crowd. "I'm really better without him."

He nodded. He'd never come here before. Bubbles, the hip martini bar, was new this summer in Albany Beach. He liked to go to bars, watch women. Let them watch him. But tonight, he'd had no ulterior motives in coming; he just wanted to relax and have a look around. He hadn't been looking for Brandy; he usually put more planning into it. He liked to follow his special women. He liked to watch them, learn their habits, get to know them, but Brandy had approached him. Divine providence?

She'd told him she had just moved into town after leaving her boyfriend. She had started a job last week as a temp at the local community hospital. He'd seen her there the other day behind the main intake desk in the ER; her blond hair had caught his eye. Apparently she'd noticed him as well; he was like that. Women noticed him, liked him.

Brandy had now been talking about her ex-boyfriend nonstop for forty-five minutes, and she was getting on the Bloodsucker's nerves. He was beginning to get antsy. He jiggled his leg on the bar stool. He wasn't the kind to sit; he needed to be moving. Thinking. Watching, all the time.

He sipped his club soda that looked like vodka to a girl who was polishing off her third martini on an empty stomach. Clear drinks. He'd learned that on TV somewhere. You can have the bartender keep bringing you another round, make it look like you're drinking alcohol right along with her, when really, you're not. Really, you're just watching her. Waiting.

"I know that," she continued, reaching with a slender hand to retrieve her drink. "And I know it's going to be hard, but once I start getting out more, you know, meeting more people with this new job . . ."

The Bloodsucker watched her tip the glass, her pouty lips brushing the edge as she drained the glass.

"I mean, I should have done it ages ago. Right? All my girlfriends told me so."

He nodded again, his eyes full of feigned understanding. He'd seen the "concerned boy-friend" or "concerned husband" look on the faces of men in made-for-TV movies and he'd practiced the expression in the mirror on the back of his bedroom door until he had it just right. Without drawing any attention to himself, he signaled to the bartender to bring another round of drinks.

"What do you think, Cory? Don't you think I should have dumped him long ago?" She swiveled on the bar stool to question the man seated on the other side of her. Her fingers, the nails painted an unnatural pink with white tips, trailed down his forearm.

The guy, a computer geek from Altoona, had come over and casually sat down and began talking to them.

The Bloodsucker didn't usually work this way. He was a loner, but a little variation now and then to his routine wouldn't hurt. It added a modest excitement to the evening. A little thrill. Not that he was one of those cretins who wanted to get caught, the kind you read about in the papers who left easily traceable clues behind. He was too smart for that. Hadn't his IQ scores proved he could have been a Mensa member if he'd wanted to? But there was no harm in having a little fun with the cops, with Chief Claire-Bear? And the women like the one on the bar stool beside him made it so easy. Like taking candy from a baby.

As for Cory, he might even come in handy.

The Bloodsucker sipped his club soda on the rocks with a twist of lime and flexed the fingers of one hand. He was getting impatient, now that he could see options opening up to him. He didn't really like this girl that much now that he had talked to her. Brandy was her name. Brandy Jones . . . Smith . . . something common like that. She smelled like cigarette smoke . . . probably tasted like it. But she had come to him. Wasn't that a sign? Didn't that mean she was meant for him?

He swallowed, trying to ease the constriction in his throat. In his groin.

The need had been building in him for days . . . no . . . longer. Ever since Jillian had left. Maybe Brandy had sensed it.

When Jillian had gotten away from him, returned to Atlanta, something curious inside him had turned over, something unfamiliar that scared him a little. It was anger. He'd never felt this way before. Not about his women. He didn't take these women, do what he did, out of anger. He wasn't one of *them*. He did it out of need.

But the anger was there again tonight, lurking just beneath the surface of his calm, nice-guy demeanor. He could feel it, tight and suffocating in his chest. He could hear it, strangulating, in his voice. But Brandy couldn't sense it, silly girl. Those around him didn't see the rage that lurked beneath the surface of his skin.

"Oh, gosh, thanks," Brandy told the bartender as he delivered her drink. She clasped the slender stem of the fresh martini glass and raised it in a toast. "To us, my newfound friends." She giggled, looking at the Bloodsucker and then Cory on the other bar stool.

"To us," the Bloodsucker echoed. As he sipped the cold club soda, he made his decision. He would take Brandy home with him tonight. By the time he set his glass down and reached for a handful of cheese fish crackers on the bar, he'd already begun to set his plan in motion.

Brandy and Cory were now deep in conversation. She was running her finger along his knee as she spoke, flirting with him, which could definitely work to the Bloodsucker's advantage. After all, he certainly couldn't walk out of the bar with Brandy on his arm. Men did that, but he was too smart to make such a blinding error.

Shortly, the Bloodsucker finished his club soda and climbed off the stool.

"Where you going, John?" Brandy spun around on the stool as she pulled a tube of lip gloss from her purse and ran it over her lips. "Little boys' room?"

"Actually, it's getting late." Suppressing the urge to chuckle over the fact that he'd been clever enough to give a false name, he checked his watch. "Sunday night. I have to work day shift tomorrow."

"I know, but you don't have to go yet, do you?" She rose off the stool, but the minute her high heels hit the floor, she swayed and grabbed onto him to keep from falling. "It's early, baby."

The Bloodsucker tensed the moment her hand touched him. His first impulse was to slap her. Punch her. Dig her blue eyes out of their sockets with something handy. A toothpick from the bar, maybe?

His jaw tightened. She was drunk, and it was not terribly flattering. Not for any woman, but certainly not a pretty blonde like her.

Granny said his mother had been a drunk.

"She's right, you should stay longer, man," Cory echoed, sipping his beer.

The Bloodsucker forced himself to relax and stepped toward the bar to pay his tab, effectively moving away from her without making it obvious. "It was great to meet you, Brandy. I'm sure I'll be seeing you around."

"Right." She backed against the bar stool to keep her balance. "Guess I will. Once I get a phone, maybe you can give me a call?"

"I'd like that." He smiled. "Well, good night."

She waved. Giggled. " 'Night."

With a casual nod in the direction of Cory, the Bloodsucker weaved his way through the loud, crowded bar and out the door into the humid night air where he could breathe better. Away from the crowd . . . all the people.

As he cut across the parking lot, he hummed confidently to himself. So what if this was impulse? April had been an impulse, too, and she had worked out just fine. He was too great a creature of habit. People were always telling him that. It was time he broadened his horizons and learned to be more spontaneous.

He got into his car, parked as far from any light as possible, and pushed the driver's seat back to get comfortable. Now all he had to do was wait.

And he didn't even have to wait long. Half an hour later, Brandy stumbled out of the bar on the arm of Cory from Altoona. The Bloodsucker watched as the computer geek pushed her up against a car and covered her mouth with his.

What was wrong with this young woman? Didn't she know the dangers of getting drunk in a bar, far from home, with men you didn't know? Didn't she realize how unsafe it was?

He licked his dry lips. Flexed his hands. He already had the latex gloves on the seat beside him. Already had the baggie with the chloroform-soaked gauze he would need to subdue her. In the trunk were the other items he would need—tape, rope, the plastic sheeting. Even though he hadn't come here tonight for Brandy, he was prepared. He took pride in the fact that he was a man who was always prepared.

"Come on," he urged under his breath, absently fingering the photo in his pocket. "Tell him no. I don't have time for this tonight. I've got work tomorrow."

If Brandy went home with Cory, that would make the night longer. It was doable, but now that he had made his decision, chosen his next guest, he was anxious to get started. Anxious to feel. To taste . . .

Brandy suddenly gave Cory a little push back, and the Bloodsucker smiled. It was dark, and the parking lot wasn't well lit, so he couldn't see exactly what had happened, but Cory must have done something to anger her.

"That's right," the Bloodsucker whispered. "He's not interested in you as a person, Brandy. Just a sex object. He ought to be ashamed of himself, treating a lady that way."

Cory tried to catch her, to push her against his car again, but she ducked under his arm. Brandy was athletic, apparently. Strong. Strong was good. Strong women lasted longer. They fought the inevitable longer.

"I'm out of here." She lifted her hand to Cory.

The Bloodsucker smiled.

"Brandy, wait!" Cory hollered.

"Good night." She stumbled through a row of parked cars, headed in the Bloodsucker's direction.

Perfect.

"Hey, you sure you can drive?" Cory asked.

The Bloodsucker scowled. Like he was going to show

concern for her now after he'd tried to take advantage
of her sexually right in the parking lot? What a jerk.

"I can give you a ride home," he said. "Come on. I'm
sorry. I just got carried away."

She continued through the parking lot. Cory hesitated, and then climbed into his car.

The Bloodsucker watched him pull out of the parking lot and then searched for Brandy again. She was
headed straight for him; apparently, she couldn't find
her car.

The Bloodsucker popped the lever on his trunk, then
opened his door, reaching for the gloves and the baggie. Timing; it was all about timing. One quick look to
see that there was no one in the parking lot and then he
called to her in his best "nice guy" voice. "Hey, Brandy,
you okay?"

She halted, looking over the roof of a sports car.

"It's John," he said, closing his car door, shutting off
the dome light.

"John?" She suddenly seemed a bit uneasy. "You're
still here?"

"Yeah." He slid his hands smoothly into the gloves, the
car between them blocking her view. "I ran into somebody I knew inside." He could see that his easygoing
tone was making her relax a little. She could see she
had nothing to fear from him. "What's the matter, can't
find your car?"

"No . . . I . . ." She laughed and leaned on the hood
of a pickup. "It's here somewhere. A white Toyota."

Cory was right. She was too drunk to drive. But that
didn't matter now; the Bloodsucker had no intention of
letting her drive. "Doesn't that make you crazy? I run
into the grocery store to grab a few things, come out,
and I can't remember where I parked. Let me help you
find it." He moved toward her quickly, lifting his arm as
if he were going to put it around her shoulder.

She turned her head toward him. Maybe his sudden haste startled her, maybe it was that unnerving instinct women seemed to have. Even drunk ones. "Hey—"

He closed his hand over her mouth and nose. To his surprise, she lifted her knee and tried to kick him. She missed him, but in the process, she knocked his elbow, sliding the gauze off her mouth.

The Bloodsucker felt an instant of panic. If she screamed. If anyone came out the bar door or pulled into the parking lot—

She opened her mouth to scream, and his reaction was as instantaneous as it was brutal. He punched her as hard as he could, right in the stomach.

Brandy grunted and doubled over. He covered her mouth and nose with the gauze and jerked her against his body. She began to relax, and then she was dead weight in his arms. His arms shaking, he carried her the couple of feet to his car, opened the trunk and dropped her in. He slipped off his gloves and threw them in on top of her as he glanced around the dark parking lot. Not a soul to be seen. He slammed the trunk. He needed to tie her up, to gag her, but he'd pull over in a mile or two and take care of that. The chloroform would last that long.

Calmer now, feeling good about himself, the Bloodsucker walked to the front of the car and climbed in. Started the engine. He had never hit anything before. Never harmed a fly. Certainly not a woman.

It had felt surprisingly good.

The Bloodsucker pulled up beside the barn and then backed his car up to the door. As he climbed out, he spotted his dog on the back porch of the house, waiting faithfully. "It's okay, boy," he called, patting his knee. "Car's stopped moving. It's safe. Come on, boy!"

The well-trained dog flew off the old porch and barreled across the dark yard. Reaching his master, he barked and jumped until the Bloodsucker scratched behind his ears and told him what a good boy he was. Then, with a pat on his rump, he dismissed the dog. "Okay, boy, that's enough. We have a guest I need to attend to."

The dog backed down immediately, stepping aside to allow his master to pass.

The Bloodsucker had already popped the hatch before he got out of the car, so when he walked around to the rear, soft light glowed around the edges of the trunk. Laying his hand on the warm metal, he hesitated a moment, taking the time to enjoy the little trill of pleasure that shot through him. That was the problem with people today. He'd heard Dr. Phil say so on *Oprah*. No one took the time to enjoy the little delights in life, the small accomplishments.

Unable to resist a smile, the Bloodsucker slowly lifted the lid of the trunk. Soft light from the interior bulb illuminated Brandy's blond hair. He couldn't see her face, but that was all right. It was better this way, actually. Lying in the trunk, ankles and wrists tied together, hair falling over her face, she took his breath away. She looked like a sleeping angel.

The Bloodsucker lingered over the trunk another moment, then went into the barn. He found the lighter and a camp lantern right on the shelf inside the door. There was no electricity in the barn; it was too old. But he liked it that way; it made it kind of cozy at night, just him and his guest and the glow of the Coleman lantern.

The Bloodsucker used the lighter to find the valve, turned on the gas, and lit the wick. He liked the little hiss the gas made as it flowed. He added the clear glass globe and then carried the lantern to the picnic table in the middle of the largest part of the barn. Everything was already there, already set up and waiting. Now all he needed was Brandy to join him.

* * *

"Why are you doing this?" Brandy whispered, her eyes wild with fear.

He stood beside the picnic table, snapping up the clear plastic suit he had bought for the occasion. It was disposable, used by painters. Quite effective for blood splatter, especially when you added the shoe coverings, hat, and face shield. It was amazing the things you could buy over the Internet.

The four vodka martinis Brandy had drunk at the bar had worn off, and now she was sober. He'd taken the gag off when she'd promised not to scream. Not that it would matter. No one would hear her. The barn was insulated with bales of musty straw the Bloodsucker had stacked against the walls more than a story high; it had taken him days, but was quite effective at muffling any sounds inside the barn. Quite clever.

"Please. What is it you want?" she begged, tears running down her face, leaving ugly blue and black streaks of mascara and eye shadow. "Money? Sex? I'll give you whatever you want. If it's a blow—"

He reached out and slapped her hard across the face. It startled her. It startled him. It also shut her up.

"That will be enough of that talk," he said sternly, looking down at his hand, now spotted with blood. He stared at it for a moment in fascination. He hadn't expected blood yet.

A little added bonus.

He glanced up and saw that it came from her lip. Fortunately, he had already donned the surgical gloves. There would be no trace of his DNA left on her skin. Not that this little old podunk town of Albany Beach had easy access to DNA testing, but he liked to be careful just the same.

The Bloodsucker returned to the task of snapping up the jumpsuit. "You ought to be ashamed of yourself, a pretty young woman talking trash like that."

"I'm sorry," she sobbed. "I'm sorry. Please. I feel sick."
She let her head fall forward for a moment and she
slumped in the chair he had tied her to.

"I'm sorry, it's the chloroform. The feeling will wear
off," he told her. "Just give it a little time."

He ran his hand over his chest, and satisfied that he
was properly covered, he turned to retrieve the tray of
supplies he'd prepackaged at the house. He'd gotten
fresh gauze and sterile water, and he'd boiled the scalpel
in a pot to rid it of any of Kristen's blood cells. On impulse, he'd also picked up another tool in the kitchen
that might be handy. Intriguing. Something he had
watched late on TV the other night had given him the
idea.

Hearing him start toward her, Brandy lifted her head.
She struggled against the ropes that bound her in the
plastic deck chair. This was a change; he had used a
wooden one before, but wood was porous and more
likely to hold trace evidence. Even with all the plastic
sheeting, it didn't hurt to be extra careful.

"Please don't hurt me anymore," she begged, turning her face away as if there were any way she could
avoid him.

Her words made him feel bad. Ashamed. His gaze
fell to the freshly spread sawdust at his feet. He *had* hurt
her. He'd punched her back in the parking lot. Hit her
again and given her a bloody lip.

*But she'd made him do it, hadn't she? Women were like
that. They made you do things you didn't want to do.*

The Bloodsucker lifted his head in determination.
"Hold still and be quiet," he ordered, setting the tray
aside on a small table. He didn't have a lot of time
tonight. He needed to get a good night's sleep, go to
work fresh and ready to do his job. He wouldn't do
much tonight, just have a little fun. He reached for the
scalpel.

Brandy screamed and, without thinking, he belted her

so hard that her head flew back and her neck snapped with a satisfying crack. "I told you before that you had to be quiet," he barked, reaching impatiently for the tape to gag her again. "You're ruining everything," he said, barely able to contain his rage. "Now, just shut up."

It's what Granny had always said. You're ruining everything.